"LOOK AT ME, GWENDOLYN."

"Gwen," she snapped.

"Gwen," he acquiesced right before he kissed her.

Heat lightning, she thought, *his touch is electrifying.* Attraction sizzled between them, and she knew he felt it too, because he drew back and looked at her strangely. Then, nudging her lips apart with his thumb, he opened her mouth and brushed his lips back and forth over hers.

Yes, she thought, *this is what I want.* She slid her hands up the rippling muscles of his arms, over his shoulders, then locked them firmly behind his neck. She hadn't gone to Scotland, fallen in a hole, and met a madman. She'd died and gone to heaven. He closed his hands on her waist, then slid them upward as he deepened the kiss.

DELL BOOKS BY
KAREN MARIE MONING

Kiss of the Highlander

The Highlander's Touch

To Tame a Highland Warrior

Beyond the Highland Mist

KISS
of the
HIGHLANDER

KAREN MARIE
MONING

A DELL BOOK

Published by
Dell Publishing
a division of
Random House, Inc.
1540 Broadway
New York, New York 10036

Dell® and its colophon are registered trademarks of
Random House, Inc.

ISBN: 0-440-23655-X

Printed in the United States of America

Published simultaneously in Canada

September 2001

10   9   8   7

OPM

This one's for you, Mom.
When I raged, you listened
When I wept, you held me
When I ran away, you brought me back
When I dreamed, you believed.
Woman of immeasurable wisdom and grace
You have been all that a mother could be
And more.

*"I cannot believe God plays dice
with the Cosmos."*

—ALBERT EINSTEIN

*"God not only plays dice.
He sometimes throws the dice where they
cannot be seen."*

—STEPHEN HAWKING

PROLOGUE

"The MacKeltar is a dangerous man, Nevin."

"What are you going on about this time, Mother?" Nevin looked out the window and watched the grass rippling in the early morning sun beyond their hut. His mother was reading fortunes, and were he foolish enough to turn around and meet Besseta's gaze, she would interpret it as encouragement, and he would be lured into yet another conversation about some bewildering prediction. His mother's wits, never the sharpest blade in the armory, were dulling daily, eroded by suspicious imaginings.

"My yew sticks have warned me that the laird presents a grave danger to you."

"The laird? Drustan MacKeltar?" Startled, Nevin glanced over his shoulder. Tucked behind the table near the hearth, his mother straightened in her chair, preening beneath his attention. Now he'd done it, he thought with an inward sigh. He'd gotten himself snagged in her conversation as securely as he'd gotten his long robes entangled in a thorny bramble a time or two, and it would require finesse to detach himself now without things degenerating into an age-old argument.

Besseta Alexander had lost so much in her life that she clung too fiercely to what she had left—Nevin. He repressed a desire to fling back the door and flee into the serenity of the Highland morning, aware that she would only corner him again at the earliest opportunity.

Instead, he said gently, "Drustan MacKeltar is not a danger to me. He is a fine laird, and 'tis honored I am to have been chosen to oversee the spiritual guidance of his clan."

Besseta shook her head, her lip trembling. A fleck of spittle foamed at the seam. "You see with a priest's narrow view. You can't see what I see. This is dire indeed, Nevin."

He gave her his most reassuring smile, one that, despite his youth, had eased the troubled hearts of countless sinners. "Will you cease trying to divine my well-being with your sticks and runes? Each time I am assigned a new position, you reach for your charms."

"What kind of a mother would I be, if I didn't take interest in your future?" she cried.

Brushing a lock of blond hair from his face, Nevin crossed the room and kissed her wrinkled cheek, then swept his hand across the yew sticks, upsetting their mysterious design. "I am an ordained man of God, yet here you sit, reading fortunes." He took her hand and patted it soothingly. "You must let go of the old ways. How will I achieve success with the villagers, if my own dear mother persists in pagan rituals?" he teased.

Besseta snatched her hand from his and gathered her sticks defensively. "These are far more than simple sticks. I bid you, accord them proper respect. He *must* be stopped."

"What do your sticks tell you the laird will do that is so terrible?" Curiosity trumped his resolve to end this conversation as neatly as possible. He couldn't hope to curtail the dark wanderings of her mind if he didn't know what they were.

"He will soon take a lady, and she will do you harm. I think she will kill you.

Nevin's mouth opened and closed like a trout stranded on the riverbank. Although he knew there was no truth to her ominous prediction, the fact that she entertained such wicked thoughts confirmed his fears that her tenuous grasp on reality was slipping. "Why would anyone kill me? I'm a priest, for heaven's sake."

"I can't see the why of it. Mayhap his new lady will take a fancy to you, and evil doings will come of it."

"Now you truly *are* imagining things. A fancy to me, over Drustan MacKeltar?"

Besseta glanced at him, then quickly away. "You are a fine-looking lad, Nevin," she lied with motherly aplomb.

Nevin laughed. Of Besseta's five sons, only he had been born slender of build, with fine bones and a quietude that served God well but king and country poorly. He knew what he looked like. He had not been fashioned—as had Drustan MacKeltar—for warring, conquering, and seducing women and had long ago accepted his physical shortcomings. God had purpose for him, and while spiritual purpose might seem insignificant to others, for Nevin Alexander it was more than enough.

"Put those sticks away, Mother, and I don't want to hear any more of this nonsense. You needn't fret on my behalf. God watches over—" He stopped midsentence. What he'd nearly said would encourage an entirely new, and at the same time very old and very lengthy, discussion.

Besseta's eyes narrowed. "Ah, yes. Your God certainly watched over all of my sons, didn't He?"

Her bitterness was palpable and made him heartsick. Of all his flock, he'd failed most surely with his own mother. "I might remind you that quite recently He was *your* God, when I was granted this position and you were well-pleased with my promotion," Nevin said lightly. "And you will not harm the MacKeltar, Mother."

Besseta smoothed her coarse gray hair and angled her nose toward the thatched roof. "Don't you have confessions to hear, Nevin?"

"You must not jeopardize our position here, Mother," he said gently. "We have a solid home among fine people, and I hope to make it permanent. Give me your word."

Besseta kept her eyes fixed on the roof in stubborn silence.

"Look at me, Mother. You must promise." When he refused to retract his demand or avert his steady gaze, she finally gave a shrug and nodded.

"I will not harm the MacKeltar, Nevin. Now, go on with you," she said brusquely. "This old woman has things to do."

Satisfied that his mother wouldn't trouble the laird with her pagan foolishness, Nevin departed for the castle. God willing, his mother would forget her latest delusion by dinner. God willing.

Over the next few days, Besseta tried to make Nevin understand the danger he was in, to no avail. He chided her gently, he rebuked her less gently, and he got those sad lines around his mouth she so hated to see.

Lines that clearly pronounced: *My mother's going mad.*

Despair settled into her weary bones, and she knew that it was up to her to do something. She would *not* lose her only remaining son. It wasn't fair that a mother should outlive all her children, and trusting God to protect them was what had gotten her into this bind to begin with. She refused to believe she'd been given the ability to foresee events only to sit back and do nothing about them.

When shortly after her alarming vision a band of wandering Rom arrived in the village of Balanoch, Besseta struck upon a solution.

It took time to barter with the proper people; although *proper* was hardly a word she'd use to describe the people with whom she was forced to deal. Besseta might read yew sticks, but simple scrying paled in comparison to the practices of the wild gypsies who wandered the Highlands, selling spells and enchantments cheek by jowl with their more-ordinary wares. Worse still, she'd had to steal Nevin's precious gold-leafed Bible, which he used only on the holiest of days, to trade for the services she purchased, and when he discovered the loss come Yuletide he would be heartbroken.

But he would be alive, by the yew!

Although Besseta suffered many sleepless nights over her decision, she knew her sticks had never failed her. If she didn't do something to prevent it, Drustan MacKeltar would take a wife and that woman would kill her son. That much her sticks had made clear. If her sticks had told her more—mayhap how the woman would do it, when, or why—she might not have been seized by such desperation. How would she survive if Nevin were gone? Who would succor an old and useless woman? Alone, the great yawning darkness with its great greedy maw would swallow her whole. She had no choice but to get rid of Drustan MacKeltar.

A sennight later, Besseta stood with the gypsies and their leader—a silver-haired man named Rushka—in the clearing near the little loch some distance west of Castle Keltar.

Drustan MacKeltar lay unconscious at her feet.

She eyed him warily. The MacKeltar was a large man, towering and dark, a mountain of bronzed muscle and sinew, even when flat on his back. When she shivered and nudged him gingerly with her toe, the gypsies laughed.

"The moon could fall on him and he wouldn't waken," Rushka informed her, his dark gaze amused.

"You're certain?" Besseta pressed.

" 'Tis no natural sleep."

"You didn't kill him, did you?" she fretted. "I promised Nevin I wouldn't harm him."

Rushka arched a brow. "You have an interesting code, old woman," he mocked. "Nay, we did not kill him, he but slumbers, and will eternally. 'Tis an ancient spell, laid most carefully."

When Rushka turned away, instructing his men to place the enchanted laird in the wagon, Besseta heaved a sigh of relief. It had been risky—slipping into the castle, drugging the laird's wine and luring him to the clearing near the loch—but all had gone according to plan. He'd collapsed on the bank of the glassy lake and the gypsies had set about their ritual. They'd painted strange symbols upon his chest, sprinkled herbs and chanted.

Although the gypsies made her uneasy and she'd longed to flee back to the safety of her cottage, she'd forced herself to watch, to be certain the canny gypsies would keep their word, and to assure herself Nevin was finally safe—forever beyond Drustan MacKeltar's reach. The moment the final words of the spell had been uttered, the very air in the clearing had changed: she'd felt an uncommon iciness, suffered a sudden, overwhelming weariness, even glimpsed a strange light settling around the laird's body. The gypsies indeed possessed powerful magic.

"*Truly* eternally?" Besseta pressed. "He will ne'er awaken?"

"I told you, old woman," Rushka said impatiently, "the man will slumber, frozen, utterly untouched by time, ne'er to awaken, unless both human blood and sunshine commingle upon the spell etched upon his chest."

"Blood and sunshine would wake him? That must never happen!" Besseta exclaimed, panicking all over again.

"It won't. You have my word. Not where we plan to hide his body. Sunlight will ne'er reach him in the underground caverns near Loch Ness. None will e'er find him. None know of the place but us."

"You must hide him very deep," Besseta pressed. "Seal him in. He must *never* be found!"

"I said you have my word," Rushka said sharply.

When the gypsies, wagon in tow, disappeared into the forest, Besseta sank to her knees in the clearing, and murmured a prayer of thanks to whatever deity might be listening.

Any idle feelings of guilt were far outweighed by relief, and she consoled herself with the thought that she hadn't *really* hurt him.

He was, as she had promised Nevin, unharmed.

Essentially.

· 1 ·

Gwen Cassidy needed a man.

Desperately.

Failing that, she'd settle for a cigarette. *God, I hate my life*, she thought. *I don't even know who I am anymore.*

Glancing around the crowded interior of the tour bus, Gwen took a deep breath and rubbed the nicotine patch under her arm. After this fiasco, she deserved a cigarette, didn't she? Except, even if she managed to escape the horrid bus and find a pack, she was afraid she might expire from nicotine overdose if she smoked one. The patch made her feel shaky and ill.

Perhaps before quitting she should have waited until she'd found her cherry picker, she mused. It wasn't as if she was drawing them like flies to honey in her current mood. Her virginity was hardly presented in its best light when she kept snarling at every man she met.

She leaned back against the cracked seat, wincing

when the bus hit a pothole and caused the wiry coils of the seat to dig into her shoulder blade. Even the smooth, mysterious, slate-gray surface of Loch Ness beyond the rattling window that wouldn't stay closed when it rained—and wouldn't stay open otherwise—failed to intrigue her.

"Gwen, are you feeling all right?" Bert Hardy asked kindly from across the aisle.

Gwen peered at Bert through her Jennifer Aniston fringed bangs, expensively beveled to attract her own Brad Pitt. Right now, they simply tickled her nose and annoyed her. Bert had proudly informed her, when they'd begun the tour a week ago, that he was seventy-three and sex had never been better (this said while patting the hand of his newlywed, plump, and blushing bride, Beatrice). Gwen had smiled politely and congratulated them and, since that mild show of interest, had become the doting couple's favorite "young American lassie."

"I'm fine, Bert," she assured him, wondering where he'd found the lemon polyester shirt and the golf-turf-green trousers that clashed painfully with his white leather dress shoes and tartan socks. Completing the rainbow ensemble, a red wool cardigan was neatly buttoned about his paunch.

"You don't look so well, there, dearie," Beatrice fretted, adjusting a wide-brimmed straw hat atop her soft silvery-blue curls. "A little green about the gills."

"It's just the bumpy ride, Beatrice."

"Well, we're nearly to the village, and you must have a bite to eat with us before we go sightseeing," Bert said firmly. "We can go see that house, you know, the one where that sorcerer Aleister Crowley used to live. They say it's haunted," he confided, wiggling bushy white brows.

Gwen nodded apathetically. She knew it was futile to protest, because although she suspected Beatrice might have taken pity on her, Bert was determined to ensure that she had "fun." It had taken her only a few days to figure out that she should never have embarked upon this ridiculous quest.

But back home in Sante Fe, New Mexico, as she'd peered out the window of her cubicle at the Allstate Insurance Company, arguing with yet another injured insured who'd managed to amass an astounding $9,827 worth of chiropractic bills from an accident that had caused a mere $127 in damage to his rear bumper, the idea of being in Scotland—or anywhere else, for that matter—had been irresistible.

So she'd let a travel agent convince her that a four-teen-day tour through the romantic Highlands and Lowlands of Scotland was just what she needed, at the bargain price of $999. The price was acceptable; the mere thought of doing something so impulsive was terrifying, and precisely what she needed to shake up her life.

She should have known that fourteen days in Scotland for a thousand dollars *had* to be a senior citizens' bus tour. But she'd been so frantic to escape the drudgery and emptiness of her life that she'd only cursorily glanced through the itinerary and not given her possible traveling companions a second thought.

Thirty-eight senior citizens, ranging in age from sixty-two to eighty-nine, chatted, laughed, and embraced each new village/pub/bowel movement with boundless enthusiasm, and she knew that when they returned home they would play cards and regale their elderly and envious friends with endless anecdotes. She wondered what stories they would tell about the twenty-five-year-old virgin who had traveled with them.

Prickly as a porcupine? Stupid enough to try to give up smoking while taking the first real vacation in her life and simultaneously trying to divest herself of her virginity?

She sighed. The seniors really were sweet, but sweet wasn't what she was looking for.

She was looking for passionate, heart-pounding sex.

Sex that was down and dirty, wild and sweaty and hot.

Lately she ached for something she couldn't even put a name to, something that made her restless and anxious when she watched *10TH Kingdom* or her favorite star-crossed lovers' quest, *Ladyhawke.* Were she still alive, her mother, renowned physicist Dr. Elizabeth Cassidy, would assure her it was nothing more than a biological urge programmed into her genes.

Following in her mother's footsteps, Gwen had majored in physics, then worked briefly as a research assistant at Triton Corp. while completing her Ph.D. (before her Great Fit of Rebellion had landed her at Allstate). Sometimes, when her head had been swimming with equations, she'd wondered if her mother wasn't right, if all there was to life could be explained by genetic programming and science.

Popping a piece of gum in her mouth, Gwen stared out the window. She certainly wasn't going to find her cherry picker on this bus. Nor had she entertained even a modicum of success in the prior villages. She had to do something soon, because if she didn't, she would end up going back home no different than she'd arrived, and frankly that thought was more terrifying than the idea of seducing a man she hardly knew.

The bus lurched to a halt, pitching Gwen forward. She struck her mouth on the metal frame of the seat in front of her. She cast an irate glance at the rotund, bald bus driver, wondering how the old folks always seemed to anticipate the sudden stop, when she never could. Were they simply more cautious with their brittle bones? Strapped into the seats better? In cahoots with the ancient, portly driver? She dug in her backpack for her compact and, sure enough, her lower lip was swelling.

Well, maybe that will entice a man, she thought, poking it out a little more, as she dutifully followed Bert and Beatrice off the bus and into the sunny morning. Sucker lips: Didn't men fixate on plump lips?

"I can't, Bert," she said, when the kindly man tucked her arm in his. "I need to be alone for a little while," she added apologetically.

"Is your lip swollen again, dear?" Bert frowned. "Don't you wear your seat belt? Are you sure you're okay?"

Gwen ignored the first two questions. "I'm fine. I just want to go for a walk and gather my thoughts," she said, trying not to notice that Beatrice was regarding her from beneath the wide brim of her hat with the unnerving intensity of a woman who had survived multiple daughters.

Sure enough, Beatrice pushed Bert toward the front steps of the inn. "You go on, Bertie," she told her new husband. "We girls need to chat a moment."

While her husband disappeared into the quaint, thatch-roofed inn, Beatrice guided Gwen to a stone bench and pulled her down beside her.

"There *is* a man for you, Gwen Cassidy," Beatrice said.

Gwen's eyes widened. "How do you know that's what I'm looking for?"

Beatrice smiled, cornflower-blue eyes crinkling in her plump face. "You listen to Beatrice, dearie: Fling caution to the wind. If I were your age and looked like you, I'd be shaking my bom-bom everywhere I went."

"Bom-bom?" Gwen's eyebrows rose.

"Petunia, dear. Booty, behind," Beatrice said with a wink. "Get out there and find a man of your own. Don't let us spoil your trip, dragging you about. You don't need old folks like us around. You need a strapping young man to sweep you off your feet. And *keep* you off them for a good long while," she said meaningfully.

"But I can't find a man, Beatrice." Gwen blew out a frustrated breath. "I've been searching for my cherry picker for months now—"

"Cherry . . . *Oh!*" Beatrice's round shoulders, swathed in pink wool and pearls, shook with laughter.

Gwen winced. "Oh, God, how embarrassing! I can't believe I just said that. That's just what I started calling him in my mind because I'm the oldest living . . . er—"

"Virgin," Beatrice supplied helpfully, with another laugh.

"Mm-hmm."

"Doesn't a pretty young woman like you have a man back home?"

Gwen sighed. "In the past six months I've dated *oodles* of men. . . ." She trailed off. After her prominent parents had been killed in a plane crash in March, returning from a conference in Hong Kong, she'd turned into a veritable dating machine. Her only relative, her grandfather on her father's side, had Alzheimer's and hadn't recognized her in forever. Lately, Gwen felt like the last Mohican, wandering around, desperate for someplace to call home.

"And?" Beatrice prodded.

"And I'm not a virgin because I'm trying to be," Gwen said grumpily. "I can't find a man I want, and I'm beginning to think the problem is me. Maybe I expect too much. Maybe I'm holding out for something that doesn't even exist." She'd voiced her secret fear. Maybe grand passion *was* just a dream. With all the kissing she'd done in the past few months, she'd not once been overcome with desire. Her parents certainly hadn't had any great passion between them. Come to think of it, she wasn't sure she'd ever seen grand passion outside of a movie theater or a book.

"Oh, dearie, don't think that!" Beatrice exclaimed. "You're too young and lovely to give up hope. You never know when Mr. Right may walk in. Just look at me," she said with a self-deprecating laugh. "Over-the-hill, overweight, in a dwindling market of men, I'd resigned myself to being a widow. I'd been alone for years, then one sunny morning my Bertie waltzed into the little diner on Elm Street where the girls and I breakfast every Thursday, and I fell for him harder than the fat lady at the circus takes a tumble. Dreamy as a young girl again, fussing with my hair and"—she blushed—"I even bought a few things at Victoria's Secret." She lowered her voice and winked. "You know you've got hanky-panky on your mind when perfectly respectable white bras and panties suddenly won't do anymore, and you find yourself buying pink ones, lilac ones, lime green and the like."

Gwen cleared her throat and shifted uncomfortably, wondering if her lilac bra showed through her white tank top. But Beatrice was oblivious, chatting away.

"And I'll tell you, Bertie certainly wasn't what I thought I wanted in a man. I'd always thought I liked simple, honest, hardworking men. I never thought I'd get involved with a dangerous man like my Bertie," she confided. Her smile turned tender, dreamy. "He was with the CIA for thirty years before he retired. You should hear some of his stories. Thrilling, positively *thrilling*."

Gwen gaped. "Bertie was CIA?" *Rainbow Bertie?*

"You can't judge the contents of the package by the wrapper, dearie," Beatrice said, patting her cheek. "And one more piece of advice: Don't be in too much of a rush to give it away, Gwen. Find a man who is worthy. Find a man you want to talk with into the wee hours, a man you can argue with when necessary, and a man who makes you *sizzle* when he touches you."

"Sizzle?" Gwen repeated doubtfully.

"Trust me. When it's right, you'll know," Beatrice said, beaming. "You'll feel it. You won't be able to walk away from it." Satisfied that she'd said her piece, Beatrice planted a pink-lipsticked kiss on Gwen's cheek, then rose, smoothing her sweater over her hips, before disappearing into the gaily painted inn. Gwen watched her retreat in thoughtful silence.

Beatrice Hardy, age sixty-nine and a good fifty pounds overweight, walked with confidence. Glided with the grace of a woman half her size, swayed her ample bottom and serenely displayed her cleavage.

In fact, she walked like she was beautiful.

Worthy. Hmph!

At this point, Gwen Cassidy would settle for a man who didn't require a stiff dose of Viagra.

Gwen paused to rest atop the small mountain of rocks she'd climbed. After discovering she couldn't check into her room at the inn until after four o'clock, and firm in her resolve to not march into the nearest shop and buy a pack of that-word-she-wasn't-saying-anymore, she'd grabbed her backpack and an apple and trotted off into the hills for an introspective hike. The hills above Loch Ness were dotted with outcroppings of stone, and the group of rocks upon which she stood extended for nearly half a mile, rising in breakneck hills and falling in jagged ravines. It had been a tough climb, but she'd relished the exercise after being cooped up in the stale air of the bus for so long.

There was no denying that Scotland was lovely. She'd tromped gingerly through patches of hawthorn, skirted prickly thistles, paused to admire a rowan tree's bright red berries, and kicked about a few spiky green horse chestnuts that heralded autumn with their tumble to the ground. She'd stood long moments admiring a field of cross-leaved heath that ascended and blended with a hillside of purple-pink heather. She and a dainty red deer had spooked each other as she'd passed through the woodland clearing in which it grazed.

Peace had settled over her, the higher she'd hiked into the lush meadows and rocky hills. Far beneath her, Loch Ness stretched twenty-four miles long, over a mile wide, and, in places, a thousand feet deep, or so said the brochure that she'd read on the bus, highlighting the fact that the loch never froze in the winter because of its peaty, slightly acid content. The loch was a huge silvery mirror shimmering beneath the cloudless sky. The sun, nearly at its zenith, marked the approaching noon hour and felt delicious on her skin. The weather had been unusually warm for the past few days and she planned to take advantage of it.

She flopped down on a flat rock and stretched out, soaking up the sunshine. Her group was scheduled to remain in the village until seven-thirty the following morning, so she had ample time to relax and enjoy nature before reboarding the tour bus from hell. Although she'd never meet an eligible prospect up here in the foothills, at least there were no phones ringing, with irate insureds on the other end, and no senior citizens casting nosy glances her way.

She knew they gossiped about her; the old folks talked about *everything*. She suspected they were making up for all the times they'd held their tongues when they were young, invoking the impunity of advanced age. She found herself rather looking forward to senior immunity. What a relief it would be to say exactly what she thought for a change.

And what would you say, Gwen?

"I'm lonely," she muttered softly. "I would say that I'm lonely and I'm damn tired of pretending that everything's fine."

How she wished something exciting would happen!

It just figured that the one time she'd tried to *make* something happen, she'd ended up on a senior citizens' bus tour. She may as well face it, she was doomed to live a dry, uneventful, and lonely life.

Eyes shut against the bright rays, she groped for her backpack to get her sunglasses but misjudged the distance and knocked the bag off the rock. She heard it bounce amid the clatter of loose stones for several moments, then a protracted silence, and finally a solid thump. Tucking her fringed bangs behind one ear, she sat up to see where it had fallen. She was dismayed to discover that it had tumbled off the rock, down a gully, and to the bottom of a narrow, forbidding precipice.

She moved to the lip of the aperture, eyeing it warily. Her patches were in her pack, and she certainly couldn't be expected to remain a non-that-word-she-wasn't-thinking without something to take the edge off. Gauging the depth of the rocky cleft to be no more than twenty-five to thirty feet, she decided she was capable of retrieving it.

She had no alternative; she *had* to go down after it.

Lowering herself over the edge, she felt for toeholds. The hiking boots she'd laced on that morning had rugged, gripping soles that made the descent a little easier; however, as rough stone grazed her bare legs, she found herself wishing she'd worn jeans instead of her favorite pair of khaki Abercrombie & Fitch short-shorts that were so in vogue. Her lacy white tank top was comfortable for hiking, but the faded denim button-down she'd tied around her waist just kept getting tangled about her legs, so she paused a moment to untie it and let it waft down onto her backpack. Once she reached the bottom, she'd tuck it in her pack before climbing back up.

It was slow, strenuous going, but half her life was in that pack—and it was arguably the better half. Cosmetics, hairbrush, toothpaste, floss, panties, and many other items that she'd wanted on her person in case her luggage got lost. *Oh, admit it, Gwen,* she thought, *you could live out of that pack for weeks.*

The sun beat down on her shoulders as she descended, and she started to sweat. It figured that the sun had to shine directly into that crack at that moment, she thought irritably. Half an hour earlier or later, and it wouldn't have penetrated there.

Near the bottom, she slipped and inadvertently kicked her bag, wedging it firmly at the bottom of the narrow crevice. Squinting up into the sun, she muttered, "Come on, I'm trying to quit smoking down here, you could help me anytime now."

Easing herself down the last few feet, she placed one foot on the ground. There. She'd made it. Hardly enough room to turn around in the tight space, but she was there.

Lowering her other foot, Gwen grabbed her button-down and stretched her fingers toward the strap of her pack.

When the ground gave way beneath her feet, it was so sudden and unexpected that she scarcely had time to gasp before she plunged through the rocky bottom of the crevice. She fell for a terrifying few seconds, then landed with such force that the impact knocked the air from her lungs.

As she struggled to draw a breath, crushed rock and dirt showered her where she lay. Adding insult to injury, the backpack fell through the hole after her and thumped her in the shoulder before rolling off into the darkness. She finally managed a ragged breath, spit hair and dirt out of her mouth, and mentally assessed her condition before attempting to move.

She'd fallen hard and felt bruised from head to toe. Her hands were bleeding from her panicked attempt to catch herself as she'd plunged through the jagged opening, but, blessedly, it didn't appear she'd broken any bones.

Gingerly, she turned her head and gazed up at the hole through which she'd fallen. A stubborn ray of sunshine filtered down on her.

I will not panic. But the hole was an impossible distance above her head. Worse still, she'd not passed any other hikers during her climb. She might yell herself hoarse, yet never be found. Shaking off a nervous shiver, she peered into the gloom. The shadowy blackness of a wall loomed a few yards away, and she could hear the faint trickle of water off in the distance. Obviously, she'd fallen into an underground cavern of sorts.

But the pamphlet said nothing of any caves near Loch Ness—

All thought ceased abruptly as she realized that whatever she was lying upon was not rock or soil. Stunned by the abrupt fall, she'd naturally assumed she'd landed on the hard floor of a cavern. But while it was hard, it was certainly not cold. Warm, rather. And given that until a few moments ago no sunlight had penetrated this place, what were the odds that something could be warm in this cool, damp cave?

Swallowing, she remained utterly still, trying to decide what she was lying on without actually looking at it.

She nudged it with a hipbone. It gave slightly, and it did *not* feel like soil. *I'm going to be sick,* she thought. *It feels like a person.*

Had she fallen into an old burial chamber? But, then, wouldn't it be nothing but bones? As she debated further movement, the sun reached its zenith, and a brilliant shaft of sunlight bathed the spot where she'd fallen.

Summoning all her courage, she forced herself to look down.

Gwen screamed.

· 2 ·

She'd fallen on a body. One that, considering she hadn't disturbed it, must be dead. *Or,* she worried, *perhaps I killed it when I fell.*

When she managed to stop screaming, she found that she'd pushed herself up and was straddling it, her palms braced on its chest. Not its chest, she realized, but *his* chest. The motionless figure beneath her was undeniably male.

Sinfully male.

She snatched her hands away and sucked in a shocked breath.

However he'd managed to get here, if he was dead, his demise had been quite recent. He was in perfect condition and—her hands crept back to his chest—warm. He had the sculpted physique of a professional football player, with wide shoulders, pumped biceps and pecs, and washboard abs. His hips beneath her were lean and powerful. Strange symbols were tattooed across his bare chest.

She took slow, deep breaths to ease the sudden tightness in her chest. Leaning cautiously forward, she peered at a face that was savagely beautiful. His was the type of dominant male virility women dreamed about in dark, erotic fantasies but knew didn't *really* exist. Black lashes swept his golden skin, beneath arched brows and a silky fall of long black hair. His jaw was dusted with a blue-black shadow beard; his lips were pink and firm and sensually full. She brushed her finger against them, then felt mildly perverse, so she pretended she was just checking to see if he was alive and shook him, but he didn't respond. Cupping his nose with her hand, she was relieved to feel a soft puff of breath. *He isn't dead, thank God.* It made her feel better about finding him so attractive. Palm flush to his chest, she was further reassured by his strong heartbeat. Although it wasn't beating very often, at least it was. He must be deeply unconscious, perhaps in a coma, she decided. Whichever it was, he couldn't help her.

Her gaze darted back up to the hole. Even if she managed to wake him and then stood on his shoulders, she still wouldn't be near the lip of the hole. Sunshine streamed over her face, mocking her with a freedom that was so near, yet so impossibly far, and she shivered again. "Just what am I supposed to do now?" she muttered.

Despite the fact that he was unconscious and of no use, her gaze swept back down. He exuded such vitality that his condition baffled her. She couldn't decide if she was upset that he was unconscious, or relieved. With his looks he was surely a womanizer, just the kind of man she steered away from by instinct. Having grown up surrounded by scientists, she had no experience with men of his ilk. On the rare occasions she'd glimpsed a man like him sauntering out of Gold's Gym she'd gawked surreptitiously, grateful that she was safely in her car. So much testosterone made her nervous. It couldn't possibly be healthy.

Cherry picker extraordinaire. The thought caught her off guard. Mortified, she berated herself, because he was injured and there she was, sitting on him, thinking lascivious thoughts. She pondered the possibility that she'd developed some kind of hormone imbalance, perhaps a surfeit of perky little eggs.

She eyed the designs on the man's chest more closely, wondering if one of them concealed a wound. The strange symbols, unlike any tattoos she'd ever seen, were smeared with blood from the abrasions on her palms.

Gwen leaned back a few inches so a ray of sunshine spilled across his chest. As she studied him, a curious thing happened: the brightly colored designs blurred before her eyes, growing indistinct, as if they were fading, leaving only streaks of her blood to mar his muscled chest. But that wasn't possible . . .

Gwen blinked as, undeniably, several symbols disappeared entirely. In a matter of moments all of them were gone, vanished as if they'd never existed.

Perplexed, she glanced up at his face and sucked in an astonished breath.

His eyes were open and he was watching her. He had remarkable eyes that glittered like shards of silver and ice, sleepy eyes that banked a touch of amusement and unmistakable masculine interest. He stretched his body beneath hers with the self-indulgent grace of a cat prolonging the pleasure of awakening, and she suspected that although he was rousing physically, his mental acuity was not fully engaged. His pupils were large and dark, as if he'd recently had his eyes dilated for an exam or taken some drug.

Oh, God, he's conscious and I'm straddling him! She could imagine what he was thinking and could hardly blame him for it. She was as intimately positioned as a woman astride her lover, knees on either side of his hips, her palms flat against his rock-hard stomach.

She tensed and tried to scramble off him, but his hands clamped around her thighs and pinned her there. He didn't speak, merely secured and regarded her, his eyes dropping to linger appreciatively on her breasts. When he slid his hands up her bare thighs, she seriously regretted having put on her short-shorts this morning. A slip of a lilac thong was all that was beneath them, and his fingers were toying with the hem of her shorts, perilously close to slipping inside.

His heavy-lidded gaze reflected a languor that had nothing to do with having just awakened, and there was no doubt what was on his mind. *But this is no safe cherry picker,* Gwen thought, growing more concerned by the moment. *This man looks like a cherry tree chopper-downer.*

"Look, I was just about to get off you," she babbled. "I didn't plan to sit on you. I fell through the hole and landed on you. I was hiking and accidentally knocked my backpack down a crevice, and when I went to rescue it the ground gave way beneath me and here I am. On that note, why didn't my falling on you wake you?" More important, she thought, how *long* had he been awake? Long enough to know that she'd copped a few perverted feels?

Confusion flickered in his mesmerizing eyes, but he said nothing.

"I'm usually groggy when I first wake up too." She tried for a reassuring tone.

He shifted his hips, subtly reminding her that she

didn't wake up quite like him. There was something happening beneath her and, like the rest of him, it was in-your-face male.

When he smiled at her, revealing even, white teeth and a slight cleft in his chin, the part of her brain that made intelligent decisions melted like chocolate taffy left by the pool on a hot summer day. Her heart raced, her palms felt clammy, and her lips were suddenly parched. For a moment, she was too stupefied to feel anything but relief. So *this* was mindless sexual attraction. It *did* exist! Just like in the movies!

Her relief was doused by anxiety when he dragged her forward against his chest, cupped her bottom with both hands, and ground her pelvis against his. He buried his face in her hair and thrust upward, rubbing against her like a sleek and powerful animal. A hiss of breath escaped her, an involuntary reaction to a surge of desire that was far too intense to be sane. She was drowning in sensations: the possessive crush of his arms, the testosterone-laden scent of man, the sensual scrape of his shadow beard against her cheek when he caught the lobe of her ear with his teeth, and *oh*—that wildly erotic rhythm of his hips. . . .

He squeezed her bottom, kneading and caressing, then one hand slid upward, lingering deliciously over the hollow where her spine met her hips, inching ever upward until he palmed the back of her head and guided her lips nearer his.

"Good morrow, English," he said, a breath from her lips. The words were delivered in a thick brogue that sounded roughened by too much whisky and peat smoke.

"Let me go," she managed, angling her face away from his. He'd fitted his erection snugly between her thighs, and a firm hand splayed across her bottom kept her locked precisely where he wanted her. He was rock-hard and hot through the lightweight fabric of her shorts. Expertly, he thrust against the most perfect spot nature had bestowed upon a woman, and Gwen coughed to camouflage a moan. If he treated her to a few more of those cocky strokes, she might have her first real orgasm without even sacrificing her cherry.

"Kiss me," he murmured into her ear. His lips braised her neck; his tongue tasted her skin with lazy sensuality.

"I am *not* kissing you. I can understand how you might have gotten the wrong impression, waking up to find me sprawled on top of you, but I told you that I didn't mean to land on you. It was an accident." *Aw, kiss him, Gwen,* clamored a hundred perky eggs. *Shut up,* she rebuked. *We don't even know him, and until moments ago we thought he was dead. That's no way to start a relationship.*

Who's asking for a relationship? Kisskisskiss! her babies-in-waiting insisted.

"Lovely lass, kiss me." He planted a hungry, open-mouthed kiss in the sensitive area between her collarbone and the base of her throat. His teeth closed gently on her skin, his tongue lingered, sending chills up her spine. "On my mouth."

She shuddered as the velvety stroke made her nipples pearl against his chest. "Uh-uh," she said, not trusting herself to say too much.

"Nay?" He sounded surprised. And undeterred. He nibbled the underside of her chin while splaying his hand intimately between the cleft of her behind.

"No. No way. *Nay.* Understand? And get your hand off my butt," she added with a squeal, when he squeezed again. "*Oooh.* Stop that!"

Lazily, he slid his hand up from her hips to her head, availing himself of the opportunity to thoroughly caress every inch in between. Burying both hands in her hair, he gripped her near the scalp and tugged her head gently back so he could search her eyes.

"I *mean* it."

He arched a dubious brow but, to her surprise, he proved to be a gentleman and slowly relinquished his grip. She scrambled off him. Unaware that they'd been lying on a slab of stone that was several feet above the floor of the cavern, she stumbled to her knees on the floor.

He sat up on the slab gingerly, as if every muscle in his body was stiff.

He swept his gaze about the cavern, shook his head with the vigor of a drenched dog casting off rain, then gave the interior of the cave a second, thorough glance. He flipped his long dark hair over his shoulder and narrowed his eyes. Gwen witnessed the precise moment the confusion of deep slumber quit his mind. The seductive gleam in his gaze faded, and he folded his muscular arms across his chest. He glanced at her with an expression both startled and angry. "I doona recall coming here," he said accusingly. "What have you done? Did you bring me here? Is this witchery, lass?"

Witchery? "No," she said hastily. "I told you, I fell in through that hole"—she jerked her thumb up in the direction of the shaft of sunlight—"and you were already in here. I landed on you. I have no idea how you got here."

His cool gaze roamed over the jagged opening, the loose stones and dirt scattered around the slab, the blood on her hands, her disheveled condition. After a moment's hesitation, he appeared to deem it a plausible story. "If you did not come seeking my personal attentions, why are you so shamelessly attired?" he said flatly.

"Perhaps because it's hot out?" she shot back, tugging defensively at the hem of her khakis. Her shorts weren't *that* short. "It's not like you have much on yourself."

"'Tis natural for a man. 'Tis not natural for a woman to cut off her chemise at the waist and doff her gown. Any man would make the assumption I did. You are wantonly clad, and you were draped most intimately across my loins. When a man first awakens, it sometimes takes several moments before he starts thinking clearly."

"And here I thought it took several years, perhaps a lifetime for the average man's intellect to kick in," she said snidely. *Chemise? Doff?*

He snorted, shaking his head again, vigorously enough that it was giving *her* a headache. "Where am I?" he demanded.

"In a cave," she muttered, feeling less than charitable toward him. First, he'd tried to have sex with her, then he'd insulted her clothing, and now he was behaving as if *she'd* done something wrong to *him*. "And you should apologize to me."

His brows arched with surprise. "For waking up to find a half-clad woman lying on top of me and thinking she wished me to pleasure her? I doona think so. And I am not simple," he chided. "'Tis clear I'm in a cave. In what part of Scotland does this cave reside?"

"Near Loch Ness. Near Inverness," she said. She backed away from him a few steps.

He blew out a relieved breath. "By Amergin, 'tis not too much of a fankle. I am but a few days and not many leagues from home."

Amergin? Fankle? Who'd taught the man English? His brogue was so thick that she had to listen intently to decipher what he was saying, and even then not all of it made sense. Could the glorious man have grown up in some obscure Highland village where time stood still, cars were twenty years out of date, and the old ways and manner of speech were still revered?

When he was silent for several minutes, she wondered if perhaps he really was hurt in some way and had been resting in the cave. Maybe he'd struck his head; she hadn't explored that part of him. *Damn near the only part you didn't,* she thought. Gwen scowled, feeling vulnerable in the cavern with the dark, sexual man who occupied too much space and was using more than his fair share of oxygen. His confusion was only adding to her unease.

"Why don't you show me the way out, and we can talk outside," she encouraged. Perhaps he'd be less attractive in broad daylight. Perhaps it was merely the dim, confined atmosphere of the cave that made him seem so large and dizzyingly masculine.

"You vow you had nothing to do with how I came to be here?"

She raised her hands in a gesture that said, *Why don't you just take a good hard look at little ole' me, and then look at you?*

"There is that," he agreed with her wordless rebuke. "You doona amount to much."

She refused to dignify his comment with a response. When he rose from the slab she realized that, contrary to her initial impression, he wasn't wearing unfashionably long plaid shorts, like some of her elderly tourmates had worn, but was clad in a length of patterned fabric fastened about his waist. It brushed above his knees, and his feet and calves were encased in soft boots. She tipped her head back to look up at him and, disconcerted by how he towered over her, blurted, "How tall *are* you?" She could have kicked herself when it came out sounding awed. Standing beside him, few people would amount to much. Although she'd never get involved with a man like him, it was impossible to remain unaffected by his incredible height and powerfully developed body.

He shrugged. "Taller than the hearth."

"The . . . hearth?"

He stopped his intent perusal of the cave and glanced at her. "How am I to think with you chattering away? The hearth in the Greathall, the one Dageus and I vied to outgrow." An expression of deep sadness crossed his face at the mention of Dageus. He fell silent a moment, then shook his head. "He never did. Missed by so much." He demonstrated the space of an inch with his finger and thumb. "I'm taller than my father, and taller than two of the stones at *Ban Drochaid*."

"I meant in feet," she clarified. Speaking of the mundane gave her a measure of calm.

He eyed his boots a moment and appeared to be doing some rapid calculations.

"Forget it. I get the picture." *Six and a half feet, perhaps taller.* And to a woman five foot three inches on her best day, daunting. She stooped and grabbed her backpack, sliding a strap over her shoulder. "Let's go."

"Hold. I am yet unprepared for travel, lass." He moved to a pile by the wall, which Gwen had thought was a jumble of rocks. She watched nervously as he retrieved his belongings. He did something she didn't quite follow with the blanket thingie he was wearing, where part of it ended up over one shoulder. After fastening a pouch about his waist, he draped wide bands of leather over each shoulder so that they crossed in an X over his chest. These he secured at his waist with another wide band of leather that belted them snugly in place, then he donned a fourth band that encircled his pecs.

Was he dressing in some old costume? Gwen wondered. She'd seen something similar to his attire in a castle her group had toured yesterday, on one of the medieval sketches in the armory. Their guide had explained that the bands fashioned a sort of armor, adorned in critical places—such as above the heart and over the abdomen—with ornate metal discs.

As she watched, he fastened similar leather bands that stretched from wrist to elbow around his powerful forearms. She stared in silence when he began tucking dozens of knives away—knives that looked alarmingly real. Two went into each wristband, handle down toward his palm, ten on each crossband. When he bent to the dwindling pile and hefted a massive double-bladed ax, she flinched. *Cherry tree chopper-downer, indeed.* Definitely not a man a woman could take any chances with. He raised an arm and lowered it behind his right shoulder, sliding the handle into the bands across his back. Last, he sheathed a sword at his waist.

By the time he was done she was aghast. "Are those real?"

He turned a cool silver gaze on her. "Aye. You can scarce kill a man otherwise."

"Kill a man?" she repeated faintly.

He shrugged and eyed the hole above them and said nothing for a long while. Just when she was beginning to think he'd forgotten her entirely, he said, "I could toss you that high."

Oh, yes, he probably could. With one arm. "No, thank you," she said frostily. Small she might be, a basketball she was not.

He grinned at her tone. "But I fear that doing so might cause more rocks to collapse upon us. Come, we will find the way out."

She swallowed. "You *really* don't remember where you came in?"

"Nay, lass, I'm afraid I doona." He measured her for a moment. "Nor do I recall why," he added reluctantly.

His response troubled her. How could he not know how or why he'd entered the cave, when he had obviously come in, removed his weapons, and piled them neatly before lying down? Did he have amnesia?

"Come. We must make haste. I care naught for this place. You must put your clothes back on."

Her hackles rose and she barely resisted the urge to hiss like a cat. "My clothes *are* on."

He raised a brow, then shrugged. "As you will. If you are comfortable strolling about in such a fashion, far be it from me to complain." Crossing the chamber, he took her wrist and began dragging her along.

Gwen allowed him to tug her behind him for a short distance, but once they'd left the cavern, all light disappeared. He was guiding them by feeling his way along the wall of the tunnel, his other hand latched about her wrist, and she began to fear they might plunge into another crevice, hidden by the darkness. "Do you know these caves?" she asked. The blackness was so absolute that it was crowding her in, suffocating her. She needed light and she needed it now.

"Nay, and if you are telling me the truth and you fell through the hole, then you doona either," he reminded. "Have you a better idea?"

"Yes." She tugged on his hand. "If you'll just stop a moment, I can help."

"Have you fire to light our way, wee English? For 'tis what we sorely need."

His voice was amused, and it irritated her. He'd taken her measure, deemed her helpless, and that pissed her off. And why did he keep calling her English? Was it the

Scottish version of American, and perhaps they called people from England British? She knew she had a trace of an English accent because her mother had been raised and schooled in England, but it wasn't *that* pronounced. "Yes, I do," she snapped.

He stopped so suddenly that she ran into the back of him, striking her cheekbone on the handle of his ax. Although she couldn't see him, she felt him turn, smelled the spicy male scent of his skin, then his hands were on her shoulders.

"Where have you fire? Here?" He sifted his fingers through her long hair. "Nay, perhaps here." His hand brushed her lips in the dark, and if she hadn't clamped them shut he would have slipped the tip of his finger between them. The man was positively outrageous, hell-bent on seduction with a single-mindedness that made her fear for her resolve. "Ah, here," he purred, sliding his hand over her derriere, then yanking her against him. He was still erect. *Unbelievable*, she thought dazedly. He laughed, a husky, confident sound. "I doona doubt you have fire, but 'tis naught that might help us escape this cave, though it would undoubtedly make it vastly more amenable."

Oh, definitely mocking now. She twisted away from his liberty-taking hands. "You are *so* arrogant. Have all those steroids eaten away your brain cells?"

He was silent a moment, and his lack of response unnerved her. She couldn't see him and wondered what he was thinking. Was he preparing to pounce on her again? Finally he said slowly, "I doona understand your question, lass."

"Forget it. Just let go of me so I can get something out of my pack," she said stiffly. She slipped it off her shoulder and thrust it at him. "Hold this a minute." While she'd been willing to discard her cigarettes, throwing away a perfectly good lighter had seemed wasteful. Besides, she'd quit before, and then when she started again, she had to buy a new lighter every time. Rummaging in one of the external pockets, she sighed with relief when her fingers closed on the silver Bic. When she pressed the little button, he roared and leaped back. His heavy-lidded eyes, glittering with banked sensuality, widened in amazement.

"You *do* have fire—"

"I have a lighter," she interrupted defensively. "But I don't smoke," she hastened to add, not in the mood to entertain the disdain of a man who was clearly an athlete of some kind. She'd taken up smoking two years ago during the Great Fit of Rebellion, right after she and her parents had quit speaking permanently, and then she'd ended up addicted. Now, for the third time, she'd quit, and by God she was going to be successful this time.

His fingers closed over the lighter, and he assumed possession of it. As she stood beside him in the darkness, as he took her lighter away and the flame flickered out, she sensed that he would do the same with anything he wanted. Casually assume possession. Wrap his strong hand around it and claim it.

She was surprised when he fumbled for several moments before he managed to press the little button that released the flame. How could he not know how to use a lighter? Even a health fanatic would have seen someone light a cigar or a pipe, if only on TV or in a movie. She suffered another attack of the shivers. When he resumed the pace, she followed him—the only alternative to remain by herself in the dark, and that was no alternative at all.

"English?" he said softly.

"Why do you call me that?"

"You haven't given me your name."

"I don't call you Scotty, do I?" she said irritably. Irritated by his strength, his arrogance, his blatant sexuality.

He laughed, but it didn't sound like his heart was in it. "English, what is the month?"

Oh, boy, here we go, she thought. *I* did *fall down one of Alice's rabbit holes.*

· 3 ·

Drustan MacKeltar was worried. Although there
was nothing he could put his finger on—apart from the
remarkable fire she possessed, her shameless attire, and
her unusual manner of speaking—he couldn't shake the
feeling that an even more significant fact was eluding
him. Initially, he'd thought mayhap he was no longer in
Scotland, but then she'd informed him he was a mere
three-day hike from his home.

Mayhap he'd lost several days, even a week. He shook
his head, trying to clear it. He felt the same as he
had once before when as a young lad he'd had a high
fever and woken over a week later: confused, thick-wit-
ted, his normally lightning-fast instincts slowed. His re-
actions were further dulled because lust was thundering
though his veins. A man couldn't think clearly when he
was aroused. All his blood was being sucked to one part

of his body, and while it was one of his finer parts, *cool* and *logical* didn't describe it.

The last thing he remembered, prior to awakening with the English lass sprawled so wantonly atop him, was that he had been racing toward the little loch in the glen behind his castle and growing unnaturally weary. From there, his memories were blurred. How had he ended up in a cave, a three days' hike away from his home? Why couldn't he remember how he had gotten here? He didn't seem to have suffered any injury; indeed, he felt hearty and hale.

He struggled to recall why he had been running toward the loch. He paused, as a tide of fragmented memories washed over him.

A sense of urgency . . . distant voices chanting . . . incense and snatches of conversation: *He must never be found,* and a curious reply, *We will hide him well.*

Had his petite English been there? Nay. The voices had been oddly accented, but not like hers. He quickly discarded the possibility that she had aught to do with his plight. She didn't seem the brightest lass, nor particularly strong. Still, a woman of her beauty didn't need to be; nature had given her all the gifts she needed to survive. A man would use all his skills as a warrior to protect such lush beauty, even had she been deaf and mute.

"Are you all right?" English nudged his shoulder. "Why did you stop, and please don't let the light go out. It makes me nervous."

Skittish as a foal, she was. Drustan pressed the tiny button again and flinched only mildly this time when the flame issued forth. "The month?" he asked roughly.

"September."

Her reply hit him like a fist in his stomach: the last afternoon he recalled had been the eighteenth day of August. "How near Mabon?"

She regarded him strangely, and her voice was strained when she said, "Mabon?"

"The autumnal equinox."

She cleared her throat uncomfortably. "It is the nineteenth of September. The equinox is the twenty-first."

Christ, he'd lost nearly a month! How could that be? He pondered the possibilities, sorting and discarding until he struck upon one that horrified him because it seemed the only explanation that fit the circumstances: once he'd been lured to the clearing, he'd been abducted. But assuming he had been abducted, how had he lost an entire month?

The unnatural exhaustion he'd experienced while running toward the glen suddenly made sense. Someone had drugged him in his own castle! That was how his captors had managed to take him, and apparently they'd been keeping him drugged.

And that someone could even now be returning to the cave to force him to slumber again. They would not find him so easy to take captive a second time, he vowed silently.

"Are you all right?" she asked hesitantly.

He shook his head, his thoughts grim. "Come," he warned before he dragged her along behind him.

She was so small that it would have been easier to toss her over his shoulder and run with her, but he sensed that she would vociferously resist such treatment and he cared not to waste time arguing. She was fine-boned and petite, yet prickly as a hungry boar. She was also lushly curved and scandalously clad and stirred a cauldron of lustful urges in him.

He glanced over his shoulder at her. Whoever she was, wherever she was from, she was unaccompanied by a man, and that meant she was going home with him. The lass made his heart pound and his blood roar. When he'd awakened to find her on top of him, he'd responded fiercely. The moment he'd touched her, he'd been loath to let go, had slipped his hands up her silky legs and been captivated by the notion that mayhap she removed *all* her body hair. He would find out as soon as his plight permitted.

In the fierce Highlands of Scotland, possession was nine-tenths of the law, and Drustan MacKeltar was the other one-tenth: Drustan was *brehon*, or lawgiver. He could recite the lineage of his clan back for millennia, directly to the ancient Irish Druids of the *Tuatha de Danaan*—a feat worthy of a Druid bard. No one questioned his authority. He'd been born to rule.

"Whence do you hail, English?"

"My name is Gwen Cassidy," she said stiffly.

He repeated her name. "'Tis a good name; Cassidy is Irish. I am Drustan MacKeltar, laird of the Keltar. My people made their home in Ireland for many centuries, before we took these Highlands as our home. Have you knowledge of my clan?"

Why had he been abducted? And once taken, why not killed? What must his father be making of his disappearance? Then a worse thought occurred to him: Was his father still alive and unharmed?

Fear for his father's safety gripped him, and he repeated his question impatiently, "Have you news of my clan?"

"I've never heard of your cl—family."

"You must hie from across the border. How came you here?"

"I'm on vacation."

"On what?"

"Vacation. I'm visiting," she clarified.

"Have you clan in Scotland?"

"No."

"Then whom do you visit? Who accompanies you?" Women did not travel without escort or clan, and certainly not dressed as she was. Although she'd knotted a blue fabric about her waist before they'd left the main cavern, it failed to conceal her shocking undergarments. The woman had no shame at all.

"No one accompanies me. I'm a big girl. I do perfectly well on my own."

There was a defiant note in her voice. "Have you any clan left alive, lass?" he asked more gently. Mayhap her family had been massacred and she displayed her body reluctantly, in hopes of finding a protector. She comported herself with the stiff bravado of an orphaned wolf cub, conditioned by savagery and starvation to snap at any hand, no matter that it might hold food.

She glared at him. "My parents are dead."

"Och, lass, I'm sorry."

"Shouldn't you be busy trying to find a way out of here?" she changed the subject swiftly.

He found the display of toughness, affected by a woman so obviously wee and helpless, touching. It was evident that the loss of her clan was still difficult for her to speak of, and far be it from him to press such a discussion. He knew too well the pain of losing a loved one. "Och, but 'tis just ahead. See the daylight sifting through the stones? We can break through there." He let the flame go out, and they were swallowed by darkness, broken by a few thin trickles of light a dozen yards ahead.

As they drew nearer, Gwen eyed the rubble blocking the tunnel with disbelief. "Even *you* can't move those boulders."

She knew so little about him. The only question was whether he would do it using his body or his other . . . arts. Eager to be quit of the cave, he knew using his Druid skills would be the fastest way out.

It would also be the fastest way to ensure he would *never* get her in his bed. A display of such unnatural power had driven three of his betrotheds from his life. The fourth had been killed two weeks past—nay, he amended, a month and a half ago if it was truly almost

Mabon—with his brother Dageus, who'd been escorting her to Castle Keltar for the wedding. He closed his eyes against a fresh wave of grief. It still *felt* like two weeks to him.

He'd never met his bride-to-be. Although he mourned her death, he grieved the loss of a potential wife, grieved the cutting short of so young a life, not the woman herself.

Dageus, on the other hand . . . Ah, that was a bitter and burning grief within his breast. He closed his eyes, firmly corralling the pain to be dealt with at a later time.

Since his brother had died, it was even more critical that he beget an heir. And soon. He was the last MacKeltar left to sire sons.

He glanced speculatively at Gwen.

Nay. He would use no Druid magic to move the stones in her presence.

He studied the stone blockade for a few moments before launching a simple physical assault. But he didn't merely put his arms into the job, he put his entire body into it, aware that she had dropped to her knees on the floor of the tunnel and was watching his every move. He might have flexed a bit more than necessary, to demonstrate what a prize she might enjoy in her bed. Anticipation was an important part of bed play and heightened the woman's ultimate satisfaction immeasurably. *Never* let it be said he wasn't an expert and attentive lover. The seduction began long before he removed a woman's clothing. Women might not like the thought of wedding with him, but they vied in masses for the pleasure of his bed.

Digging them out was a time-consuming task. From how tightly the stones were packed, the crevices between them sealed with the dust of time, he guessed this branch of the tunnel had collapsed a long time ago and been forgotten. He dug and tossed and cleared out the smaller rocks before turning his attention to the larger ones, using his ax as a lever to push and roll them. Before long, he had cleared a small passage. Thick foliage camouflaged the opening, and he could see why the tunnel had been forgotten. What had once been an entrance lay secluded between boulders and covered by bramble. Who would think to look for a cave in such a place? It was apparent that he hadn't been brought in via this tunnel. That much foliage *couldn't* have grown in a month.

He glanced over his shoulder at her. She raised a guilty gaze from his legs, and he grinned. "You have naught to fear," he assured her. "Freeing us is easy. 'Tis the hike that will be tiring."

"What hike?"

He didn't bother to answer her but returned to his labor. The sooner they got out, the sooner he could devote attention to her seduction. Of course it would have to happen while they were traveling back to his castle, for he dare not waste time. After widening the opening, he used his sword to hack through the dense overgrowth obscuring the entrance. When he'd finally cleared a passage he deemed safe enough to accommodate them, she hurried to his side. He realized she would bolt out the opening and sprint away if he gave her the opportunity.

"Step back while I go through," he commanded.

"Ladies first," she said sweetly.

He shook his head. "You would bound off faster than a hare if I were such a fool." He grasped her shoulders and pulled her close. "I would advise against running from me. I would catch you easily, and the chase would only arouse me." When she tried to shrug his hands off her shoulders, he said, "Is this the fashion in which you thank me for freeing you?" he teased. "You might grant me a boon for my efforts." He rested his gaze on her lips, making it clear what boon he had in mind. When she wet them nervously, he dropped his head closer, taking it as a sign of compliance.

But the contrary lass flattened her wee palms on his cheeks and held him at bay. "Fine. Go first, then. Age before beauty," she added sweetly.

"Arrogant lass," he said with a snort, grudgingly admiring her audacity. "Give me your pack." After producing the remarkable fire from within it, he was confident she wouldn't try to flee him without it in her possession.

"I'm *not* giving you my pack."

"Then you're *not* moving," he said flatly. "And the longer I stand here, in such tempting proximity—"

She smacked him in the chest with it, hard, and he laughed. Her cheeks flushed when he said, "Temper, temper, wee English. 'Tis truly most becoming to you." What a lovely spitfire she was, scarce taller than a child but voluptuously curved and plainly old enough for carnal pleasure.

Aye, he'd take her back to Castle Keltar; mayhap she would prove an amenable companion, mayhap more. Mayhap she could be his *fifth* betrothed, he thought wryly, and perchance he'd actually get her to the altar. He'd not met a woman so uncowed by him. It was refreshing. With his height and size, not to mention whispers circulating about the MacKeltar in the Highlands, he frightened lasses more oft than not.

He maneuvered himself through the opening, then took her hands and helped her scramble through, enjoying the feel of her small hands in his. Transferring his grip to her waist, he lifted her out. He didn't lower her to her feet right away but gazed challengingly into her eyes as he slid her down his body, enjoying the firm thrust of her nipples against his chest. The friction was delicious, and he felt her knees wobble for a moment before she found her feet.

If retreat was the measure of her desire, she desired

him fiercely. She scrambled away from him with an alarmed expression the moment her toes touched the ground. He stared at her nipples, now puckered peaks beneath her chemise. She glanced down and defiantly crossed her arms across her lovely breasts, baring her teeth in a ferocious little scowl. He laughed, because she succeeded only in pushing the generous mounds together and up, increasing his desire to bury his face in her plump cleavage tenfold.

"I said doona run from me," he reminded. "You could not hope to outdistance me." He looked her up and down. Her skin—and he was seeing a splendid amount of it—was smooth and unscarred, bearing no sign of disease. Her waist was slim, her belly had the slight swell he adored on a wench, and although her hips were lush, he suspected she'd not yet born bairn. The harsh light of day—oft unflattering to a wench—paid this one naught but tribute, and he bit back a groan. He'd not felt so intensely desirous of a woman ever before in his life.

"Stop looking at me like that," she snapped.

His gaze collided with hers; she had eyes the color of a wild Scottish sea, and there was clear evidence of a storm brewing in the icy blue depths. "Why are you so prickly, English? Is it because I am a Scot?"

"It's because you are overbearing, domineering, and pushy."

"I am a man," he replied easily.

"If men are allowed to behave in such an atrocious fashion, how are women supposed to act?"

"Appreciative. And among my clan we like them demanding in bed," he added with a smile. When her gaze grew even cooler, he said, "You do not respond well to a jest. Be easy, Gwen Cassidy. I seek but to lighten your fears. You need fear naught, lass. I will care for you, despite your bad blood. Even the English can learn. On occasion," he added, just to provoke her.

She growled—actually growled low in her throat, as if he'd so irritated her that she'd like nothing more than to kick him. He found himself hoping she would. He was aching for an excuse to tussle with her and take her soft body down beneath his. Then he'd make her growl low in her throat for an entirely different reason: a moan of desire as he buried himself between her thighs.

But feeble-minded though she might be, she knew better than to provoke contact—he could see it in her storm-filled eyes. Her lack of intelligence didn't seem to have precluded common sense. He drew a deep breath of fresh air and smiled. He was free of the cave, alive, and would soon be home. He would uncover the traitors and reward himself with the feisty Briton. *Life was rich,* thought the laird of the MacKeltar.

· 4 ·

Not a woman prone to violence, Gwen was taken aback by her desire to kick Drustan MacKeltar. Not to slice and dissect him verbally, which would have been the mature thing to do, but to punch him, maybe even bite him the next time he touched her. Her mind went on instant, extended sabbatical, just looking at him. She'd never met a man so hopelessly chauvinistic. He provoked the worst in her, dragging her down to a level as base and primitive as his own. She wanted to launch herself at him and pummel him. He was behaving as if, because he'd found her atop him, he owned her. Scottish lords obviously hadn't changed much over the centuries.

She hadn't missed his proclamation that he was an authentic "laird"; rather, she'd chosen to ignore it. He'd seemed to expect a curtsy or maidenly swoon, and she would not pander to his conceit. It appeared that centuries of submission to the English hadn't taught the Scots one damn thing about submission. He was likely one of those stuffy aristocrats who was fighting to restore Scotland's independence so he could swagger about in his kilt and regalia like a little king. He even preferred the archaic manner of speech affected centuries past.

And he was definitely a womanizer. Smooth-talking, sexy, and entirely too touchy-feely. Probably dumb as a box of rocks, however, because all that brawn couldn't possibly couch too much brain.

"I have to return to the inn now," she informed him.

"There's no need for you to seek shelter in a common tavern. You will be generously housed in my demesne. I will see to your needs." Possessively, he cupped his hand at the nape of her neck, tangling his fingers in her hair. "I like the way you keep your hair. 'Tis unusual, but I find it most . . . sensual."

Bristling, she tossed her bangs out of her eyes. "Let's get something straight, MacKeltar. I am not going home with you. I am not going to bed with you, and I am *not* wasting one more moment arguing with you."

"I promise not to mock you when you change your mind, lass."

"*Oooh.* Contrary to what you might think, arrogance does not work as an aphrodisiac on me." It was only a small lie. Arrogance alone didn't, but this particular arrogant man was a walking lollipop, and she was certain that latching her lips onto any part of him would satisfy the relentless oral craving she'd been fighting for ten days, seven hours, and forty-three minutes, not that she was counting.

"Aphro-di-si-ac," he repeated slowly, brows furrowed. He was silent a moment, then he said, "Ah, Greek: Aphrodite and *akos*. Mean you a love potion?"

"Sort of." How could he not know that word? she

wondered, eyeing him warily. And why break it into *Greek* parts?

When he grinned cockily, she dropped her gaze and pretended a sudden fascination with her cuticles. The man was too damn sexy for his own good. And standing *way* too close.

He slid his hands into her hair and tugged gently, forcing her to look at him. His silver eyes glittered. "Tell me you doona feel mating heat between us. Tell me you doona desire me, Gwen Cassidy." His gaze dared her to lie.

Dismayed, she realized he could sense how much she wanted him, just as she could sense that he wanted to be all over her, so she did what handling insurance claims had taught her to do best: Deny, deny, deny.

"I *doona* desire you," she mocked lightly. Yeah, right. The sexual tension between them nearly qualified as a fifth force of nature.

He inclined his head. A dark eyebrow rose and his gaze was amused, as if he were somehow privy to her internal dissenting opinion. One corner of his mouth lifted in a faint smile. "When you finally speak the truth, it will be so sweet, wee English. It will make me hard as stone, the mere words upon your lips."

She felt it imprudent to point out that he already was. When he'd buried his hands in her hair, he'd brushed that part of him against her. She was shocked to realize she was actually contemplating having impulsive sex with him, trying to decide what was the worst that could happen if she did as many people she knew did— just hopped into bed with a stranger. God, he was so tempting. She wanted to experience passion, and when he looked at her the way he was looking at her right now, she felt an epiphany might be a hot, slippery kiss away.

But he was headstrong, too gorgeous for anyone's peace of mind, a wildly unpredictable variable in a risky equation, and she knew what those could do—create chaos. The nervous flutter in her stomach, the desire she felt was too novel a sensation for her to act upon it without careful consideration.

Although she wanted to change her life and was determined to lose her virginity, she was beginning to realize that it wasn't as easy to change one's ways as she'd thought it would be. *Thinking* about having sex with a virtual stranger was a whole lot different than actually plunging right into the heat and nakedness and rawness of it. Especially when that virtual stranger was so much man, a little odd, and a lot overwhelming. Her newfound feelings of desire scared her. The intensity of her body's reaction to him scared her.

Perhaps she could do it with him on the last day of her trip, she mused. He was certainly willing. She could have what she knew would be heart-pounding sex, then fly back home and never have to see him again. She'd bought condoms before leaving the States, and they were tucked safely in her pack. . . .

Sheesh! Was madness contagious? What on earth was she thinking?

A brisk shake of her head restored her sanity.

"Come," he said.

I'd like to, but you're way too dangerous, she thought with a sigh.

Since he was heading down the hill in the general direction of the inn, she followed. "You don't have to hold my hand," she protested. "I'm not going to run off."

His eyes crinkled with silent amusement as he released her. "I enjoy holding your hand. But you may walk beside me," he informed her.

"I wouldn't walk anywhere else," she muttered. Behind would feed his ego, although she'd get to watch his incredible body, unobserved. In front, she'd be miserable, feeling his gaze on her. Beside him was the only tolerable place.

He took long strides, his natural pace a lope for her, but she refused to complain. The faster he walked, the more quickly she could surround herself with the safety of the teeming village. She'd never dreamed she'd be so grateful to see a busload of senior citizens in her life.

Busy plotting her polite but hasty retreat from his presence, she didn't realize he'd stopped until he was quite some distance behind her. She turned and gestured impatiently, but his eyes were on the village below.

"Come on," she shouted. He didn't appear to hear her. She called for him again, waving her arms to get his attention, but he remained motionless, his gaze locked on the view.

Fine, she decided, *this is a great time to leave, and I have a head start.* She broke into a sprint down the sloping hillside. Stretching her legs, as if running for her very life, she suddenly felt silly. If the man had truly planned to harm her, he could have done so long before now. Still, she couldn't shake the feeling that she was leaving something incredibly dangerous behind her on the hillside—far more than a simple man—and it was wiser that she did so now.

She ran for several seconds before the missile blasted her from behind. She stumbled and landed on her stomach in a springy patch of purple vetch, trapped beneath his body. He stretched her hands above her head and pressed her against the ground. "I said doona run from me," he gritted out. "Which word did you have difficulty with?"

"Well, you stopped moving," Gwen argued. "I called for you. And ouch, dammit, now I hurt all over."

When he didn't respond, only raised his body slightly off hers so she could breathe, she became aware of a subtle change in him. His heart was thundering against her back, his breathing was shallow, and his hands were trembling atop hers.

"Wh-what's wrong?" she asked faintly. What horror could make such strong hands tremble?

He pointed to a car, disappearing down the winding road beneath them. "What in the name of all that is holy is *that*?"

Gwen squinted. "It looks like a VW, but I can't tell from this distance. The sun's in my eyes."

"A what?"

"Volkswagen."

"A *what* wagon?"

"*Volks*wagen. A car." Was the man going deaf?

"And that?"

His cheek brushed her temple as she turned her head to gaze where he pointed. "What?" She blinked owlishly. He appeared to be pointing at the inn. "The inn?"

"Nay, that bright thing with colors such as I have never seen. And what of all those leafless trees? What has happened to the trees? And why have they tied cords between them? Think you they will run away if not tethered? Never have I seen oaks so shamed!"

Gwen eyed the neon sign above the inn and the telephone poles in wary silence.

"Well, lass?" He took several slow deep breaths, then said unsteadily, "None of this was here before. I have seen naught of such oddities. It looks as if half the clans in Scotland have settled about Brodie's loch, and I am quite certain he wouldn't approve of all this. He is a most private man." He rolled off her and flipped her over, then pulled her up so she was on her knees facing him. He cupped her shoulders and shook her. "What is a car? What purpose has it?"

"Oh, for heaven's sake—you know what a car is! Stop pretending. You've been pretty convincing as the archaic lord, but don't play any more games with me." Gwen glared at him, but beneath her anger he was frightening her. He had the most bewildered expression on his face, and she thought she glimpsed a hint of fear in his brilliant eyes.

"What is a car?" he repeated softly.

Gwen began to make a caustic comment, then hesitated. Perhaps he was sick. Perhaps this situation was infinitely more dangerous than she thought. "It's a machine powered by . . . er . . . battery and gas." She abruptly decided to humor him, giving him the short answer. "People travel in them."

Soundlessly, his lips formed the words *battery* and *gas*. He was very still a moment, then, "English?"

"Gwen," she corrected.

"Are you truly English?"

"No. I'm American."

"*American.* I see—well, not truly, but . . . Gwen?"

"*What?*" His questions were starting to scare her.

"In what century do I find myself?"

The breath locked in her throat. She massaged her temples, assailed by a sudden headache. It figured that a man who dripped such raw sex appeal had to be fatally flawed. She had no idea what to say to him. How did one answer such a question? Dare she get up and simply walk away, or would he tackle her again?

"I said, what century is it?" he repeated evenly.

"The twenty-first," she said, closing her eyes. Was he playing a game? The bold block letters of a newspaper headline blossomed against the insides of her eyelids, crowding out all rational thought:

DROPOUT DAUGHTER OF WORLD-RENOWNED PHYSICISTS ABDUCTED BY ESCAPED MENTAL PATIENT. SUBTITLED: SHE SHOULD HAVE LISTENED TO HER PARENTS AND STAYED IN THE LAB.

He fell silent, and when she opened her eyes he was scanning the village below: the boats on the loch, the buildings, the cars, the bright lights and signs, the bicyclists in the streets. He cocked his head, listening to the *blat* of horns honking, the buzz of motorbikes, and, from some café, the rhythmic bass of rock and roll. He rubbed his jaw, his gaze wary. After some time he nodded, as if he'd resolved an internal debate he'd been having. "Christ," he half-whispered, aristocratic nostrils flaring like a cornered animal. "I haven't lost a mere moon. I've lost *centuries*."

A mere moon? Centuries? Gwen pinched her lower lip between her finger and thumb, riveted.

Then he looked back at her, eyed her shirt, her pack, her hair, her shorts, and finally her hiking boots. He tugged her foot out from beneath her, held it in his hands and studied it for a long moment before raising his eyes to hers again. His dark brows dipped.

"You name your stockings?"

"What?"

He ran his finger over the words *Polo Sport* stitched on the thick woolen cuff of her sock. Then his gaze fixed on the small tab on her hiking boots: *Timberland*. Before she could form a reply, he said, "Give me your pack."

Gwen sighed and started to hand it to him, then unzipped the main pouch first, not in the mood to get into a discussion about zippers. Considering the one on her shorts—if he truly didn't know how they worked—she wasn't in a hurry to teach him. Women should sew padlocks on their zippers with him around.

He took the pack and dumped the contents on the ground. When her cell phone fell out, she was momentarily furious with herself for forgetting it, until she recalled that it wouldn't work in Scotland anyway. As he withdrew it from the jumble of her belongings, she realized it wouldn't work—ever again. The plastic casing had been crushed in one of her many falls, and it broke into pieces in his hands. He eyed the tiny technology inside with fascination.

He sorted through her cosmetics, pried open a compact, and regarded himself in the small mirror. Her protein bars were tossed aside along with the box of condoms (thank heavens), and when he spied her toothbrush, his bewildered gaze swept from her long, thick hair to the tiny brush and back to her hair again. One brow arched in an expression of doubt. He picked up the latest issue of *Cosmopolitan*, eyed the picture of the half-clad model on the cover, then fanned rapidly through it, gawking at the brilliantly colored pictures. He ran his fingers over the pages as if stunned. "And Silvan thinks his illuminated tomes are lovely," he muttered. When he started sorting through her brightly colored panties, she'd had enough. She closed her fist over the lime silk thong he was currently examining and firmly shook her head.

But when he looked at her, she realized that for the first time since they'd met, seduction was not on his mind. Her desire to flee was abruptly vanquished by the look of anguish on his face, and she wasn't so certain anymore that he was playing with her. If he was, he was a consummate actor.

Plucking the magazine from his hands, she pointed out the date in the corner. His eyes widened even further. "What century did you think it was?" she asked, disgusted with herself for being a sucker for a gorgeous man. He evidenced no intellect, had no redeeming qualities, yet drew her like a fluttery moth to a flame, and so what if she made ashes of her wings?

"The sixteenth," he replied hollowly.

He sounded so distraught that she touched him, brushing her fingers against his chiseled jaw, lingering longer than was wise. "MacKeltar, you need help," she soothed. "And we'll find you help."

He closed his hand over hers, turned his head, and kissed her palm. "My thanks. I am pleased you come so swiftly to my aid."

She withdrew her hand quickly. "Come with me to the village, and I'll get you to a doctor. You probably fell and have a concussion," Gwen said, hoping it was true. The alternative was that he had been wandering around, God only knew how long, thinking he was some medieval lord, and she just couldn't reconcile the powerful, arrogant man with a delusional paranoid schizophrenic. She didn't want him to be sick. She wanted him to be just as he appeared to be: competent and strong and healthy. It seemed impossible that a mental case could be so . . . commanding, regal.

"Nay," he said softly, his gaze drifting to the date on the magazine again. "We go not to your village, but to *Ban Drochaid*," he said finally. "And we haven't much time. It will be a hard journey, but I will tend you gently when we arrive. I shall see you handsomely rewarded for your assistance."

Oh, God, he meant to take her to his *castle*. He really *was* over the top. "I'm not going to those stones with you," she said as calmly as she could under the circumstances. "Let me take you to a doctor. Trust me."

"Trust *me*," he said, as he pulled her to her feet beside him. "I need you, Gwen. I need your help."

"And I'm trying to give it to you—"

"But you doona understand."

"I know you're sick!"

He shook his dark head, and in the late-afternoon light his silver eyes were clear, level, and intelligent. No crazed glimmer lurked there, only concern and determination. "Nay. I am well and in no way touched as you are thinking. You will simply have to see for yourself."

"I'm not coming with you," she said firmly. "I have other things to do."

"You must forgo them. The Keltar takes precedence, and in time you will understand. Now, I ask you a last time, do you come with me of your own free will?"

"Not a chance in hell, barbarian."

When he wrapped his hand about her wrist, she realized that while they were arguing he'd removed a chain of sorts from somewhere on his body. When he closed the metal links about her wrist and bound her to him, she opened her mouth to scream, but he clamped a powerful hand over her mouth.

"Then you come with me of my will alone. So be it."

· 5 ·

Nearly five hundred years, **Drustan brooded. How** could that be? He felt as if only yestreen he'd gone riding in the heather-filled Highland meadows of his home. His mind reeled from shock, and try though he might to deny it, he knew it was true. He knew it with a gnostic bone-deep knowing that was unquestionable. Her time felt different, the natural rhythm of the elements was frenetic, fractured. Her world was not a healthy one.

Centuries had passed, and he had no idea how it had happened. Probing his memory had yielded no additional facts. Five centuries of slumber seemed to have muted his memory, dimmed the events that had occurred just prior to his abduction. All he knew was that he'd been lured into some sort of ambush in which a number of people had participated. There had been armed men. There had been chanting and fragrant smoke, which reeked of witchcraft or Druidry. He'd obviously been drugged, but then what? Enchanted by a sleep spell? And if he'd been spelled, by whom? Still more important, why? The why of it would tell him if his entire clan had been targeted.

An icy finger of dread brushed his spine as he considered the possibility that they'd been attacked for the lore they protected.

Had someone finally believed the rumors and come seeking proof?

The Keltar males were Druids, as their ancestors had been for millennia. But what few knew was that they were not simple Druids, struggling with mostly incomplete lore since the loss of so much of it in the fateful war millennia ago. The Keltars possessed *all* the lore and were the sole guardians of the standing stones.

If after he'd been abducted, his father, Silvan, had been killed by his abductors, the sacred lore would be lost forever, and the knowledge they protected—to be used only when the world had dire need—vanquished utterly.

He glanced at Gwen. If she hadn't awakened him, he might well have slumbered for eternity! He murmured a silent prayer of thanks.

Pondering his situation, he realized that for now the how and why of his abduction were irrelevant. He would find no answers in her time. What mattered was action: He'd been blessed enough to have been awakened and had both the chance and the power to correct things. Yet to do so, he must be at *Ban Drochaid* by midnight on Mabon.

He glanced at her again, but she refused to look at him. Dusk had long since fallen, and they'd made good time, putting many miles between them and the horrifying, noisy village. In the moonlight her smooth skin shimmered with the warm richness of pearl. He indulged himself, envisioning her nude, which wasn't hard to do when she wore so little. She was all woman and brought out the most primitive man in him, a fierce need to possess and mate. Her nipples were clearly visible beneath her thin shirt, and he ached to suckle them in his mouth. She was a fiery wee lass with a spine of steel and curves that would lure even his devout priest Nevin's gaze. He'd gotten hard the moment he'd opened his eyes and looked at her and had been uncomfortably erect since. One flirtatious glance from her would return him to a painful state, but he didn't worry overmuch that she might cast him such a look. She hadn't spoken to him in hours, not since he'd refused for the hundredth time to release her. Not since he'd told her he would toss her over his shoulder and carry her if he had to.

It intrigued him—that she'd neither screamed, nor fainted, nor pleaded for release. His first impression of her had not been entirely accurate; although it was difficult to discern, what with her strange manner of speaking, she *did* possess a dash of intelligence. She'd demonstrated fine reasoning abilities while trying to talk him out of taking her along, and when she'd realized there was no possibility of him relenting, she'd treated him as if he simply didn't exist. *Bravo, Gwen,* he thought. *Cassidy is Irish for clever. Gwendolyn means goddess of the moon. Quite a fascinating lass you're turning out to be.*

Whereas initially he'd thought her an orphan or survivor of a clan massacre, a woman willing to barter her body to secure a protector—thus explaining her clothing and demeanor—it had since occurred to him that she might simply be typical of her time. Mayhap in five centuries women had changed this much, become tenaciously independent. Then why, he wondered, did he sense a silent sadness, a brush of vulnerability in her that belied her bravado?

He knew she thought that he'd dragged her off because he desired her, and would that it were that simple. There was no denying that he found her mesmerizing and was impatient to bed her, but things were suddenly much more complicated. Once he'd discovered he was stranded in the future, he'd realized he *needed* her. When they arrived at the stones—if the worst was true and his castle was gone—there was a ritual he must perform, his conscience be damned. There was a possibility the ritual would go wrong, and if that happened, he needed Gwen Cassidy standing by his side.

She was growing weary, and he felt a pang of regret for causing her distress. When she stumbled over a tree root and fell against him, only to hiss and jerk away, he softened. He would give her this one night, for after tomorrow there would be no stopping. She nearly fell where she stood, so he cupped one arm behind her shoulders, the other behind her knees, and deposited her on the mossy trunk of an enormous tree that had fallen to the floor of the forest. Perched upon the massive trunk, with her feet dangling several inches above the ground, she looked wee and delicate. Warrior hearts did not always come in warrior-strong bodies, and although he could hike three days without rest or food, she would not fare well under such conditions.

He boosted himself up onto the trunk beside her.

"Gwen," he said gently.

There was no response.

"Gwen, I truly will not harm you," he said.

"You already have," she retorted.

"You're speaking to me again?"

"I'm chained to you. I had planned to never speak to you again, but I've decided that I don't feel like making things easy for you, so I'm going to tell you incessantly and in vivid detail precisely how miserable I am. I'm going to stuff your ears with my shrill complaints. I'm going to make you wish you'd lost your hearing when you were born."

He laughed. This was his scornful English again. "You are free to torment me at every opportunity. I regret causing you discomfort, but I must. I have no choice."

She arched one brow and regarded him with disdain. "Let me be certain I understand this situation. You think you are from the sixteenth century. What year, exactly?"

"Fifteen hundred and eighteen."

"And in fifteen hundred and eighteen, you lived somewhere near here?"

"Aye."

"And you were a lord?"

"Aye."

"And how is it that you ended up sleeping in a cave in the twenty-first century?"

"That is what I must discover."

"MacKeltar, it's impossible. You seem relatively sane to me, this delusion excluded. A bit chauvinistic, but not too abnormal. There is no way a man can fall asleep and wake up nearly five centuries later. Physiologically, it's impossible. I've heard of Rip Van Winkle and Sleeping Beauty, but those are fairy tales."

"I doubt the fairy had aught to do with it. I suspect gypsies or witchcraft," he confided.

"Oh, now, that's infinitely reassuring," she said, too sweetly. "Thank you for clarifying that."

"Do you mock me?"

"Do you believe in fairies?" she countered.

"Fairy is merely another name for the *Tuatha de Danaan*. And yes, they exist, although they keep their distance from mortal man. We Scots have always known that. You have lived a sheltered life, have you not?" When she closed her eyes, he smiled. She was so naive.

She opened her eyes, favored *him* with a patronizing smile, and changed the subject as if not wont to press his fragile mind too hard. He bit his lip to prevent a derisive snort. At least she was talking to him again.

"Why are you going to *Ban Drochaid,* and why do you insist on taking me with you?"

He weighed what he might safely tell her without driving her away. "I must get to the stones because that is where my castle is—"

"Is, or was? If you expect to convince me you are truly from the sixteenth century, you're going to have to do a little better with your verb tenses."

He glanced at her reprovingly. "Was, Gwen. I pray it stands still." It must be so, for if they arrived at the stones and there was no sign of his castle, his situation would be dire indeed.

"So you're hoping to visit your descendants? Assuming, of course, that I'm playing along with this absurd game," she added.

Nay, not unless his father, at sixty-two, had somehow managed to breed another bairn after Drustan had been abducted, which was highly unlikely since Silvan had not tupped a woman since Drustan's mother had died, as far as Drustan knew. What he was hoping for was some of the items in the castle. But he couldn't tell her any of that. He couldn't risk scaring her off when he needed her so desperately.

He needn't have bothered searching for a suitably evasive reply, because when he hesitated too long for her liking, she simply forged ahead with another question. "Why do you need me?"

"I doona know your century, and the terrain between here and my home may have changed," he offered the incomplete truth smoothly. "I need a guide who has knowledge of this century's ways. I may need to pass through your villages, and there could be dangers I would not perceive until it was too late." That sounded rather convincing, he thought.

She was regarding him with blatant skepticism.

"Gwen, I know you think that I've lost my memory, or am ill, and am having fevered imaginings, but consider this: What if you are wrong, and I am telling the truth? Have I harmed you? Other than making you come along with me, have I injured you in any way?"

"No," she conceded grudgingly.

"Look at me, Gwen." He cupped her face with his hands so she had to look directly into his eyes. The chain rattled between their wrists. "Do you truly believe I mean you ill will?"

She blew a strand of hair out of her face with a soft puff of breath. "I'm chained to you. That worries me."

He took a calculated risk. With an impatient movement he released the links, counting on the mating heat between them to keep her from outright fleeing. "Fine. You are free. I misjudged you. I believed that you were a kind and compassionate woman, not a fainthearted lass who cannot abide anything that she does not immediately understand—"

"I am not fainthearted!"

"—and if a fact doesn't adhere to your perception of how things should be, then it cannot be." He gave a derisive snort. "What a narrow vision of the world you have."

"Oh!" Gwen scowled, scooting away from him on the fallen tree trunk. She swung one leg across it, straddling the massive trunk, and sat facing him. "How dare you try to make me feel bad for not believing your story? And I assure you, I do *not* have a narrow view of the world. I'm probably one of the few people who doesn't. You might be astounded by how broad and well-informed my vision of the world is." She massaged the skin on her wrist, glaring at him.

"What a contradiction you are," he said softly. "At moments I think I see courage in you, then at others I see naught but cowardice. Tell me, are you always at odds with yourself?"

A hand flew to her throat and her eyes widened. He'd struck something sensitive. Ruthlessly he pursued it: "Would it be so much to ask that you give a bit of your precious time to help someone in need—the way they wish to be helped, rather than the way you think they *should* be helped?"

"You're making it sound like everything is my fault. You're making it sound like *I'm* the one who's crazy," she protested.

"If what I say is true, and I vow it is, you do seem most unreasonable to me," he said calmly. "Has it occurred to you that I find your world—without any knowledge of the ancients, with limbless, leafless trees and clothing with formal appellations—as unnatural as you find my story?"

Doubt. He could see it on her expressive face. Her stormy eyes widened further, and he glimpsed that mysterious flash of vulnerability beneath her tough exterior. He disliked provoking her, but she didn't know what was at stake and he couldn't possibly tell her. He didn't have time to go out into her world and seek another person. Besides, he didn't wish any other person. He wanted her. She'd discovered him, she'd awakened him, and his conviction that she was supposed to be involved in helping him correct things increased with each passing hour. *There are no coincidences in this world, Drustan,* his father had said. *You must see with the eagle's eye. You must detach, lift above a conundrum, and map the terrain of it. Everything happens for a reason, if you can but discern the pattern.*

She massaged her temples, scowling at him. "You're giving me a headache." After a moment, she blew out a resigned breath, fluffing her bangs from her eyes. "Okay, I give up. Why don't you tell me about yourself. I mean, who you *think* you are."

A rather begrudging invitation, but he would work with what he could get. He hadn't realized how tense he had been, awaiting her response, until his muscles smoothed beneath his skin. "I have told you that I am the laird of my clan, despite the fact that my father, Silvan, still lives. He refuses to be laird anymore, and at three score and two I can scarce blame him. 'Tis a long time to bear such responsibility." He closed his eyes and took a deep breath. "I had a brother, Dageus, but he died recently."

He didn't mention that his betrothed had been killed while accompanying Dageus back to Castle Keltar for the wedding. The less said about any of his betrotheds to another woman, the better. He was touchy about the entire subject.

"How?" she asked gently.

"He was returning from the Elliott's estate when he was killed in a clan battle that wasn't even our own but between the Campbell and the Montgomery. Most likely, he saw the Montgomery was severely outnumbered and tried to make a difference."

"I'm so sorry," she said softly.

He opened his eyes to find compassion shimmering in her gaze, and it warmed him. When he lowered himself from the massive trunk of the fallen tree and pulled her leg over the trunk so she faced him, she didn't resist. With him standing on the ground and her perched upon the trunk, they were at equal eye level, and it seemed to make her feel more comfortable. "Dageus was like that," he told her with a mixture of sorrow and pride. "He was ever one to fight others' battles. He took a sword through the heart, and one bitter morn I woke up to the sight of my brother, trussed across the back of his horse, being escorted home by the captain of the Elliott guard." *And grief rips at my heart. Brother of mine, I failed both you and Da.*

Her brows puckered, mirroring his sorrow. "Your mother?" she asked gently.

"My father is widowed. She died in childbirth when I was fifteen; neither she nor the babe survived. He has not remarried. He vows there was only one true love for him." Drustan smiled. His da's sentiment was one he understood. His parents' match had been made in heaven: he a Druid and she the daughter of an eccentric inventor who'd scoffed at propriety and educated his daughter better than most sons. Unfortunately, educated lasses were hardly in abundance in the Highlands, or anywhere else for that matter. Silvan had been lucky indeed. Drustan had longed for such a match himself, but time had worn him down, and he'd given up hope of finding such a woman.

"Are you married?"

Drustan shook his head. "Nay. I would not have tried to kiss you were I betrothed or wed."

"Well, score one point for men in general," she said dryly. "Aren't you rather old never to have been married? Usually when a man hasn't married by your age, there's something wrong with him," she provoked.

"I've been betrothed," he protested indignantly, not about to tell her the number of times. It wasn't a fine selling point, and she was closer to the truth than he would have liked. There was indeed something wrong with him. Once women spent a bit of time with him, they packed up their bags and left. It was enough to make a man feel uncertain of his charms. He could see she was about to press the issue, so he said hastily, hoping it would end the discussion of the subject, "She died before the wedding."

Gwen winced. "I'm so sorry."

They were silent a few moments, then she said, "Do you *want* to get married?"

He arched a teasing brow. "Are you offerin' for me, lassie?" he purred. If only she would, he'd like as not snatch her up and marry her before she could change her mind. He found himself more intrigued by her than he'd ever been with any of his betrotheds.

She flushed. "Of course not. I'm merely curious. I'm just trying to figure out what kind of man you are."

"Aye, I wish to wed and have bairn. I simply need a good woman," he said, flashing her his most charming grin.

She wasn't unaffected by it. He saw her eyes widen slightly in response and she seemed to forget the question she'd been about to ask. He breathed a silent thank you to the gods who'd gifted him a handsome face and white teeth.

"And what would a man like you consider a good woman?" she said after a moment. "Wait"—she raised a hand when he would have spoken—"let me guess. Obedient. Adoring. Definitely not too bright," she mocked. "Oh, and she'd just have to be the most gorgeous woman around, wouldn't she?"

He cocked his head, meeting her gaze levelly. "Nay. My idea of a good woman would be one I loved to look at, not because another found her lovely, but because her unique characteristics spoke to me." He brushed the corner of her mouth with his fingers. "Mayhap she would have a dimple on one side of her mouth when she smiled. Mayhap she would have a witch-mark"—he slid his hand up to the small mole on her right cheekbone—"high upon one cheek. Mayhap she would have stormy eyes that remind me of the sea I so love. But there are other characteristics far more important than her appearance. My woman would be one curious about the world, and like to learn. She would want children and love them no matter what. She would have a fearless heart, courage, and compassion."

He spoke from the heart, his voice deepening with passion. He freed what was bottled up inside him and told her exactly what he wanted. "She would be one who would talk with me into the wee hours about anything and everything, who would savor all the tempers of the Highlands, who would treasure family. A woman who could find beauty in the world, in me, and in the world we could make together. She would be my honored companion, adored lover, and cherished wife."

Gwen drew a deep breath. The skeptical look in her eyes faded. She shifted uncomfortably, glanced away from him, and was silent for a time. He didn't interrupt, curious to see how she would respond to his honest declaration.

He smiled wryly when she cleared her throat and glibly changed the subject.

"Well, if you're from the sixteenth-century Highlands, why don't you speak Gaelic?"

Give nothing away, lass, he thought. *Who or what hurt you that makes you so conceal your feelings?* "Gaelic? You wish Gaelic?" With a wolfish smile, he told her exactly what he wanted to do to her once he removed her clothing, first in Gaelic, then in Latin, and finally in a language that had not been spoken in centuries—not even in his time. It made him hard, saying the words.

"That could be gibberish," she snapped. But she shivered, as if she'd sensed the intent behind his words.

"Then why did you test me?" he asked quietly.

"I need something to prove it," she said. "I can't just go on blind faith."

"Nay," he agreed. "You doona seem to be a woman who could."

"Well, *you* had proof," she countered, then added hastily, "of course, pretending that what you claim is true. You saw cars, the village, my phone, my clothing."

He gestured at his attire, his sword, and shrugged.

"That could be a costume."

"What would you consider sufficient proof?"

She folded her arms across her chest. "I don't know," she admitted.

"I can prove it to you at the stones," he finally said. "Beyond any doubt, I can prove it to you there."

"How?"

He shook his head. "You must come and see."

"You think your ancestors might have some record of you, a portrait or something?" she guessed.

"Gwen, you must decide whether I am mad or I am telling the truth. I cannot prove it to you until we reach our destination. Once we reach *Ban Drochaid*, if you still doona believe me, there at the stones, when I have done what I can to offer you proof, I will ask nothing more of you. What have you to lose, Gwen Cassidy? Is your life so demanding and full that you cannot spare a man in need a few days of your time?"

He'd won. He could see it in her eyes.

She looked at him in silence for a long time. He met her gaze steadily, waiting. Finally she gave a tight nod. "I will make sure you get to your stones safely, but that doesn't mean for a minute that I believe you. I am curious to see what proof you can offer me that your incredible story is true, because if it is . . ." She trailed off and shook her head. "Suffice it to say, such proof would be worth hiking across the Highlands to see. But the moment you show me whatever it is you have to show me, if I still don't believe you, I'm done with you. Okay?"

"Okay?" he repeated. The word meant nothing to him in any language.

"Do you agree to our deal?" she clarified. "A deal you agree to honor *fully*," she stressed.

"Aye. The moment I show you the proof, if you still doona believe, you will be free of me. But you must promise to stay with me until you actually *see* the proof." Deep inside, Drustan winced, loathing the carefully phrased equivocation.

"I accept. But you will not chain me, and I must eat. And right now I am going for a short walk in the woods, and if you follow me it will make me very, *very* unhappy." She hopped down from the fallen tree trunk and skirted around him, giving him wide berth.

"As you wish, Gwen Cassidy."

She stooped and reached for her pack, but he moved swiftly and wrapped his hand around her wrist. "Nay. If you go, it stays with me."

"I need a few things," she hissed.

"You may take one item with you," he said, reluctant to interfere if she had womanly needs. Mayhap it was her time of the moon.

Angrily, she dug in the pack and withdrew two items. A bar of something and a bag. Defiantly, she stuffed the bar in the bag and said, "See? It's only one thing now." She turned abruptly and headed for the woods.

"I'm sorry, lass," he whispered when he was certain she was out of hearing range.

He had no choice but to make her his unwitting victim. Larger issues than his own life depended upon it.

Gwen hurriedly used the "facilities," anxiously scanning the forest around her, but it didn't appear that he had followed her. Still, she didn't trust a thing about her current situation. After relieving herself, she devoured the protein bar she'd grabbed. She rummaged through her cosmetics bag, flossed, then dabbed a touch of toothpaste to her tongue. The taste of mint boosted her flagging spirits. A swipe of a medicated pad over her nose, cheeks, and forehead nearly made her swoon with pleasure.

Sweaty and exhausted, she felt more alive than ever. She was beginning to fear for her own sanity, because there was a part of her that wanted to believe him, wanted desperately to experience something outside of her everything-can-be-explained-by-science existence. She wanted to believe in magic, in men who made her feel hot and weak-kneed, and in crazy things like spells.

Nature or nurture: Which was the determining factor? She'd been obsessing over that question lately. She knew what nurture had done to her. At twenty-five, she had a serious intimacy problem. Aching for a thing she couldn't name, and terrified of it at the same time.

But what was her nature? Was she truly brilliant and cold like her parents? She recalled all too well the time she'd been foolish enough to ask her father what love was. *Love is an illusion clung to by the fiscally challenged, Gwen. It makes them feel life might be worth living. Choose your mate by IQ, ambition, and resources. Better yet, let us choose him for you. Already I have several suitable matches in mind.*

Before she'd indulged in her Great Fit of Rebellion, she'd dutifully dated a few of her father's choices. Dry, intellectual men, they'd regarded her more often than not through eyes red-rimmed from constant peering into a microscope or textbook, with little interest in her as a person, and great interest in what her formidable parents might do for their careers. There'd been no passionate declarations of undying love, only fervent assurances that they would make a brilliant team.

Gwendolyn Cassidy, the sheltered daughter of famous scientists who had elevated themselves from stark poverty as children to esteemed positions at Los Alamos National Laboratory doing top-secret quantum research for the Department of Defense, had had a nearly impossible time getting a date outside of the cliquish scientific community in which she'd been raised. At college it had been even worse. Men had dated her for three reasons: to try to get in good with her parents, to see if she had any theories worth stealing, and, last but not least, for the prestige of dating the "prodigy." Those few who'd been attracted by her other endowments (translated: generous C cups) hadn't lingered long after learning who she was and what courses she was acing while they were hardly managing to skate by.

She'd been frighteningly cynical by twenty-one.

She'd dropped out of the doctorate program at twenty-three, carving an irrevocable schism between herself and her parents.

Lonely as hell by twenty-five. A veritable island.

Two years ago, she'd thought changing jobs—taking a nice, normal, average job with nice, normal, average people who weren't scientists—would fix her problems. She'd tried so hard to fit in and build a new life for herself. But she'd finally realized it wasn't her career choice that was the problem.

Although she'd told herself that she'd come to Scotland to shuck her virginity, the small deception was how she concealed her deeper and much more fragile motives.

The problem was—Gwen Cassidy didn't know if she had a heart.

When Drustan had spoken so passionately of what he was looking for in a woman, she'd nearly flung herself at him, madman or no. Family, talking, taking quiet pleasure in the simple lush beauty of the Highlands, having children who would be loved. Fidelity, bonding, and a man who wouldn't kiss another woman if he were wed. She sensed that Drustan was a bit of an island himself.

Oh, she knew why she'd really come to Scotland— she needed to know if love really was an illusion. She was desperate to change, to find something to shake her up and make her *feel*.

Well, this certainly qualified. If she wanted to become a new person, what better way to start than to force herself to completely suspend disbelief, throw caution to the wind. To toss aside all that she'd been raised to believe and plunge into life, messy as it was. To rescind control over what was happening around her and entrust that control to a madman. Raised in an environment where intellect was prized above all else, here was her chance to act impulsively, on gut instinct.

With a *gorgeous* madman, at that.

It would be good for her. Who knew what might come of it?

She could feel a perfectly vicious cigarette craving coming on.

"Come," he said, when she returned. He'd built a fire in her absence, and she considered asking for her lighter back but was too exhausted to summon up the energy for a potential ownership dispute. Violating her privacy utterly, he'd rummaged through her pack and created a paltry bed by strewing her previously clean clothing upon the ground. A recent acquisition—a vibrantly crimson thong, adorned with black velvet silhouettes of romping kittens—poked out from between a sweatshirt and a pair of jeans. She spent a moment calculating the odds that he would pull out the only thong she'd bought but never worn—the thong she planned to wear when she lost her virginity.

Inconceivable. She glared suspiciously at him, certain he'd displayed her panties on purpose, but if so, he was the picture of innocence.

"I cannot procure food for you this night," he apologized, "but we will eat in the morning. For now, you must sleep."

She said nothing, merely cast an irritable glance at her clothes, strewn across twigs, leaves, and dirt. Further irritating her, he was standing at the perimeter of the light cast by the flames, making it difficult to see him clearly. But she didn't miss that lazily sensual, lionlike toss of his head that sent his silky dark hair falling over his shoulder. It *screamed* come hither, and pissed her off even more.

He met her glare with a provocative smile and gestured toward her clothing. "I made you a pallet upon which to sleep. In my time I would spread my plaid for you. But I would also warm you with the heat of my naked body. Shall I remove my plaid?"

"No need to bother," she sputtered hastily. "My clothes are fine. Wonderful. Really."

Despite the abysmal lowlands of her emotions and feverish highlands of her hormones, she was bone-weary and desperate for the plateau of sleep. She'd gotten more exercise today than she got in a month at home. The small pile of her clothing near the fire suddenly seemed as inviting as a down bed. "What about you?" she asked, reluctant to sleep if he was going to be awake.

"Although you doona believe me, I slept for a very long time and find I am most reluctant to close my eyes again. I shall stand watch."

She regarded him warily and didn't move.

"I would be pleased to give you something to help you relax," he offered.

Her brows furrowed. "Like what? A drug or something?" she asked indignantly.

"I have been told I have a calming effect with my hands. I would rub your back, caress your hair until you drifted peacefully."

"I don't think so," she said icily.

A quick white flash of teeth was the only indication she had that he was amused. "Then I bid you, lie down before you fall down. We must cover a great deal of ground tomorrow. Although I could carry you, I sense you would not appreciate it."

"Damn right, MacKeltar," she muttered, as she relented and dropped to the ground near the fire. She bundled her button-down into a pillow of sorts and stuffed it under her head.

"Are you warm enough?" he asked softly out of the darkness.

"I am downright toasty," she lied.

And in truth, she shivered for only a short time before inching closer to the fire and falling into deep and dreamless oblivion.

Drustan watched Gwen Cassidy sleep. Her blond hair, streaked with darker and lighter highlights, shimmered in the firelight. Her skin was smooth, her lips lush and pink, the lower one quite a bit fuller than the top. Kissably full. Above almond-shaped eyes, her dark-blond brows arched upward at the outer edges, adding an aristocratic disdain to the scowl she so frequently wore. She was lying on her side, and her plump breasts pressed together in dangerously tempting curves, but it wasn't her physical attributes alone that stirred him.

She was the most unusual woman he'd ever encountered. Whatever had shaped her temperament, she was a curious blend of cautiousness and audacity, and he'd begun to realize she had a clever and quick mind. So wee, she was unafraid to thrust her chin in the air and shout at him. He suspected that audacity was more her nature, while her cautiousness was a learned thing.

Her audacity would serve her well in the trials to come, and there would be many. He poked at his memory fragments, which were still frighteningly incomplete. He had two days to reclaim perfect recall. It was imperative that he isolate and study every detail of what had happened prior to his enchantment.

With a heavy sigh, he turned his back to the fire and stared out into the night at a world he didn't understand and had no desire to be a part of. He found her century unsettling, felt bombarded by the unnatural rhythm of her world, and was comforted by the knowledge that he wouldn't have to spend too much longer in it. As he listened to the unfamiliar sounds of the night—a humming in the air few would hear, a strange intermittent thunder in the sky—he reflected upon his training, sifting through neatly compartmentalized vaults of information stored in his mind.

Precision was imperative, and he subdued a surge of unease. He'd never done what he would soon have to do, and although his upbringing had prepared him for it, the possibility for error was immense. His memory was formidable, yet the purpose for which he'd been trained had never taken into account the possibility that he would not be at Castle Keltar when he performed the rite, and thus would not have access to the tablets or any of the books.

Although it was widely believed that Druidry had waned—leaving only inept practitioners of lesser spells—and that the ancient scholars had forbidden writing of any kind, both beliefs were myths that had been cultivated and spread by the few remaining Druids themselves. It was what they *wished* the world to believe, and Druids were ever adept at illusion.

On the contrary, Druidry thrived, although the prone-to-melodrama British Druids scarce possessed the knowledge to cast an effective sleep spell, in Drustan's estimation.

Many millennia ago, after the *Tuatha de Danaan* had left the mortal world for stranger haunts, their Druids—mortals and unable to accompany them—had vied among themselves for power.

There had ensued a protracted battle that had nearly destroyed the world. In the horrifying aftermath, one bloodline had been selected to preserve the most sacred of the Druid lore. And so the Keltar's purpose had been mapped out. Heal, teach, guard. Enrich the world for the wrong they'd done it.

The fabulous and dangerous knowledge, including sacred geometry and star guides, had been carefully inked in thirteen volumes and upon seven stone tablets, and the Keltar Druids guarded that bank of knowledge with their souls. They tended Scotland, they used the stones only when necessary for the world's greater good, and they did their best to quell the rumors about them.

The ritual he would perform at *Ban Drochaid* required

certain formulas that must be without error, and he was uncertain of three of them. The critical three. But who would ever have believed he would be trapped in a future century? If they arrived at the stones and Castle Keltar was gone and the tablets were missing—well, that was why he needed Gwen Cassidy.

Ban Drochaid, his beloved stones, were the white bridge, the bridge of the fourth dimension: time. Millennia ago, Druids had observed that man could move in three ways: forward and back, side to side, up and down. Then they'd discovered the white bridge, whereupon they could move in a fourth direction. Four times a year the bridge could be opened: the two equinoxes and the two solstices. No simple man could avail himself of the white bridge, but no Keltar had ever been simple. From the beginning of time, they had been bred like animals to be anything but.

Such power—the ability to travel through time—was an immense responsibility. Thus they adhered unfailingly to their many oaths.

She thought him mad now; she would surely abandon him if he overburdened her mind with more of his plans. He couldn't risk telling her anything else. His Druid ways had made too many women flee him already.

For what time they had left together in her century, he'd like to continue seeing that glimmer of desire in her gaze, not revulsion. He'd like to feel like a simple man with a lovely woman who wanted him.

Because the moment he finished the ritual, she would fear him and mayhap—nay, assuredly—hate him. But he had no other choice. Only the ritual and a fool's hopes. His oaths demanded he return to avert the destruction of his clan. His oaths demanded he do whatever was necessary to accomplish that.

He closed his eyes, hating his choices.

If Gwen had awakened during the night, she would have seen him, head tossed back, gazing up at the sky, speaking softly to himself in a language dead for thousands of years.

But once he'd spoken the words of the spell to enhance sleep, she slept peacefully until morning.

· 6 ·

Gwen had never felt so acutely five foot two and three-quarter inches in her life as she did trailing behind the behemoth who didn't understand the concept of physical limitations.

As she stretched her legs, swinging her arms to generate greater forward momentum—fully aware of how futile the effort was because momentum was contingent upon mass, and his mass was three times hers, ergo, he could outwalk her to infinity barring any unforeseen complications—her temper snapped. "MacKeltar, I'm going to *kill* you if you don't slow down."

"I am curious to know how you plan to do so, when you can't even pace me," he teased.

She was not in the mood for teasing. "I'm tired and I'm *hungry!*"

"You ate one of those bars from your pack a scarce

quarter hour past, when we stopped to examine your map and plot the fastest course," he reminded.

"I'm hungry for real food." *And I'm going to need it,* she thought with a sinking feeling, for the tourist map in her pack had indicated the fastest course from their current location to *Ban Drochaid* was eighty miles, cross-country.

"Shall I snare and spit a rabbit for you?"

A bunny? Was he serious? *Eww.* "No. You should stop at the next village. I can't believe you didn't let me go into Fairhaven. We were right there. There was coffee there," she added plaintively.

"To reach *Ban Drochaid* by tomorrow, we must travel without pause."

"Well, *you* keep stopping to pick up those stupid stones," she grumbled.

"You will understand the purpose of my stupid stones tomorrow," he said, patting his sporran, where he'd stored them.

"Tomorrow. You'll show me tomorrow. Everything will be explained tomorrow. I don't live for tomorrow, and you require a lot of faith, MacKeltar," she said, exasperated.

He glanced over his shoulder at her. "Aye, I do, Gwen Cassidy. But I give much in return to those people who have faith in me. I could carry you, if you wish."

"I don't think so. Why don't you just slow down a bit?"

He stopped, evidencing the first hint of impatience she'd glimpsed. "Lass, if that map you have is correct, we have until the morrow's eve to travel a distance of nearly eighty miles. That is three of your miles per hour, without stopping to sleep. Although I could run much of the way, I know you cannot. If you can manage four miles each hour, you may rest later."

"That's impossible," Gwen gasped. "The fastest mile

I've ever run on a treadmill was ten and a half minutes and I nearly died. And it was only *one* mile. I had to rest for hours and eat chocolate to revive myself. MacKeltar, we need to rent a car," she tried again. Earlier, upon discovering the length of the hike he planned, she'd proposed the alternative, but he'd simply clammed up and dragged her off at a brisk pace. "We could travel eighty miles in one *hour* in a car."

He glanced at her and shuddered. "I trust my feet. No wagons."

"Come on," she nearly wailed. "I can't keep up with you. It would be a simple matter. We can go down into the next village, rent a car, drive to your stones, and you can show me whatever it is this afternoon."

"I cannot show you until tomorrow. It would be without merit to arrive today."

"You said you needed to stop at the castle. If we walk the whole way, that's not going to give you any time to visit your old stomping ground," she pointed out.

"I doona stomp there, nor do I stomp much of anywhere, woman. *You* drive me to stomp." A muscle in his jaw jumped. "You must walk more quickly."

"You're lucky I'm moving at all. Haven't you heard of Newton's First Law of Motion? It's *inertia*, MacKeltar. An object that's at rest wants to *stay* at rest. I can't be expected to overcome laws of nature. That's why exercising is so difficult for me. Besides, I think you're afraid." Gwen felt a little guilty for playing fast and loose with Newton, but most people had no idea what she was talking about when she brought up the laws of motion, and rather than reveal their ignorance and argue with her, they usually dropped the subject. Dirty pool, but startlingly effective. She'd avail herself of anything that would get her out of walking eighty *freaking* miles.

He was staring at her strangely, with a mixture of

startlement and confusion. "I know naught of this Newton, but 'tis clear he failed to attain a complete understanding of objects and motion. And I am hardly afraid of one of your foolish wagons."

He'd never heard of Isaac Newton? Where had the man been living? In a cave?

"Wonderful," she pounced. "If you're not afraid, then let's return to Fairhaven and I'll rent a car. I'll even pay for it myself. We'll be at your castle by lunchtime."

He swallowed hard. He really did have an aversion to cars, she realized. Exactly the kind of aversion a man from five hundred years in the past might evidence. Or, she thought cynically, the type of aversion displayed by an actor who had given his performance much thought, down to the minute details. A small, wicked part of her longed to wedge the oversize package of testosterone into a little bitty compact car and see just how far he would carry the performance.

"Let me help you, MacKeltar," she coaxed. "You asked for my help. All I'm trying to do is get you to the castle faster than you could possibly get there yourself. Besides, there's no way I'm going to be able to walk for two days straight. Either we get a car, or you can just forget about me."

He blew out a frustrated breath. "Fine. I will travel in one of your wagons. You are right in thinking that I need time to prepare, and 'tis plain to see that you doona intend to exert any effort to increase your pace."

Gwen smiled all the way back to Fairhaven. She would get Band-Aids for the blisters on her heels where her hiking boots chafed. She would get coffee and chocolate and scones for breakfast. She would buy him clothes, rent a car, and return him to his family, who would figure out what was wrong with him. It was shaping up to be an acceptable day after all, she thought, sneaking a glance at the luscious man who was walking much slower now—in fact, dragging his feet beside her. He looked miserable. She didn't laugh, because she knew she must have worn an identical expression when they'd been traveling in the opposite direction.

The morning was steadily improving. The patch she'd put on earlier while she'd freshened up in the woods was working nicely. Nicotine hummed through her veins and she was no longer quite so worried that she might, in a fit of irritability, hurt the next person she saw or, worse, suffering oral withdrawal, do something with, or to, some part of Drustan MacKeltar she would regret. She was going to survive and she was again in control.

Control is everything, her mother, Elizabeth, had often said in that dry, chilly British voice of hers. *If you control the cause you own the effect. If you don't, events will unfold like dominoes toppling and you will have no one to blame but yourself.*

Oh, do hush up, Mother, Gwen thought mulishly. Her parents were dead and still running her life. Still, Elizabeth had been making a valid point. It was only because Gwen had been distracted by the state of her emotions—a thing Elizabeth had never permitted—that she'd carelessly plunked her backpack down without first examining her surroundings. Had she been paying attention, she would not have placed the pack in such a precarious position. But she had, and it had fallen out of reach, and she'd ended up in a cave. That single moment of carelessness had gotten her stuck in the Highlands with a very ill or very deranged man.

It was too late for regret. She could only exercise damage control. Now she was the one stretching her legs, urging him to walk faster. He did so in brooding silence, so she used the quiet time to firm her resolve that he was *not* a potential cherry picker.

They made it back to Fairhaven in under an hour, and

she sighed with relief at the sight of cozy inns, bike and car rentals, coffee shops, and stores. She was no longer alone with him, confronted by the constant temptation to part with her virginity or start smoking again, or both. They would zip into the stores and collect—*oh*!

She stopped and eyed him with dismay. "You can't come any further, MacKeltar. There's no way you can walk into the village looking like that." Sinfully gorgeous, the half-clad warrior could not mingle with tourists looking like a medieval terrorist.

He glanced down at himself, then at her. "More of me is covered than you," he said with an indignant and utterly regal sniff.

Figured the man would even *sniff* like royalty. "Maybe. But you're covered all wrong. Not only are you a walking weapon factory, you have nothing but a blanket wrapped around you." When he scowled, she hastened to assure him, "It's a very nice blanket, but that's not the point."

"You will not leave me, Gwen Cassidy," he said quietly. "I will not have it."

"I gave you my word that I would help you get to your stones," she reminded.

"I have no way of gauging the sincerity of your word."

"My word is good. Besides, you have no other choice."

"But I do. We walk." He took her hand and started to drag her back the way they'd come.

Gwen panicked. There was no way she was walking for two days. No way in hell. "All right," she cried. "You can come. But you've got to get rid of those weapons. You can't saunter into Fairhaven with an ax on your back, a sword at your waist, and fifty knives."

His jaw tightened and she could see he was preparing a list of protests.

"No," she said, raising a hand to cut him off. "One knife. You may keep one knife and that's it. The rest of it stays here. We will come back for it once we have a car. I can explain your costume by telling people you are working on one of those battle-reenactment thingies, but I will not be able to explain so many weapons."

With a gusty sigh, he removed his weapons. After depositing them beneath a tree, he moved reluctantly toward the village.

"Uh, excuse me," she said to his back.

"What *now?*" He stopped and glanced back at her, clearly exasperated.

She gazed pointedly at the sword, which he hadn't removed.

"You said one knife. You didn't specify what size it should be."

There was a dangerous glint in his gaze and, realizing she'd pushed him as far as he would bend, she acquiesced. She'd just say the sword was part of the costume. She glanced at it, wishing those glittering gems in the hilt looked less real. They could end up getting mugged for some silly fake sword.

At the rental agency, Gwen leased the last, dilapidated little car and arranged to collect it in an hour, which would give them ample time to purchase clothing, food, and coffee before leaving for Alborath. Guiding him past the curious stares of the onlookers, and occasionally tugging on his arm when he stopped to stare, she finally got him into Barrett's, a sporting-goods store that had the obligatory tourist's miscellany of other items.

In no time he would be presentable. People would

stop gawking at him as he passed before turning their scrutiny to her, as if trying to figure out what a perfectly normal-looking, albeit a bit grubby, American was doing strolling about with such a barbarian. They would stop drawing attention to themselves—a thing Gwen despised—and they would take a nice drive to Alborath. Perhaps have lunch with his family while she explained how she'd found him. She'd entrust him to his familial bosom and then catch up with her tour group in the next village.

Do you really want to leave him? Return to the seniors?

After last night she was no longer certain she would be able to leave him. Perhaps she'd linger for a time near his home and see how he fared before moving on. It wasn't as if there was anything in the States she was in a hurry to get back to. Not her job, not the exquisite, sprawling house on Canyon Road in Santa Fe she'd avoided since her parents' death. Too many memories, still fresh and painful.

Perhaps she would check into a bed-and-breakfast near Drustan's home for a while; it would be the compassionate thing to do.

"Where are you going?" she hissed when he swept past her, trailing his hand over a rack of purple running suits. He brushed his hand over a lavender sweatshirt, then stared at a lilac sweatband, ignoring her. She shook her head but, after a moment's vacillation, decided he should be harmless enough wandering the store while she selected something for him to wear.

She turned her attention to choosing clothing for a man who had the overly developed body of a professional athlete. Although Barrett's carried a variety of clothing, few men had his height and muscle. She tucked some jeans beneath an arm, eyed a denim button-down, and glanced at his wide shoulders. It'd never fit. A V-neck T-shirt might do, in stretchy cotton, but definitely not white. It would contrast entirely too nicely with his silky dark hair and deep golden skin. The sight of a white tee stretched across his muscular chest might persuade her to catapult her cherry at him.

She *felt* him return to her. The hair on the back of her neck tingled the moment he stepped beside her, but she refused to glance at him. At the same moment, a feminine purr from the other side of her asked, "May I help you?"

Gwen glanced up from the pile of T-shirts to find a tall, leggy, thirtyish saleslady, librarian glasses perched on her nose above a lushly pursed mouth, looking past her, eyeing the MacKeltar with fascination. "Wearing the old dress, are you now?" she spoke with a lilting burr, ignoring Gwen entirely. "Such a lovely weave. I've no' seen the pattern before."

Drustan folded his arms across his chest, his body rippling beneath the leather bands. "And you won't," he said. "'Tis the Keltar's alone."

There went the lionlike toss of his head, which on a woman would have looked coy but on him was an irresistible come-hither-if-you-think-you-can-handle-me. Gwen didn't wait for the saleslady to start drooling. Or go hither. She thrust a pile of jeans and shirts into Drustan's arms, forcing him to unfold his arms and drop the he-man pose.

"Allow me to show you to a fitting room," the saleslady purred. "I'm quite confident we'll find something to satisfy your . . . desires . . . at Barrett's."

Oh, choke me on innuendo, Gwen thought, not caring one bit for the interest in the woman's eyes. He might be crazy, but he was *her* deluded hunk. *She'd* found him.

Blocking the aisle to prevent—she glanced at the

woman's name tag—Miriam from latching on to him, she nudged Drustan toward the dressing room. Miriam sniffed and tried to step around her, but Gwen engaged her in a determined, irritated little dance in the narrow aisle until she heard Drustan close the dressing-room door behind her. Plunking her fists on her waist, Gwen looked down her nose up at leggy Miriam and said, "We lost our luggage. His costume was all he had in his carry-on. We don't need any help."

Miriam glanced at the fitting room, where Drustan's muscular calves were visible beneath the short white slatted door, then contemptuously examined Gwen, from her not-very-recently shaped eyebrows to the muddy toes of her hiking boots. "Found yourself a Scotsman, did you now, wee *nyaff*? You Americans are given to samplin' our men with the same thirst you turn to our whisky, and you canna handle our whisky either."

"I can most certainly handle my *husband* from here," Gwen snapped, louder than she would have liked.

Miriam directed a pointed look at her ringless hand and arched a meticulously shaped brow that made Gwen feel she had small, unruly bushes growing above her eyes, but she refused to be humbled and returned the stare in icy silence. When Gwen made no effort to explain why she sported no wedding band and displayed no inclination to quit blocking the aisle, Miriam moved off in a snit to fluff and tidy the sweaters Gwen had messed up on the display table.

Swallowing a catlike growl, Gwen moved to stand guard outside the fitting room, tapping her foot impatiently. A *swoosh* of fabric alerted her that he'd removed his plaid, and Gwen tried hard not to think about him standing behind the flimsy door, nude. It was harder than trying not to think about a cigarette, and her disobedient thoughts handled it as badly: The more she tried to *not* think it—the more she thought it.

"Gwen?"

Dragging herself from a fantasy in which she was about to drip chocolate syrup on him, she said, "Um?"

"These trews . . . *och! By Amergin!*"

Gwen snorted. The MacKeltar was pretending to discover zippers, and if he was wearing the plaid true to the sixteenth century (according to what their tour guide had told them), he had no underwear on. She heard a few more muttered curses, then a *zzzzzp!* Yet another curse. He sounded *so* convincing.

"Come out and let me see you," she said, struggling to keep a straight face.

His voice sounded strangled when he replied, "You'll have to come in."

Sneaking a furtive glance at Miriam, who had conveniently been accosted by a pimple-faced teenage boy, Gwen entered the dressing room. He was regarding himself in the mirror and his back was to her, and, heavens, but she would have been much better off if she'd *never* seen his tight muscled ass in a pair of tight faded jeans. His long black hair rippled over his shoulders and down his back, inviting her to plunge her fingers in it and trail them down the splendid ridges of muscle—

"Turn around," she said, her mouth suddenly dry.

He did so, with a scowl.

She eyed his bare chest and, with effort, forced herself to remember she was supposed to be looking at the jeans. Her gaze skimmed downward over his rippled abdomen and lean hips and—

"*What* have you stuffed in your pants, MacKeltar?" she demanded.

"Nothing that wasn't God-given," he replied stiffly.

Gwen stared. "There's no way that's part of you. You must have gotten a sock or . . . something . . . stuck. Oh, my." She pried her gaze from his groin. A muscle worked in his jaw, and he was clearly in discomfort.

"I doona believe you *intended* to torture me—nay, I saw other men on the street in such clothing—so I will not take putative measures. However, I think the problem is much the same as my feet," he informed her.

"Your feet?" she repeated dumbly, her gaze dropping. They *were* large.

"Aye." He gestured toward hers. "In your time you bind your feet in constrictive boots, whereas we wear soft, supple leather."

"Your point?" she managed.

"They have more room to grow," he said, as if she were simpleminded.

Gwen blushed. Of all things to play a joke on her about. Stuffing socks in his pants, indeed! "MacKeltar, I do not believe for one minute that *that*"—she gestured at the bulge in his jeans—"is you. I may be gullible, but I do know what men look like, and that is *not* what men look like."

He flattened her up against the door of the dressing room, and his sensual mouth, much too close for safety, curved in a cocksure smile. "Then you will simply have to see for yourself. Touch me, lass. Feel my . . . sock." His silver gaze sizzled with challenge, as he unzipped his zipper.

"Uh-uh." She shook her head for added emphasis.

"Then find me a pair of trews that doona threaten to sever my manparts."

"Uh-huh," she agreed, trying not to think about that unzipped zipper.

"Doona let this frighten you, lass. We will fit together well when I make love to you," he purred.

Weel was how it came out, and his lovely brogue, coupled with his "sock," were nearly all the persuasion she needed to set to removing his jeans with her teeth. She closed her eyes. "Back up, bud, or I'll *help* you fit in those trews," she threatened. "With your sword, if necessary."

"Look at me, Gwendolyn," he said softly.

"Gwen," she snapped.

"Gwen," he acquiesced. Right before he kissed her.

· 7 ·

Heat lightning, **Gwen thought.** *His touch is electrifying.* Attraction sizzled between them, and she knew he felt it too, because he drew back and looked at her strangely. Then, nudging her lips apart with his thumb, he opened her mouth and brushed his firm lips back and forth over hers, creating a light and irresistible friction.

Yes, she thought. *This is what I've needed. I feel . . . ooh!* He tilted her head at the perfect angle—just like Lancelot did Guinevere in that single kiss between them in the movie *First Knight*—and sealed his mouth over hers. She shivered when his tongue plunged between her lips, hot and silky and raw man.

Take that, Miriam.

Dizzied by a rush of desire, her head plopped limply back against the dressing-room door. She slid her hands up the rippling muscles of his arms, over his shoulders, then locked them firmly behind his neck. She hadn't gone to Scotland, fallen in a hole, and met a madman. She'd died and gone to heaven, and he was her reward for putting up with her parents for so many years. He closed his hands on her waist, then slid them intimately upward as he deepened the kiss, lingering over each curve. When he flattened his palms roughly over her breasts, her thighs popped open so smoothly that she wondered why she didn't just have a placard taped across them that said SQUEEZE HERE FOR SEX. She arched her back, rubbing her hard nipples against his callused palms. The sock she'd accused him of having was the hardest sock she'd ever felt and dangerously close to being smack-dab between her thighs.

And she wanted him there, by God.

She wanted to feel him silky and hot inside her, naked, with nothing between them.

He brushed her nipples with his thumbs as his tongue glided deeper, slick and hungry, so deep it coaxed soft little mewling noises from her throat. With a subtle turn of their bodies, he shifted his erection into the vee of her thighs and thrust his hips with the same ruthless, insistent rhythm as he thrust his tongue into her mouth. When he cupped her bottom and lifted her against him, she vaulted happily onto him, wrapped her legs around his waist, and kissed him frantically.

She arched against him, trying to get as close as possible, with so much irritating, restrictive clothing between them. She threaded her fingers into his silky hair, she suckled his tongue, desperate for more of him. He made a kind of laughing, satisfied male sound deep in his throat, clamped her head between his hands, and kissed her so hard he drew her breath into his body. His tongue glided into her mouth, withdrew, and returned. She felt her skin rippling with kinetic energy where he touched her; she was soaking it up and growing hotter at the core. This man knew her natural frequency and was making her resonate to perfect pitch. And as fine crystal, if vibrated continuously at its natural frequency, would shatter, she hovered mere caresses away from a similar explosion.

"Might I find you a different size or style?" chirped Miriam beyond the dressing-room door, inspiring the only benevolent feeling Gwen would ever entertain about her, for rescuing her before she shucked her virginity on a fitting-room floor to a madman. With a door that ended a foot above the floor.

Drustan groaned, then deepened the kiss.

How embarrassing! Gwen's sanity returned in degrees. *The man kisses me and I just hop right on him like he's the hottest new ride at Disneyland. Have I lost my mind?* She dug her fingernails into his shoulders and bit his tongue.

"*Ouch.* I doona think that was necessary," he whispered, passion blazing in his eyes, coupled with irritation that someone had dared interrupt them. He was clearly not a man who liked to stop anything he'd begun. He looked downright dangerously aroused.

"Ma'am?" Miriam said in a pinched tone.

Gwen was mortified to realize she was making soft panting noises. She took a deep breath, forced herself to unwrap her legs, and slid down his body. His hands tightened on her hips, until she threatened his shoulders with her nails again. Reluctantly, he lowered her to the floor, then promptly tried to kiss her again. "Stop it," she whispered furiously.

After drawing another shaky breath she called to Miriam, "Yeah. Um. Clothes, right. How about . . . uh, a pair of those khakis. The loose-fit brand in a thirty-two—wait a minute." She shook her head, trying to clear it. To accommodate his muscular thighs, they would have to be loose on his waist. "Bring a thirty-four, thirty-six-, and thirty-eight-inch waist," she corrected.

"And a belt." She closed her eyes and drew several more deep breaths. Her heart was thundering like a battering ram against the wall of her chest.

"Ma'am?" Miriam cooed so sweetly that only another woman would have heard the bitchiness.

"Yes?"

"I realize Americans are . . . *different* . . . and perhaps your feet were no longer on the floor because you were perched on the chair admirin' the state-of-the-art videocams we recently installed, but there are children in the store, and in Scotland we take the upbringin' of them seriously. These dressing rooms are not coed."

Her face flamed. "Get off me, you oaf," she hissed, pushing at his chest. He gave her a look that promised they would continue where they'd left off—and soon—before stepping back.

"As you wish. *Wife*," he purred, then opened the door with a flourish and a courtly bow.

Gwen blushed. So much for hoping he hadn't heard her snap at Miriam earlier. She stepped out, and there stood the infernal Miriam, staring past her at Drustan MacKeltar clad in tight unzipped jeans and no shirt. "Oh, my." Miriam wet her lips. "I'll just get those khakis."

But Miriam didn't move an inch, and Gwen wanted to kick her. Better yet, smack her eyeballs back into her head.

"You were going to get those pants," Gwen reminded stiffly.

"Oh, yes," Miriam said, flustered. "If the khakis don't cover . . . er, fit . . . perhaps he could try running pants. They're quite . . . roomy." She flashed a brilliant smile at Drustan, her gaze darting from the barely covered bulge at his groin to his ringless hand.

"Fine. Bring some of those too." Gwen glared at

Drustan, then pulled the door tightly shut. She leaned back against it and sighed, trying to collect herself.

"I want purple trews, lass," Drustan called over the door.

"No," she said irritably.

"And a purple shirt."

Absolutely not, she thought. His black hair and dark skin would look incredible offset by such a vibrant color. Maybe black would make him look drab. One could always hope. When, after a few moments and unintelligible curses later, she heard his jeans hit the floor, she imagined him nude and wondered if someone might have slipped her an aphrodisiac in the past twenty-four hours.

Find a man you want to talk with into the wee hours, a man you can argue with when necessary, and a man who makes you sizzle when he touches you, Beatrice had said. Well, the sizzle was there, and they certainly could argue. . . .

She shook her head, refusing to entertain the notion that a madman might be her potential soul mate.

Might he have a point about his feet? Did things truly grow larger if unconfined? It certainly hadn't felt like a sock. More like that can of tennis balls on the shelf behind the cash register. She glanced down at her breasts. Should she stop wearing a bra and start wearing snugger panties?

How was she going to look at him now?

The running pants were tolerable, Drustan decided, relieved. The blue trews had clearly been a torture device and would have strangled a man's seed. Mayhap men were fashioned differently in her time. He hadn't seen one other bulge out there on the street; mayhap they all had wee carrots in their trews. Mayhap there were hundreds of unsatisfied women in this century. Although at the moment, only one woman's satisfaction was of paramount interest to him, and he was rapidly becoming obsessed with her.

Gwen Cassidy did something unnatural to him. Made him feel weak-kneed and powerful at the same time. Made him feel the potency and virility of his Druid blood hammering in his veins. When he touched her, everything in the world made perfect sense, as if constructed of elegant mathematical equations. He should fear her because, when holding her, he forgot everything he should be worrying about.

Druids maintained that the larger an object, the more impact that object had upon the space in which it existed, and the greater the pull it exerted on other objects. Drustan had always considered himself walking proof of such a postulation; but Gwen, tiny Gwen, had very little mass, yet a monumental impact on his world. She defied the laws of nature.

Sighing, he forced his thoughts away from her firm little body and studied himself in the mirror. The black trews (named Adidas) were fitted yet baggy, with remarkable, stretchy stuff at the waist and ankles. They were by far the most suitable selection. He admired the black fabric, densely woven; he suspected it might repel water. Purple would have been better, but black was acceptable. Not royal—still, not serf colors.

The blue trews had been painful, and a terrible dye job to boot, as if the color hadn't set in. No weaver in his clan would have owned up to such terrible craft. And those bland "khaki" trews, although a reasonable fit, would have branded him a crofter, which the Keltar wasn't. His own plaid of royal purple and black, shot with costly silver threads, he rolled neatly around three of his leather bands and stuffed under his arm. Her people clearly did not adhere to *brehon* law. There'd been racks of purple attire, for simply anyone to purchase, arrayed throughout the store. The Keltar, centuries past and with much pomp and ceremony, had been gifted the full use of the seven colors by a Gael king. The MacKeltar lairds were entitled to wear purple so long as a Keltar lived.

And by God, he did—live, that is. Mayhap none other of his clan did, but he was alive, and once he got to his stones he would find out what had gone wrong. He was apprehensive about this world of hers, this wagon of hers, but to arrive at Castle Keltar today he would have ridden a fire-breathing dragon.

He prayed that by some miracle Silvan might have lived and fathered children—even at his advanced age, it wasn't impossible—and that he would find descendants alive and well. He prayed that if not, he would at least find his castle unscathed by time, that he would secure the tablets and by midnight tomorrow eve be standing safely in his own century again. No abrasive noises, no awful odors, no unnatural rhythm of Gaea herself.

Kicking aside the hard white shoes with strings that she'd thrust under the door moments ago, he put his boots back on. He balled his fists inside the T-shirt, having absolutely no idea why it was called a T-shirt as opposed to an A-shirt or a B-shirt, and stretched the fabric so it wasn't quite so restrictive around his neck and chest.

Opening the door, he paused a moment and swept his gaze over her petite, shapely body. They would fit well, although he suspected she wouldn't believe that until he demonstrated, and he hoped to demonstrate many times.

He *liked* Gwen Cassidy—prickly, stubborn, a touch domineering and bossy—in addition to aching to rip her clothes off and push her down on her back in sweet heather. Spread her legs and tease until she begged for him. Bury his face between her breasts and taste her skin. Their kiss had only whetted his appetite for her and he groaned, recalling how difficult it had been to peel those blue trews down over his swollen shaft.

He stood in the doorway, looped his sporran about his hips, fastened one of his leather bands atop it, and thrust his sword through it. He moved silently behind her and closed his hands on the slender span of her waist. Grinning, he slipped his hands lower. She had a luscious ass, soft and womanly and shaped like a plump upside-down heart, and he'd take advantage of every opportunity to touch it. He was about to press a finger intimately between her twin globes when she tensed and shot out of his grasp.

He arched a brow at the saleslady. "My *wife* is still growing accustomed to me. We haven't been wed long." Hmm, he quite liked the way "wife" had sounded on his tongue, he thought, eyeing Gwen.

"Nice sword," the saleslady purred, looking nearly a foot to the left of it.

Gwen pivoted on her heel. "Come on," she said to Drustan. "*Husband*." The look he gave her sizzled with passion, and she was beginning to wonder just how long she was going to be able to keep him under control. *If* she'd ever really had him under control to begin with.

"*I'd* like to grow accustomed to you," Miriam murmured, as she watched the magnificent man guide his wife out the door with a possessive palm to the small of her back.

He tossed her a flirtatious grin over his shoulder.

Gwen's spirits lifted a few blocks from the café, buoyed by the tantalizing aroma of fresh-ground coffee beans wafting on a gentle breeze. In a matter of moments she would be ordering cappuccino and chocolate bread. Cranberry-and-orange scones. Gwen released a heartfelt sigh of pleasure as they entered the café.

"Lass, there are so many people," Drustan said uneasily. "Does the entirety of this village belong to one laird?"

Gwen glanced at him and decided she should have gone with the white T-shirt, because Drustan MacKeltar, clad from head to toe in unbroken black, was, as her girlfriend Beth would say, *just downright fuckable*. She was still experiencing shivers of resonance from their kiss that were never going to stop unless she quit looking at him, so she glanced hastily around the shop. Families with children, seniors, and young couples—mostly tourists—were seated at dozens of small tables. "No, they're probably all from different families."

"And they're *peaceable*? All these different clans eat together and are *happy* about it?" he exclaimed, at sufficient volume that several people turned to look at them.

"Shh . . . you're drawing attention to us."

"I always draw attention. Even more so in this time. Wee little folks, the lot of you."

She glared at him. "Just be quiet, behave, and let me order."

"I *am* being have," he muttered, then moved away to gawk at the shiny silver machines grinding and perking and steaming.

Being have, with a long *A*? His command of language baffled her. But then she thought about it a moment: be good—being good; be quiet—being quiet; behave—being have. There was an unsettling consistency to his madness. What was it Newton had said? *I can calculate the motion of heavenly bodies but not the madness of people.*

While Gwen ordered, Drustan circled the interior

of the coffee shop, missing nothing. He seemed fascinated by everything, picking up stainless-steel mugs, turning them around and upside down, sniffing the bags of coffee beans, poking at the straws and napkins. Then he found the spices. She caught up with him at the condiment stand just as he was slipping the little jars of cinnamon and chocolate in the pocket of his running pants.

"*What* are you doing?" she whispered, removing the lids from their coffee. She angled her back so the patrons of the café couldn't see that he was breaking the law. "Take those out of your pocket!"

He scoffed. "These are valuable spices."

"You would steal?"

"Nay, I'm no thief. But this is cinnamon and cocoa. 'Tis not so easy to come by, we're nearly out, and Silvan loves it."

"But it's not yours," she said, trying to be patient.

"I am the MacKeltar," he said, clearly trying to be patient. "Everything is mine."

"Put them back."

His grin was pure male challenge. "*You* put them back."

"I am not rooting around in your pockets."

"Then they stay where they are."

"You are *so* stubborn."

"I am? I? Woman who insists everything be her way?" He fisted his hands at his waist and shifted his voice into a higher octave, imitating her: "You must wear hard white shoes. You must remove your weapons. You must travel in a car. You must not kiss me even though I wrap my legs around you when you do." Shrugging irritably, he reverted to his deep brogue. "Must must *must*. I weary of that word."

Cheeks flaming over the jibe about her unruly legs,

Gwen thrust her hand in his pocket and closed her fingers around the small glass bottles.

"Silvan will be most unhappy," he said, stepping closer with a wolfish smile.

"Silvan died five centuries ago, according to you." The moment she said the words, she regretted them. A flash of pain crossed his face, and she could have kicked herself for being so callous. If he was ill, he might genuinely believe everything he was telling her, and if so, the death of his "father"—real or imagined—would hurt him.

"I'm sorry," she said quickly. She sprinkled cinnamon on their frothy cappuccinos. Then, to atone for her unkind words, she slipped the bottle back in his pocket, trying to ignore the dually disturbing facts that she was aiding and abetting a criminal and that she was so close to his "sock," which rhymed nicely with *cock*, and oh, it had been an eyeful in those jeans.

Angrily, he plunged his hand into his pocket, pulled both bottles out, and plunked them on the little condiment stand. Without a word, he turned his back to her and stalked out the door.

Gwen hastened after him, and as she passed a table where a distinguished-looking man sat with his wife and son, she heard the boy say, "Can you believe they were going to steal the cinnamon and chocolate? They didn't look poor. Did you see his sword? Wow! It was better than the Highlander's!"

Embarrassed, Gwen tucked the bag of pastries beneath her arm, juggled both cups of coffee, and struggled with the door.

"Drustan, wait. Drustan, I'm sorry," she called to his broad, stubborn back.

He stopped midstep, and when he turned around he was smiling. Was that how brief the duration of his anger? She caught her breath and held it. He was simply the most beautiful man she'd ever seen, and when he smiled . . .

"You like me."

"I do not," she lied. "But I didn't mean to hurt your feelings."

He was undaunted. "Aye, you like me, lass. I can tell. You called me by my given name and you are frowning, with dewy eyes. I forgive you for being cruel and thoughtless."

She changed the subject hastily and addressed something that had been bothering her since they'd left Barrett's and that snooty Miriam. "Drustan, what does *nyaff* mean?"

He looked startled, then laughed. "Who dared call you a wee *nyaff*?"

"That snotty woman in Barrett's. And quit laughing at me."

"Och, lass." More laughter.

"Well, what does it mean?"

"Do you wish the whole gist of it, or a simple one-word summary? Not that I can think of one at the moment," he added. "It's a uniquely Scots word."

"The whole gist of it," she snapped.

Eyes sparkling, a brow mischievously arched, he said, "As you wish. It means one who is irritating, much like a midge, one whose capacity to annoy and inspire contempt exceeds her diminutive size but not the cockiness that accompanies it."

Gwen was seething by the time he finished. She turned around and stomped back toward Barrett's to tell perfectly plucked Miriam precisely what she thought of her.

"Hold, lass," he said, catching up with her and closing his hand about her upper arm. " 'Tis plain to see she was merely jealous of you," he told her soothingly, "for having a fine braw man such as me at your side, especially after she beheld me in those blue trews."

Gwen plunked her fists at her waist. "Oh, could you *be* any more pleased with yourself?"

"You're no *nyaff*, lass," he said, gently tucking a strand of hair behind her ear. "She was like as not far more envious of the look on my face when I gaze upon you."

Well. Her sails deflated. Gwen felt suddenly much more charitable toward Miriam, and it must have shown on her face because he smiled arrogantly.

"Now you like me even more."

"I do not," she said, stiffly pulling her arm from his grasp. "Let's go get that rental car and get out of here."

God forgive her, she was beginning to more than like him. She was feeling territorial, protective, and downright lusty.

· 8 ·

One flat tire—in the company of a man who had
no idea how to change one, and no jack—a pit stop for
his weapons, three rest stops, four coffees, and a very
late lunch later, they arrived at the outskirts of Alborath
just as dusk was falling.

Gwen sneaked a glance at him and wondered if the
color would ever return to his face. She'd pushed the
shuddering car up to seventy but quickly relented when
he'd gripped the sides of his seat so tightly that if
she'd tapped him with a fingernail, he might have shattered.

It was a good thing she'd slowed down, because the
tire had gone flat two miles outside of Fairhaven, and
they'd had to walk back and get a person from the rental
agency to arrange for a serviceman to get the tire
changed. She'd tried to rent a different vehicle, but as all

were under contract, it was this one or none until to-morrow evening.

Tire changed, they'd resumed their drive, and eventually he'd relaxed enough to turn his attention to the coffee and pastries. After complaining because she'd gotten no kippers and tatties, he'd consumed the coffee and chocolate with gusto. The pleasure he'd exhibited over such mundane items had further irritated her. God help her, but she was nearly beginning to believe him. They hadn't talked much on the drive, although not for her lack of trying. He simply hadn't seemed able to relax enough to speak.

Now, as the lights of Alborath came into view, nestled in a lush valley, his complexion was ghastly in the gloaming.

"Would you like to stop in the village?"

"Nay," he replied tersely. He pried his fingers from the edge of the seat and pointed to a road north of the village. "You must guide this metal beast to the crest of that ben."

Gwen eyed the mountain to which he pointed. There were two hundred seventy-seven mountains in Scotland, so said her brochure, that exceeded three thousand feet, and he was pointing to one of them. Sighing, she circled the village, downshifting when she reached the mountain. She'd been hoping to coax him to have dinner and secure a reprieve before confronting the extent of his delusions.

"Tell me about your home," she urged. The day had been a trial for both of them, and she felt a sudden spear of concern. She was about to take him "home," and what if there wasn't one there? What if the next few hours critically stressed his already damaged mind? She was supposed to stay with him until tomorrow night to see his proof, although technically she'd fulfilled her end of the bargain: She'd gotten him safely to *Ban Drochaid.*

She had a feeling *technically* didn't mean much to a man of his ilk.

"Doona think you'll be leaving me now," he said, placing his hand over hers on the gear stick.

Gwen glanced sharply at him. "What are you? A mind reader?"

He half-smiled. "Nay. I'm merely reminding you that your bargain with me was that you would stay to see my proof. I will not let you fail me now."

"What are you going to do, chain me again?" she said dryly.

When he didn't answer, she took another look at him. God above, but the man looked dangerous. His silver-metal eyes were cool and frighteningly calm and—yes, he would chain her again. For a split second, in the eerie, bruised half light of gloaming, he looked as if he had truly stepped forward five centuries, a barbaric warrior intent on his quest, and nothing or no one would get in his way.

"I have no intention of reneging," she said stiffly.

"I assume *reneging* means to act with dishonor?" he said flatly. "Good, for I would not permit it."

They drove in silence for a time.

"Do you enjoy a bard's rhymes, Gwen?"

She glanced sharply at him. "I have been accused of enjoying poetry from time to time." *Romantic poetry, the kind never read at Chez Cassidy when I was a child.*

"Would you grant me a boon?"

"Sure, why not," she said with a sigh a martyr would envy. "I've already done fifty gazillion, what could one more possibly hurt?"

He gave her a faint smile, then spoke quietly and clearly: *"Wither thou goest, there goest I, two flames sparked from but one ember; both forward and backward doth time fly, wither thou art, remember."*

She shrugged, confused. It had started out rather

romantic, but hadn't ended that way. "What does it mean?"

"Have you a good memory, Gwen Cassidy?" he evaded.

"Of course I do." *Oh, God, he was losing it.*

"Re-say it to me."

She looked at him. His face was pale, his hands fisted in his lap. His expression was deadly serious. For no other reason than to appease him, she made him repeat it, then repeated it without error. "Is there a point to this?" she asked when she'd said it three times, perfectly. It was permanently etched in her mind.

"It made me happy. Thank you."

"That seems to have become my purpose in life," she said dryly. "Is this another one of those things that will become clear to me in time?"

"If all goes well, nay," he replied, and something in his voice made a shiver kiss her spine. "Pray you need never understand."

She changed the subject uneasily, and for the duration of the ride they spoke of innocuous things while her tension mounted. He described his castle lovingly, first the grounds, then the interior and some of the recent renovations. She spoke of her mindless job but said little else of significance. Gwen had been conditioned not to overdisclose: The more a man knew about her, the less he ended up liking her, and for reasons she couldn't explain to herself, she wanted Drustan MacKeltar to like her. It seemed they were both suddenly eager to fill the silence or it would swallow them alive.

By the time they reached the top of the mountain, Gwen's hands were trembling on the steering wheel, but when he lifted a hand to rake his hair from his face she saw that his were too. She didn't miss the significance of the fact: He was not playing with her. He genuinely hoped to find his castle at the top of this mountain. Firmly grounded in his delusion, he also feared that it might no longer stand. Sneaking cautious peeks at him, she grudgingly conceded that he was not suffering amnesia or playing some strange game. He believed he was what he claimed he was. The realization was far from reassuring. A physical injury would heal, a mental aberration was much more difficult to cure.

Steeling herself, she backed off the gas, reluctant to complete the journey. She wished she'd hiked it with him, so she wouldn't have to face this moment now. If she'd done it his way, she could have postponed it for another twenty-four hours.

"Turn north."

"But there's no road there."

"I see that," he said grimly. "And considering the ones upon which we've traveled thus far, one would think there should be, a fact that concerns me."

She turned left, and the headlights of the car limned a grassy knoll.

"Up the hill," he urged softly.

Drawing a deep breath, Gwen obeyed. When he snapped at her to stop, she didn't need the command, for she'd monkeyed the clutch and was about to stall anyway. The tips of the towering stones of *Ban Drochaid* loomed over the crest of the hill, black against a misty purple sky.

"Um, I don't see a castle, MacKeltar," she said hesitantly.

"'Tis beyond the fell; the mon conceals it because it sits farther back, past the stones. Come. I will show you." He fumbled with the door latch, then burst from the car.

Fell *and* mon *must mean* hill or crest, she decided as she killed the lights and joined him. The tremor in her hands had spread to the rest of her body, and she was suddenly chilled. "Wait, let me grab my sweatshirt," she said. He waited impatiently, his gaze fixed upon the tops of the stones, and she knew he was desperate to get up over the crest to see if his castle still stood.

No more eager than she was to delay it. "Do you want a bite to eat before we go?" she said brightly, reaching for the salmon patties and celery they'd boxed up at the last stop.

He smiled faintly. "Come, Gwen. Now."

With a resigned shrug, she slammed the car door shut and trudged to his side. When he took her hand in his, she didn't even try to pull away but inched closer, as much for her support as his.

They hiked the remainder of the incline in silence, unbroken but for the chirping of crickets and the melodic hum of tree frogs. At the top she drew in a sharp breath. Against the backdrop of pink-and-purple-streaked sky, a gentle breeze ruffled the grass within the circle of stones. She counted thirteen of them, ranged about a great slab in the center. The megaliths reared up, black against the brilliant horizon.

There was nothing beyond the stones.

Oh, a few pines, and, granted, there were several gentle slopes that might block one's vision, but nothing that a castle could crouch mischievously behind.

They moved forward in silence, cutting through the circle of stones, much more slowly now, for ahead of them, past stumps of what had once been lofty and ancient oaks, was the clear foundation of a castle that no longer stood.

She refused to look at him. She would *not* look at him.

When they reached the perimeter of the outer wall, he sank to his knees.

Gwen eyed the tall grass in the center of the ruin, the chunks of stone and mortar in crumbling piles, the night sky beyond the silent castle grave, anything but him, dreading what she would see. Anguish? Horror? Realization that he truly was mentally unbalanced flickering in those beautiful silver eyes that seemed so misleadingly clear?

"Och, Christ, they're all dead," he whispered. "Who destroyed my people? Why?" He drew a shuddering breath. "Gwen." The word was strangled.

"Drustan," she said softly.

"I bid you return to your wagon for a time."

Gwen hesitated, torn. Half of her wanted nothing more than to tuck tail and run; the other half felt that he needed her desperately here and now. "I'm not leaving now—"

"*Go.*"

He sounded so anguished that Gwen flinched and looked at him. His eyes were dark and unreadable but for a shimmer of moisture.

"Drustan—"

"I beg of you, leave me now," he whispered. "Leave me to mourn my clan alone."

The faintness of his voice deceived her. "I promised not to just abandon—"

"Now!" he thundered. When she still didn't move, his eyes blazed. "*You will obey me.*"

Gwen noticed three things in the time it took him to utter the command. First, although she knew it was impossible, his silvery eyes seemed to blaze from deep within like something she'd once seen in a sci-fi movie. Second, his voice was different, sounded like a dozen voices layered upon one another, obliterating any conscious choice, and third, she suspected if he'd ordered her to walk off a cliff in such a voice, she might.

Her legs broke into an instinctive sprint even as her brain was processing those startling observations.

But a few paces inside the stones, the eerie compulsion receded and she stopped and glanced back. He'd entered the ruin and climbed the highest pile of collapsed stone; a black silhouette on his knees, back arched, chest canted skyward, he shook his fist at the indigo sky. When he tossed his head back and roared, the blood curdled in her veins.

Was this the same man who'd kissed her in the fitting room? The one who'd gotten her hotter than a volcano and as prone to imminent explosion and made her think there might be an equation for passion her parents had never taught her?

No. This was the man who wore fifty weapons on his body. This was the man who carried a double-bladed ax and a sword.

This was the man to whom she'd begun losing a little piece of an organ that she'd been raised to believe was merely an efficient pump. The realization startled her. Madman or no, frightening or not, he made her feel things she'd never felt before.

MacKeltar, she thought, *what on earth am I going to do with you?*

Drustan wept.

The worst was true. He lay on his back in the Greathall, one knee bent, arms spread wide, his fingers laced in the tall grass, and thought of Silvan.

You have only one purpose, son, as do I. Protect the Keltar line and the knowledge we guard.

He'd failed. In a moment of carelessness he'd been taken unaware, enchanted, stolen from his time, and buried for centuries. His disappearance had triggered the destruction of his castle and clan. Now Silvan was dead, the Keltar line extinguished, and who knew where the tablets and volumes were? The possibility of such knowledge falling into the wrong hands dragged him down into a deep black place beyond fear. He knew that a greedy man could reshape, control, or destroy the entire world with such knowledge.

Protect the line. Protect the lore.

It was imperative that he successfully return to his time.

Although he had not changed so much as one hair, five hundred years had passed, and nothing remained to speak of his existence or the life of his father and his father's father before him. Millennia of training and discipline, all gone in the blink of an eye.

Tomorrow night he would enter the stones and perform the ritual.

Tomorrow night he would not exit the stones. One way or another, he would no longer be in the here and now.

And God willing, tomorrow her century would matter no more, for with luck, by Mabon-high he would have undone all the wrong that had been done.

Still, for the time he had remaining in the twenty-first century, his people were as dead as his castle was destroyed, naught more than ancient dream dust blowing ignobly across Scotland. Roughly dragging the back of his hand across his cheeks, he pushed himself to his feet and spent the next hour wandering the ruin, looking for graves. He uncovered not one new marker in the chapel yard. Where had his clan gone? If they'd died, where had they been buried? Where was Silvan's marker? Silvan had made it painstakingly clear that he wished to be interred beneath the rowan behind the chapel, yet no stone marker proclaimed his name.

Dageus MacKeltar, beloved brother and son.

He swept shaking fingers over the stone that marked his brother's grave. Unable to comprehend the passage of five centuries, Drustan suffered the fever-hot grief of having buried Dageus only a fortnight past. His brother's death had made him crazed. They'd been close as two people could be. When he'd lost his brother, he'd argued endless hours with his father.

What good is it to have the knowledge of the stones if I cannot go back and undo Dageus's death? he'd shouted at Silvan.

You must never travel to a point within your own life, Silvan had snapped, weary and red-eyed from weeping.

Why can I not return to a time within my own past?

If you are too close in proximity to your past self, one of you—either your past or present self—won't survive. We have no way of foretelling which one lives. There have been times when neither survived. It seems to stress the natural order of things, and nature struggles to correct itself.

Then I'll choose a time in the past when I was across the border in England, Drustan snarled, refusing to accept that Dageus was irrevocably gone.

No one knows how far away is far enough, son. Besides, you are forgetting that we may never use the stones for personal reasons. They are to be used only for the greater good of the world—or in extreme circumstances to ensure the succession of the MacKeltar. One of us must always live. But these are not extreme circumstances, and you know what would happen if you abused the power.

Aye, he knew. Legend handed down over the centuries claimed a Keltar who used the stones for personal reasons would become a dark Druid the moment he passed through. Lost to honor and compassion, he would relinquish his very soul to the blackest forces of evil. Become a creature of irreverent destruction.

The hell with the legend! he'd thundered defiantly. But even in his grief, he'd known better. Whether or not the legend was true, he would not be the first MacKeltar to trespass on such sacred territory. Nay, he would accept, as all his ancestors had accepted, and honor his oaths. He had not been given unfathomable power to abuse it or use it for personal gain. He couldn't justify using the stones to mend his own heart.

If he saved Dageus and became a dark Druid, what then would he do when Silvan grew ever older? Cheat fate again? A man could go crazy with so much power and no limits. Once he crossed such a line, there would be no turning back; he would indeed become a master of the black arts.

And so he'd bid farewell to Dageus and resworn his oath to his father. *I will never use the stones for personal reasons. Only to serve and protect, and to preserve our line, should it be threatened with extinction.*

As it was now.

Drustan ran a hand through his hair, exhaling. Dageus was dead. Silvan was dead. He was the only remaining Keltar, and his duty was clear. For five hundred years the world had been unprotected by a Keltar–Druid. He had to return and do whatever was necessary to restore a concurrent succession of the Keltar. At any cost.

And what about the price the woman will pay? his conscience chided.

"I have no choice," he muttered darkly. He plunged his hands into his hair and massaged his temples with the heels of his palms.

He knew by rote the formulas for the thirteen stones, but he did not know the critical three, the ones that would specify the year, the month, the day. It was imperative that he return to the sixteenth century shortly after his abduction. Whoever had lured him beyond the castle walls would not be able to penetrate the fortress of Castle Keltar—even with a full army—for at least several days. The castle was too well-fortified to be taken easily. So long as he returned a day, or even two, after his abduction, he should still have time to save his clan, castle, and all the information within its walls. He would defeat his enemy, marry, and have a dozen children. With Dageus dead, he finally understood the urgency Silvan had tried to impart to his sons to rebuild the Keltar line.

Drustan, you must learn to conceal your arts from women and take a wife—any wife. I was blessed with your mother; 'twas a miraculous and uncommon thing. Though I wish the same for you, 'tis too dangerous to have so few Keltar.

Aye, he'd learned that the hard way. He rubbed his eyes and exhaled. He had a minuscule target at which to aim, and he'd never studied the symbols he now needed. He'd been forbidden to travel within his lifetime, so there had been no reason for him to commit to memory the symbols spanning his generation.

Yet . . . in a dark moment of weakness and longing, he'd looked up the ones that would have taken him back to the morning of Dageus's death—and from those forbidden symbols he could attempt to derive the shapes and lines of the three he needed now.

Still, it would be a guess. An incredibly risky guess, with dire consequences if he didn't get them right.

Which brought him back to the tablets. If Silvan had

been able to hide them somewhere on the grounds before he'd suffered whatever fate had befallen him, Drustan wouldn't have to guess—he could calculate the symbols he needed from the information on the tablets, with no fear of error. He felt fairly certain that if he returned himself to the day *after* his abduction, the leagues between his future self and his enchanted body, coupled with the thick stone walls of the cave, would be enough distance between them.

He had no choice but to believe that.

Drustan glanced around the ruins. While he'd brooded, full night had fallen and it was too dark to conduct a thorough search, which left him tomorrow to hunt for the tablets and try to recall the symbols.

And if the tablets weren't there?

Well, then, that was why there was wee, sweet, unsuspecting Gwen.

Wee, sweet, unsuspecting Gwen perched on the hood of the car, munching celery sticks and salmon patties and absorbing the remaining warmth of the engine. She glanced at her watch. Nearly two hours had passed since she'd left Drustan at the ruin.

She could leave now. Just hop in the car, slam it into reverse, and squeal off to the village below. Leave the madman alone to sort out his own problems.

Then why didn't she?

Pondering Newton's Law of Universal Gravitation, she considered the possibility that since Drustan's mass was so much greater than hers, she was doomed to be attracted to him—so long as he was in her near vicinity—as much a victim of gravity as the earth orbiting the sun.

Lost in thought, she hummed absently as she huddled on the hood, shivering as the indigo sky deepened to black cashmere, arguing with herself and reaching no firm conclusions.

She couldn't shake the feeling that she was overlooking one or more critical facts that might help her figure out what had happened to him. She'd never given any credence to "gut instinct"; she'd believed the gut controlled hunger and waste, nothing gnostic. But in the past thirty-six hours, something in her gut had found a voice, it was arguing with her mind, and she was baffled by the discord.

She had remained in the stones and watched him for some time before she'd sought the warmth of the hood of the car. She'd studied him with the remote candor of a scientist observing a test subject in an experiment, but her study of him had only revealed more contradictions rather than resolving any.

His body was powerfully developed, and a man didn't get a body like that without extraordinary discipline, effort, and a mind capable of sustained focus. Wherever he had been before she'd found him in the cave, he'd lived an active, balanced life. He'd either worked hard or played hard, and she decided it was more work than play, because his hands were callused, and no stuffy, jock-type aristocrat had calluses on fingers and palms. His silky black hair was too long to be considered apropos on a twenty-first-century lord and gentleman, but it was glossy and well cut. His teeth were even and white, more evidence of care for his body. People who devoted attention to their physical health were usually healthy in mind as well.

He walked with a gait that bespoke confidence, strength, and the ability to make hard decisions. He was reasonably intelligent and well-spoken—his strange inflection and vocabulary aside.

He hadn't known the way out of the cave, and when they had emerged, Gwen hadn't missed the significance of the collapsed tunnel and the overgrowth of foliage.

Och, Christ, they're all dead, he'd whispered.

She shivered. The engine had cooled, the remnants of heat gone.

Occam's Razor promulgated that the simplest explanation that fit the majority of the facts was most likely true. The simplest explanation here was . . . he was telling the truth. He'd somehow been put into a deep sleep five hundred years ago against his will, perhaps via some lost science, and she'd awakened him by falling on him.

Impossible, her mind exclaimed.

Tired of trying to coax the jury to deliver a consensus, she reluctantly accepted the hung verdict and admitted that she couldn't leave him. What if the impossible was possible? What if tomorrow he offered her some concrete proof that he had been frozen in time for nearly five hundred years? Perhaps he planned to show her how it had been done, some advanced cryogenics that had been lost over time. She wasn't vacating the premises if there was even a remote possibility of finding out such a thing. *Oh, admit it, Gwen, despite having "dropped out" on the profession that has been eternally crammed down your throat, despite refusing to continue your research, you're still fascinated by science, and you'd love to know how a man could somehow sleep for five centuries and wake up healthy and whole. You'd never publish it, but you'd still love to know.*

But it was more than just scientific curiosity, and she suspected it had something to do with his sock and her eggs and a desire she couldn't attribute solely to the mandate programmed into her genes that clamored for survival of her race. No other man had ever incited such a response in her.

Science couldn't explain the tenderness she'd felt at the sight of tears in his eyes. Nor the desire she'd had to cradle his head against her chest—not to have her cherry once and truly plucked, but for his comfort.

Oh, her heart was engaged, and it both alarmed and elated her.

Tucking her bangs behind an ear, she slid off the hood and started up the hill. He'd had enough time alone. It was time to talk.

*

"Drustan." Gwen's voice cut like a light through the darkness around him.

He met her gaze levelly. The poor wee lass looked terrified, yet bristled with resolve.

She looked directly into his eyes then and, if she felt fear, she rose above it. He admired that about her, that despite her misgivings she forged on with the valor of a knight entering battle. When he'd chased her off, he worried that she might simply jump in her metal beast and drive away. The relief he'd felt when he glimpsed her heading toward him through the stones had been intense. Whatever she'd decided to think of him, she'd resolved to stick by his side—he could see it in her eyes.

"Drustan?" Hesitant, yet firm.

"Aye, lass?"

"Are you feeling better now?" she asked warily.

"I have made a tentative peace with my feelings," he said dryly. "Fear not, I doona plan to leap up and avenge the loss of my people." *Yet*.

She gave him a brisk nod. "Good."

He could tell that she didn't wish to discuss it, and rather than accuse him of being deluded when he was clearly distraught, she was going to scuttle around it in some circuitous manner. He narrowed his eyes, wondering what she was up to.

"Drustan, I memorized your poem, now it's your turn to grant me a favor."

"As you wish, Gwen. Only tell me what you want of me."

"A few simple questions."

"I will answer them to the best of my ability," he replied.

"How much dirt is in a hole a foot wide, nine inches long, and three and a half feet deep?"

"That is your question?" he asked, baffled. Of all things she might have asked . . .

"One of them," she said hastily.

He smiled faintly. Her question was one of his favorite puzzles. His priest, Nevin, had agonized for half an hour trying to calculate exactly how much dirt would be in such a space before seeing the obvious. "There is no dirt in a hole," he replied easily.

"Oh, well, that was a trick puzzle and doesn't tell me much. You may have heard it before. How about this one: A boat lies at anchor with a rope ladder hanging over the side. The rungs in the rope ladder are nine inches apart. The tide rises at a rate of six inches per hour and then falls at the same rate. If one rung of the ladder is just touching the water when the tide begins to rise, how many rungs will be covered after eight hours?"

Drustan ran through a swift series of calculations, then laughed softly, at a time when he thought he might not laugh again. He suddenly understood why she had chosen such questions, and his regard for her increased. When an apprentice petitioned a Druid to be accepted and trained, he was put through a similar series of problems designed to reveal how the lad's mind worked and what he was capable of.

"None, lass, the rope ladder rises with the boat upon the water. Do my powers of reason convince you that I am not mad?"

She regarded him strangely. "Your reasoning abilities seem untouched by your peculiar . . . illness. So what is 4,732.25 multiplied by 7,837.50?"

"37,089,009.375."

"My *God*," she said, looking simultaneously awed and revolted. "You poor thing! I asked the first question mostly to see if you were thinking clearly, the second to see if the first had been a fluke. But you did that math in your head in five seconds. Even I can't do it that fast!"

He shrugged. "I have always had an affinity for numbers. Did your questions prove anything to you?" They had proved something to him. Gwen Cassidy was the most intelligent lass he'd ever met. Young, seemingly fertile, an extraordinary mating heat between them, *and* smart.

His certainty that fate had brought her to him for a reason increased tenfold.

Mayhap, he thought, she might not fear him after tomorrow eve. Mayhap there *was* such a love for him as his father had known.

"Well, if you're a candidate for bedlam, you're the smartest madman I've ever met, and your delusions seem confined to one issue." She blew out a breath. "So, what now?"

"Come, lass." He held his arms out to her.

She eyed him warily.

"Och, lassie, give me something to hold in my arms that's real and sweet. I will not harm you."

She trudged to his side and sank down in the grass beside him. She kept her face averted for several moments, gazing up at the stars, then her shoulders slumped and she looked at him. "Oh, bother," she said, and stunned him by reaching out to cradle his head in her arms, pulling him to her breast.

His slid his hands around her waist and pulled her onto his lap. "Lovely Gwen, 'tis thanking you once again I am. You are a gift from the angels."

"I wouldn't be so sure about that," she muttered against his hair. She seemed awkward holding him, as if she hadn't had much practice. Her body was tense, and he sensed if he moved suddenly that she would jerk away, so he breathed slowly and kept still, allowing her time to grow accustomed to the intimacy.

"I guess this means you won't be able to prove anything to me tomorrow, huh?"

"As promised, on the morrow I will prove to you my story is true. This changes nothing, or little. Will you stay of your own volition? Mayhap help me explore the grounds tomorrow?"

Hesitantly, she slipped her wee hands into his hair and he half-sighed, half-groaned with pleasure when her nails lightly grazed his scalp. "Aye, Drustan MacKeltar," she said, with as good a lilt as any Scots lass. "I'll be stayin' wi' ye 'til the morrow."

He laughed aloud and pulled her closer. He craved her touch, wanted desperately to make love to her, but sensed that if he pressed her now, he would lose the comfort of her embrace. "That was fine, lass. Yer no bampot, and I'm thinkin' we may make a wee douce Highland lass out o' ye yet."

Gwen slept that night curled in the arms of a Highlander, in a field of sillar shakles and gowan, beneath a silvery spoon of a moon, peaceful as a lamb. And if Drustan was feeling wolfish, he bid himself be content merely to hold her.

· 9 ·

They searched all day but didn't find the tablets.

When the sky darkened to indigo, pierced by glitter-ing stars, Drustan gave up and constructed a bonfire within the circle of stones so he would have light by which to perform the ritual.

If the worst occurred tonight, he wanted her to know as much about what had happened to him as possible. And her backpack would be an added boon. While dig-ging in the ruins, he'd told her everything that had transpired just prior to his abduction.

One disbelieving brow arched, she'd nevertheless lis-tened as he explained how he'd received a note bearing an urgent summons to come to the clearing behind the little loch *if ye wish tae ken the name of the Campbell who murdered yer brother.* His grief fever-hot, he'd donned his weapons and rushed off, without summoning his guard;

the thirst to avenge his brother's death had overridden all intelligent thought.

He told her how he'd grown light-headed and weary while racing toward the loch and that he now believed he'd somehow been drugged. He told her how he'd collapsed just outside the forest on the banks of the loch, how his limbs had locked, his eyes had closed as if weighted by heavy gold coins. He told her he'd felt his armor and weapons being removed, then symbols being painted on his chest, then felt nothing more until she'd wakened him.

Then he told her of his family, of his brilliant and bristly father, of their beloved housekeeper and substitute mother, Nell. He told her of his young priest, whose nagging, fortune-telling mother was wont to chase him ceaselessly about the estate trying to get a look at his palm.

He forgot his sorrow for a time and regaled her with tales of his childhood with Dageus. When he spoke of his family, her skeptical gaze had softened a bit, and she'd listened with marked fascination, laughing over the antics of Drustan and his brother, smiling gently over the ongoing sparring between Silvan and Nell. He deduced from her wistful expression that, even when her family had been alive, there'd not been much laughter and loving in her life.

Have you no brothers and sisters, lass? he'd asked.

She'd shaken her head. *My mother had fertility problems and had me late in life. After she had me, the doctors said she couldn't have any more.*

Why have you not wed and had bairn of your own?

She'd shifted and averted her gaze. *I never found the right man.*

Nay, she'd not had much pleasure in her life, and he'd like the chance to change that. He'd like to make her eyes sparkle with happiness.

He wanted Gwen Cassidy. He wanted to be her "right man." The mere scent of her as she walked by brought every inch of him to attention. He wanted her to become so familiar with his body and the pleasure he could give her with it that a simple glance would make her limp with desire. He wanted to pass a fortnight, uninterrupted, in his bedchamber, exploring her hidden passion, unleashing the eroticism that simmered just beneath her surface.

But it might never come to pass, because once he performed the ritual and she discovered what he was, and what he'd done to her, she would have every reason to despise him.

Still, he had no other choice.

Casting a worried glance at the arc of the moon against the black sky, he inhaled deeply, greedily, of the sweet Highland night air. The time was nearly upon them.

"Let it rest, Gwen," he called. He was moved that she refused to give up. Mad though she might think him, she was still digging about in the ruins. "Come join me in the stones," he beckoned. He wanted to spend what might be his last hour with her, close to the fire, holding her in his arms. His druthers were to strip off her clothes and bury himself inside her, brand himself into her memory with what time he had left, but that seemed as likely as the tablets suddenly manifesting themselves in his hands.

"But we haven't found the tablets." She turned toward him, smudging dirt on her cheek when she pushed back her hair.

"'Tis too late now, lass. The time is nearly upon us, and that tube of light"—he gestured at her flashlight—"won't help us see what isn't there to be found. 'Twas a vain and foolish hope that they might have survived intact on the estate. If we haven't found them yet, the next hour will accomplish naught. Come. Spend it with me." He held out his arms.

She'd slept within them last night, and he'd awakened to the lovely sight of her face, trusting and innocent in repose. He'd kissed her full, lush lips, and when she'd awakened, sleep-flushed, with crease marks on her cheek from being pressed to his wrinkled T-shirt, he'd felt a rush of tenderness he'd not felt for a woman before. Lust, ever at a boil within him when she was near, had simmered into a more intense, complexly layered feeling, and he'd recognized that given time he could fall deeply in love with her. Not merely ache to keep her in bed without respite but develop a real and lasting emotion, equal parts passion, respect, and appreciation, the kind that bound a man and a woman together for life. She was everything he wanted in a woman.

Gwen trudged into the circle, clearly reluctant to give up when there was even one stone unturned, another trait he admired in her.

"Why won't you tell me what you plan to do?" All day she'd tried to coax it out of him, but he'd refused to tell her anything more than that they were looking for seven stone tablets inscribed with symbols.

"I said I'd give you proof, and I will." A stunning, irrevocable amount of proof.

The hours had dragged on as they searched, tossing rocks and rubble, and his hope had steadily faded with each broken chip of pottery, each timeworn memento of his dead clan.

At one point futility had nearly overwhelmed him, and he'd sent her down to the village with a list of items to pick up so he would have time to think, undistracted. During her absence, he'd meditated upon the symbols, working through complex calculations, and derived his best guess at the last three—the guess that would be put to the test in less than one hour. He was aiming for two weeks after his brother's death, plus one day. He was almost certain they were correct and believed there was only a minute chance the worst would happen.

And if the worst happened, he had prepared her well and need only remind her what to say and do to restore complete, merged memory to the past version of himself. 'Twas why he'd bid her memorize the spell.

She'd picked up several jugs of water, along with flashlights, coffee, and food, and now sat beside him near the fire, cross-legged, cleaning her hands with dampened towels, emitting little sighs of pleasure as she scrubbed at her face with tiny pads from her pack.

While she freshened up, he broke open the stones he'd collected during their hike. Inside each was a core of brilliant dust, which he scraped carefully into a tin and blended with water to form a thick paste.

"Paint rocks," she said, intrigued enough to pause in her ablutions. She'd never seen one but knew the ancients had used them to paint with. They were small and craggy, and deep in the center a dust formed over time that made brilliant colors when mixed with water.

"Aye, 'tis what we call them as well," he said, rising to his feet.

Gwen watched as he moved to one of the megaliths and, after a moment's hesitation, began etching a complex design of formulas and symbols. She narrowed her eyes, studying it. Parts of it seemed somehow familiar yet alien, a perverted mathematical equation that danced just out of her reach, and there was little that did that to her.

A beat of nervous apprehension thudded in her chest, and she watched intently as he moved to the next stone, then the third and the fourth. On each of the stones he etched a different series of numbers and symbols upon their inner faces, pausing occasionally to glance up at the stars.

The autumnal equinox, she reflected, was the time when the sun crossed the planes of the earth's equator, making night and day of approximately equal length all over the earth. Researchers had long argued over the precise use of the standing stones. Was she about to find out their real purpose?

She eyed the megaliths and pondered what she knew about archaeoastronomy. When he finished sketching upon the thirteenth and final stone, her breath caught in her throat. Although she recognized only parts of it, he'd clearly stroked the symbol for infinity:

$$\infty$$

beneath it. The lemniscate. The Möbius strip. *Apeiron.* What knowledge did he have of it? She scanned the thirteen stones and felt a peculiar itchy sensation in her mind, as if an epiphany was trying to burrow into her overcrowded brain.

Watching him, she was struck by a stunning possibility. Was it possible that he was smarter than *she* was? Was that his madness?

Gorgeous *and* smart? *Be still, my beating heart. . . .*

As he turned away from the last stone, she shivered. Physically, he was irresistible. He was wearing his original costume of plaid and armor again, having shed "such trews that doona let a man hang properly and an inar that canna conceal an oxter knife" as soon as he'd awakened that morning. Hang properly, indeed, she thought, gaze skipping over his kilt, mouth going dry as she imagined what was hanging beneath it. Was he in that seemingly permanent state of semi-arousal? She'd like to kiss him until there was nothing "semi" about it . . .

With effort, she dragged her gaze to his face. His sleek hair was a wild fall about his shoulders. He was the most intense, exciting, and erotic man she'd ever met.

When she was around Drustan MacKeltar, inexplicable things happened to her. When she looked at him, his powerful body, his chiseled jaw, the flashing eyes and sensual mouth, she heard Pan's distant pipes and suffered an irresistible compulsion to tithe to Dionysus, the ancient god of wine and orgy. The tune was seductive, urging her to cast aside restraint, don her crimson kitten thong, and dance barefoot for a dark forbidding man who claimed he was a sixteenth-century laird.

He glanced back at her, and their gazes collided. She felt like a time bomb ready to explode, ticking, ticking.

Her face must have betrayed her feelings, because he inhaled sharply. His nostrils flared, his eyes narrowed, and he went quiet, with the perfect stillness of a mountain lion before hurling itself at its prey.

She swallowed. "What are you doing with those stones?" she forced herself to ask, flustered by the intensity of what she was feeling. "Don't you think it's time you tell me?"

"I have told you all I can." His eyes were cool slate, the crystalline light that usually danced within them subdued.

"You don't trust me. After all I've done to help, you still don't trust me." She didn't try to conceal that it hurt her feelings.

"Och, lass, doona be thinking such. 'Tis merely that some things are . . . forbidden." Not really, he amended silently, but he simply couldn't risk revealing his plans yet, lest she abandon him.

"Bullshit," she said, impatient with his evasions. "If you trust me, nothing is forbidden."

"I do trust you, wee lass. I am trusting you far more

than you know." *With my life, possibly even with my clan's very existence. . . .*

"How am I supposed to believe in you, when you won't confide in me?"

"Ever the doubter, are you not, Gwen?" he chided. "Kiss me, before I sketch the final symbols. For bonny fortune," he urged. Shards of crystal glittered in his eyes, reminding her that although sometimes he banked his passionate nature, it was always simmering just beneath the surface.

Gwen started to speak, but he laid a finger to her lips. "Please, lass, just kiss me. No more words. There have been enough of them between us." He paused before adding quietly, "If you have aught to say to me, let your heart speak now."

She took a deep breath.

There was no question what her heart was saying. Earlier that afternoon, when she'd gone down to the village, she'd dug her crimson thong out of her pack and, after washing up, had put it on. Then she'd peeled off her nicotine patch, preferring outright withdrawal to having to explain its presence on her body. She was not going to make love for the first time with a patch on. Besides, once she'd made the decision, a remarkable calm had settled over her.

She knew what she was going to do.

Truth be told, she'd probably known the moment he'd opened his eyes that she was going to give him her virginity. The past two days had been nothing more than her way of growing accustomed to the thought, so she would be less apprehensive when she finally did it.

She wasn't simply attracted to him, she was drawn to him on every level—mentally, emotionally, and physically.

She wanted him in a way that had no rhyme or reason. She felt things when he spoke to her and touched her that originated from a unique place inside her. It no longer mattered to her that he might be mentally unbalanced. During the passage of the day, digging beside him in the ruins of the castle while he talked of the various members of his clan, she'd realized that she was going to stick by him until he worked out whatever reality problem he was having. She *liked* him. She wanted to know more about him. She'd begun to respect him, despite his delusions. If she had to check him into a hospital, hold his hand, and sit by his side until he recovered, she was going to do it. If she had to walk around Scotland for months clutching a photograph of him until she found someone who could identify him and shed light upon his condition, she was going to do it.

She tucked her bangs behind her ear and looked at him levelly. Her voice hardly shook when she said, "Make love to me, Drustan."

Mad or not, she wanted him to be her first lover, here and now, on top of a mountain in the Highlands, beneath a million stars, encircled by ancient stones. Perhaps making love had some healing power. God knew, she probably needed some healing too.

His eyes flared and he went perfectly still. "I did hear that, did I not?" he said carefully. "You did say what I think you said? Or have I truly gone as mad as you accuse me of being?"

"Make love to me," she repeated quietly. There was no tremor in her voice the second time.

His silver eyes glittered. "Lass, you honor me." When he opened his arms, she leaped at him, and he swung her effortlessly into his embrace, pulling her legs around his waist. They both gasped at the intensity of the contact. A current of desire sizzled between them, zapping them both to the core. With powerful strides, he backed her to the perimeter of the stones until her spine rested against one of the megaliths. He lowered his head and kissed her, grinding his hips against her, and when she cried out, he caught it on his tongue.

"I've wanted you since the moment I saw you," he said roughly.

"Me too," she confessed, with a breathless laugh.

"Och, lass, why dinna you tell me?" he asked, kissing her jaw, her cheeks, her nose and lashes, cradling her face with his hands. "Why did you resist? Three *days* we could hae passed doin' this," he said, his burr thickened by desire.

"Not if we wanted to get to your stones," she panted, wondering why he couldn't just shut up and kiss her hard on the mouth. "Shut up and kiss me," she said.

He laughed and kissed her so hard that it unleashed ferocity in her tiny frame. She'd seen movies where people made love slowly, sinuously wrapping around each other, but theirs was a mating of wildness. Given their propensity to argue heatedly, she hadn't expected their sex to be anything less intense. She couldn't get enough of him, she wanted more tongue and more hands and more of his muscular ass. She wanted him naked against her body. Wanted to feel him pounding into her. She'd waited all her life for this, and she was ready. Just *looking* at him made her wet.

He tugged her shirt from her shorts and fumbled with her fly, kissing her urgently all the while. "Your trews, lass, get them off," he said roughly.

"I can't. My legs are wrapped around you," she mumbled. "And *ow*. Your knife is poking my breast."

"*Mmm*, sorry." He nipped her lower lip and sucked it hard. "I must put you down, lass, to get you naked. And 'tis needin' you naked I am."

But he didn't make any move to lower her, hostage to

her luscious mouth nibbling at him, her wee hands clawing at his back.

"So put me down, MacKeltar," she panted a few minutes later against his mouth, desperate to feel his skin against hers. "I have too many clothes on!"

"I'm *trying*," he said, trailing kisses down her neck and scraping his velvety tongue back up, only to arrive at her lips again, a position he could hardly fail to take full advantage of.

"Don't put me down," she whimpered when he stopped kissing her. Her lips felt naked and cold without him, her body bereft.

The minute her toes touched the ground, she reached impatiently for his clothing, but he dived for her shorts at the same moment, cursing when he bumped his jaw on her head and she got tangled up in his hair.

She fumbled with his hair, then found her way to the leather bands across his chest but was unable to fathom how he'd fastened them. Brushing her hands aside, he tugged her shirt over her head, than stared at her bra. He touched the lacy fabric with fascination. "Lass, show me your breasts. Be quit of this thing, lest I tear it to shreds in my haste."

She popped the front clasp swiftly and slipped it off. The cool air teased her nipples into puckered crests, and he drew a sharp inhalation of breath. For a moment, he didn't seem to be able to move, just stood and stared.

"You have splendid breasts, lass," he purred, cupping the plump mounds. "Splendid," he repeated stupidly, and she almost laughed. Men loved breasts—any shape or form, they just loved them.

And he was certainly loving hers. He palmed them, lifting and squeezing, and with a husky groan he buried his face in her breasts, rubbing back and forth before drawing a nipple deep into his mouth.

Gwen panted softly when he scattered scorching kisses over her breasts. She twisted and turned in his arms, wanting his mouth there . . . and there . . . and there, telling him with her body just how and where she needed him. His fingers worked at her shorts, with little success, and grunting his frustration he tugged at her zipper but succeeded only in jamming it off the track. Encountering similar resistance with his costume, she moaned frantically. She wanted skin against skin; she needed it—every last inch, pressed slick and intimate.

"Oh, just do your own and I'll do mine," she snapped, impeded desire making her downright testy. She needed him naked *now*.

He looked as relieved as she felt by the efficient solution, and as she tugged and twisted at her zipper, then kicked off her shorts, he removed his plaid, tossing knives left and right, doffing his ax and sword and finally shucking his leather armor. He stood up straight, tossing his long dark hair over his shoulders, and looked at her.

"*Christ, MacKeltar,*" Gwen breathed, stunned. Six and a half feet of sculpted naked warrior stood before her, unselfconscious in his nudity. Proud, in fact, and well he should be. He was raw and male and powerful beyond compare, and it had certainly *not* been a sock or twenty in his jeans. He was breathtaking, and he had a remarkable amount of mass that she had not been factoring into her equation of why she was orbiting him, but she certainly would be in the future. It explained a great deal.

His eyes drifted over her breasts, down her belly, then lit on her kitten thong, and he made a strangled sound. "I thought that was some strange ribbon to restrain your hair. 'Twas why I put it on your pallet that night, thinking you might plait it before you slept. But, ah, lass, I far prefer it there," he said roughly. " 'Tis wise you did not tell me that was beneath your trews, for I would have walked around hard all day thinking of removing it with my tongue."

He likes my thong, she thought, beaming. She'd always known that if she'd picked the right man to pluck her cherry, he would appreciate her good taste.

Slipping to his knees before her, he proceeded to do as he'd threatened, lifting the strap of her thong away from the smooth curve of her hip with his teeth and licking the sensitive skin beneath it. He tugged the silk down with little nips, curving his tongue beneath it. She dug her fingers into his shoulders as he licked again and again, building resonance beneath her skin. He sucked her sensitive nub through the silk, making her arch against him, begging for more. Each inch he bared he swept with a hot stroke of his tongue, alternating tiny love bites. His callused hands glided up her thighs, and the delicious friction created by his rough palms against her smooth skin awakened erogenous zones she'd never known she had. Her knees trembled and she clutched his muscled shoulders for support.

"Lovely you are," he purred, slipping his hands between her thighs, kneading and tasting her. "I doona know which part of you to taste first."

"Drustan," she moaned, pressing against him.

"What, Gwen? Do you want me?"

"God, yes!"

"Did you want me when you saw me in those blue trews?" he pushed. "Did you want me then too?"

"Yes."

"Do you feel the heat when I touch you? Does it hit you like a thunderbolt too?"

"*Yes.*"

He stripped off her thong and rose to his feet. He drank in the sight of her nude body for a long moment before dragging her into his arms.

They both cried out as skin met skin, stunned by the intensity of the contact, sizzling where they touched. He kissed her deeply, his tongue hot and hungry, plundering her mouth. She arched her back, rubbing her breasts against him. When he cupped his hands beneath her bottom, she clasped her hands behind his neck and wrapped her legs tightly around him, so his erection was firmly trapped in the vee of her thighs. She squirmed, wanting him inside her *right now*, but either he wasn't cooperating or she was too clumsy to angle them into the right position, which, she rued, given her inexperience, was possible. *But it doesn't seem that he's being particularly helpful,* she thought mulishly, breaking their kiss long enough to look at him. His silvery gaze was wicked . . . and cockily amused.

"Are you *torturing* me?"

"*My* pace, lass. You're the one who said no and wasted days. We might have done this yesterday when you stuffed me into those torturous trews. And later that afternoon. And later that night, and this morning, and—"

When she tried to reply, he kissed her so hard she forgot what she was going to say. He rocked himself against her, mimicking sex, gliding back and forth in the slick vee of her thighs. Millions of tiny nerve endings screamed for more. *Well, if he won't, I will.* She knew better than most people that forces of nature should not be resisted or subdued. She twisted against him, rubbing herself wantonly, pushing herself to the peak.

As her soft panting became more frantic, Drustan broke the kiss and looked at her. Her cheeks were flushed, her eyes brilliant and wild, her lips kiss-bruised and parted.

"That's it, lass, take your pleasure." He was riveted by her unabashed hunger for him; she was making him hotter and harder with every insistent thrust of her hips. If he wasn't careful, he'd spill without ever entering her. He doubted a woman had ever desired him so intensely.

She whimpered as she came, she purred, she rubbed against him like a love-starved kitten.

"*Yes*," he breathed, flooded with purely male, possessive triumph. When her shudders subsided and she relaxed against him, he lowered her to the ground on his plaid, then sat back on his knees and gazed at her for a long moment. Long enough that she began to squirm, and it wrought havoc upon his fleeting control. She arched her back, raising her breasts toward him, her nipples dark berries, begging to be suckled.

"Touch me," she whispered.

"Och, lass, I'll touch you," he promised. He nudged her legs wider, then drank in the sight of her, lying in wait for him, her full breasts swollen from his kisses, her thighs open and slick with her desire.

He ran his hand up the inside of her thighs, across her woman's wetness, then down the other leg. Once, twice, and a half dozen times lingering between her thighs, flicking her sensitive nub, until she was arching her hips up from the plaid.

"I'm going to toop you as you've naught been tooped before, lass."

Gwen was quite certain of that, having never been *tooped* before. "Promises, promises, MacKeltar," she provoked. "A woman could die of old age before you got around to it."

His eyes flew wide in surprise, then he laughed, a husky laugh full of dark eroticism.

Finally, she purred, when, shoulder muscles bunching sleekly, he covered her body with his.

"Have you no sense at all, that you would provoke me? I'm twice your size, you know," he murmured against her ear.

"So show me something I don't already know." She gasped, when he nipped her earlobe.

"Like this?" he asked, shifting himself between her thighs. "Or like this?" He rubbed the head of his cock back and forth and back again in her slick folds.

Gwen melted as he spoke to her then in a language she'd never heard but knew was tribute from the husky admiration in his voice. The strange accents made her wild as he purred compliments against her heated skin. She half-wondered if he was ensorcelling her, because the more he spoke in his foreign accents, the hotter she got. Or perhaps it was the smoky deep voice and the way his hands moved over every inch of her body as if memorizing the subtleties of each plane and hollow. He devoted lavish attention to her breasts, squeezing them, plumping and fondling them until she was nearly delirious with need, hovering at the brink of another orgasm.

He braced himself on his forearms and suckled each nipple, moving his head back and forth, chafing her with his shadow beard, and just when she thought one couldn't take the erotic teasing anymore, he would turn his attention to the other. He kissed her breasts, the sides of her breasts, the soft warm place beneath them, pushed them together and kissed the plump cleavage, dragging his tongue roughly between them, then returned to her hard nipples and took them alternately with his teeth. Nipping and suckling and drawing her into his mouth. She nearly screamed from the exquisite pleasure of it.

He trailed kisses over her ribs, down her abdomen, then glided his tongue across her belly, playfully flickering into her belly button. Then, suddenly, he dragged his tongue across her swollen bud and she cried out.

"There's my lass," he purred, burying his face between her thighs.

The man has a magic tongue, she thought, writhing beneath him. He cupped his hands beneath her bottom, raised her to his mouth, and Gwen filled the night with tiny whimpers as he kissed and licked her, then plunged his tongue deep inside her. As his hot tongue stroked her in places that had never been touched before, she came in spasms, and he lapped her as she shuddered over and over again. Then, just when she thought it was over, he gently nipped her, wringing a tinier series of spasms from her trembling body.

Resonance—I am crystal and I am shattering, she thought feverishly.

As she arched her hips against him, crying out, Drustan growled and pressed himself against the ground. He wanted this to last as long as it could. Wanted to pleasure her like no other man ever had. Gritting his teeth, he pressed himself against the plaid, remaining perfectly still, trying to convince his cock that it needed to wait just a bit longer, because at least he could give her this.

At least he could have this. This perfect moment with her, if naught else. She whimpered softly as the spasms stopped, and he gently lapped her again, playfully warning her that she would have many more peaks of pleasure before he was through with her.

She was so beautiful and open to him. She was the most sensuous woman he'd ever met in his life, every inch of her body sensitive to his caresses, and although he'd bedded scores of bawdy women in his life, none had nudged him past the edge of reason, until now. His stomach was shaky from the intensity of his desire, and his cock was so hard it was painful. His breathing sounded harsh to his own ears, the beat of his heart was the thunder of a hundred horses, the blood boiled in his veins and reality narrowed down to: Just. One. Thing.

Her.

He could wait no longer.

He rained kisses up the gentle swell of her stomach, over her breasts, and dragged the edge of his teeth back and forth across her nipples. Positioning himself between her legs, he did not take her immediately but kissed her thoroughly, a kiss of demand and dominion, of raw possession.

"Tell me," he demanded. She didn't play shy or coy, a thing he liked. She let him read her hunger in her face, in her expressive stormy eyes, hiding nothing. But would she speak of her desire? Would she be audacious and whisper words to him that would tell him how to fulfill her wildest needs?

"Tell me," he insisted.

His wee Gwendolyn said a thing to him then that he'd never heard a woman say before, neither high-born nor whore, and the baseness of her words slammed into him as if he'd swallowed a double dose of a Rom lust potion.

He'd *never* had a woman say *that* to him. They used gentler words, but what Gwen had asked of him was exactly what he wanted to do. Their attraction to each other was primitive and went far beyond reason.

If she could voice such raw desires, what more might she confront bravely? Who and what he was? Might she possess such courage?

She lay beneath him, shivering with desire, her lips glistening in the moonlight, wet from his kisses, and he realized he was falling for her harder than a mighty oak cleaved in two by a lightning bolt would crash to the forest floor.

He plunged inside her.

And stopped.

Not by choice—oh, nay, not by his choice—but because there was something in his way.

"Oh, just *push*," she cried. "I know it's going to hurt at first. Just do it! Get it over with."

He was stunned. Fragments of thoughts collided in his head: *She is untouched by any man; how could this woman have survived a maiden so long? Are the men in her century utterly fools?* Then, *Ah, she chose no other, but she chose me!*

What a gift!

A more noble man might have backed off, a more noble man who knew that even a minute possibility existed that he might disappear that night would surely have refused, but there was something about Gwen Cassidy that drove him far past nobility. He wanted her, by fair means or foul. And if the worst happened tonight, the loving between them might make her more able to face what she may have to confront. Mayhap help her complete all the things he might need her do, and mayhap—he could entertain the outlandish dream—she could be persuaded to find a happy future in his past. For like it or not, the only future she was going to have after tonight was in his past.

He would make it up to her, he vowed. Her happiness would be his first priority. He would give her anything she wanted, heap her with mountains of gifts, attention, and devotion, as befitted a queen. He would wait on her hand and foot. And mayhap loving could work out the uncertainties in his plan that no amount of careful and cautious orchestration could accomplish.

"I may be little," she coaxed softly when he hesitated, "but I'm tougher than you think." And she repeated her previous request that had sent all the blood in his body rushing to his groin.

Inflamed, he plunged through the barrier, claiming her.

"Yes," she screamed, and he drank her cry into his mouth, kissing her savagely, pushing deep within her. She matched his urgent rhythm, and although he knew it had caused her pain, her desire quickly surpassed the tearing of her maidenhead.

He gave himself to her with intensity he'd not given a woman before, burying himself so deep inside her he thought he must be touching the lip of her womb, then gliding out, slowly, only to thrust again. His entire world, his every breath and heartbeat, was focused on the woman in his arms.

Slipping her legs over his shoulders, he angled himself to drive back into her. He took the move achingly slowly, knowing how wee she was and that he would stretch her to her limits, but he needed to be so deep inside her that he no longer knew where he began and she ended. He slid into her, inch by inch, his body straining from such sweet torture.

"Drustan," she cried, tossing her head from side to side, tangling her silky hair. He suckled her nipples as he withdrew and returned, and when he felt her contract around him, he clamped his teeth lightly on a nipple and tugged. He drove himself into her hard and fast and deep, over and over until he was nearly mindless with savage need.

"Och, lassie," he said roughly, caught up in her spasms, "I canna ride out this storm again." And as he thrust inside her so hard it nearly hurt him, his husky voice mingled with her sweet cries. They peaked in perfect rhythm, each shuddering contraction of her body drawing forth his seed.

He purred to her as he came, in an ancient tongue he knew she wouldn't understand. He said foolish things, heartfelt things, deep and weighty things he could never acknowledge otherwise. He called her his goddess of the moon and praised her courageous spirit and fire. He asked her for babies. Christ, he talked like a fool.

Gwen shuddered against him, listening to his strange accents, and somehow she knew that every word he uttered was praise. When he finally stilled against her, she stroked his back and shoulders, marveling, buoyant, elated and sated beyond compare.

"You are beautiful, lass," he whispered, brushing his lips back and forth over hers tenderly.

She squealed when he thumped inside her, a final flexing from their love play.

"Did I hurt you, sweet Gwen?" he asked, with such concern in his eyes that it touched her heart.

"A bit," she confessed. "But no more than I expected after seeing that . . . *sock* you have there."

He smiled, his eyes dancing. "I told you it was God-given. You would hear none of it." He sucked her lower lip. "I didn't mean to hurt you, lass. I fear I was without sense for a time there."

"No more than I. I think I said something really bad," she worried, nibbling her lip.

"It aroused me immensely," he growled. "Never have I had a woman say such a thing to me, and it made me hard as stone."

"You are *always* hard, MacKeltar," she teased. "Don't think I don't see that permanent bulge in your clothing."

"I know," he said smugly. "Your glance drifts there often." He sobered suddenly. "But now I know why you were naysaying me. Gwen, why did you not tell me you had known no man before me?"

She closed her eyes and sighed. "I was afraid you would say no," she finally admitted. "I wasn't sure you would make love to a virgin."

Make love, she'd said. She'd saved herself from all others but chosen to give herself to him. *You care for me,* he thought, hoping she would say the words. He was disappointed when she didn't, but in her touch—her hands tracing gentle circles on his chest—he felt a tenderness that meant much to him.

And she'd given him her maidenhead.

He felt himself hardening again, moved by the depth of her gift. Although he hadn't given her proof that he was telling the truth, she'd given of herself freely to him, that which she'd given to no other man. She had feelings for him, he was sure of it, as sure as he was that Gwen Cassidy didn't give of herself lightly.

She'd honored him in so many ways.

There was no question in his mind: She was the one for him. The woman he'd wanted all his life—and so what if he'd had to come five hundred years into the future to find her? He would give her the words and begin the Druid binding, and mayhap in a few hours, if all was well, she might freely give the words back to him.

And if all doesn't go well?

He shrugged mentally. If all didn't go well, and he didn't survive tonight, the sixteenth-century version of him would find her druggingly irresistible, even before she said the spell to merge their memories. He could see no harm in that, doubted it would come to pass anyway.

She'd given him a precious gift; this was all he had to offer her in return. The gift of his eternal love.

He placed the palm of his right hand on her chest over her heart, the palm of his left above his, and looked deep into her eyes. When he spoke, his voice was low and firm: "If aught must be lost, 'twill be my honor for yours. If one must be forsaken, 'twill be my soul for yours. Should death come anon, 'twill be my life for yours." He drew a deep breath and finished it, completing the spell that would haunt him for life. "I am Given." He shuddered as he felt the irrevocable bond take root within him—a bond that could never be severed. He was now connected to her by gossamer strands of awareness. Were he to walk into a room of people, he would be drawn to her side. Were he to enter a village, he would know if she was in it. Emotion welled up within him, and he struggled to hold it back, astonished by the intensity. Feelings crashed over him, feelings he'd never imagined.

She was so beautiful—made a thousand times more so by his having opened himself completely to her.

Her eyes were wide. "What did you mean by that?" she asked, with a shaky little laugh. He'd spoken in that strange voice again, the one that held the resonance of a dozen voices, the soft rumble of spring thunder. It had sounded terribly romantic—a little serious and scary too. His words had been almost like a living thing, brushing her with warm fingers. She had a nagging sensation that there was something she should say back to him but had no idea what or why.

He smiled enigmatically.

"Oh, I get it. It's another one of those things—"

"That will become clear in time," he finished for her. "Aye. It's rather like, I will protect you should the need ever arise." *It's more like, you are mine forever, should you agree and give me the words back. And now I am yours forever, whether you agree or not.* It was a risky thing he'd just done, of a certain, because if she never agreed, Drustan MacKeltar would ache endlessly for her. His heart trapped by the binding spell, he would sense her eternally, would love her eternally. But should she one day choose to freely give the words back, the bond would intensify a thousandfold. He could live for such a hope.

Her eyes widened further when she felt him stiffen inside her. "Again?"

"Are you too tender?" he asked gently.

She arched a brow. "I told you, I'm tougher than you think," she said, running the tip of her pink tongue over her lower lip.

He groaned and caught it between his lips. "Then, aye, lass, and again and again," he said, as he began to glide back and forth inside her. "We MacKeltars were bred for stamina."

And since he knew she was the disbelieving type, a woman disinclined to accept anything but firm proof, he proceeded to give her hard evidence of his claim, telling her with his body all the words he so longed to say.

· 10 ·

Gwen stretched languorously, her hands skimming the muscles of Drustan's back. She felt sleepily sated and sexy and tender and, oh . . . so much more complex than she had before. She felt brand new somehow.

Gwen Cassidy had finally been well and truly plucked.

An indefinable sense of peace and rightness nestled in her belly, her heart was full, her mind at ease.

But breathing beneath his weight was a challenge even the new and improved Gwen wasn't up to, so with a gentle nudge she eased him off her. He rolled onto his back and she slipped astride him, straddling him the same way she had the day she'd found him but with one highly erotic and delightful difference: They were both nude. There was so much she wanted to do with him. She wanted to make love on top of him, beside him, with him behind her. . . .

"Drustan," she murmured, studying his face, so beautiful in the silvery light of the moon. His eyes opened, hot-metal silver, lazily seductive. "Thank you," she said softly. He'd made her first time a beautiful, passionate, intense experience, and if for some unfathomable reason she never got to make love with him again, she knew he would be the standard by which she judged men for the rest of her life.

She was falling head over heels in love. And it felt incredible.

He caught her face in his hands and pulled her down for a hungry kiss. "Never thank me, lass. Only ask me for more. That's the finest praise a man can hear from a woman. That and this"—he slipped a hand between her legs—"woman's dew that tells a man how much she desires him."

He smiled at her, and at precisely the same moment noticed the carriage of the moon in the sky. His smile faded abruptly and his body tensed beneath hers. The passion receded from his eyes, replaced by panic.

"Christ," he swore, "'tis nearly too late!" Rolling her off him, he leaped to his feet, grabbed his plaid, and raced to the stone slab. "Come," he commanded.

Befuddled by her rapid dismount, still feeling sexy and sleepy and soft, she stared blankly at him.

"'Tis nearly midnight," he said urgently. "Come."

She reached for her clothing, and he snapped, "No time to dress. But you must bring your pack, Gwen."

Puzzled by his comment, and not completely comfortable with her nudity, she grabbed her backpack and hurried to join him at the slab nevertheless, the scientist within her intensely curious to discover how he planned to prove his claims true. Besides, she told herself, there would be time for more lovemaking afterward.

He worked swiftly, stealing intermittent glances at

the sky as he dipped his fingers in the paint and sketched the final symbols on the slab.

"Take my hand."

She slipped her hand into his. He studied the designs a moment, then shook his head and exhaled loudly.

"Pray Amergin, let them be right. Stand close to me, Gwen. Here."

Gwen positioned herself where he indicated and tried to peer around him to see the last symbols, but he angled his body between them, blocking her view.

"What do you think is going to happen, Drustan?" she asked, glancing at her watch, surprised that anything had remained on her body in the frenzy of their lovemaking. She nearly laughed when she realized that it, and the strap of the pack over her shoulder, were all she now wore. The second hand moved with an audible *tick-tick-tick*.

"Gwen, I—" He broke off, and looked at her.

Her gaze flew to his. Had he felt it too when they'd made love? Being inexperienced in lovemaking, she was uncertain if the emotion she felt when she looked at him was a temporary side effect of physical intimacy. She suspected it was of more significant duration but wasn't in any hurry to make a fool of herself. But if he was feeling it too, she might believe that what existed between them was every bit as real and valid as any mathematical equation. His gaze swept over her body, in such a way that he made her feel beautiful, not short and . . . *all right, a little plump*. She'd always felt inadequate in a world that plastered leggy, slim cover models on every magazine and in every movie.

But not with him. In his eyes, she saw a reflection of herself that was perfection.

"Would that we had an eternity," he said sadly.

Her fingers tightened around his hand, silently

encouraging him to continue. When her watch chimed the hour of midnight with tiny metallic tings, she flinched. *One. Two. Three . . .*

"You are magnificent, lass," he said, tracing his finger down the curve of her cheek. "Such a fearless heart."

Five. Six. Seven.

"Have you come to care for me, if only a bit, Gwen?"

Gwen nodded, her throat suddenly thick, not trusting herself to speak. He looked so sad that she was afraid she might blurt out silly sentimental things and make a fool of herself. She'd already said one thing during their lovemaking she'd never thought would slip past her lips, and now if she wasn't careful she'd get disgustingly mushy on him.

Nine.

"That, and my faith in you, must be enough. Would you aid me, were I in danger?"

"Of course," she said instantly. Then, more hesitantly, "What about me?"

"My life for you," he said simply. "Lass, doona fear me. No matter what happens, promise me you will not fear me. I am a good man, I vow I am."

Stricken by the pain in his voice, she brushed his jaw with her fingers. "I *know* you are, Drustan MacKeltar," she said firmly. "I don't fear you—"

"But things might change."

"Nothing can change that. *Nothing* could make me fear you."

"Would that it could be true," he said, his eyes dark.

Twelve.

Thirteen?

He cried out then, dragged her roughly into his arms, and kissed her, a deep soul kiss—and the world as Gwen Cassidy knew it began to unravel at the seams.

She began gyrating in his arms, bobbing and spinning like a cork in a whirlpool, up and down, side to side, back and forward . . . then a new direction that wasn't a direction at all.

Space-time shifted, her very existence within it changed, and somehow she melted from Drustan's arms.

Her backpack slipped from her shoulder and went sailing off into a vortex of light.

As if from a great distance, she saw her hands reaching for it, but there was something wrong with them. They had an added dimension her mind couldn't comprehend. She wiggled her fingers, struggling to grasp their new quality. Her palms, her wrists, her arms were so . . . different.

She thought she saw Drustan spinning past and then she thought she heard a distant sonic boom, but a sonic boom would have meant that she was moving faster than the speed of sound, and she wasn't moving at all, unless one counted the fact that she felt as ineffectual as a butterfly batting fragile wings against the gale-force winds of a tornado. She fancied she could feel the tips of those delicate appendages tearing off. Besides, she thought dimly, struggling for some core of sanity, the person moving faster than the speed of sound didn't hear the sonic boom. Only those standing still did.

Then a flash of white encompassed her, so blinding that she lost all sense of time and space and self. Whiteness filled her: She choked on it, breathed it, felt it beneath her skin, soaking into her cells and rearranging them according to some alien design. *Terminal velocity for the average skydiver,* the scientist within her recited in a chilly voice, *averages ninety-three to one hundred twenty-five miles per hour. Sound travels seven hundred sixty miles per hour, on a humid day. Escape velocity is the speed required to exit the earth's atmosphere and achieve interplanetary travel, or twenty-five thousand miles per hour. Light travels one hundred eighty-six thousand miles per second.* Then the peculiar thought: *A cat always lands on its feet. Maintain an angular momentum of zero.*

There was no sense of motion, yet there was a horrible vertigo. There was no sound, yet the silence was deafening. There was no fullness of body, yet there was no emptiness. Escape velocity achieved and exceeded, white and whiter, she was—in? on? off?—a long bridge or tunnel. She had no body to instruct to run.

The white was gone so abruptly that the darkness hit her like a brick wall. Then there was blessed sight and sound, and feeling in her hands and feet.

Maybe not so blessed, she decided. Taste was a bitter metallic bile in the back of her throat; weight was a sickening pressure after the terrible vacuum.

Stifling the urge to vomit, she lifted a head that weighed two tons and felt as swollen as an overripe tomato.

Around her, the night exploded. Driving hail pelted the ground, gouging tendrils of mist from the soil. The wind wailed and keened, flung leaves and snapped branches. Large chunks of ice stung her bare skin.

"Drustan!" she cried.

"Here, lass." He stumbled to her side, then slipped on the hail-covered terrain and fell to his knees.

"Drustan, what's happening?" As he drew himself erect, she saw that his face was pale and drawn; lines she'd never noticed before etched sharp grooves around his mouth. He was looking down at his hands with horror. Her gaze flew to them, wondering what was wrong with them. Whatever he saw, she couldn't see. They seemed to disappear into the mist.

"I erred when I sketched the final symbols," he yelled hoarsely. A large ball of ice struck his cheekbone, raising an immediate welt. "I went back too far. I thought I could come with you, but I cannot. Forgive me, lass, it wasn't supposed to be this way!"

"What?" Gwen could scarcely hear him, so deafening was the wind. Strands of her hair stung the skin of her neck as the wind whipped it wildly about her face. The gale was so lashing, it felt it was raking the skin from her cheekbones. The hail was bruising her scalp; her head ached in dozens of spots. She inched toward him and clutched at his arm. It felt curiously insubstantial beneath her fingers, although she could see the muscles in his arms bulging. He tried to close his misty hand around hers, but it sort of slid through hers.

"What's *happening* to you?" she wailed.

"Save me. Save my clan, lass," he yelled. "Keep the lore safe." *Christ, he could feel himself being torn in two. Talking to her, simultaneously trying to reason with his past self. It wasn't working. It took immense effort merely to move his lips and form words. He was coming apart . . . two places in one time, and all the while reeling because he finally understood the next dimension . . . and he had to tell her what to say and do! He must tell her how to use the spell he'd taught her!*

"*What* are you talking about?" she cried. "Ouch!" she cried, as a chunk of hail struck her forehead.

But he didn't answer, just flickered in a way that terrified her, as if he was fading but fighting to stay. Nearly hysterical, Gwen tried to cling to him, but he slid through her hands.

His silver eyes flashed, he looked wild, forbidding, a dark sorcerer from eons past. He thrust his plaid at her, wordlessly demanding she take it.

She closed trembling fingers over the fabric.

"Listen," he cried. His gaze swept over her and passion blazed in his eyes. Then he cocked his head as if hearing something she couldn't hear and glanced beyond her as if seeing something she couldn't see. His lips moved one last time.

The moment you see him you must tell him . . . show him—

"What?" she cried. "Tell who what?" Flying leaves and limbs rained down upon them. When he ducked and shielded his face to avert a blow from a particularly large branch, she missed most of what he was saying. Tell and show who *what?*

Abruptly, he was gone. Vanished as completely as the symbols had vanished from his chest in the cave days ago.

With his disappearance, the maelstrom died and the hail ceased abruptly. The night fell silent, the mist dissipated on a last, bitter gust of wind.

Gwen remained frozen, in shock, bruised and windburned and aching.

She didn't trust herself to take even one step on a leg that moments ago had not been her leg at all but her leg *and* something else, something the bristling scientist was still pacing back and forth in a white lab coat protesting stridently. She wasn't certain any part of her would obey simple orders, so knotted up was her mind.

"Drustan," she called weakly. Then louder: *"Drustan!"*

A terrible silence greeted her. She shivered uncontrollably, belatedly remembering she was nude. Woodenly, she pulled his plaid around her and scrambled across the slippery ground toward the fire.

But there was no fire. The storm must have put it out.

She dropped to her knees on the hail-covered ground, clutching his plaid, huddling within it for warmth. Dazedly, she glanced about and was astonished to see the hail was so thick on the ground that it looked as if the heavens had opened up and simply iced the top of the mountain. It could take hours for it to melt in the warm autumn night. And then she fell still and thought no more about the strange storm, as she replayed their entire encounter through her mind, finally seeing the pattern.

He had said he would *prove* to her that he was telling the truth, but he could only do it at the stones. He'd said that if she didn't believe him, she would be free of him. She now realized he'd always chosen his words cautiously, couching double meanings.

Now she understood exactly what he'd meant. "You *left* me," she whispered. "You really showed me, huh?" She snorted and started crying at the same time. "Incontrovertible proof. Uh-huh. Ever the doubter here, that's me."

He'd bullied her into guiding him through her time to the stones, made incredible love to her, proved his story true, then returned himself to his own time—leaving her in the twenty-first century, alone.

He hadn't been deranged after all. She'd had a genuine time-traveling sixteenth-century warrior in her arms, and she mocked him at every turn. Treated him with disbelief, even patronized him on occasion.

Oh, she'd screwed this one up royally. She'd fallen for him at terminal velocity. In the space of three days, she'd grown attached to him as she'd never thought possible. She'd been building a life with him in her mind, rationalizing away his delusions, weaving him into her world.

And he'd *left* her. He'd not even offered to take her with him!

Would you have gone? Would you have said yes? the scientist asked dryly. *Plunged into a century you knew nothing about? Left this one behind for good?*

Hell, yes, I would have said yes! What do I have here? I was falling in love, and I'd go anywhere, do anything for that!

For a novel change, the scientist within her had no caustic comeback.

Gwen cried, feeling suddenly old, regretting the loss of a thing she'd not truly appreciated and understood while she'd held it in her hand.

She had no idea how long she lay in the clearing, re-playing things through her mind, lingering over their lovemaking, seeing everything in a different light.

When she finally sat up, she was trembling. Her knees were frozen from huddling on the ice, and her toes were stinging. *I feel, MacKeltar. You taught me that. I hope you're happy with yourself—showing me I had a heart by hurting me.*

She pushed herself up and slipped around the circle, searching for her clothes in the dark. Shaking off a fresh desire to weep, she blew out a breath. Where the hell were her boots? For that matter, where were her back-pack and her flashlight? She was starting to suffer a se-vere nicotine craving; emotional distress always made her crave a cigarette.

How was she ever going to get over him? How would she cope with the knowledge that the man she'd lost her heart to had been dead for hundreds of years?

Panic gripped her as she circled the stone slab, search-ing for her belongings. They were gone. Could the freakish and violent windstorm have carried it all off?

Stunned, she glanced about, then up at the sky, and caught a glimpse—for the first time since Drustan had disappeared—of what lay beyond the stones.

Where previously there had been nothing, tons upon tons of stone rose up from the earth.

She gaped in astonishment, her gaze drifting from tower to turret, to bigger stone tower, past walls capped by those toothy stone things one saw on castles every-where in Scotland, and to yet another turret and a square tower again. Blinking, she looked left to right and back again.

An alarm went off in her brain, but she couldn't re-spond to it. She couldn't respond to anything. She started hyperventilating; tiny breaths slammed into each other and piled up in her throat.

A monstrous castle lay beyond the circle of stones.

Huge, forbidding, yet beautiful, it was fashioned of massive gray stone walls that vaulted smoothly skyward. A center rectangular tower stood tallest and had two smaller round towers flanking it. Wings spread east to west consuming the horizon, with large square towers at the farthest east and west ends. A milky fog dusted the ridges and capped the turrets.

Her jaw dropped.

Still as the cold stones that encircled her, she stared.

Could it be that she had not lost him after all?

With a painful surge of adrenaline that made her heart beat much too fast, she bolted from the circle of stones and burst into a terraced courtyard. Pathways forked in various directions, one leading straight to the front steps of the castle itself.

She spun in a slow circle, heedless of her icy toes. Dimly, her mind registered the fact that the hail had fallen only within the circle of stones. The ground beyond it was warm and dry.

He'd told her that in his century, the stones of *Ban Drochaid* had been enclosed within the perimeter walls of his estate, but the *Ban Drochaid* she'd entered an hour ago had resided in the midst of a wasteland of crumbled stone and grass.

Yet now she was completely encircled by high walls, within a veritable fortress.

She glanced at the night sky. It was dense black with no distant glow on the horizon in any direction, which was impossible, because Alborath lay in the valley beyond, and only last night, while sitting on the hood of the rental car, she'd rued that the lights of the village spoiled her view of the stars.

Turning back to the castle that hadn't been there five minutes ago, she fingered the folds of his plaid. Suddenly, the words he'd shouted—words she'd ignored because they hadn't made any sense at the time—now made perfect sense.

I went back too far. I thought I could come with you, but I cannot.

Save my clan.

Oh, God, Drustan, she thought, *you didn't go back in time. You sent me back to save you!*

"When I consider the small span of my life absorbed in the eternity of all time, or the small part of space which I can touch or see engulfed by the infinite immensity of spaces that I know not and that know me not, I am frightened and astonished to see myself here instead of there . . . now instead of then."

—BLAISE PASCAL

"For those of us who believe in physics, this separation between past, present, and future is only an illusion, however tenacious."

—ALBERT EINSTEIN

JULY 18
1518

·11·

The nightmare was beyond anything Drustan MacKeltar's slumbering mind had ever managed to conjure, replete with a taste so vile, he knew it for what it was: the taste of death.

Shadowy images taunted him at the periphery of his vision, and he felt a monstrous leech suckle onto him, and they grappled, then suddenly there were two discrete yet similar beings inside his body.

I am possessed of a demon, the sleeping Drustan thought, struggling to spew the atrocity forth. *I will not permit this.* Enraged, he resisted the new presence violently, lashing out to destroy it without even trying to identify it. It was foreign and as strong as he was, and that was all he needed to know.

He focused his mind, isolating the intruder, cocooning it with his will, and with immense effort thrust it from his body.

Then suddenly there were two of him in his nightmare, but the other him looked older, and anguished. Mortally weary.

Get thee hence, devil, Drustan shouted.

Listen to me, you fool.

Drustan clamped his hands over his ears. *I will hear none of your lies, demon.* Somewhere in the distance—in the nightmare place that defied his mind's ability to either comprehend or fabricate—Drustan scented a woman. She was indistinct, but he could feel her, even smell the fragrant heat of her skin. A rush of longing consumed him, nearly shattering his resolve to hold the other him at bay.

Sensing the weakness, the replica leaped forward, but Drustan flexed his will and knocked him aside.

They glared at each other, and Drustan wondered at the play of emotions on the replica's face. Fear. Sorrow so deep it might cleave a man asunder. And as he watched, a sudden understanding flickered in the false Drustan's eyes, even as the replica seemed to be losing solidity.

You would fight me to the death, the counterfeit's lips moved soundlessly. *I see. I see now why only one lives. 'Tis not Nature, which is innately indifferent, but our own fear that causes us to destroy each other. I beg you, accept me. Let us both be.*

I will never accept you, Drustan roared.

The replica faded, then grew more solid, then faded around the edges again. *You are in terrible danger—*

Speak no more! I will believe naught you say! Drustan lashed out at the shadow-him viciously.

The shadow-him glanced over his shoulder and shouted to someone Drustan couldn't see: *The moment you see him you must tell him the first rhyme I taught you, remember it? The verse in the car, and show him the backpack and all will be well.*

Be gone, demon! Drustan roared, shoving at him with his will.

The other him speared Drustan with his gaze. *Love her,* the counterfeit whispered, and then he vanished.

Drustan shot bolt upright in bed, gasping for air.

He clawed at his throat, pounded his fists on his chest, and finally managed to suck in a painful breath. He was sweating. Icy and feverish at the same time, he'd shredded his linens in his sleep. Previously soft animal skins were now mere tufts of sweat-slicked fur, and his head pounded.

He fumbled for the mug of wine at his bedside. It took him several attempts before he succeeded in wrapping his fingers securely around it. Trembling, he drank deep, until the mug was empty. He dragged the back of his hand across his mouth.

His heart thundered and he felt as if he'd just been more bitterly threatened than ever in his life. As if something had crept into his body and tried to claim territorial rights.

He plunged shaking hands into his hair, lunged from the bed, and began to pace. He glanced back at the bed warily, expecting a succubus to be lurking in the pile of destroyed linens.

By Amergin! What strange dream had been visited upon him? He could recall naught of it now but a bitter sense of violation, and a hollow sense of victory.

His attention was snared by a brilliant flash of light beyond the window of his bedchamber. A low growl of thunder followed it, and he tugged aside the tapestry and gazed out through the glass into the night.

Drustan stood by the window for a long time, taking slow, deep breaths and trying to regain a measure of calm. He rarely suffered nightmares and preferred to forget this one, for the dream reeked of madness. He firmly corralled it in a deep, dark place in his mind, burying it where it would never see the light of day.

The storm died as suddenly as it had arisen, and the Highland night fell still and silent again.

Think think think, Gwen berated herself. *You're supposed to be so brainy, use it.* But her brain felt numb and clumsy. After the day she'd just had—the incredible passion, the bizarre storm, the fuzziness of her mind from nicotine withdrawal—she was in no condition to be brilliant. She was hardly in any condition to manage average.

Pacing gingerly upon the melting hail, she tallied the tangible facts, because the intangible ones, at the moment, scared the bejeezus out of her. She was desperate to find some factual, logical conclusion to explain away the illogic of her whereabouts.

She shivered, eyeing the castle. The prospect of confronting what it held both fascinated and terrified her.

But there was something she had to do first. Not that she was the disbelieving type, no way, not her. But she did prefer to view hard evidence with her own two eyes.

Drawing a bracing breath, she plunged into the darkness beyond the circle and sped away from the castle. When she reached the estate wall, she flung herself up on a pile of casks, pressed her cheek to a narrow slit in the wall, and peered out into the valley at the city of Alborath.

It wasn't there. Suspicion confirmed.

Her shoulders slumped. She hadn't expected it to be, but its absence was shocking nonetheless.

I went back too far.

In other words, she mused, sorting through what she knew about the theories of time travel, he'd probably tried to go back to shortly after he'd been abducted, but had gotten the symbols wrong. He'd returned to a time when the past him was there in the castle, and common theory held that if time travel were possible, the fabric of the universe would not suffer two identical selves in a single moment. The future him had somehow been canceled out.

Time travel! the scientist shouted in her head. *Analyze!*

We have to save him. Analyze that. We'll contemplate the ramifications of multiverses later.

If the future him had been canceled out, that meant the Drustan she'd fallen in love with no longer existed, but she would find him in the castle, pre-enchantment, and with no knowledge of her whatsoever.

That thought made her heart hurt. She was in no rush to look into his silvery eyes, which had gazed at her so intimately but an hour ago, and see an utter lack of recognition.

Promise me you will not fear me.

Fear him? Why would she have feared him? Because he could manipulate time? Sheesh, that only increased her fascination with him!

Save my clan.

She would *not* fail him.

Squaring her shoulders, she hurried back through the stones, toward the castle, and flew up the stairs. Fisting her hand, she knocked on an enormous door that made her feel like a shrunken Alice in a hostile Wonderland. Once, twice, and again. "Halloo, halloo!" she cried. She flung her small frame at it, pounding with her shoulder.

There was no answer. No convenient doorbell either. Her mind duly noted more tangible evidence that what she was knocking on was not a twenty-first-century door. She would contemplate the medieval door later. From the inside. At the moment, she was feeling as if she might faint at any moment. The strangeness of it all left her feeling utterly overwhelmed. And so what if she was a physicist, supposedly capable of heightened comprehension—she was totally freaked out.

"Oh, puh-lease!" she cried, turning around and using her bottom as a battering ram on the thick door. *Thump-thump, thump-thump.* It hurt her more than it hurt the door, and made about as much noise as a downy pillow. She'd be damned if she was getting sent back to save him, only to be denied entrance.

She stepped back and eyed the windows. Perhaps she could toss something through the glass?

Not exactly a wise way to petition shelter from strangers, she decided. Someone might shoot at her. Arrows, or something equally archaic. Perhaps toss boiling oil down the walls.

She cast a glance about and spied a pile of chopped wood. She scurried over to it, freed a wedge, and slammed one end against the door. "Please, open up," she called.

"I'm coming," a sleepy voice replied. "I heard ye the first time. Impatient, aren't ye?" There was the sound of metal sliding against wood, and the door was finally, blessedly opened. Gwen sank to her knees with relief.

A buxom fortyish woman clad in a long gown and lacy cap stood in the doorway, blinking sleep from her eyes. Her eyes widened as she took in the sight huddling on the doorstep, nearly naked.

She whisked Gwen through the door with a strong grip and slammed it behind them. "Och, lassie," she crooned, gathering her in her arms. "Nell's got ye now. For the love of Columba, what gives ye cause to be wandering so on such a night? An English wench, no less! How came ye here? Did a man have at ye? Did he harm ye, wee lass?"

As the woman drew her to her ample bosom, Gwen thought, *So this is Drustan's Nell,* and sagged against her. She was exactly as he'd described. Assertive and gruffly kind, pretty—past the flush of youth, but with a timeless beauty that would never fade.

Beyond coherent thought, she was dimly astonished to realize her brain was shutting off, as if someone had flipped the main breaker and, circuit by circuit, all systems were going down.

She couldn't crash now! She needed to know what date it was. But her body, overwhelmed and madly off-kilter from her jaunt through the centuries, had other ideas.

"Nell, what's all the commotion?" A man called from somewhere in the perimeter of her awareness.

"Help me with the lass, Silvan," Nell murmured. "'Tis the oddest thing, but she's chilled and her feet are near frozen."

Gwen tried desperately to ask, "What's the date" and "Is he okay?" But damn it all, she was passing out.

Her fading consciousness chuckled richly when she thought she glimpsed Albert Einstein, the greatest theoretical physicist of all time, bending over her, wiry white hair and wrinkled impish face, a mischievous light in his eyes. If she was dying, she was going to be in fine company, indeed. He bent his face close to hers and she managed to whisper, "Drustan."

"Fascinating," she thought she heard him remark. "Let's get her warmed up and put her in the Silver Chamber."

"But that chamber adjoins Drustan's," Nell protested. " 'Tis not proper."

"Propriety be damned. 'Tis the most suitable."

Gwen didn't listen further.

Drustan was alive and they were putting her near him. She would rest for a moment.

· 12 ·

"**Why must ye live all the way up here, Silvan?**
Yer like the bald eagle nestin' on the mount," Nell said,
nudging open the door to his tower chamber—one hundred and three steps above the castle proper—with her
hip. "Had to settle on the highest limb, dinna ye?"

Silvan MacKeltar popped his head up out of a book
with a bemused expression. A silvery-white mane was
sleek about his face, and Nell found him terribly handsome in a sage way, but she'd never tell him that. "I am
not bald. I have quite a lot of hair." He lowered his head
again and resumed reading, running his finger across the
page.

The man was completely in his own world most of
the time, Nell mused. Many were the times she'd wondered how he'd managed to get sons on his wife. Had
the woman slammed his tomes shut on his fingers and
dragged him off by the ear?

Now, there was a fine idea, she thought, watching him through eyes that did not nor had ever, in the twelve years she'd been there, betrayed one ounce of her feelings for him.

"Drink." She plunked the mug down on the table next to his book, careful not to spill a drop on his precious tome.

"Not another of your vile concoctions, is it, Nell?"

"Nay," she said, stony-faced, "'tis another of my splendid brews. And ye need it, so drink. I'm not leaving until the mug is empty."

"Did you put any cocoa in it?"

"Ye know we're nearly out."

"Nell," he said with a put-upon sigh, flipping a page in his book, "go on with you. I'll drink it later."

"And ye might as well know yer son is up and about," she added, hands on her hips, foot tapping, waiting for him to drink. When he didn't reply, she forged on. "What do ye wish me to do with the lass who appeared last eve?"

Silvan closed his tome, refusing to look at her lest he betray how very much he enjoyed looking at her. He appeased himself with the promise of safely stealing several surreptitious glances when she walked out the door. "You're not going to leave, are you?"

"Not until ye drink."

"How is she?"

"She's sleeping," Nell told his profile. The man rarely looked at her that she noticed; she'd been speaking to his profile for years. "But she doesn't seem to have suffered lasting injury." *Thank the saints,* Nell thought, feeling fiercely protective toward the lass who'd arrived with no clothing and the blood of her maidenhead on her thighs. Neither she nor Silvan had missed it when they tucked the wee unconscious lass into bed. They'd glanced uneasily at each other, and Silvan had fingered the fabric of his son's plaid with a perplexed expression.

"Has she said anything about what happened to her last eve?" he asked, rubbing his thumb idly over the symbols embossed on the leather binding of the book.

"Nay. Although she mumbled in her sleep, naught of it made sense."

Silvan's eyebrows rose. "Think you she was . . . er, harmed in some way that has affected her mind?"

"I think," Nell said carefully, "the fewer questions ye ask her for now, the better. 'Tis plain to see she needs a place to stay, what with having no possessions nor clothing. I ask ye grant her shelter as ye did me that eve, many years past. Let her story come out when she's ready."

"Well, if she's aught like you, that means I'll never know," Silvan said with studied casualness.

Nell caught her breath. In all these years he'd not once asked what had happened the night she was given sanctuary at Castle Keltar. For him even to make such an offhand reference to it was rarer than a purple pine marten. Privacy was ever honored at the MacKeltars'— sometimes a blessing, ofttimes a curse. The Keltar men were not wont to pry. And many were the times she'd wished one of them had.

When, a dozen years ago, Silvan had found her lying in the road, beaten and left for dead, she hadn't felt like talking about it. By the time she'd healed and been ready to confide, Silvan—who'd held her hand and fought for her while she'd lain fevered—had retreated coolly from her bedside and never spoken of it again. What was a woman to do? Blurt out her woeful tale as if she were looking for sympathy?

And so a polite and infinite distance had formed between housekeeper and laird. As should be, she reminded herself. She cocked her head warily, warning herself not to read too much into his mild statement.

When she said nothing, Silvan sighed and instructed that she procure suitable clothing for the lass.

"I already dug out some of yer wife's old gowns. Now, would ye please drink? Dinna be thinking I've not noticed that ye haven't been feeling yerself of late. My brew will help if ye quit dumping it in the garderobe."

He flushed.

"Silvan, ye hardly eat, ye scarce sleep, and a body needs certain things. Will ye just try it and see if it doesn't help?"

He raised one white brow, giving her a satyrlike look. "Pushy wench."

"Cantankerous old fox."

A faint smile played about his lips. He raised the mug, held his nose, and tipped the contents back. She watched his throat work for several minutes before he grimaced and plunked it down. For a brief moment, their eyes met.

She turned around and swept toward the door. "Dinna be forgetting about the lass," she reminded stiffly. "You need to see to her, assure her she has a place here for however long need be."

"I shan't forget."

Nell inclined her head and stepped out the doorway.

"Nellie."

She froze, her back to him. The man hadn't called her Nellie in years.

He cleared his throat. "Have you done something different with yourself?" When she didn't reply, he cleared his throat again. "You look . . . er, that is you look rather . . ." He trailed off, as if regretting even beginning.

Nell spun back around to face him, her brows drawn together, lips pursed. He opened and closed his mouth several times, his gaze drifting over her face. Might he truly have noticed the wee change she'd made? She thought he *never* noticed her. And if he did, would he think she was a silly old woman fussing with herself? "Rather *what?*" she demanded.

"Er . . . I do believe . . . the word might be . . . fetching." Softer somehow, he thought, his gaze skimming her up and down. Ye Gods, but the woman was temptingly soft to begin with.

"Have ye lost yer mind, old man?" she snapped, thoroughly discombobulated, and when Nell was thoroughly discombobulated, she wielded crankiness like a sword. "I look the same as I do every day," she lied. Straightening her spine, she forced herself to glide regally out the door.

But the moment she knew she was out of sight, she rushed down the stairs, skirts a-flying, hair tumbling loose, hands to her throat.

She patted at the wispy strands of hair she'd snipped shorter that morn—similar to the wee lass's, admiring the look. If such a minor change drew—by God, a compliment!—from Silvan MacKeltar, she might just stitch herself that new gown of softest lapis linen she'd been considering.

Fetching, indeed!

Gwen awakened slowly, surfacing from a montage of nightmares in which she'd been running around nude (naturally, at her heaviest weight, *never* after a week of successful dieting), chasing Drustan, and losing him through doors that disappeared before she could reach them.

She took a deep breath, sorting through her thoughts. She'd left the States because she despised her life. She'd embarked upon a trip to Scotland to lose her virginity, see if she had a heart, and shake up her world.

Well, she'd certainly accomplished all her goals.

No simple cherry picker for me, she thought. *I get a time-traveling genius who comes with a world of problems and sends me back through time to fix them.*

Not that she minded.

She'd decided the words *soul mate* and *Drustan Mac-Keltar* were synonymous. She'd finally met a man who made her feel with an intensity she'd never imagined, was brilliant, yet wasn't cold in his brilliance. He knew how to tease and be warm and passionate. He found her beautiful, and he was a phenomenal, erotic lover. Simply, she'd met the perfect man and lost him, all in three days. He'd awakened more emotions in her in that short time than she'd felt in her entire life.

Slowly, she opened her eyes. Although the room was dim, the muted golden light of a fire spilled about the chamber. She blinked at the profusion of purple surrounding her, then recalled Drustan's fascination with the purple running suits in Barrett's. His insistence on purple trews or a T-shirt, a request she'd refused.

That sealed it. She was definitely in Drustan's world now.

A sumptuous violet velvet coverlet was tucked beneath her chin. Above her, a lavender canopy of sheer gauzy stuff draped the elegantly carved cherry bed. A lilac sheepskin—*oh really,* she thought, *I know there are no lilac sheep*—was spread across her feet. Purple pillows with silver braided trim were strewn about the headboard.

Small curio tables were draped in orchid and plum silks. Brilliant plum and black tapestries in complicated patterns adorned the two tall windows, and between them hung an enormous ornate gilt-framed mirror. Two chairs were arranged before the windows, centered around a table that held silver goblets and plates.

Purple, she mused, with sudden insight. Such an electrifying, energetic man would naturally choose to surround himself with the color that had the highest frequency in the spectrum.

It was a hot color, vivid and erotic.

Like the man himself.

She pressed her nose into the pillow, hoping to catch his scent in the linens, but if he'd slept in this bed it had been too long ago, or the coverings had been changed. She turned her attention to the frame of the exquisitely carved bed in which she lay. The headboard had numerous drawers and cubbyholes. A sweeping footboard was etched with delicate Celtic knotwork. She'd seen a bed like it once before.

In a museum.

This one was as new as anything one might find in a modern-day furniture gallery. Raking her bangs out of her face, she continued surveying the room. Knowing she was in the sixteenth century and *seeing* it were two very different things. The walls were fashioned of pale gray stone, the ceiling was high, and there were none of those moldings or baseboards that always looked so out of place in "renovated" castles frequented by tourists. Not one outlet, not one lamp, merely dozens of glass bowls filled with oil, topped by fat, blackened wicks. The floor was planked of honey-blond wood, polished to a high sheen, with rugs scattered about. A lovely chest sat near the foot of the bed, topped with a pile of folded blankets. More cushioned chairs were arranged before the fire. The fireplace was fashioned of smooth pink stone, with a massive hewn mantel above it. In it, a peat fire steamed, sheaths of heather stacked atop the dried bricks scenting the room. All in all, it was a deliciously warm room, rich and luxurious.

She glanced at her wrist to see what time it was, but apparently her watch had wafted off into the same quantum foam that had devoured her clothing and backpack.

She was momentarily distracted by the garment she was wearing: A long, sheer white chemise edged with lace, it looked positively old-fashioned and frivolous.

She shook her head, swung her legs over the edge of the bed, and felt painfully short when her toes dangled a foot above the floor. With an exasperated hop, she dropped down out of the high bed and hurried to the window. She pulled the tapestry aside to find the sun shining brightly beyond the paned windows. She fumbled with the latch a moment, then pushed it open and breathed deeply of the fragrant air.

She was in sixteenth-century Scotland. *Wow.*

Beneath her stretched a lovely terraced courtyard, enclosed by the four inner walls of the wing of the castle she was in. Two women were beating rugs against the stones, chatting as they kept an eye on a gaggle of children kicking a lopsided sort of ball about. She peered at it, squinting. *Eeew*, she thought, recalling that Bert had said he'd read that medieval children had played with balls fashioned from bladders of animals and such.

She shook herself abruptly. She needed to know what the date was. While she stood gaping out the window, peril could be drawing ever nearer her Highland lover.

She was about to tug the coverlet off the bed and don it toga-style when she noticed a gown—lavender, of course—lying across the stuffed armchair near the fire, aside a miscellany of other items.

She hurried to the chair, where she fingered the items, trying to decide the order in which she was supposed to put them on.

And there were no panties, she realized with dismay. She could hardly be expected to swish around, bare-bottomed beneath her gown. She glared at the clothing, as if irritation alone might conjure a pair of panties from thin air. She glanced about the room with an entrepreneur's eye but reluctantly concluded that even if she snatched up a table covering, she'd have to knot it about her like a diaper.

She slipped off her nightgown, then slid the soft white undergarment over her head. A simple shift, it clung to her body and fell to midankle. Over it went the gown, then the sleeveless overtunic of darker purple, embroidered with silver threads. Stunned that it didn't drag on the floor, she plucked up the hem and snorted when she saw it had been neatly sheared off. Apparently people had already noted how short she was. She tied the laces on the overtunic beneath her breasts.

The slippers were a joke, sizes too big, but would have to do. She swiped the silk swath from a table and ripped the sheer fabric. As she was balling it up and stuffing it in the toes, her stomach growled mightily, and she remembered that she hadn't eaten since yesterday afternoon.

But she couldn't just stroll out into the corridor without a plan.

Order of the day: a bathroom, coffee, then at the earliest possible opportunity find Drustan and tell him what had happened.

Tell him . . . what danger he is in was probably what he'd been saying before he'd melted in the circle of stones. *Show him . . .* had obviously meant her backpack. She sighed, wishing she had it. But Drustan was a brilliant man with a fine logical mind. Surely, he would see the truth in her story.

In retrospect, it infuriated her that Drustan hadn't told her the whole truth. However, she grudgingly acknowledged, chances were good that if he *had* told her, she would have, with infinite condescension, debated the implausibility of time travel for however long it had taken her to drive him to the nearest psychiatric ward.

She would never have believed he knew how to move in the fourth dimension. Who and what was this man to whom she'd given her virginity?

There was only one way to find out. Find him and talk to him.

Yo, Drustan. You don't know me, but a future you will be enchanted, wake up in the twenty-first century, and send me back to save you and keep your clan from being destroyed.

She frowned. It wasn't something *she'd* believe, if a man showed up in her time with such a story, but Drustan must have known what he was talking about. It was clear that he'd wanted her to tell the "past" him the truth. There was nothing else he could have been trying to say.

She was starved, both for food and a glimpse of Drustan.

And it was urgent that she discover the date.

Jamming the slippers on her feet, she hurried out into the corridor.

· 13 ·

Sleeping past sunrise was not a thing Drustan did often, but troubled dreams had disrupted his slumber and he'd slept until long past dawn.

He'd pushed the vague memories away and concentrated instead on the pleasant thoughts of his upcoming wedding. Silvan longed to hear the castle filled with voices again, Nell would be delighted by wee ones scampering about, and Drustan MacKeltar wanted bairn of his own. He would teach his sons to fish and calculate the motion of heavenly bodies. He would teach his daughters the same, he vowed.

He wanted children, and by Amergin, he would get his bride to the altar this time! No matter that he knew naught of her. She was young, of child-bearing age, and he would lavish her with respect and courtesy. Double it, for having him.

And mayhap one day she might come to have feeling

for him. Mayhap she was young enough that she might be . . . er, trainable like a young foal. If she couldn't read and write, she might like to learn. Or she could be weak of sight and not notice the eccentricities of the occupants of Castle Keltar.

And mayhap his wolfhounds would take to sailing longboats across the loch, sporting Viking attire. Waving flags of surrender. Ha.

Anya was his last chance, and he knew it. Because they were Highlanders who kept much to themselves, because of the centuries of rumors, because of the string of broken betrothals, fathers of well-bred young ladies were loath to pledge their daughters to him. They sought for their daughters safe, respectable men to whom rumors didn't cling as tenacious as burrs on a woolen.

Yet the Elliott, laird of an ancient clan of noble lineage, had decided to overlook it all (for two manors and a fair amount of coin) and a match had been promised. Now Drustan merely had to hide his unusual abilities long enough to make Anya Elliott care for him, or at least long enough to get a few bairn. He knew better than to hope for love. Time had taught him that well.

Love, he mused. What would it be like to have a woman look at him with admiration? Appreciate who he was? Each time he'd begun to believe a woman might care about him, she'd seen or heard something that had frightened her witless and abandoned him, crying, *Pagan! Sorcerer!*

Bah. He was a perfectly respectable Christian. He just happened to be a Druid too, but he suffered no conflicts of faith. God was in everything. As He'd granted His beauty to mighty oaks and crystal lochs, He'd also brushed the stones and the stars with it. Absorbed in the simple perfection of an equation, Drustan's faith deepened, not weakened. Recently, he'd begun regularly attending mass again, intrigued with the intelligent young priest who'd taken over the services at the castle. Endowed with a gentle manner, a quick wit, an addled mother for whom he couldn't be blamed, and an open-mindedness rare in men of the Kirk, Nevin Alexander didn't condemn the MacKeltars for being different. He saw past the rumors to the honorable men within. Mayhap in part because his own mother practiced a few pagan rites.

Drustan was pleased the young priest would be performing the wedding ceremony. Work restoring the lovely chapel in the castle had been accelerated, to have all in readiness.

In anticipation of his future wife's arrival at Castle Keltar, he'd taken precautions. Not only had he warned Silvan and Dageus about unusual displays of talent and mind-boggling conversations, but he'd had the "heretical" tomes removed from the library and toted up for secure storage in Silvan's tower chamber. God willing, she'd be so busy with her aunts and maids who were to accompany her that she wouldn't notice anything odd about any of them. He would not make the same mistakes with Anya Elliott as he'd made with his first three betrotheds. Surely his family could present their best boots forward for only a fortnight!

He would not fail this time, he vowed optimistically.

Unfortunately, no one else in the castle seemed optimistic this morn.

Upon awakening, hungry, and unable to a find a single kitchen lass about, he'd wandered down the corridor to the kitchens, calling for Nell, until she'd finally poked her head out of the buttery to see what he wanted.

What did any man want in the morning, he'd teased, *besides an energetic tussle between the sheets? Food.*

She hadn't smiled and teased back. Casting him sidewise and oddly scathing glances, Nell had complied, following him back to the Greathall and slapping down crusty, week-old bread, flat ale, and a pork pie that he'd begun to suspect contained parts of a pig he'd prefer not to think about.

Where were his treasured kippers and tatties, fried crispy golden? Since when had he, Nell's favorite, rated such meager fare in the morning? On occasion Dageus had been treated in such a poor fashion—usually when he'd done something Nell hadn't appreciated, involving a lass—but not Drustan.

So now he sat alone, wishing someone, anyone, even young Tristan, the bright lad they were training in basic Druidry, might saunter in with a *hullo* or a smile. He was not a man given to dark moods, yet this morning his entire world felt off-balance, and he couldn't shake a niggling sense of foreboding that it was about to get worse.

"So?" Silvan said, popping his head into the Greathall, skewering him with his intense gaze. "Where were you last night?" The rest of him followed at a more leisurely pace. Drustan smiled faintly. If he lived to be a hundred, he'd never get used to his father's gait. Headfirst, the rest of him trailing behind, as if he tolerated his body only because it was necessary to tote his head about from place to place.

He took a swill of flat ale and said dryly, "Good morning to you too, Da." Was everyone out of sorts this morn? Silvan hadn't even bothered with a greeting. Just a question that had sounded much like an accusation and had made him feel like a lad again, caught slipping back in from a nocturnal dalliance with a serving wench.

The elderly Keltar paused inside the doorway, leaned back against the stone column, and folded his arms across his chest. Too busy pondering the mysteries of the universe and scribbling in his journals to indulge in training or swordplay, Silvan was nearly as tall as Drustan, but much narrower of frame.

Drustan forced himself to swallow a mouthful of what he was becoming convinced was pig-tail pie. *Crunch-*

crunch. By Amergin, what had Nell put in the thing? he wondered, trying not to look at the filling overmuch. Did she bake horrid things in advance to ply upon whomever upset her in some fashion?

"I said, where were you?" Silvan repeated.

Drustan frowned. Aye, Silvan was definitely out of sorts. "Sleeping. And you?"

He plucked an unidentifiable from his plate and offered it to one of the hounds beneath the table. Curling its lip, the animal growled and backed away. Drustan frowned dubiously at the pie before glancing back at his father. Silvan looked his age this morning, and that depressed and irritated Drustan.

Depressed him because Silvan *was* his age, all of three score and two. Irritated him because recently his father had taken to wearing his hair loose around his shoulders, which, in Drustan's opinion, made him look even older, and he didn't like to be reminded of his father's mortality. He wanted his children to have their grandfather around for a very long time. Silvan's hair was no longer the thick black of his prime, but shoulder length, snowy white, and possessed of a personality of its own. Coupled with the flowing blue robe he favored, he projected an unkempt, mad-philosopher look.

Tugging the leather thong from his hair, he tossed it at his father and was relieved to see his da was still spry enough to catch it with a hand above his head.

"What?" Silvan asked peevishly, glancing at it. "What would I be wanting with this?"

"Tie it back. Your hair is making me mad."

Silvan arched a white brow. "I like it this way. For your information, the priest's mother quite likes my hair. She told me so just last week."

"Da, stay away from Nevin's mother," Drustan said, making no attempt to conceal his distaste. "I vow, that woman tries to read my fortune every time I see her.

Ever creeping about, spouting gloom and doom. She's daft, Besseta is. Even Nevin thinks so." He shook his head and popped a crust of bread in his mouth, then washed it down with a swig of ale. The pork pie had defeated him. He shoved the platter away, refusing to look at it.

"Speaking of women, son, what have you to tell me about the wee one that appeared here last eve?"

Drustan lowered his mug to the table with a thump, in no mood for one of his father's cryptic conversations. He slid the pork pie down the table toward his father. "Care for some pie, Da?" he offered. Silvan probably wouldn't even notice anything wrong with it. To him, food was food, necessary to keep the body toting the head around. "And I doona know what lass you're talking about."

"The one who collapsed on our steps yestreen, wearing naught but her skin and your plaid," Silvan said, ignoring the pie. "The chieftain's plaid, the only one that's woven with silver threads."

Drustan stopped brooding over his measly breakfast, his attention fully engaged. "Collapsed? Indeed?"

"Indeed. An English lass."

"I've seen no English lass this morning. Nor last eve." Mayhap the lass Silvan was going on about was the reason he'd gotten the offensive pork pie. Nell had a soft heart, and he'd bet one of his prized Damascus daggers that if an abused lass had appeared on the doorstep, she was the one dining on golden kippers and tatties and soft poached eggs. Mayhap even Clootie dumplings, oatcakes, and orange marmalade. On more than one occasion women from other clans had sought refuge at the castle, seeking employment or the chance to start life anew with people who didn't know them. Nell herself had found such refuge there.

"What does the lass say happened to her?" Drustan asked.

"She was in no condition to answer questions when she appeared, and Nell says she hasn't yet awakened."

Drustan eyed his father a moment, his eyes narrowing. "Are you insinuating that *I'm* responsible for her presence?" When Silvan made no move to deny it, Drustan snorted. "Och, Da, she may have found one of my old plaids anywhere. It was like as not threadbare and had been tossed in the stables to be cut up into birthing rags for the sheep."

Silvan sighed. "I helped carry her to her chamber, son. She had the blood of her maidenhead on her thighs. And she was naked, and she had *your* plaid wrapped around her. A crisp new one, not an old one. Can you see how I might be perplexed?"

"So *that's* why Nell served me week-old fare." Drustan pushed back his chair and rose, bristling with indignation. "Surely you doona believe I had aught to do with it, do you?"

Silvan rubbed his jaw wearily. "I'm merely trying to understand, son. She said your name before she swooned. And last week Besseta said—"

"Doona even think of telling me what some twig-reading fortune-teller—"

"That there is a darkness around you that worries her—"

"Such a fortuitous choice of words. A *darkness*. Which, conveniently, could be anything that comes to pass. A bad stomach from a pork pie, a wee cut in a sword fight. Doona you see how vague that is? You should be ashamed of yourself, a man of learning, the senior Keltar no less."

They glared at each other.

"Stubborn, ungrateful, and bad-tempered," Silvan snapped.

"Conniving, interfering, and bristly-haired," Drustan shot back.

"Disrespectful and impotent," Silvan thrust neatly.

"I am not! I am perfectly virile—"

"Well, you certainly couldn't prove that by your seed, which—*if* it's being scattered—isn't taking root."

"I take precautionary measures," Drustan thundered.

"Well, *stop*. You've a score and ten, and I've double that. Think you I'll be livin' forever? At this point, I'd welcome a bastard. And you can rest assured that should the lass turn out to be pregnant, I'll be calling the bairn MacKeltar."

They scowled at each other, then Silvan suddenly flushed, his gaze fixed on a distant point beyond Drustan's shoulder.

Drustan froze, as he *felt* a new presence in the room. The hair on the back of his neck stood on end.

He spun around slowly, and time seemed to stop when he saw her. His breath slammed to a halt in his chest, and he positively sizzled beneath the heat of her stare.

Christ, Drustan thought, staring into eyes that were stormy and lovely as the fierce Scottish sea, *she's wee, and vulnerable-looking, and utterly beautiful. No wonder she's got Da and Nell in such a fankle.*

She was a walking siren song, humming with mating heat. One hand was on the elegant marble banister of the stair, the other hand pressed to her abdomen, as if pondering the possibility that she might be pregnant.

Would that he had taken her maidenhead, but he hadn't—he'd not taken any woman's maidenhead—and furthermore he would never have left her wandering about outside afterward.

Nay, he thought, staring at her, he would have kept this woman tucked securely in his bed, in his arms, warm and slippery from his loving. And loving. And more loving. She did some witchy thing to his blood.

Silver-blond hair fell in a straight sheen past her shoulders and halfway down her back. She had strange, fringed lenths of hair over her forehead that she puffed from her eyes with a soft exhalation of breath, which made her lower lip look even poutier. Small of stature, but with curves that could make a grown man weak at the knees— and indeed his had turned to water—she was wearing a gown of his favorite color that did lovely things to her breasts. It was sheer enough to reveal her nipples, cut low enough to frame her curves in timeless temptation. Her cheekbones were high, her nose straight, her eyebrows winged upward at the outer edges, and her eyes . . .

Christ, the way she was staring at him was enough to make his skin steam.

She was staring as if she knew him intimately. He doubted he'd ever seen such an intense and unashamed look of desire in a woman's eyes.

And, of course, his ever-astute father didn't miss it.

"Now, tell me again you doona know her, lad," Silvan said wryly. "For of a certain she seems to know you."

Drustan shook his head, bewildered. He felt a fool, standing and staring, but try as he might he could not drag his gaze away from hers. Her eyes turned gently imploring, as if she was hoping for something from him or trying to communicate a silent message. Where had such a wee beauty come from? And why was she having such a profound effect upon him? Granted, she was lovely, but he'd known many lovely women. His betrotheds had been some of the most beautiful women in the Highlands.

Yet none had ever made him feel quite so virile and hungry and intensely possessive.

Such stirrings did not bode well for his plans of impending marital bliss.

After an interminable silence, he spread his hands, confused. "I vow, I've never seen her before in my life, Da."

Silvan crossed his arms over his chest and scowled at Drustan. "Then why is she staring at you like that? And if you didn't bed her last night, how do you explain the condition she arrived in?"

"Oh, my," the lass sputtered then. "You think he—*oh*. I hadn't considered that." She heaved a huge sigh and pinched her lower lip, staring at them.

About time she spoke up to clear his name, he thought, waiting.

"Well?" Silvan encouraged. "Did he tup you last eve?"

She hesitated a moment, glancing between the two men, then gave an uncertain wobble of the head, which Drustan promptly interpreted as a "no."

"See? I told you so, Da," Drustan said, relieved that she'd finally looked away from him. Righteous indignation flooded him. "I doona have to seduce maidens, not with so many experienced lasses vying for the pleasure of my bed." Women might not want to wed him, but that certainly didn't prevent them from crawling into his bed at every opportunity. Ofttimes he suspected the very rumors about him that drove them from the altar were the same lure that enticed them to seek his bed. Fickle like that, lasses were. Attracted to danger for a night or two, but of no mind to live with it.

When the tiny lass glared at him, he flashed her a puzzled look. Why would she be offended by his prowess with the wenches?

"Forgive my indelicate question, lass," Silvan said, "but who removed your . . . er, maidenhead? Was it one of our people?"

Typical that his father couldn't let it go. It hadn't been *him*, and that was all Drustan needed to hear. Under normal circumstances he would have scoured the estate for the erstwhile suitor who'd deflowered and callously abandoned her, and seen to it she was granted whatever recompense she wished, were it one of their own, but his da had thought *he* had taken her maidenhead, and that offended him.

Dismissing her from his thoughts—in large part to prove to himself that he *could*—he turned away to find Nell, clear this matter up with her, and procure an edible breakfast, but froze in his tracks when she spoke again.

"*He* did," she said, sounding both petulant and irritated.

Drustan pivoted slowly. She looked nearly as shocked by her own words as was he.

She wilted beneath the stress of his regard, then mumbled, "But I wanted him to."

Drustan was incensed. How dare she accuse him falsely? What if his betrothed heard tell of it? If Anya's father heard of this wee woman claiming he'd callously deflowered her, then renounced her, he might call off the nuptials!

Whoever she was—she was *not* going to wreak havoc on his unborn children.

Growling, he crossed the space between them in three swift strides, scooped her up with one arm, and tossed her over his shoulder, a controlling hand splayed on her rump.

A controlling hand that didn't fail to appreciate that rump, which made him angrier still.

Ignoring his father's protests, he stalked to the door, jerked it open, and tossed the lying wench out, headfirst, into a prickly bush.

Feeling simultaneously vindicated and like the sorriest rogue in all of Alba, he slammed the door shut, slid the bolt, backed himself against it, and folded his arms over his chest, as if he'd barred the door against something far more dangerous than a simple lying lass. As if Chaos herself was currently wedged in his hedges, clad in irresistible lavender and mating heat.

"And that's the end of *that*," he told Silvan firmly. But it didn't come out sounding quite as firm as he'd intended. In truth, his voice rose slightly at the end, and his assertion bore a questioning inflection. He scowled to more properly punctuate it, while Silvan gaped at him, speechless.

Had he ever seen his father speechless before? he wondered uneasily.

Somehow, he had a feeling that dumping the lying lass out into the prickly bush hadn't put an end to anything.

Indeed, he suspected that whatever was going on, it had only begun. Were he a more superstitious man, he might have fancied he heard the creaking wheels of destiny as they turned.

· 14 ·

Gwen sputtered indignantly as she backed out of the bush, plucking prickly leaves from her hair. There she was, less than twelve hours later, on her hands and knees on the confounded doorstep *again*.

Incensed, she threw her head back and yelled, "Let me in!"

The door remained firmly shut.

She sat back on her heels and pounded a fist on the door. The argument that had erupted inside the castle was so loud that she knew they'd never hear her over such a racket.

She took a deep breath and reflected upon what she'd just done, thinking that a cigarette would go a long way toward clearing her mind, and a cup of strong coffee might just restore her sanity.

Okay, she admitted, *that was abjectly stupid.* She'd said singularly the worst thing she could have said, guaranteed to piss him off.

But she'd been through a lot in the past twenty-four hours, and logic hadn't exactly been the ruling planet in her little universe when Drustan turned his back on her. Emotion, that great big unexplored planet, had been exerting an irresistible pull on her wits. She didn't have enough practice with emotions to handle them with finesse, and by God, the man made her feel so many that it was simply bewildering.

When she'd first seen him, she stood at the top of the stairs for several moments, gazing at him with her heart in her eyes, scarcely hearing the conversation going on below.

He was devastating in any century. Even when she'd thought him mentally unhinged, she'd found him dangerously appealing. In his natural element, he was twenty times as irresistible. Now that she knew he was a genuine sixteenth-century lord, she wondered how she could have ever believed otherwise. He dripped regal authority as blatantly as he wore his sexuality. He was a man who thoroughly enjoyed being a man.

Ecstatic that he was alive and well and that she'd arrived in time to save him, she'd rushed down the stairs. Then Drustan's father, Silvan, the man she'd mistaken for Einstein, had mentioned something about her being pregnant, flummoxing her. Confronted with a possible pregnancy before even latching her lips to the rim of a cup of Starbucks, she'd stood, stupefied.

It's not enough just to buy condoms, Cassidy; you have to use them.

And then Drustan had tossed his silky mane over his shoulder and looked right at her, and although his eyes had flared as if he'd found her attractive, there had been no spark of recognition.

She'd expected it.

She'd *known* he wouldn't know her. Still, her heart had not understood how awful it was going to feel when he turned that silvery, sexy gaze on her, as distant and cold as a stranger.

Rational or not, it had hurt, and then he'd made that wise-ass comment about women vying for the pleasure of his bed.

Then, as if he hadn't poked every one of her raw nerves already, he'd turned his back on her, dismissing her.

It was at that point that she'd reacted blindly. She'd blurted out the *one* thing she knew would make him turn back around and look at her again. She'd sacrificed long-term goals for instant gratification.

She was appalled by what she'd done. It was no wonder her mother had so stridently counseled against being emotional. Emotion apparently made fools of even geniuses.

She needed him to listen to her, and he wasn't going to be in any mood to hear her now. By telling him they'd been lovers *before* telling him the whole story, she'd irritated and provoked him.

"Let me in." She pounded on the door. "I need to tell you the whole story." But they were still arguing so loudly that she might as well have been whispering.

Brushing leaves from her gown, she rose to her feet. She scowled at the door. Since no one would answer and the argument showed no signs of abating, she tipped her head back, eager to see the castle in daylight, but she was too close to it. She felt like a flea trying to get a good look at an elephant while perched upon its forehead. Curious, she decided she may as well take a short walk.

Tucking her bangs behind her ear, she turned around. And froze.

Her heart slammed into her throat. *Impossible*, her mind wailed.

But there he was, plain as day. Sinfully, heart-stoppingly sexy Drustan.

Sauntering up the steps toward her, clad in leather trews and a linen shirt, casually unlaced, revealing a mouth-watering amount of hard, bronzed chest. Although the brilliant morning sun was behind him, shadowing his features, his smile was dazzling.

Yet, behind her in the castle, Drustan was yelling. She could *hear* him.

According to her understanding of physics, both of them couldn't exist at the same time. But obviously they did. What would happen if they met? Would one of them just blip out of existence?

If Drustan-behind-the-door was the one that didn't know her, she reasoned, then Drustan-on-the-steps who looked so happy to see her must be *her* Drustan.

What was she going to do with two Drustans?

A kinky part of her proposed something unmentionable . . . and rather fascinating. Really, if they were both *him,* it wouldn't be like she was cheating on anyone.

Blushing, she ogled him from head to toe. *Her* Drustan didn't scowl at her. He arched a brow in that oh-so-familiar way of his and grinned, opening his arms wide.

She didn't hesitate.

With a shriek of delight, she launched herself at him. He caught her midleap and pulled her legs around his waist, just like in her century.

He laughed when she covered his face with little kisses. She had no idea what she would do with two of them, or how it could be possible, she knew only that she'd missed him more in the past twelve hours than she'd ever missed anyone in her entire life. "Kiss me," she said.

"Och, English, I'll be kissing you most thoroughly," he purred against her lips. Clamping her head between his hands, he slanted his mouth hungrily over hers.

Gwen melted against him, parting her lips. There was no doubt about it; the man was an expert kisser. His kiss was demanding, aggressive, silky, hot, and hungry . . . and any minute now she'd feel the sizzle.

Any minute now, she thought, kissing him back with all of her heart.

He tasted of cinnamon and wine, and he kissed her with single-minded intensity, and still . . . no sizzle.

"*Mmph,*" she said against his mouth, meaning, *Wait a minute, something's not right.* But if he heard her, he paid no mind and deepened the kiss.

Gwen's head spun. Something was seriously wrong. Something about Drustan was different, and his kiss wasn't affecting her as it usually did. Distantly, she heard the door open behind them and tried to draw back, but he wouldn't let her.

Then she heard a roar and was dragged off Drustan by the other Drustan, with one steely arm about her waist, another around her neck.

She glanced rapidly between them, blinking and hoping her double vision would go away. They were glaring at each other. Would they fight? If she saw her own double she'd probably be tempted to punch it once or twice. Especially today. For being so stupid.

"What's wrong with you?" Passion and irritation glittered in leather-trew-clad Drustan's eyes.

"What's wrong with *me?* " kilt-clad Drustan snapped. "What's wrong with me is that this wench here, who was kissing you so ravenously, accused *me* of taking her virginity!" Kilt-clad Drustan dumped her on her feet between them. "I'm trying to save you, before she tangles you in her deceitful web."

"I *liked* her deceitful web. It was hot and slippery, and all a lass should be," Drustan-of-the-leather-trews growled.

Kilt-clad Drustan launched into a diatribe with a burr

so thick she could scarcely understand a word he was saying, and Drustan of the trews began yelling back, and then Silvan poked his nose out of the castle to observe the fracas.

She'd lost her mind, she thought, watching with wide eyes. They stood nose to nose, arguing, while she plucked nervously at her gown, backed up a few steps, and listened, hoping to catch a word or two she might understand.

Observe. There is a logical explanation for this, the scientist insisted.

"Drustan. Dageus," Silvan said reprovingly. "Stop your arguing this moment."

Dageus! A ray of enlightenment pierced her confusion.

Her nostrils flared and her eyes narrowed. It was one more thing Drustan hadn't bothered to tell her—that he and his brother were identical twins. It seemed there were oodles of things he'd overlooked. He'd nearly given her a heart attack over this one. He certainly hadn't made saving him easy.

She kicked the real Drustan in the shin. "You didn't tell me you and your brother were twins."

He continued arguing with Dageus as if she'd barely touched him, and no wonder with such flimsy little slippers. What she wouldn't give for her hiking boots.

And now I have two problems, she thought. Dageus was still alive, which meant she had to prevent his death too. She was elated to have the opportunity to save Dageus, but she was beginning to feel a little overwhelmed. Discovering the date was a serious priority, and she had to get her hands on Dageus's itinerary. There was no way he could go anywhere near the Elliott's estate.

Now that they were standing side by side, she could discern differences and would not mistake the two of them again. They weren't quite identical, probably half-identical; polar body twins, giving them about seventy-five percent of the same DNA. Had the sun not been so bright behind him as he'd walked up, she might not have erred in the first place. Dageus was indeed an inch or two shorter, which still made him at least six foot four. His hair—which she hadn't been able to see when he'd been walking toward her—pulled back in a thong as it was— was much longer, falling to his waist, and so black it was nearly blue. And their eyes were different, she thought, sidling closer between them, ducking wildly gesturing arms, to get a good look. *Oh, and how,* she thought, for as silvery as Drustan's were, Dageus's were yellow-gold.

Wow. All in all, two of the most gloriously handsome men she'd ever seen.

Drustan stopped cursing and glowered at her. "Who *are* you?" he demanded, finally rubbing his shin.

"I've been trying to tell you, but the moment you hear something you don't like, do you ask questions to try to clear it up?" she demanded, hands on her hips and glaring back at him. "No. Not even one. You behave like a barbarian." Not that she'd done much better, but wiser to go on the offensive than justify her own failings. "I thought you were smarter than that."

Drustan opened his mouth and closed it again. *Ha,* she thought smugly, the offensive had worked.

Dageus's brows rose and he laughed. "I must say, for being such a wee—"

"I am *not* a *nyaff,*" she said defensively.

"—lass, she certainly has fire."

"And it's a fire you can keep your hands off," Drustan snapped. He looked bewildered by his own words and added hastily, "I doona want you to get snared in her trap. 'Tis apparent she's looking for someone to marry her."

"I am not looking for someone to marry me," Gwen said firmly. "I'm looking for someone with a modicum of intellect."

"*Ahem*. That would be me, m'dear," Silvan said mildly, raising an ink-spotted hand.

Drustan scowled at his father.

"Well, that *would* be," Silvan said, crossing his arms over his bony frame and leaning back against the door-jamb. "You doona see *me* standing out there shouting my head off when a few simple questions might clear things up nicely."

"I'd say that qualifies," Gwen said, tucking her arm through Silvan's. She wasn't going to get anything accomplished trying to talk to Drustan right now. Let him cool off outside for a while. She swept into the castle, towing Silvan along, and kicked the door shut with her heel.

"I can't tell you," Gwen told Silvan for the third time, already regretting having come inside with him. The moment they'd entered the castle, the inquisition had begun, and until she talked to Drustan, she dare not tell Silvan a thing. She'd already made one mistake this morning. She was not going to make another. She would tell Drustan and only Drustan. He could tell whomever he trusted.

"Well, what can you tell me? Anything?"

Gwen sighed. She'd taken an instant liking to Silvan MacKeltar—another of those baffling gut instincts—the moment she'd seen him standing in the hall interrogating his son, with so much love in his eyes. She'd felt a twinge of envy, wondering what it must feel like to be the focus of such parental concern. Not only did he resemble Einstein, with his white hair, olive-toned skin, curious brown eyes feathered by wrinkles, and deep grooves bracketing his mouth, but he demonstrated a similar acuity of mind.

Perched on the hearth in the Greathall, she glanced at the door, hoping Drustan would saunter in. Angry or not, she needed desperately to talk with him. "I told you my name," she hedged.

"Rubbish. That tells me naught but that you're English with Irish ancestors, and a damned odd accent. How do you know Drustan?"

She regarded him glumly.

"How am I supposed to help you, m'dear, if you refuse to tell me a thing? If my son took your maidenhead, 'tis wedding you he'll be. But I can't force him if you doona tell me who you are and a bit about what happened."

"Mr. MacKeltar—"

"Silvan," he interrupted.

"Silvan," Gwen amended, "I don't want you to force Drustan to marry me."

"Then what do you want?" he exclaimed.

"More than anything right now?"

"Aye."

"I'd like to know what the date is." She hated asking it so baldly, but she needed to know. She drew some comfort from the fact that Dageus was still alive—it meant she'd arrived in time. But she wouldn't feel entirely safe until she knew precisely, to the minute, how long she had.

Silvan went very still, his dark eyes narrowed, head cocked at an angle. She suddenly had the eerie feeling he was listening with more than his ears, and watching with more than his eyes.

And she knew she was right when he murmured softly, "Och, m'dear, you're from a far far place, aren't you, now? Nay, no need to reply. I doona understand what I sense, but I know you're a stranger to this land."

"What are you doing, reading my mind? Can you *do* that?" She might believe anything of a man who'd fathered a son who could manipulate time.

"Nay. 'Tis but a bit of deep listening in the old way, something neither of my sons are adept at, although I've tried to teach them. So 'tis the date you're needing," he said slowly. "I'll trade you answers, what say you, Gwen Cassidy?"

"I'm not going to get them any other way, am I?"

He shook his head, a faint smile playing at his lips.

"I'll answer your questions as honestly as I can," she conceded, "but there are bound to be some that I can't answer just yet."

"Fair enough. As long as you doona lie to me, m'dear, we'll get on fine. If you can't tell me what transpired last eve, then tell me *why* you can't."

That was reasonably safe. "Because I must talk to Drustan first. If, once I talk with Drustan, he chooses to, he can tell you everything."

Silvan held her gaze, weighing her words for truth.

" 'Tis the nineteenth day of July," he said finally.

About a month, Gwen thought, relieved. When Drustan had discovered that he was in the future, he said, *Christ, I haven't lost a mere moon. I've lost centuries.* Translation: Initially he thought he had been in the cave for a month or so, which meant he'd been abducted somewhere in mid-August. He'd also said that Dageus had died "recently." She'd had no idea how recent his grief had been and had assumed he'd meant several months or even a year ago. But apparently Dageus would die at some point in the next few weeks. She needed to know exactly when Dageus planned to leave for the Elliott's; she had to prevent him from going at all.

"Fifteen eighteen?" She hated wasting a question, but had to be sure. Considering that Drustan had gotten the month and day wrong, she supposed it was possible he'd messed up on the year too.

Silvan's eyes evinced utter fascination. He leaned forward, elbows on his knees and peered at her. "Where are you from?" he breathed.

She sighed and averted her gaze, half-afraid the canny man could read the answers in her eyes. She blinked, momentarily distracted by her first real look at the Greathall. When she'd come downstairs, she'd scarce seen past Drustan. The hall was elegant and lovely as her chamber had been, the floor fashioned of spotlessly scrubbed pale gray stones, the walls lined with brilliant tapestries. Two hounds snored softly beneath a large masterpiece of a table. Heavy velvet drapes were pulled back from tall paned windows, and the rosy marble double staircase gleamed in the morning light. A panel of stained glass was inset above the massive door, and silver shields and weapons adorned the walls on either side. "It's a country you've never heard of," she demurred, not about to say the good old U.S. of A. That would start a whole other conversation that could go on indefinitely.

"Tell me, or you'll get no answers from me. Really, where you're from can hardly be too revealing, can it, now?"

She blew out a frustrated breath. "America. Far across the ocean."

Again, he assessed her with his steady stare. "Fifteen eighteen," he agreed. "And I know of the Americas. We doona call it that, but we Scots discovered it centuries ago."

"You did not," she scoffed. "Christopher Columbus—"

"Merely followed the Sinclair's path, after he got his hands on the old maps left to the Templars."

"*Oooh.* You Scots have got to be the most arrogant—"

"What a conundrum you are proving—"

"Do you always talk over people?"

He snorted with laughter. "You do it rather well yourself," he said, smiling and patting her hand. "I think I'm going to like you quite a lot, lass. So, when do you plan to tell Drustan, so I may hear the whole story?"

"The minute he walks in. And thanks for giving me an easy question."

"That's not fair, that wasn't a—"

"Uh-uh. No way you're reneging now. That was too a question."

"Aye, but not really and you know it," Silvan grumbled. He averted his nose in a snit, a flicker of admiration in his eyes. "You're a clever lass, aren't you, now? Next?" he said dryly.

"Is Dageus planning to take any trips soon?"

"What a very odd question," Silvan remarked, stroking his chin. "I must say you've got my curiosity in quite a lather. Aye, he is to go to the Elliott's soon. Did Drustan take your virginity?"

She blew out a breath slowly. "It's a very complicated story," she evaded, "and I must speak to Drustan as soon as possible. Your son is in danger. I believe he trusts you completely; however, he must decide what to tell you. I can't say any more than that until he and I talk. Please respect that," she added softly.

He arched a brow, but nodded.

When he took her hand between his and patted it, she felt funny inside. She couldn't recall her own father ever doing such a thing. He held her hand for a few moments, his eyes narrowed, his expression pensive. She had the distinct, unsettling sensation that he was peering right into her soul. Was that possible? she wondered.

"All right, m'dear," Silvan said. "You win. No more questions until you speak with Drustan. But if I know my son, he'll not cooperate."

"He must, Silvan," Gwen said desperately. "We don't have all that much time."

"Is he truly in danger?"

Gwen closed her eyes and sighed. "You all are."

"Then we will make him listen to you."

Gwen opened her eyes and scowled. "And how do you plan to make him do that? Lock him in a room with me?"

Silvan smiled faintly, deepening the lines about his mouth. Elderly though he was, he was a handsome man with no small amount of charisma. She wondered why he'd never married again. Surely not for lack of women being interested.

"Not a bad idea, m'dear. Will you do as I say?"

After a moment's hesitation, she nodded.

And he bent his head close to hers and began whispering.

· 15 ·

Hours later, an anxious Gwen paced before the fire in the Silver Chamber. The day had dragged endlessly on with no sign of Drustan. If he'd only return, she'd clear things up and they could set about figuring out who the enemy was.

After a scrumptious breakfast of poached eggs, potatoes, and dried, salted fish in the hall with Silvan, Nell had given her a brief tour, pointing out garderobes and the like. She'd spent a few hours in the library, then had retired to her chamber to await Drustan.

Dageus had ridden in a few hours ago, without him. He said they'd parted ways at the tavern. Silvan had drawn his younger son—younger by a mere three minutes—into their plan, and Dageus, grinning and casting Gwen steamy glances—did he *have* to drip as much raw sex appeal as Drustan?—now held the door to the corridor ajar a crack, watching for Drustan's approach. He'd been spotted riding into the stable a quarter hour past.

"I can't believe you placed her in the chamber that adjoins Drustan's," Dageus said over his shoulder.

Silvan shrugged defensively. "She said his name last night, and besides, 'tis the third nicest in the castle. Yours and Drustan's are the only two more lavishly furnished."

"I'm not certain she should be sleeping so close to him."

"Where should I move her? Nearer to your chamber?" Silvan countered. "Drustan denies knowing her. You kissed her. Who poses more of a threat to her?"

Gwen flushed, grateful that Dageus didn't point out that she'd *demanded* he kiss her. He glanced at her sidewise and flashed her a seductive look. God, he was gorgeous, she thought, watching his glossy waist-length hair slide silkily as he angled his head to argue over his shoulder with Silvan. How could two such devastating men exist in one castle? Not that she was attracted to him, but she'd have to be dead not to appreciate his raw male virility.

"Why are you helping me?" she asked Silvan, nudging the conversation in a less disconcerting direction.

He smiled faintly. "Doona fash yourself over my motives, m'dear."

"You would be wise to fash yourself over his motives, lass," Dageus cautioned dryly. "When Da bothers to involve himself, he always has ulterior motives. Schemes within schemes. And inevitably, he knows more than he lets on."

"Do you?" She peered at the charming, grandfatherly man.

"Innocent as a little lamb ambling the hillside, m'dear," Silvan said mildly.

Dageus shook his head at her. "Doona believe a word

of it. But nor should you waste your breath trying to get more out of him. He's quiet as the grave with his little secrets."

"I'm not the only one who keeps secrets around here, lad," Silvan said with a sharp glance. Father and son battled with their gazes a few moments, then Dageus dropped his eyes and looked back out into the corridor.

An awkward silence reigned, and Gwen wondered what she was missing, what secrets a man like Dageus kept. Feeling like the perpetual outsider-looking-in, she changed the subject again. "Are you sure he won't listen? Are you certain we need to go to such extremes?" A pile of wood planks and bolts lay near the adjoining door, and the longer Gwen looked at it, the more nervous she became.

"M'dear, you accused him of taking your maidenhead. Nay, he'll not speak to you if he can avoid it."

Dageus nodded agreement. "He's coming," he warned them.

"Into the boudoir with you, m'dear," Silvan urged. "When you hear him enter his chamber, count to ten, then join him. I'll block this door and Dageus will take the other. We won't permit him to leave until you've had your say."

Squaring her shoulders, Gwen drew a deep breath and plunged into the boudoir. She listened intently for the sound of Drustan's door opening and realized to her chagrin that she was trembling.

She flinched when she heard the door open, and counted to ten slowly, giving Dageus time to sneak out of her chamber and blockade the door from the corridor.

Silvan had chuckled when he'd told her that if Drustan refused to listen, he and Dageus would do their best to bar him in from the outside by hammering a plank or two over the doors. God, she hoped it didn't come to that!

Time was up. She turned the handle and quietly opened the door.

His back was to her, and he was facing the fire, staring into it. He'd changed into snug leather pants, a billowy linen shirt, and boots. His silky black hair spilled unbound over his shoulders and down his back. He looked as if he'd stepped straight off the cover of one of those romance novels she ordered from Amazon.com so she didn't have to be embarrassed by some supercilious male clerk in the bookstore.

Ha, she thought. When she returned to her time, she was going to start buying them flagrantly, with no apologies. She'd never seen a man blush while buying *Playboy*.

But she had to survive the wrath of Drustan Mac-Keltar first.

Murmuring a silent prayer, she closed the door behind her.

He spun around the moment it clicked shut, and when he saw her, his silver eyes glittered dangerously.

Shaking a finger, he stalked toward her, and she skittered away from the door in case he planned to toss her out it again. He followed like a magnet to steel.

"Doona even think, English, that I'll be tolerating more of your lies," he said with silky menace. "And best you get out of my chamber, because I've had enough whisky that I'm of a mind to taste the crime of which I've been accused." His gaze drifted meaningfully to the massive bed, draped in silk and covered with velvet pillows.

Gwen's eyes widened. Indeed, his expression was a combination of fury and raw lust. The raw lust was perfectly wonderful; the anger she'd cheerfully do without.

She was going to be cool and rational this time. No stupid comments, no emotional outbursts. She would tell him what had happened, and he would see reason.

She hastened to reassure him. "I'm not trying to get you to marry me—"

"Good, because I won't," he growled, closing the distance between them, using his body to intimidate her.

She planted her feet and held her ground. Given that her nose came only to his solar plexus, it wasn't as easy as she made it look.

"What's this?" he purred softly. "You doona fear me? You should fear me, English." He closed his hands around her upper arms like bands of steel.

Silvan and Dageus must be pressing their ears to the doors, waiting for his explosion, she thought, but they'd misjudged him. This was not a man who exploded—he seethed quietly and infinitely more dangerously.

"Answer me," he demanded, shaking her. "Are you such a fool that you have no fear of me?"

She'd rehearsed her speech a dozen times, yet when he stood so close to her, it was difficult to remember where she'd decided to begin. Her lips parted as she stared up at him. "Please—"

"Please what?" he said silkily, lowering his head to hers. "Please kiss you? Please take you the way you accuse me of already having had you? I've had a long time to think today, English, and I must confess that I find myself fascinated by you. I rode for hours before stopping in the tavern. I drank for hours, yet fear all the whisky in fair Alba wouldn't cleanse you from my mind. Have you spelled me, witch?"

"No, I have not spelled you, I am not a witch, and please *don't* kiss me," she managed. God, she wanted him! Whether he knew her or not, it was *her* Drustan, damn it all, just a month and five centuries younger.

"Och, that's a rare request from a woman," he mocked. "Especially one who says she's already tasted my loving. Do you now disparage my intimate attentions?" His gaze was silver ice, challenging. "Was I less than satisfying? You claim we're lovers; mayhap we should be again. It would seem I've left a less than favorable impression." He closed his hand about her wrist and tugged her toward the bed. "Come."

She dug her heels in, a feat in soft slippers on a planked wood floor.

Her protests whooshed from her lungs when he scooped her into his arms and tossed her onto the bed. She landed on her back, sank deep into velvet-covered feather mattresses, and, before she could scramble away, he was on top of her, his body stretched the length of hers, pinning her with his weight.

She closed her eyes to shut out the sight of his beautiful, angry face. She would *never* be able to carry on a meaningful conversation with him in this position.

"Drustan, please listen to me. I'm not trying to trap you into marriage, and there's a reason why I said what I said this morning, if you'll just listen," she said, eyes squeezed tightly shut.

"There's a reason why you lied? There's *never* a reason to lie, lass," he growled.

"Does that mean *you* never lie?" she said snidely, opening her eyes a slit and peeping at him. She was still miffed that he hadn't told her the entire truth before sending her back.

"Nay, I doona lie."

"Bullshit. Sometimes, not telling all of the truth is exactly the same thing as lying," she snapped.

"Such language from a lady. But you're no lady, are you?"

"Well, you're certainly no gentleman. This lady didn't *ask* you to throw her in your bed."

"But you like being beneath me, lass," he said huskily. "Your body tells me much your words deny."

Gwen stiffened, horrified to realize she had hooked her ankles over his legs and was rubbing a slipper against one muscular calf. She pushed at his chest. "Get off me. I can't talk to you when you're squishing me."

"Forget about talking," he said roughly, lowering his head to hers.

Gwen shrank back deeper into the pillows, knowing the moment he kissed her she would be lost.

Just as his lips brushed hers, the boudoir door opened and Silvan stepped briskly in.

"*Ahem.*" Silvan cleared his throat.

Drustan's lips froze against hers. "Get out of my chamber, Da. I will handle this as I see fit," he growled.

"But you didn't tup her last eve, eh?" Silvan remarked mildly, his gaze sweeping over them. "Things look cozy to me, for being strangers and all. Aren't you forgetting something? Or should I say *someone*? The lass told me you were in danger; the only danger I perceive is that of you botching yet another perfectly good—"

"*Haud yer wheesht!*" Drustan roared. Stiffening, he pushed himself off her and sat back on his heels on the bed. "Da, you are no longer chieftain here, remember? I am. You quit. Get out." He flung an impatient hand toward the door. "Now."

"I merely came to see if Gwen required assistance," Silvan said calmly.

"She requires no assistance. She wove this web with her lies. Doona be blaming me for knotting her up in it."

"M'dear?" Silvan asked, eyeing her.

"It's all right, Silvan. You can go," she said softly. "Dageus too."

Silvan regarded her a moment more, then inclined his head and backed out of the room. When the door closed again, Drustan got off the bed and stood several paces away from her.

"What did Silvan mean by 'someone'?" she asked. "Botching a perfectly good what?"

He eyed her in stony silence.

She scrambled up and eyed him warily and, although she could see desire glittering in his gaze, she could also see that he'd thought better of trying to have sex with her for the moment. She was both relieved and disappointed.

"Talk. Why have you come here, and what is your purpose?" he asked stiffly.

When she was seated before the fire, Drustan poured a glass of whisky and leaned back against the hearth, facing her. He took a generous swallow, studying her discreetly over the rim of his glass. He had a difficult time thinking clearly in her presence, partly because she was so damn beautiful and partly because she'd put him on the defensive with her outrageous claim the moment he'd laid eyes on her. The intensity of his attraction to her upset him more greatly even than her lie. She was the last thing he needed, right before his wedding. Walking—nay, lushly sauntering—temptation to make a fankle of things.

Initially, he'd meant merely to intimidate her by pushing her back on the bed, but then he'd touched her and she'd looped her ankles over his calves, and he'd gotten lost in the welcoming softness of her body beneath him. Had his father not interrupted, he'd like as not still be atop her. The moment he'd walked into the castle tonight, he'd *felt* the wee English within his walls. He responded fiercely to her; all it took was one glance at her to stir feelings in him he couldn't explain.

He'd told the truth when he said he couldn't get her out of his mind. Not for one moment. He knew the scent of her, had been able to recall it even while sitting amidst the smelly ale-soaked rushes in the tavern. Hers was a clean, cool, and sensual fragrance, a blend of spring rain, vanilla, and mysteries. As he'd sat in the tavern, he realized that somehow he knew she had a dimple on one side of her luscious mouth when she smiled, although he couldn't recall having seen her smile.

"Smile," he demanded.

"What?" She looked at him as if he'd lost his mind.

"I said smile," he growled.

She smiled weakly. Aye. Plain as day. A dimple on the left side. He sighed heavily.

His gaze drifted over her features, lingering on the witch-mark on her cheekbone, and he wondered how many others she had, in more intimate places. He'd like to search, connect the patches with his tongue, he thought, his gaze lingering on the creamy expanse of cleavage above the scooped bodice of her gown.

He shook his head impatiently. "Out with it. What's so important, English, that you lied to gain my attention this morn?"

"Gwen," she corrected absently. She was pinching her plump lower lip between her thumb and forefinger, and the gesture was making him damn uncomfortable.

Goddess of the moon, he translated silently, and she looked every inch a goddess.

"You already know my name, and since you claimed such familiarity with me, I won't stand on ceremony and insist you call me 'milord.' "

Her immediate scowl made his lips twitch, but he kept his face impassive. She did not respond to his comment. Her self-control chafed him; he'd far prefer her off-balance, reacting blindly. Then *he'd* feel more in control.

She eyed him warily. "I don't know where to begin, so I ask that you hear me out completely before you start getting angry again. I know once you hear my whole story, you'll understand."

"You're going to tell me something else to upset me? What else have you left? You've already accused me of taking your maidenhead, yet you claim you doona seek to trap me into marriage. What *do* you seek?"

"Do you promise to hear me out? No interruptions until the end?"

After a moment's consideration, he conceded. Silvan had said she claimed he was in some kind of danger. What harm was there in listening? If he left the room without letting her have her say, he'd have to be on constant guard lest Silvan lock him in the garderobe so she might shout at him through the door. And until he'd cleared things up, he was quite certain he wasn't going to see a single batch of kippers and tatties from Nell. There'd been none of his thick, black exotic coffee all day either. Nay, he had to set things to rights. He enjoyed his comforts and didn't intend to suffer one more day without them. Besides, the sooner he cleared things up, the sooner he could pack her off and get her out of his sight.

Shrugging, he gave his pledge.

She nibbled her lip, hesitating a moment. "You're in danger, Drustan—"

"Aye, I am well aware of that, though I suspect we're not referring to the same thing," he muttered darkly.

"This is serious. Your life is in danger."

He grinned faintly, gaze skimming her from head to her toes. "Och, wee one, and next you'll tell me you plan to save me, eh? Mayhap fight off my attackers yourself? Bite them in the knee?"

"*Oooh.* That wasn't nice. And if you're too stupid to listen to me, I'll have to," she snapped.

"Consider me warned, lass," he placated her. "I've listened, now go on with you," he said abruptly, dismissing her. "Tell Silvan I heard you out, so he'll call off his little siege. I have things to do."

At the earliest opportunity he would have Nell secure her a position in the village, far from the castle. Nay, mayhap he'd have Dageus cart her off to Edinburgh and find her work there. One way or another, he had to get the bewitching lass out of his demesne before he did something foolish and irrevocable.

Like toss her into bed and tup her until neither one of them could move. Until his muscles ached from loving her. Would she score his shoulders with her nails? he wondered. Arch her neck and make sweet mewling noises? He stiffened instantly at the thought.

He turned his back on her, hoping it might lessen whatever spell she'd cast upon him.

"Don't you even want to know what kind of danger?" she asked incredulously.

He sighed and glanced over his shoulder, one sardonic brow arched. What would it take, he wondered irritably, to make the wee lass cower? A sword at her throat?

"You said you'd hear the whole story. Was that a lie? You who claim you don't lie?"

"Fine," he said impatiently, turning back around. "Tell me all of it and have it done with."

"Maybe you should sit down," she said uneasily.

"Nay. I will stand and you will speak." He folded his arms across his chest.

"You're not making this easy."

"I doona intend to. Speak or leave. Doona waste my time."

She took a deep breath. "Okay, but I'm warning you, it's going to sound pretty far-fetched at first."

He exhaled impatiently.

"I'm from your future—"

He stifled a groan. The lass was a bampot, addled,

soft in the head. Wandering about naked outside, accusing men of tupping her, thinking she was from the future, indeed!

"—the twenty-first century, to be precise. I was hiking in the hills near Loch Ness when I fell into a cave and discovered you sleeping—"

He shook his head. "Cease this nonsense."

"You said you wouldn't interrupt." She jumped to her feet, much too close for his comfort. "It's hard enough for me to tell you this."

Drustan's eyes narrowed, and he backed up a step lest she touch him and he turn into a lustful beast again. She stood there, head tossed back. Her cheeks were flushed, her stormy eyes flashing, and she looked ready to pummel him, despite her diminutive size. She had courage, he'd give her that.

"Go on," he growled.

"I found you in the cave. You were sleeping, and funny symbols were painted on your chest. Somehow, my falling on you woke you. You were confused, you had no idea where you were, and you helped me get out of the cave. You told me the strangest story I'd ever heard. You claimed you were from the sixteenth century, that someone had abducted and enchanted you, and you slept for nearly five centuries. You said the last thing you recalled was that someone had sent you a message to go to some glen near a loch if you wished to know who'd killed your brother. You said you went, but someone had drugged you and you started getting very tired."

"Enchanted?" Drustan shook his head in amazement. The lass had an imagination that could compete with the finest bard. But she'd made her first mistake: He didn't *have* a dead brother. He had only Dageus, who was alive and hale.

She took a deep breath and continued, undaunted by his blatant skepticism. "I didn't believe you either,

Drustan, and for that I'm sorry. You told me that if I accompanied you to *Ban Drochaid*, you would prove to me that you were telling the truth. We went to the stones, and your castle"—she swept a hand around the room—"this castle was a ruin. You took me into the circle." She deliberately omitted the intense passion they shared therein, not wishing to alienate him further. With a wistful sigh, she continued. "And you sent me here, to your castle, in your century."

Drustan blew out an exasperated breath. Aye, she was truly a madwoman, and one who knew the old rumors well. He knew the villagers loved to repeat the old tale that their ancestors had seen two entire fleets of Templars enter the walls of Castle Keltar centuries ago, never to come out again. Apparently she'd heard that those "pagan Highlanders" could open doorways and had incorporated it into her madness.

"But before I sent you back, using the stones in some pagan fashion"—he scoffed, not about to admit to such a thing—"I took your maidenhead, eh?" he said dryly. "I must confess, you've chosen a most unique way to try to trap a man into a wedding. Choose one about whom strange rumors abound. Claim he took your virginity in the future, thus, he can never argue conclusively against it." He shook his head and smiled faintly. "I give you credit for your imagination and audacity, lass."

Gwen glared at him. "For the last time, I am *not* trying to marry you, you overbearing slack-jawed troglodyte."

"Slack-jawed—" He shook his head and blinked. "Good, because I can't. I'm betrothed," he said flatly. That would put an end to her crazed claims.

"*Betrothed?*" she echoed, stunned.

His eyes narrowed. "'Tis plain that doesn't please you. Careful lest you further betray yourself."

"But that doesn't make sense. You told me you weren't . . ." She trailed off, eyes wide.

Yet another hole in her story, he mused darkly. He'd been betrothed for over half a year. Near all of Alba knew of his upcoming nuptials and were, like as not, watching with bated breath to see if he actually succeeded this time. And he *would* succeed. "I am. The match was agreed upon last Yuletide. Anya Elliott is due to arrive within the fortnight for our wedding."

"Elliott?" she breathed.

"Aye, Dageus is going to fetch her and bring her here for the wedding."

Gwen turned her back to him, to conceal the shock and pain she knew must be etched all over her face. Betrothed? Her soul mate was going to marry someone else?

He'd told her Dageus had been killed coming back from the Elliott's. He'd told her that he'd been betrothed, but she'd died. But he hadn't bothered to tell her they'd both been killed at the same time!

Why? Had he loved his financée so much, then? Had it been too painful for him to speak of?

Her heart sank to her toes. *Not fair, not fair,* she wailed silently.

If she saved Dageus, she would be saving Drustan's future wife. The woman he wanted to marry.

Gwen drew a shaky breath, hating her choices. This wasn't how things were supposed to go. She was supposed to tell him her story, together they would unmask the villain, get married, and live happily ever after. She'd planned it all out this afternoon, even down to the details of her medieval wedding dress. She wouldn't mind staying in the sixteenth century for him; willingly she'd forfeit her Starbucks, tampons, and hot showers. So what if she couldn't shave her legs? He had sharp daggers, and eventually she'd quit nicking herself. Yes, it might be a bit rustic, but on the other hand, what did she have to go back to?

Nothing. Not a damn thing.

Empty, lonely life.

Tears pressed at the backs of her eyes. She dropped her head, hiding behind her fringed bangs, reminding herself that she hadn't cried since she was nine and crying wouldn't help now. "This is *so* not happening," she muttered dismally.

You can't let his clan be destroyed, no matter the price, her heart said softly.

After a time she turned around and looked at him, swallowing the lump in her throat, acknowledging that there was no way she could stand by and watch him be abducted and his family be destroyed. So what that it might rip her to pieces in the process?

So much for falling in love, she thought dismally.

"Drustan," she said, striving for the calmest tone of voice she could muster, when inside she was unraveling at every seam, "in the future, the last thing you said was for me to tell the past you the whole story and to show you something. The something I was supposed to show you was my backpack, because it had things in it from my century that would have convinced you—"

"Show me this pack," he demanded.

"I can't," she said helplessly. "It disappeared."

"Why does that not surprise me?"

She bit her lip to keep from screaming with frustration. "The future you seemed to think you would be smart enough to believe me, but I'm beginning to realize the future you gave you a whole lot more credit than you deserve."

"Cease and desist with your insults, lass. You provoke the very laird upon whom your shelter depends."

God, that was true, she realized. She *was* dependent

upon him for her shelter. Although she was a smart woman, she suffered more than a few concerns about how a misplaced physicist might fend for herself in medieval Scotland. What if he *never* believed her? "I know you don't believe me, but there is something you must do, whether you believe me or not," she said desperately. "You can't let Dageus go get your fiancée yet. Please, I'm begging you, postpone the wedding."

He arched one dark brow. "Och, have out with it, lass. Ask me to marry you. I'll say nay, then you can hie yourself back whence you came."

"I am not trying to get you to postpone it so you'll marry me. I'm telling you because they're going to *die* if you don't do something. In my time, you told me Dageus was killed in a clan battle between the Montgomery and the Campbell when returning from the Elliott's. You also told me that you'd been betrothed, but that she died. I think she must have been killed coming back here with Dageus. According to you, he tried to help the Montgomery because they were outnumbered. If he interferes with that battle, they will both die. And you'd believe me then, wouldn't you? If I foretold those deaths? Don't make it cost that much. I saw you grieve—" She broke off, unable to continue.

Too many mixed emotions were crashing over her: disbelief that he wouldn't believe her, pain that he was engaged, exhaustion from the stress of the entire ordeal.

She cast him a last pleading glance, then darted into her bedchamber before she turned into the emotional equivalent of Jell-O.

After she'd slipped inside and closed the door, Drustan gazed blankly at it. Her plea for his brother had sounded so sincere that he'd gotten chills and suffered an eerie sense of disagreeable familiarity.

Her story couldn't be true, he assured himself. Many

of the old tales hinted that the stones were used as gates to other places—legends never forgotten, passed down through the centuries. She'd like as not heard the gossip and, in her madness, made up a story that held a purely coincidental bit of truth. Had she faked the blood of her virginity? Mayhap she was pregnant and in desperate need of a husband. . . .

Aye, he could travel through the stones, that much of it was true. But everything else she claimed reeked of wrongness. If he'd ever gotten trapped in the future he would never have behaved in such ways. He would never have sent a wee lass back through the stones. He couldn't begin to imagine the situation in which he might take a lass's maidenhead—he'd vowed never to lie with a virgin unless 'twas in the marriage bed. And he would *never* have instructed her to tell his past self such a story and expected himself to believe it.

Och, thinking all this future self, past self was enough to give a man a pounding head, he thought, massaging his temples.

Nay, were he to get into such a situation, he would have simply come back himself and set things aright. Drustan MacKeltar was infinitely more capable than she'd made him out to be.

There was no point in getting unduly upset about her. His primary problem would be keeping his hands to himself, because addled or no, he desired her fiercely.

Still, he mused, mayhap he should send a full complement of guard with Dageus on the morrow. Mayhap the country wasn't as peaceful as it appeared from high atop the MacKeltar's mountain.

Shaking his head, he strode to the boudoir door and slid the bolt from his side, locking her in. Then he grabbed the key from a compartment in the headboard of his bed, left his chamber, and locked her in from the corridor as well. *Nothing* would jeopardize his wedding. Certainly not some wee lass scampering about unattended, spouting nonsense that he'd taken her virginity. She would go nowhere on the estate unaccompanied by either him or his father.

Dageus, on the other hand, he didn't plan to allow within a stone's toss of her.

He turned on his heel and stalked down the corridor.

Gwen curled up on the bed and cried. Sobbed, really, with hot tears and little choking noises that gave her a swollen nose and a serious sinus headache.

It was no wonder she hadn't cried since she was nine. It *hurt* to cry. She hadn't even cried when her father had threatened that if she didn't return to Triton Corp. and finish her research, he would never speak to her again. Maybe a few of those tears leaked out now as well.

Confronting Drustan had been more awful than she'd imagined. He was *betrothed*. And by saving Dageus, she was saving Drustan's future wife. Her overactive brain busily conjured torturous images of Drustan in bed with Anya Elliott. No matter that she didn't even know what Anya Elliott looked like. It was clear from the way things were going that Anya would be Gwen's antithesis—tall and slim and leggy. And Drustan would touch and kiss tall leggy Mrs. MacKeltar the way he'd touched and kissed Gwen in the stones.

Gwen squeezed her eyes shut and groaned, but the horrid images were more vivid on the insides of her eyelids. Her eyes snapped open again. *Focus*, she told herself. *There is nothing to be gained by torturing yourself, you have a bigger problem on your hands.*

He hadn't believed her. Not a word she'd said.

How could that be? She'd done what he'd wanted her to do, told him what had happened. She'd believed telling him the whole story would make him see the logic inherent, but she was beginning to realize that six-teenth-century Drustan was not the same man that twenty-first-century Drustan had thought he was. Would the backpack have made that much of a differ-ence? she wondered.

Yes. She could have shown him the cell phone, with its complex electronic workings. She could have shown him the magazine with the modern articles and date, her odd clothing, the waterproof fabric of her pack. She'd had rubber and plastic items in there; mate-rials that even a medieval whatever-he-was—genius?—wouldn't have been able to dismiss without further consideration.

But the last time she'd seen the damn pack, it was spi-raling off into the quantum foam.

Where do you suppose it ended up? the scientist queried, with childlike wonder.

"Oh, hush, it's not here, and that's all that really signi-fies," Gwen muttered aloud. She was not in the mood to think about quantum theory at the moment. She had problems, all kinds of problems.

The odds of her identifying the enemy without his help weren't promising. The estate was vast, and Silvan had told her that, including the guards, there were seven hundred fifty men, women, and children within the walls, and another thousand crofters scattered about. Not to mention the nearby village. . . . It could be any-one: a distant clan, an angry woman, a conquering neighbor. She had at most a month, and as recalcitrant as he was—not even willing to admit he could travel through the stones—she certainly couldn't expect him to be forthcoming with other information.

Woodenly, she undressed and crawled beneath the covers. Tomorrow was another day. Eventually she'd get through to him somehow, and if she couldn't, she'd just have to save the MacKeltar clan all by herself.

And then what will you do? her heart demanded. *Catch the bouquet at his freaking wedding? Hire on as their nanny?*

Grrr . . .

"Well?" Silvan demanded, strolling into the Greathall. "Does she still claim you took her maidenhead?"

Drustan leaned back in his chair. He quaffed the remains of his whisky and rolled the glass between his palms. He'd been gazing into the fire, thinking of his future wife, trying to keep his mind off the temptress in the chamber that adjoined his. As the spirits had slid into his belly, his worries had eased a bit and he'd begun to see dark humor in the situation. "Oh, aye. She even has a reason why I remain blissfully unaware of my breach of honor. 'Twould seem I tupped her in my future."

Silvan blinked. "Come again?"

"I tupped her five hundred years from now," Drustan said. "And then I sent her back to save me." He couldn't hold it in any longer. He tossed his head back and laughed.

Silvan eyed him strangely. "How does she claim you came to be in the future?"

"I was enchanted," Drustan said, shoulders shaking with mirth. It really was quite amusing, now that he reflected upon it. Since he wasn't currently looking at her, he wasn't worried that he might lose control of his lust and could see the humor more easily.

Silvan stroked his chin, his gaze intent. "So she claims she woke you and you sent her back?"

"Aye. To save me from being enchanted in the first place. She also mumbled some nonsense about you and Dageus being in danger."

Silvan closed his eyes and rubbed his index finger in the crease between his brows, a thing he did often when thinking deeply. "Drustan, you must keep an open mind. 'Tis not entirely impossible on the face of it," he said slowly.

Drustan sobered swiftly. "Nay—on the face of it, it's not," he agreed. " 'Tis once you get into the details that you realize she's a wee bampot with little grasp on sanity."

"I admit it's far-fetched, but—"

"Da, I'm not going to repeat all the nonsense she spouted, but I assure you, the lass's story is so full of holes that were it a ship, 'twould be kissing the sandy bed of the ocean."

Silvan frowned consideringly. "I scarce see how it could hurt to take precautions. Mayhap you should pass some time with her. See what else you might learn about her."

"Aye," Drustan agreed. "I thought to take her to Balanoch on the morrow, see if anyone recognizes her and can tell us where to find her kin."

Silvan nodded. "I will bide a wee with her myself, study her for signs of madness." He cast Drustan a stern look. "I saw the way you looked at her and know that, despite your misgivings, you desire her. If she's daft as you say, I won't abide her being taken advantage of. You must keep her out of your bed. You have your future wife to think of."

"I know," Drustan snapped, all trace of amusement vanishing.

"We need to rebuild the line, Drustan."

"I know," he snapped again.

"Just so you know where your duties lie," Silvan said mildly. "Not betwixt an addlepate's thighs."

"I *know*," Drustan growled.

"On the other hand, if she weren't daft—" Silvan began, but stopped and sighed when Drustan stomped from the room.

Silvan sat in pensive silence after his son had gone. Her story was nigh impossible to believe. How was one to countenance someone knocking upon one's door, claiming to have spent time with one in one's future?

The mind summarily rejected it—it was too chafing a concept for even a Druid to wrap his mind about. Still, Silvan had swiftly run through a few complex calculations, and the possibility existed. It was a minuscule possibility, but a good Druid knew it was dangerous to ignore *any* possibility.

If her story were true, his son had cared for the lass so much that he'd taken her maidenhead. If her story were true, she knew Drustan had powers beyond most mortal men and had cared for him enough to both give him her virginity and come back to save him.

He wondered how much Gwen Cassidy truly knew about Drustan. He would speak with Nell and have her casually mention a few things, observe the lass's reaction. Nell was a fine judge of character. He would spend time with her himself as well, not to question her—for words were without merit, lies easy to fabricate—but to study the workings of her mind as he would study an apprentice. Between the two of them, they would discern the truth. Drustan was clearly not demonstrating a levelheaded response toward the lass.

His eldest son could be so stubborn sometimes. After three failed betrothals, he was so blinded by doubts about himself, so hell-bent on wedding, that he was unwilling to entertain anything that might seem to threaten his upcoming nuptials. He was going to marry, and tarry not in the process.

Although Silvan knew they needed to rebuild the Keltar line, he suspected marriage between Drustan and the Elliott lass would entail a lifetime of deception that would inevitably result in misery for both of them.

A wee bampot, was she, this Gwen Cassidy? Silvan wasn't so certain about that.

· 16 ·

Besseta Alexander fumbled above the mantel for her yew sticks, dread coiling like a venomous snake in the pit of her stomach. A deeply superstitious woman, her charms were as necessary to her as the air she breathed. Of late she'd taken to scrying daily, frantic to discover what threat was moving ever nearer her son.

When she and Nevin had first moved to Castle Keltar, she'd been thrilled to return to the Highlands. No flat-lander was she; she'd ached for many years to return to the misty caps, shimmery lochs, and heathery moors of her youth. The Highlands were closer to the heavens, even the moon and stars seemed within reach atop the mountains.

Nevin's post was a prime one, priest to an ancient and wealthy clan. Here he could live out his life in security and contentment, with no risk of the kind of battles in which she'd lost her other sons, for the MacKeltar housed the second-finest garrison in all of Alba, second only to the King.

Aye, for the first fortnight she'd been elated. But then, shortly after their arrival, she'd cast her yew sticks and seen a dark cloud on her horizon rolling inexorably nearer. Try as she might, she'd been unable to coax her sticks *or* her runes *or* her tea leaves to tell her more.

Just a darkness. A darkness that threatened her only remaining son.

And then, the last time she'd read them, the darkness had extended to one of Silvan's sons, but she'd been unable to determine which one.

Sometimes she felt that great sucking darkness was reaching for *her*, trying to drag her into it. She would sit for hours, clutching her ancient runes, tracing their shapes, rocking back and forth until the panic eased. Vague fear had been her lifelong companion, even as a small lass. She dare not lose Nevin, lest those shadows gain substance and tear at her with wicked claws.

Sighing, she smoothed her hair with trembling fingers, then cast the sticks upon the table. Had she cast them with Nevin in the hut, she would have gotten yet another tedious lecture about God and His mysterious ways.

Thank you very much, lad, but I trust my sticks, not your invisible God who refuses to answer me when I ask Him why He gets four of my sons and I get only one.

Studying the design, the coil in her belly tightened. Her sticks had fallen in the identical pattern they'd formed last week. Danger—but she had no way of knowing from what quarter. How was she to prevent it if she knew not whence it came? She *dare* not fail with her fifth and final son. Alone, that hungry blackness would get her, carry her off into what must surely be the oblivion of hell.

"Tell me more," she beseeched. "I can't do anything until I know which lad presents the danger to my son."

Despairing, she gathered them, then suddenly changed her mind and did something a good fortune-teller rarely risked lest evil forces, ever attuned to fear and despair, cunningly ply a false design upon the limbs. She cast them again, a second time, in quick succession to the first.

Fortunately, the fates were inclined to be gentle and generous, for when the sticks clattered upon the table, she was granted a vision—a thing that had happened only once before in her life. Etched in her mind's eye, she clearly saw the eldest MacKeltar lad—Drustan—scowling, she heard the sound of a woman weeping, and she saw her son, blood dripping from his lips. Somewhere in the vision she sensed a fourth person but couldn't bring that person's face into focus.

After a moment, she decided the fourth person must not be relevant to Nevin's danger since she couldn't see him or her. Mayhap an innocent onlooker.

The woman weeping must be the woman her sticks had told her would kill her son—the lady that Drustan MacKeltar would wed. She squeezed her eyes shut but could glimpse only a wee form and golden hair, not a woman she'd e'er seen before.

The vision faded, leaving her shaking and drained.

She had to somehow put a stop to things before Drustan MacKeltar wed.

She knew he was betrothed—all of Alba knew he was betrothed for the fourth time—but Nevin was infuriatingly closemouthed about the occupants of Castle Keltar. She had no idea when the wedding was to be, or even when the bride would be arriving.

Of late, the more she pried for news from her son, the more recalcitrant he became. He was hiding things from her, and that frightened her. When they'd first arrived, he'd spoken freely about the castle and its occupants; now it was rare for him to mention anything about his days at the castle but for tedious details concerning his work on the chapels.

The Alexander's hut nestled in a valley on the outskirts of Balanoch, nearly twenty furlongs from the castle proper. Nevin, overseeing the renovation of two chapels on the estate, walked each day, but such a tiring journey was beyond her aching joints and swollen limbs. Walking to Balanoch, a furlong to the south, was possible, and on good days she could manage five or more, but twenty and back again were impossible.

If she couldn't wheedle the information from her son, mayhap, if the weather held, she could walk to the village.

Nevin was all she had left, and no one—not the MacKeltar, not the church, nay, not even God—was taking her last son away.

※

"Here, horse, horse, horse," Gwen cooed.

The creature in question peeled back its lips, showing frightfully large teeth, and she hastily retracted her hand. Ears flattened, tail swishing, it regarded her balefully.

Ten minutes ago the groom had brought two horses out of the stable and tied them loosely to a post near the door. Drustan had led the largest one off without a backward glance, leaving her alone with the other. It had taken every bit of her nerve to trudge up to it, and there she stood near the door of the stables, trying to *woo* the infernal thing.

Mortified, she glanced over her shoulder, but Drustan was several yards away, conversing with the stable master. At least he wasn't watching her make a fool of herself. She was city born and raised, by God. How was she supposed to know what to do with a thousand pounds of muscle, hair, and teeth?

She tried again, this time with no tempting appendage proffered, merely a sweet murmur, but the obstinate creature nonchalantly lifted its tail and a warm stream hissed on the ground.

Hastily snatching her slippered foot from the line of fire, she arched a brow, nostrils flaring. So much for thinking this day was going to be better than last night.

It had begun with promise. A half dozen maids had toted up a steaming bath and she'd gratefully soaked her still-tender-from-lovemaking body. Then Nell had brought breakfast and coffee to her chamber. Fueled by caffeine-induced optimism after gulping the dark, delicious brew, she'd dressed and strolled off to find Drustan, to continue her efforts to convince him of the danger he was in. But the moment she'd walked into the Greathall, Drustan had informed her they were going to the village. On horses.

Gwen cast a dubious glance at the beast. She'd never met a horse in person, and now she was supposed to entrust her small self to that monstrous, muscular, haughty creature? It reminded her of Drustan in both stature and demeanor. And it didn't like her any more than she trusted it.

Oh, the horse was beautiful, and at first she'd admired its lovely doelike eyes and silky nose, but it also had sharp hooves, big teeth, and a tail that—*ouch!* Kept flicking her across the rump every time she got too close.

"Here, horse, horse, horse," she muttered, tentatively extending her hand again. She held her breath as the horse made a soft whinnying sound and nudged its nose toward her fingers. At the last minute her resolve slipped and, envisioning strong white teeth neatly nipping her fingers off, she fisted her hand, and the horse, of course, turned away and flattened its ears again.

Swish!

Behind her, Drustan watched with amazement.

"Have you never seen a horse before, lass? They doona answer to 'horse.' They have no idea they are horses. 'Tis like sauntering into the forest, saying, 'Here, boar, boar, boar. I should like to roast you for dinner.' "

She shot a startled, embarrassed look over her shoulder. "Of *course* I've seen a horse before." Her brows puckered and she added sheepishly, "In a book. And don't get all cocky on me; you should have seen your face when you saw a car for the first time."

"A car?"

"In my time we have . . . wagons that need no horses to pull them."

He scoffed and dismissed her statement completely. "So you've never ridden a horse," he remarked dryly, tossing himself up into his saddle. It was a lovely motion, full of casual grace, supreme confidence, and male power to the Nth degree.

It made her downright irritable. "Show-off."

He tossed her a lazy grin. "Although I've not heard that before, 'twould seem you weren't complimenting me."

"It means arrogant and smug, flaunting your skill."

"One must work with what one has." His eyes lingered on her lips, then dropped to her breasts, before he dragged his gaze away.

"I saw that. Don't look at me like that. You're betrothed," she said stiffly, resenting Anya Elliott clear down to the marrow in her bones.

"Och, but I'm not yet wed," he muttered, looking at her from beneath his brows.

"*That* is a despicable attitude."

He shrugged. " 'Tis the way of men." He wasn't about to discuss his true beliefs on the issue with her. His true beliefs were one reason why his attraction to her disturbed him so much. He'd far prefer to be chaste for at least a few weeks before his wedding, and once wed would not stray. Yet she was an irresistible temptation.

But he was strong. He would resist her. To prove it, he smiled down at her.

What was his deal today? Gwen wondered suspiciously. She knew he hadn't decided to believe her—she'd overheard him talking with Dageus before he'd seen her entering the hall. He'd said he was taking her to the village to see if anyone recognized her.

"I can walk," she announced.

"It's a day's walk," he lied, and shrugged again. "But if you wish to walk twenty furlongs . . ." Without further ado, he turned his mount and slowly started off. She trailed along behind him, muttering under her breath.

Ha, he thought she didn't know what a furlong was, but she knew all kinds of measurements. A furlong was roughly an eighth of a mile, which meant the village was approximately two and a half miles, and while it certainly wouldn't take her all day, there was her predisposition toward inertia to consider.

He stopped and tossed her a look that said *last chance.* Shielding her eyes from the sun with her hand against her brow, she scowled up at him. Again, he wore leather trews, that cased his powerful thighs, a linen shirt, his leather bands, and leather boots. There was just something irresistible about a well-muscled man in leather. His dark hair spilled unbound over his shoulders, and as she gazed at him he gave that achingly familiar lionlike toss of his mane, and her hormones roared in response. She refused to think about what she knew lay in his snug leather trews. Knew from personal experience. Because she'd had her hand wrapped around it. Because she'd like to wrap her lips around it. . . .

She tucked her bangs behind her ear with a dismal sigh.

When he nudged his mount near, she skittered back.

A corner of his lip rose in a mocking smile. "So there *are* some things you fear, Gwen Cassidy."

She narrowed her eyes. "There's a difference between fear and lack of familiarity. Anything one does for the first time can be daunting. I have no experience with horses, therefore I have not yet developed proper responses. *Yet* is the significant word there."

"Then come, O brave one." He extended his hand. " 'Tis apparent you won't be able to ride on your own. If you doona ride with me, you'll have to walk. Behind me," he added, just to irritate her.

Her hand shot up toward his.

With a snort of amusement, he clamped his fingers about her wrist and lifted her, deftly sliding her into position on the saddle in front of him. "Easy," he murmured to his mount. Or was it to her? She wasn't sure which of them was more skittish.

He adjusted her lightweight cloak and encircled her waist with his arms. Gwen closed her eyes as a wave of longing flooded her. He was touching her. All over. His chest was pressed against her back, his arms around her to guide the tethers, his thighs pressing against hers. She was in heaven. The only thing that could make it better would be for him to remember her, to know her and look at her the same way he had their last night together in the circle of stones.

Was it possible that the memory was somewhere in him and, if she only found the right words, he would recall? On a cellular level, wouldn't he *have* to possess the knowledge? Perhaps deeply buried, forgotten and ethereal as a misty dream?

She silently savored the contact, then realized that neither he nor the horse was moving. His breath was warm, fanning the nape of her neck. It took all her will not to shift in the saddle and plant a deep, wet kiss on those lips that were only a turn of her head away.

"Well? Don't we move forward or something?" she asked. If they stayed still, touching like this, she couldn't be held responsible for her actions. Some of his silky hair had fallen forward over her shoulder, and she fisted her fingers to prevent them from reaching up and caressing it. What was he doing back there? It wouldn't do her any good to start fantasizing about him. This Drustan was a month younger than hers and a *lifetime* short of a lick of common sense. He was taking her to Balanoch to see if anyone recognized her, the dolt!

"Aye," he said hoarsely. His thighs tensed and he spurred the horse into motion.

Gwen nearly lost her breath as the animal moved beneath her. It was frightening. It was dizzying. It was exhilarating. Mane ruffling in the breeze, the horse made occasional soft horsey grunts as it galloped over the emerald and heather-filled field.

It was an incredible experience. In her mind's eye, she envisioned herself bent low over its back, soaring through the meadows and hills. She'd always wanted to learn to ride, but her parents had dictated her strenuous educational curriculum, and it had permitted no outside activities. The Cassidys were thinkers, not doers.

There was one more way she could distance herself from them, she decided. She could become a doer, and think as little as possible.

"I would like to learn to ride," she informed him over her shoulder. She was going to be there awhile, after all, and it certainly couldn't hurt to acquire some medieval skills. She couldn't bear being without the freedom of transportation. In her century, when her car was in the shop, she felt trapped. She suspected it would be wise to gain all the independence she could. What if he *never* believed her? Married his bimbo and refused to return her to her own time? Panic flooded her at that thought. She definitely needed some basic skills.

"Mayhap the stable master can fit you into his schedule," he said against her ear. "But I hear tell he makes his apprentices shovel out the stables."

She shivered. Had his lips brushed it deliberately, or had the horse's gait pressed him suddenly forward?

"Perhaps Dageus could teach me," she countered waspishly.

"I doona think Dageus will be teaching you a blethering thing," he said in a dangerous voice, and that time his lips did brush her ear. "And I bid you keep your lips off my brother, lest I confine you to your chambers."

What game was he playing? Had that been jealousy lacing his deep brogue, or wishful thinking on her part?

"Besides, as long as you fear the horse, he can sense it and will not respond well. You must respect him, not fear him. Horses are sensitive, intelligent creatures, full of spirit."

"Kind of like me, huh?" she said cheekily.

He made a sound of strangled laughter. "Nay. Horses do as they're told. I doubt you ever do. And you certainly have a lofty opinion of yourself, doona you?"

"No more so than you."

"I see spirit in you, lass, but you demonstrate naught else, and so long as you continue to lie to me, respect will never be part of it. Why not tell the truth?"

"Because I already did," she snapped. "And if you don't believe me, then why don't you take me *back* through the stones?" Gwen suggested, inspired by a sudden thought. If he would only take a short one-day jaunt into the future, she could show him her world, her cars, show him where she'd found him. Why hadn't she thought of that last night?

"Nay," he said instantly. "The stones may *never* be used for personal reasons. 'Tis forbidden."

"Ha! You just admitted that you *can* use them," she pounced.

Drustan growled near her ear.

"Besides, for what other reasons would you use them? On some secret mission?" she scoffed. "And it wouldn't be personal reasons; it would be to save your clan," she added. "I think that's important enough to merit using them."

"Enough, lass. I will not continue this discussion."

"But—"

"Enough. No more buts. And quit squirming."

They rode the rest of the way to the village in silence.

Balanoch, although they called it "the village," was in truth a thriving city. Drustan believed a more prosperous and peaceful city had never existed, and those who resided in Balanoch kept quiet about it when they traveled, to preserve the serenity of their Highland home.

The Keltar–Druids kept a careful watch over Balanoch, performing the ancient rituals to ensure fertility of clan and crop. They'd also placed strategic formations, known as *wards*, about the countryside, which worked to dissuade the curious traveler from venturing too far up the mountain.

It was their city; they would always nurture and protect it.

Aye, he thought, his gaze skimming the thatched rooftops, it was a lovely village. Centuries ago, hundreds had settled in the rich vale protected by the Keltar. Over the centuries, hundreds had become thousands. Far enough away that they had few visitors, yet near enough to the sea to trade, Balanoch housed four Kirks, two mills, chandlers, tanners, weavers, tailors, potters, blacksmiths, an armorer, shoemakers, and sundry other craftsmen.

It was to the goldsmith they were going first, so Drustan could check on the intricate gold leaf with which the talented craftsman was embellishing one of Silvan's treasured tomes.

As they entered the outskirts of the village, Drustan observed Gwen as dispassionately as possible, which was difficult with her squarely between his thighs. He'd dreaded placing her upon his horse, but there'd simply been no other alternative. It was clear the lass had never sat a horse before.

Schooling his lustful thoughts, he studied her. She craned her neck this way and that, drinking in the sights.

They rode past the tanner's and butcher's stalls, whose shops were at the perimeter of the city, where the odor from the dung used to soften the hides might more readily dissipate and the drippings from freshly butchered meat could be safely drained. On avenues further in were the sweltering ovens of the blacksmiths, set apart from the gentler merchants so the din of metal against metal would not interfere with quiet business.

The houses and shops, constructed of stone with thatched roofs and broad shuttered faces, opened to the street. The main thoroughfare housed the chandlers, clothiers, weavers, shoemakers, and such. The top shutters, which opened horizontally, were raised and propped up with poles to form an awning, while the bottom shutter lowered, and wares were laid out in enticing displays. The village had its own council that strictly enforced codes set by the Keltar, whereby they regulated trade, sanitation, and other matters of craftsmanship.

She was curious as if she'd not seen such a city before, Drustan thought, as she tried to peer in every direction at once. The moment they'd entered the town, she began firing questions. The smiths, hammering red-hot steel, sparks flying, fascinated her. She gawked at a young apprentice making wire by drawing hot metal through a template hole with pincers.

The butcher made her queasy, and she refused his of-fer of a strip of salted venison. As they passed the tan-ner, she saw steam rising from several shallow vats and bid him pause so she could watch the merchant shave a skin with a two-handled currier's knife.

His eyes narrowed. She was the most convincing little actress he'd ever encountered. Her madness seemed a sporadic thing, manifesting itself infrequently, albeit spectacularly. So long as she wasn't talking of being from the future or making wild claims about him, she seemed merely unusual, not crazed.

When she leaned back and pressed a hand against his leather-clad thigh, every muscle in his body contracted and his leg went rigid beneath her palm. He closed his eyes, telling himself it was but a hand, an appendage, ab-solutely nothing to drive him to senseless arousal, but lust had been thundering through his veins since he'd placed her on the horse. The warmth of her wee, gener-ously curved body between his thighs had kept him in a permanent state of arousal. When she was near, his mind slackened, his body stiffened, and he became use-less but for one thing.

Bed play.

He'd like to wrap his fists in the fabric of her gown and rip it down the front, baring all those rosy curves for his pleasure. She made him feel primitive as his ancient ancestors who'd taken women as barbarically and un-apologetically as they'd conquered kingdoms. For a brief moment he was flooded with the strange idea that he had every *right* to take her to his bed.

He'd bet she'd not protest o'ermuch either, he thought darkly. If at all.

"Did he make your . . . er, trews?" She gestured to-ward the tanner.

"Aye," he said roughly, pushing her hand away.

"Forgive me for touching your glorious personage," she said stiffly. "I just wondered if your trews were as soft as they looked."

He bit his lip to prevent a smile. Glorious personage, indeed. Where did she come up with her words? *My trews may be soft, lass,* he thought, *but what's in them isn't.* Had her hand crept a bit higher, she would have found that out for herself.

"Might I get a pair?"

"Of leather trews?" he said indignantly.

She turned her head to look at him, and it put her lips a breath from his. His heart beat erratically and he went motionless so he might not do something abjectly stupid, like taste those luscious lying lips.

"They look comfortable, Drustan," she said. "I'm not used to wearing dresses."

His gaze seemed to have gotten stuck on her lips, and he scarce heard her reply. Such lips as only a witch would have—hot and succulent, moist and utterly kissable. Slightly parted, revealing straight white teeth and the tip of a pink tongue. For a moment, he watched her lips moving but couldn't hear a word she said. It took a vicious shake of his head to make her voice fade back in.

"And I always wanted a pair, but in my house—ha!—my parents would have *killed* me if I'd ever worn a pair of black leather pants."

"As well they should, were their daughter to don such trews." Were he to glimpse her generously rounded bottom cased in snug-fitting black leather trews, he might just forget who he was and that he was getting married anon.

"Please? Just one pair. Aw, come on. What harm could it do?"

He blinked. For the first time since he'd met her, she sounded like a normal woman, but she wasn't begging for a pretty gown, the contrary wench wanted men's attire.

"Where's your sense of adventure?" she pressed.

Focused on your lips, he thought irritably, *with all my other damned senses.*

An image of her clad in black leather trews and nothing else, golden hair spilling in wild disarray over her generous naked breasts, loomed in his mind. "Absolutely not," he growled, spurring his horse forward and nodding farewell to the tanner. "And turn around. Doona look at me."

"*Oooh.* Now I'm not even allowed to look at you?" She snorted and sulked all the way to the goldsmith's, but he noticed that it didn't curb her curiosity. Nay, it merely meant she poked that luscious lower lip of hers out further, making him shift uncomfortably in the saddle.

When at last they arrived at the goldsmith's, he vaulted from the horse, desperate to put distance between them. He was about to knock on the door when she cleared her throat imperiously.

He glanced warily back at her.

"Aren't you going to get me off this thing?" she said sweetly.

Too sweetly, he realized. She was up to something. She was a vision, clad in one of his mother's cloaks of pale mauve, her shimmering gold hair spilling over her shoulders, her eyes bright.

"Jump," he said stiffly.

She narrowed her eyes. "You haven't had many girlfriends, have you? Get over here and help me. This beast is taller than I am. I could break an ankle. And then you'd be stuck carrying me around for God only knows how long."

Girlfriends? He puzzled over the word for a moment, breaking it into its base parts and analyzing it. Ah, she meant liaisons. Sighing, he calculated the odds that she might remain quietly mounted and give him some peace, then recalled his purpose in bringing her here. He wanted the villagers to see her, in hopes that someone would recognize her. He was certain she must have stopped in the village before walking to his castle. The sooner someone recognized her, the sooner he could put an end to her presence in his keep.

He was going to have to remove her from the horse, for wee as she was, she would indeed hurt herself jumping, and then there would be hell to pay with Silvan.

You made her jump from the horse? Silvan would exclaim.

I had to. I was afraid if I touched her, I wouldn't be able to stop touching her. Aye, that would go over well. His da would be wildly amused. He'd tell Dageus and they would laugh uproariously. He'd never live it down. Drustan MacKeltar, afraid to touch a wee wench who scarce reached his ribs. He prayed his future wife provoked similar feelings of desire in him.

"Come." He reluctantly raised his hands.

She brightened instantly, slid off the horse, and hopped into his arms.

She hit him with enough impact that it caused his breath to leave his lungs in a soft whoosh of air and forced him to wrap his arms around her to keep her from falling.

Her hair was in his face and smelled like the heather-scented soap Nell made in the kitchens. Her breasts were soft, crushed mounds against his chest, and her legs were sort of—nay, no sort of about it—they were wrapped around him.

No wonder Dageus hadn't resisted. It was a wonder his brother hadn't tupped the lass right then and there.

The muscles in his arms defied his brain's command to release her. Perversely, they tightened around her.

"Drustan?" Her voice was soft, her breath sweet, her body womanly and supple against his.

It was futile, he thought darkly. He shifted her abruptly so that her lips were accessible and did what he'd been longing to do since the moment he'd laid eyes on her. He kissed her. Punishingly. In his mind he was erasing Dageus's kiss from her lips, wiping the slate clean, imprinting himself and only himself upon her.

The moment their lips met, a frantic energy sizzled the length and breadth of his body the likes of which he'd never felt in his life.

And she kissed him back wildly. Her wee hands sank into his hair, her nails grazing his scalp. Her legs tightened shamelessly around his waist, capturing the hardness of him snugly against her woman's heat. Hers was a hotter kiss, and more carnal in nature, than aught he'd ever received.

He responded like a man starved for the touch of a woman. He cupped his hands beneath her luscious bottom, sliding the fabric of her skirt away from her legs. He kissed and kissed and kissed her, clamping her head firmly between his hands, nibbling and suckling and tasting her hot, lying mouth, wondering how it could be so sweet. Shouldn't a lying tongue taste bitter? Not like honey and cinnamon.

An image, startling in its clarity and strangeness, flashed through his mind: this woman, clad in strange garments—half a chemise and ruined trews—regarding him in a silvered glass as he struggled with a faded and dingy blue pair of trews.

He'd ne'er worn such trews in his life.

Yet his lust for her trebled at the onslaught of the image. Plunging his tongue into her mouth, he pressed his lower body against her and pulled her more tightly against his hard shaft. His wits were drugged by the scent of her, the taste of her, the raw mating heat of her.

"Milord?" a faint, startled voice said behind him.

Irritation flickered through his veins that someone

dared interrupt. By Amergin, it was his choice if he chose to hang himself! This woman had placed herself in his castle, in his arms. He wasn't married *yet!*

There was the sound of a throat being cleared, then a gentle laugh.

He closed his eyes, drew upon his Druid discipline, and thrust her away, but the wee witch sucked his lower lip as she went, causing his desire to peak feverishly. Her cheeks were flushed, her lips deliciously swollen.

And he was hard as a rock.

Disgusted with himself, he pasted a smile on his face, adjusted his sporran about his waist, and turned to greet the man who'd saved him from tupping the lass in the street without a thought for his betrothed.

"Tomas," he hailed the elderly, gray-haired gold-smith. He tugged Gwen forward by the hand and thrust her beneath the smith's nose, watching intently for any flicker of recognition. There was none.

The smith merely beamed, his gaze darting between the two of them. "Silvan must be delighted, just delighted," he exclaimed. "He's been longing for grand-children and he's finally goin' to get his wedding. I saw the two of ye out the window and simply had to come see for meself. Welcome, milady!"

As Tomas turned a beatific gaze on Gwen, Drustan realized the smith was laboring under the mistaken assumption that Gwen was his latest betrothed.

Drustan clamped his teeth around the introduction he'd been about to make, not about to disabuse him of the notion. The last thing he needed was more rumors circulating in the village that Anya might one day over-hear. Perhaps Tomas would simply forget what he'd seen or, after meeting the true bride, wisely keep his own counsel. The less said about it the better.

"I vow, in all my life I've ne'er seen Drustan Mac-Keltar escort a lass about town. He's of a certain ne'er stood and kissed one in the street for all to see. Och, but where are me wits? Addled by seein' the laird in love, they be," he said, bowing hastily. "Bidding ye welcome again, and please, do come in."

Gwen cast Drustan an arch, heated glance that seared him to the bone, before following Tomas into the shop.

He remained outside a few moments, taking longer than necessary to secure his horse, breathing deeply of the crisp, cool air. *In love, my arse,* he thought darkly. *I've been bewitched.*

· 17 ·

Gwen was ecstatic. He'd kissed her. Kissed her
just like he'd kissed her in her century, and she'd
glimpsed *her* Drustan in his eyes. And the smith had
thought they looked to be in love!

There was hope, after all. In her century, he'd claimed
he wouldn't kiss a woman were he betrothed or wed.
Well, she thought cheerily, he'd just broken that rule.
Perhaps if she dug deep enough, reminded him of
things they'd done in her time, he would somehow
remember it all, given time. She'd save him and he'd
break his engagement and marry *her*, she thought
dreamily.

Resisting the urge to fan herself, she glanced about
Tomas's cottage. Drustan was outside fiddling with the
horse, but she knew that wasn't the only reason he'd remained outside. He had responded exactly as he had in

her century, and she knew Drustan was a man of strong passion. He didn't like to stop once he got started.

She hoped he was damn uncomfortable in those comfy-looking snug leather trews he'd refused to buy for her.

It was possible that delight colored her impression of the tiny sixteenth-century cottage, but she found it lovely. It was cozy and warm, filled with a light floral scent, probably from all those herb thingies hanging upside down in the windows, she decided. A dazzling array of exquisite silver work, plates and goblets, beautifully lettered gold paternosters and religious tableaux were scattered about on tables and shelves. An illuminated manuscript lay on a long, narrow table, surrounded by half a dozen wax candles placed at a cautious distance. There were no oil globes in the room, only candles, and when she inquired, Tomas explained that the oil caused a residue when burned that was more damaging to his manuscripts and gold work than the fine candles he purchased. Indeed, he burned only certain types of wood in his hearth, to minimize the soot. His craft was so detailed and so well-loved by the laird of the MacKeltar, he'd explained, that Silvan himself had paid to have the costly glass windows installed so that he might work by brightest daylight.

"This is for Silvan," he said, beckoning her over to see the tome, eager to display his craft.

"It's lovely," she exclaimed, lifting the embossed cover with the devout care of a bookworm. The pages looked ancient and were written in yet another unintelligible language, with all kinds of symbols that danced just beyond her comprehension. The edges had been painstakingly gold-leafed, with delicate Celtic knotwork. She peered at Tomas. "What is this . . . er, tome about?"

Tomas shrugged. "Verily, I have no idea. Silvan's tomes are oft in unusual tongues."

Just then, Drustan swept into the cottage on a gust of warm, heather-scented air and closed the door with a bang. "Have you finished with it?" he said abruptly, eager to get on to the next stop to see if he could locate someone who recognized her.

Tomas shook his head. "Nay. It will take a few days more. But here's the other volume Silvan wanted. I dinna mind telling ye it took me nigh upon a year to get me hands on a legible copy."

When he offered the slim volume to Drustan, Gwen reacted instinctively and plucked it from his hand. "Oh, God," she breathed, staring at it.

She was holding a copy of Claudius Ptolemy's geocentric view of the universe, which had proposed that the sun and planets orbited the earth and would not be decisively argued in published form until 1543, with Copernicus's *On the Revolution of Heavenly Orbs*. Her eyes widened and her mouth fell open. It was all she could do not to *pet* the sixteenth-century copy.

"I'll take that," Drustan snapped, taking it from her hands.

She blinked at him, too astonished to protest. She'd had a sixteenth-century edition of Ptolemy's work in her hands, touching her skin.

"I'll stop by in a fortnight for the other tome," Drustan told Tomas. "Come," he said to Gwen.

Bidding Tomas farewell, Gwen pondered the significance of that volume. Drustan MacKeltar—sixteenth-century cosmologist? *What a hoot*, she thought. She'd tried so hard to turn her back on physics, but when her heart finally decided to get involved, it was with a man who studied planets and mathematics.

He was really going to have to start trusting her. They had so much to talk about, if he'd only trust her.

Gwen sighed as they entered the Greathall. She'd greeted the day with optimism, only to end it in defeat. She'd accomplished no more than she had last night, and she finally realized that although he was being courteous, he found her story amusing, nothing more. Three times he'd made reference to her "weakness of wit." He thought she was crazy, she realized sadly. And she began to see that the more she spoke of the future, the crazier he would think her.

Tirelessly, he'd dragged her from merchant's shop to stall, making certain everyone in the village saw her, toting her about until she was suffering medieval overload. Not once had he touched her again—in fact, he'd hardly even looked at her.

It had been an exhilarating and fascinating foray into the past, with scents and sights that had left her gaping on more than one occasion. But not once had he permitted her to steer the conversation to the issue that was most important: that he would be abducted and his clan destroyed in approximately a month.

Each time she brought it up, he'd shoved her into yet another booth or wandered off into the throng to greet someone.

On the ride back to the castle, he'd been so tense behind her that she'd finally leaned forward as far as she could and clutched the black's mane. She'd given up and simply reveled in the beauty of the sunset as it had tinted the heathery fields a deep violet. She'd glimpsed a mischievous pine marten darting about the meadow, pausing to stand with its furry little paws upon a stump, nose questioning the breeze. A luminous snowy owl had hooted softly in the branches of the forest beyond. The steady hum of frogs and crickets had filled the air with song.

Full night had fallen by the time they entered the open gates of the castle.

Don't you ever close the gates? she'd asked, frowning. The barbican, constructed of massive stones, sported a formidable portcullis that looked as if it hadn't been lowered in a century. The gate itself was fashioned of wood three feet thick and shod with steel.

And standing wide open.

Not *one* guard sat the barbican.

He'd laughed, the epitome of arrogant male. *Nay,* he'd replied easily. *Not only do the Keltar house the largest garrison beside the king's, there's been naught but peace in these mountains for years.*

Well, perhaps you should, she'd said worriedly. *Just anyone could wander in.*

Just anyone has, he'd replied with a pointed look. *The only thing within leagues of my demesne that fashes me currently rests astride my horse.*

"I am *not* a threat to you," she said, picking up the thread of the conversation where it had left off a few moments ago. "Why can't you simply consider what I've told you? You saw for yourself that no one knew me in Balanoch. For heaven's sake, if it looks like a skunk and smells like a skunk, it probably *is* a skunk," she said, exasperated.

Drustan unsheathed his sword, propped it by the door, and glanced at her with a perplexed expression. "A skunk?"

"A mammal, weasel family, one of those smelly— okay, so that probably wasn't the best metaphor." She shrugged. "What I meant was, be logical. If you simply listen and ask the right questions, you'll find that my story makes sense."

He said nothing, and she heaved another sigh. "I give up. I don't care if you believe me, if you'll just promise me two things."

"My hand in marriage is already given, lass."

Gwen closed her eyes and sighed. "Don't let Dageus go to the Elliott's."

" 'Tis too late. He rode out this morn shortly after we did."

Gwen eyes flew back open. "You must go after him," she cried.

"Doona fash yourself, lass. I sent a full complement of guard with him—"

"What if that's not enough? I don't know how big the battle was!"

"He rides with over two hundred of the finest fighting men Alba boasts. No trivial battle between clan will have such numbers. A clan dispute is usually naught more than a score or two of angry brothers and kinfolk."

Gwen eyed him. "Are you sure that it might not be a bigger battle?" He *did* know his century. Somehow, she'd gotten the idea that medieval battles were all as grand as she'd seen in *Braveheart*. Probably from watching *Braveheart*.

"The Campbell and Montgomery frequently feud, and ne'er have they sent full armies to meet one another. Even if they did, an extra two hundred on the Montgomery's side would make them victorious. My men are well-trained."

Gwen nibbled her lip worriedly. Perhaps that *was* all they needed to do to keep Dageus safe. Already things had been changed. Initially, according to what Drustan had told her in her century, Dageus had gone with only a dozen guard.

"In addition, I instructed the captain that under no circumstances may Dageus engage in battle. Robert would truss Dageus to his horse and flee battle before defying my orders." He sighed before adding, "I also told Dageus what you claimed, before he rode out. He will exercise caution. Nay," he said, when she looked at him hopefully, "not because I believe you, but because I will take no chances, however remote, with my brother's life. We will see if the battle you claimed truly does come to pass."

"Why didn't I think of that?" she exclaimed. "Will you believe me then? If it does?"

His expression grew shuttered. "Off to your chambers, lass. I will have Nell send up a bath and food."

"Oh, get real, Drustan. You don't really believe I could get two clans to go to war against each other just to make my point, do you? That's ridiculous."

His gaze swept her from hair to slippers and back again. "When I look at you, lass, I doona know what I believe and, at the moment, I'm damned weary of looking at you."

"I guess that means I don't get a good-night kiss, huh?" she said, hiding her wounded feelings behind a teasing little pucker.

He froze, his gaze fixed on her lips. Then he shook himself and scowled. "I am a betrothed man, lass," he said stiffly.

"Remind me to remind you of that the next time you kiss me like you did today," she said pointedly. "You can't just go about kissing one minute and hiding behind a fiancée the next. As you said—you aren't married *yet*."

"And as I recall you didn't care for that sentiment."

"I've changed my mind."

"And I kissed you only because you threw yourself upon me—"

"Oh, hardly. You kissed me because you wanted to," she said coolly. "I may not understand much about emotion, and I may be new to sex, but one thing I *do* know is that you want to kiss me."

She pivoted and stomped up the stairs.

His mouth suddenly dry, Drustan watched her go. He

closed his eyes and took a deep breath. She was right. He did want to. Again and again and again. Until she melted against him and begged him to take her. New to tupping? He'd like to teach her anything and everything.

And, furthermore, he didn't think he could *ever* grow weary of looking at Gwen Cassidy.

· 18 ·

She was going to seduce him.

That was the solution.

When he'd kissed her yesterday, she'd glimpsed a tiny bit of her Drustan in his eyes. She was simply going to have to *kiss* him back to his senses. Perhaps with each caress he'd reclaim a dim fragment of memory.

She rather liked that idea.

And his fiancée? her conscience whispered.

All's fair in love and war, her heart growled. *Sorry, Anya,* she appended apologetically. *I'm not really a man-stealing girl, but I've fallen in love with him and I'm not giving up without a fight.*

Eyeing herself in the mirror, she smoothed the silk gown and examined herself. The deep-indigo dress made her eyes look bluer than usual. With her cosmetics bag in God-only-knew-what dimension (the scientist briefly pondered a sort of Flatland, wouldn't that be a hoot?), she was grateful her lashes were thick and dark and her skin smooth. But she'd give a lot for her Chapstick, her toothbrush, and even one pair of panties.

Not bad, she decided, turning from side to side. She fluffed her bangs with her fingers, tousling them. She felt rather . . . soft and curvy and pretty. She hadn't realized that wearing a long silky gown might affect a woman's attitude. It made her feel far more inclined to be feminine than a lab coat ever had. It accentuated all her curves and emphasized her slim waist. The scooped bodice made much of her cleavage.

Drustan had adored her breasts, and she planned to make certain he got to see a lot of them today.

Whatever his feeling for his fiancée, it didn't seem to have diminished his attraction to her one bit.

Bending over at the waist, she cupped her hand beneath one breast, then the other, fluffing them higher in the snug chemise. When she stood back up and looked in the mirror, she blushed.

One must work with what one has, she reminded herself. He'd said so himself only yesterday.

⟡

"Good morning, Silvan. Where's Drustan?" Gwen asked brightly as she slid into a seat next to him at the table.

Nose buried in a book, Silvan didn't glance up, merely finished swallowing a bite of his porridge, then mumbled, "Be with you in a moment, m'dear."

Gwen waited patiently, knowing how much she hated being disturbed when she was reading. Hoping Drustan would saunter in soon, she tipped her head back and admired the elegant balustrade that encircled the upper floor of the Greathall, then dropped her gaze to skim the brilliant tapestries adorning the walls.

The castle was lovely and every bit as lavishly appointed as any of the modern-day castles she'd seen on the tour. Each piece of furniture she'd seen—from the dining table to the assortment of serving and end tables to the towering armoires, chests of drawers, and beds—was fashioned of burnished cherry and painstakingly embellished with intricate designs. The chairs were high, with carved arms and tall backs, topped with bright cushioned pillows and draped with soft woolen throws. The rugs were silky lambskins and woven woolens. Fragrant flowers and herbs were stitched in lace packets, tied with ribbon, and strewn about window ledges.

When she'd come down, she'd passed dozens of maids scurrying through the corridors, airing out down mattresses and beating rugs. Castle Keltar was efficiently run and well-maintained.

All in all, it was amazingly cozy and inviting. The only major difference she could see was a lack of plumbing and lights, and in the winter, of course, lack of central heating would be a nuisance.

But, she mused, with so many fireplaces—most of them tall enough to stand in—and a big brawny Highlander in her bed, a woman might forgive a lot of things. . . .

She wiped the dreamy smile off her face when Nell sailed in and placed a platter of soft poached eggs and fat strips of ham on the table beside a bowl of peach slices, berries, and nuts in a lake of sweet cream. Next, she plunked down a tray of warm oatcakes and honey.

Gwen's stomach growled as she eyed the laden table. If she had Scotch tape, she could forgo eating and just tape the stuff directly on her hips and thighs, ceding to the inevitable. Her usual bowl of raisin bran before work had never inspired appetite, nor had it inspired the scales to tip heavier.

"Put yer book down, Silvan," Nell chided. "Ye have a guest at the table."

Gwen bit her lip to hide a smile. Everything Drustan

had told her about his father and the housekeeper was true. They had a unique relationship, wherein Nell didn't mince words or defer to his position. When Nell glanced at her, Gwen smiled and asked hopefully, "Is there coffee again this morning?"

Silvan put his book down and glanced absently at Gwen. His gaze dropped to her cleavage, and a single white brow shot up. He blinked several times.

"There certainly is," Nell said, circling the table. She stopped behind Gwen and draped a linen cloth over her shoulder, so it tumbled from her neck like a bib.

"Peel yer eyes off the lass's breasts," Nell said sweetly to Silvan.

Gwen turned twenty shades of red, sneaked a hand beneath the bib, and tugged at her bodice, trying to jiggle them back down a little. Mortified, she devoted her attention to eyeing the medieval dining ware—plates and goblets made of heavy silver, a fat spoon and broad knife, and heavy blue bowls.

"She's the one who fluffed them up," Silvan protested indignantly. "I didn't mean to look, but they were . . . so . . . *there*. Like trying not to see the sun in the sky."

Nell arched a brow and circled round the table again. "I hardly think 'twas ye she fluffed 'em for, was it, lass?"

Gwen glanced up and gave an embarrassed shake of her head.

Nell bent over Silvan's plate, fetching his empty mug for a refill, and her bodice gaped. When Silvan peered down it, Gwen nearly laughed, but the laugh died in her throat when she saw Silvan's eyes change instantly.

Oh, my, she thought, going very still. Silvan might have looked at her breasts, but he'd looked at them as a man might eye a pretty flower or a well-bred mare.

Now, glancing down Nell's bodice, he wore an expression of pure hunger, a look both tender and fierce.

Gwen's smile faded and she stared, filled with a wistfulness she wasn't certain she even understood. But it had something to do with a man wanting breasts that were much older and not nearly as firm—all because of the woman they belonged to, not because of the breasts at all.

Silvan MacKeltar had deep feelings for his house-keeper.

She stole a furtive glance at Nell, who seemed oblivious to what Silvan was doing as she collected his mug and went back to the kitchen.

Silvan must have felt her gaze upon him, because he jerked slightly, as if coming out of a trance, and glanced at her.

"I wasn't looking at her breasts—" he began defensively.

"Save it for someone who didn't see the look on your face. And if you don't make any funny comments about me fluffing myself, I won't make any comments about what you feel for Nell."

"What I feel for—what I—" he sputtered, then nodded. "Agreed."

Gwen turned her attention to the platter of food, wondering why food tasted so much better in the sixteenth century. Was it the lack of preservatives? The smoky-peaty flavor of the meat? The genuine butter and cream? She slipped a knife beneath a soft poached egg and transferred it to her plate.

"So, why did you . . . er . . ." Silvan gestured toward her linen bib.

She sighed. "Because I thought Drustan might be at breakfast and I hoped he'd notice me."

"Notice you, or drag you off to tup you?"

"I might have settled for either," she said glumly, helping herself to another egg.

Silvan snorted with amusement. "Are you always so honest, m'dear?"

"I try to be. Dishonesty increases disorder exponentially. It's hard enough to communicate when you're telling the truth."

Silvan paused, his mouth halfway closed around a bite of poached egg. He withdrew the laden fork from his mouth carefully. "What did you just say?" he asked softly.

"Lies," Gwen said, her gaze on the thick slab of ham she was trying to spear with a misshapen fork. She pierced it with a tine, but it slipped off. "They increase disorder. Difficult to predict all the variables when you keep tossing more variables in." She glanced at him. "Don't you think?" she asked, with a nod for emphasis.

"Exponentially?" he asked, his brows furrowing together in a single point.

"Any positive consonant raised to a power," Gwen said, cornering the ham against the lip of the platter. "It's a function of math, used to express a large number. Like Avogadro's number, 6.023×10^{23} and represents the number of atoms in a mole of any substance—"

"Atom?"

"The smallest component of an element having the chemical properties of the element, consisting of a nucleus, containing combinations of neutrons and protons and one or more electrons—hey, maybe I shouldn't be telling you this!"

Silvan snorted. "I know of what you speak. 'Tis a hypothetical particle of matter so small to admit no division—"

No, no, no, no physics over breakfast! "Yes, but who cares? Look at this scrumptious food."

He sounded strained when he asked, "Do you play chess, m'dear?"

She brightened and, finally securing the ham, smiled. "Of course. Would you like to play?"

"On the terrace. In two hours, if you will."

Gwen beamed. Drustan's father wanted to spend time with her and play a game. She couldn't recall a time her father had ever done such a thing. Everything had been work-oriented, and the one time she'd coaxed him into a game of Pente, he'd gone off on how one could calculate every possible outcome. . . .

She shook her head, pushing that memory far to the back of her mind, and eyed Silvan speculatively. Maybe, if Drustan had told him her story, she could work on him. Perhaps he might be more inclined to listen. Winning his support would definitely help.

All while sitting in the sun and *playing* . . .

"I don't usually show so much cleavage, Nell," Gwen poked her head in the kitchen and said apologetically to Nell's back. She had some time to pass before meeting Silvan and wanted to get better acquainted with Nell. She suspected the housekeeper probably knew everything that went on in the castle and might be a source of information regarding who might wish the MacKeltars harm. Plus, she didn't want Nell to think badly of her. Next time she bared so much, she would make sure it was for Drustan and only Drustan. Her breasts were now demurely tucked beneath her bodice.

Nell glanced over her shoulder. Flour dusted her cheek and brow, and she had her hands in a mountain of dough. "I dinna think ye did, lass," she said with a gentle smile. "Despite ye showin' up bare as a babe. I know ofttimes a lass feels she has few choices. Ye needn't barter yerself for shelter and food. I suspect ye've more choices than yer thinkin' ye do."

"What kind of choices?" Gwen asked, stepping into the kitchen.

"Know ye aught about bakin', Gwen?" Nell withdrew her hands from the dough.

Gwen nibbled her lip uncertainly. "Not really, but I'm game to try." Is that what Nell meant about choices? Were they going to offer her a job in the kitchen? A dismal vision of herself cooking for Drustan and his wife made her scowl.

"Ye've two fine hands and, if ye dinna mind, I could start on the lamb. Just poke 'em in there and knead. Wash up first."

Gwen washed and dried her hands before poking tentatively at the mound. Once she'd sunk her hands in it, she decided it was rather fun. Sort of like Play-Doh, which of course she'd not been allowed to have. No Silly Putty either. Her Sunday comics (neatly removed from the paper before she ever got to it) had consisted of her father's witty drawings of black holes sucking up all the Democrats who preferred to fund the environment over the Department of Defense's obscenely expensive research projects.

"That's it, lass," Nell encouraged, watching her. She skewered a large roast on a spit. "Now, do ye wish to talk about it?"

"About what?" Gwen asked uncertainly.

"What happened the night ye arrived. If ye dinna wish to, I willna pry, but I've a willin' ear and a shoulder if yer needin' it."

Gwen's hands stilled deep in the dough and she was silent a long moment, thinking. "How long have you been here, Nell?"

"Nigh on twelve years," Nell answered proudly.

"And have you ever noticed anything . . . er, unusual about Drustan? Or any of the MacKeltars," she added, wondering how much Nell knew. A part of her longed to confide in Nell; there was no question in her mind how loyal the housekeeper was to her men. Still, it would be safer to acquire more information before revealing any.

Nell finished basting the roast, then slid it above the

fire before answering. Wiping her hands on a cloth, she regarded Gwen levelly. "Be ye meanin' their magic ways?" she said bluntly.

Magic. That was exactly what Drustan's unusual intelligence and command of cosmology would seem to a sixteenth-century woman. Heavens, it was exactly what it seemed to her. Although she knew there was a scientific theory behind his use of the stones, she couldn't begin to comprehend how he'd done it. "Yes, that's what I mean. Like the voice Drustan can use—"

"Ye've heard it?" Nell said, surprised, making a mental note to pass that tidbit on to Silvan. "The one that sounds like many voices?"

"Yes."

"He dinna use it on ye, did he?" Nell frowned.

"No. Well, once, sort of, when he asked me to leave him alone for a little while." And that other time, she thought, remembering what he'd said after they'd made love, but telling Nell about that would definitely be overdisclosing.

"I'm surprised. They're overcautious of that spell. Most often they use the healin' and protectin' spells."

Gwen gawked.

"If ye've heard Drustan use the voice, ye shouldna be too surprised. Druids have many unusual abilities." Nell let it slip casually.

Druids! The mythical alchemists and astronomers, who'd studied the sacred geometry of the ancients! They'd really existed? "I thought Druidry died out long ago."

Nell shook her head. " 'Tis what Druids wish people to believe, but nay. The MacKeltar descend from the oldest line of Druids who served the *Tuatha de Danaan.*"

"The fairy?" Gwen squeaked, remembering that Drustan had claimed they were one and the same.

"Aye, the fae. But the fae have long gone elsewhere

and now the Druids nurture the land. They tend the soil and beckon the seasons with their rituals. They honor the old ways. They scour the land after storms and heal the wee creatures harmed by the tempest. They protect the villages, and legends tell that if a grave threat should e'er come against the land, they have powers most scarce dare not whisper of."

"Oh, God," Gwen murmured, as the pieces began to slip into place. A Druid. Possessed of alchemy and sacred mathematics and magic.

There's no such thing as magic, the scientist protested.

Right, there's no such thing as time travel either, she retorted acerbically. Whatever it was, he had knowledge beyond her comprehension. Druids existed, and the man who'd taken her virginity was one.

"Tell me, lass, knowing he's a Druid, do ye still have a fondness for Drustan MacKeltar?"

Gwen nodded without hesitation.

Nell wiped her hands on her apron and propped them at her waist. "Three times now that man has been betrothed, and three times the woman has abandoned him before the formal vows. Did ye know that?"

Gwen's jaw dropped. "This is his *fourth* betrothal?"

"Aye," Nell said. "But 'tis not because he's not a fine man," she said defensively. " 'Tis because the lasses fear him. And much though he wishes otherwise, I suspect Anya Elliott will be no different. The lass has been sheltered all her young life." Her lip curled disdainfully. "Och, but he's arranged things quite tidily this time. In the past, he handfasted first, and each of the three, after passin' time at Castle Keltar, upon overseeing or overhearing somethin' that fashed 'em, packed up and left with scarce a farewell. And as braw and rich in coin and land as that man is—well, let me tell you it's left him fair uncertain of his charms. Imagine that!"

"Impossible to imagine," Gwen agreed, wide-eyed. Suddenly, quite a few things made sense. She'd wondered why Drustan hadn't told her the full truth while they were in her century. Now she knew. Her brilliant, powerful warrior had been afraid that she would leave him. He couldn't have known that she was one of few people who might have understood him—after all, she'd concealed the extent of her intelligence from him. In the past few years of working at Allstate, it had become instinctive. One didn't rhapsodize about quarks and neutrons and black holes during happy hour at Applebee's with insurance adjusters.

Three failed betrothals also explained why Drustan was so aggressively determined to wed his fourth betrothed. The Drustan she'd come to know was not a man to accept failure, and he'd made it clear that he was a man for marrying and wanted children.

"This time he's arranged to wed in a Christian ceremony, and Anya will be here but a fortnight afore the wedding. I fear he will succeed in hiding his nature until after the vows. Then she willna be able to leave him. But"—she paused and sighed—"like as not, it willna prevent her from despising him later in the marriage."

"Has it occurred to him that it's not nice to trick a woman like that?" Gwen said, grasping at straws. Maybe she could berate him for his underhanded tactics and guilt him into calling off the betrothal. Then again, she thought, maybe *she* could be underhanded, and once Anya arrived she could trick him into revealing some of his "magic" in front of his fiancée, to drive her the same route the first three had gone. Dirty pool, but all in the name of love, and that had to count for something, didn't it?

"I suspect he's preferrin' to believe he's not trickin' her but hoping that she'll one day grow to care for him. Or mayhap he thinks he can hide forever."

Gwen poked at the dough for a time. "How long has he known her?" she finally asked. *Does he love her very much?* was the question coiled on the tip of her tongue.

"He's ne'er met the lass," Nell said flatly. "The marriage was arranged between Drustan and the Elliott through messengers bearing the bride offer."

"He's never met her?" Gwen shouted. Her heart took wing; feelings of guilt about trying to break up the betrothal went up in a puff of smoke. He hadn't neglected to mention Anya because he loved Anya; he'd not mentioned her because he'd not even met her! It wasn't as if she was trying to break up a *real* relationship!

Nell smiled faintly. "Och, ye've much feelin' for him. 'Tis plain to see."

Feeling suddenly euphoric, Gwen said pertly, "Speaking of feeling that's plain to see, what about you and Silvan?"

Nell's smile faded instantly and her expression grew shuttered. "There is naught betwixt me and that canny old badger."

"Well, there may not be on your end, but there certainly is on his."

"Where do ye get yer daft ideas?" Nell snapped, leaping into a flurry of activity, banging pots and moving dishes. "Let me finish that bread, for 'tis plain that it'll be the morrow before ye've got it properly kneaded."

Gwen was unfazed. Nell's reaction told her everything. "He peeked down your bodice when you took his mug."

"He did no such thing!"

"He did. And trust me, he didn't like mine a tenth as much. Nell, Silvan has deep feelings for you."

Nell paused in her frantic kneading and bit her lip. When she looked at Gwen, her eyes were pained. "Dinna be sayin' such things," she said quietly.

"In twelve years haven't you and Silvan ever—"

"Nay."

"But you care for him, don't you?"

Nell blew out a slow breath. "I loved a laird once. It cost me my babes and nearly my life."

"What happened? I don't mean to pry . . ." Gwen trailed off uncertainly.

"What happened? Ye truly wish to know what happened?" Nell's voice rose. She punched the mound of dough several times before kneading furiously.

"Er . . . yes," Gwen said warily.

"I was a fool, 'tis what happened. I loved a laird who had a wife of his own, though there was no love betwixt them. An arranged match, it was, made on land and alliances. I resisted him for years, but the day my mam died, thick in grievin', I weakened. 'Twas not what I believed proper, but och, how I loved that man." She drew a deep breath and closed her eyes. "I suspect my mother dyin' made me realize we dinna have forever."

How true, Gwen thought. She certainly hadn't had forever. She'd always thought she and her parents would mend fences; she'd never dreamed they wouldn't live another twenty, thirty, even forty more years.

"We were discreet; still, his lady learned of our involvement. She shrieked and raged, but she'd given him no heirs, and by then I'd given him two sons." A shadow crossed her features. "Then one afternoon he was killed while hunting. That very eve, she took my children and set her kin upon me. They left me for dead near Balanoch."

"Oh, Nell," Gwen breathed, her eyes misting.

"I lost what would have been our third child in the dust. 'Twas Silvan who found me. Ne'er will I forget starin' up at the sun, waitin' to die, *wishin'* to die, only to see him"—a bittersweet smile curved her lip—"like a fierce angel, standin' o'er me. He took me in and stood by my bed and demanded that I live, in such a voice that

I feared to die and defy him." Her smile deepened. "He tended me himself, for weeks. . . ."

"What about your children?" Gwen asked hesitantly.

Nell shook her head. "As she'd had none, she claimed them as her own. 'Tis said she's barren, and my son will one day be laird, as his only heir."

"You've never seen them again?"

"Nay, but occasionally I hear bits of gossip. My Jamie is fostered outside of Edinburgh. Mayhap when she's no longer alive I'll see them again, but they willna know me. They were but one and two when I was driven out. They believe she's their true mam."

"Didn't Silvan try to get them back for you?"

"And I could give them what?" Nell snapped. Then she sighed and muttered, "I never told him what happened. And that bletherin' fool has not once asked. In twelve years! Imagine that."

"Maybe he was afraid to pry once you'd healed," Gwen suggested. "He might not have wanted to bring up painful memories. Maybe he's been waiting for you to bring it up."

"Mayhap," Nell said stiffly, blowing a wisp of hair from her face, "ye put a rosy hue on things that arena so rosy. Go on with ye, now," she said crossly. "There are some things 'tis too late for. Dinna fash yerself over me. I've passed many a peaceful day here. If ye wish to give me happier ones, fall in love with one o' those lads and give me bairn to cuddle again."

"Um . . . what if it's Drustan?" Gwen said nervously. "Would you think I was terrible if I tried to make him care about me before he marries his fiancée?"

Nell cocked her head and met Gwen's gaze levelly. "I suspect I have a few special gowns I could alter for ye, lass. He's overfond of purple, did ye know that?"

Gwen beamed.

"Now go," Nell shooed her, flipping a cloth at her.

She started to walk out, then turned back abruptly, squeezed Nell's shoulder, and kissed her floured cheek. Then she dashed hastily off, embarrassed by her impulsive display of affection.

Nell blinked and smiled, eyeing the empty corridor. Aye, she was going to like the lass a lot. She and Silvan had been worrying for months about Drustan wedding the Elliott lass. Neither of them held much hope for the match. They both sensed the quiet desperation in Drustan and knew he was plunging blindly into something that was bound to become a fankle. Duty weighed on him; he needed heirs. Anya Elliott was ten and five, and Drustan MacKeltar would patently terrify the child. Oh, he might get a bairn or two off her, but he'd pay for it with a lifetime of misery. As would the unsuspecting Anya. Drustan needed an educated lass, a lass with fire and mettle and curiosity.

Yestreen, Silvan had asked a favor of her (not looking at her, of course, as if noticing her hair earlier had been an unforgivable sin), and she had done her part as he'd requested. Gwen Cassidy now knew Drustan was a Druid.

She could scarce wait to tell Silvan how Gwen had reacted—with an open mind and heart—just as Silvan had predicted. She'd glimpsed no signs of madness in the lass—och, she was odd, but that didn't make a person mad, or the eccentric Silvan would be maddest of all.

Her smile faded at the thought of Silvan, as she recalled what Gwen had said about him having feelings for her.

Might it be? She and Silvan scarcely spoke but for conversation about the lads, the crops, or the weather. Long ago she'd once thought he'd been interested, but he'd retreated and she'd tried to forget.

She narrowed her eyes thoughtfully and glanced down at her bosom. It was still fluffable.

Had he truly glanced down her bodice? She was never comfortable looking at him when she was standing close. The man could peek anywhere he wanted and she'd not notice.

Mayhap, she mused, while stitching Gwen some tempting fashions, she might deepen the bodice of her new gown that was nearly finished.

❧

Silvan was waiting on the terrace, at a table centered in a puddle of sunshine, beneath rustling oaks.

Gwen took the seat opposite him and glanced about with delight. "It's so beautiful here," she said with a contented sigh. A brilliant yellow butterfly swooped the board, lingering a moment before fluttering off again.

"Aye, our mountain is the finest in all of Alba," Silvan said proudly, as he finished setting up the pieces.

When he was done, Gwen turned the heavy board around, reversing it.

He glanced askance at her.

"I have to be black. I don't like to go first," she explained, fingering the ebony figurines. An honest-to-God medieval chess set, she thought wonderingly. It would be worth a fortune in her time. The pieces were fashioned of ebony wood and ivory tusk. The rooks were solemn little men, the bishops had long beards and wise little faces. The knights were kilt-clad warriors on prancing destriers, the royalty wore flowing robes trimmed with fur and stood several inches above the rest. The board itself was fashioned of alternating squares of ivory and ebony. The surrounding perimeter was a solid rectangle of ebony, carved with a complex design of Celtic knotwork that represented infinity.

How on earth had the twenty-first century gotten the idea that medieval men were ignorant? she wondered. She was beginning to suspect that perhaps they were more in tune with the world than her century would ever be.

Silvan pursed his lips and narrowed his eyes. "Why do I think I might be in for a time of it?"

"Why do I think you might be able to give as good as you get?" she countered.

"How long have you been playing?"

"All my life. You?"

"All my life. Which has been considerably longer than yours," he said dryly as he moved a pawn with swift certainty.

Two games later—one win to Silvan, one to Gwen—they were into a more interesting variation. Normal chess was too much of a draw between them, so Gwen had proposed they play progressive chess, wherein pawns didn't "queen" but rather increased in power with each square they advanced. In progressive chess, a pawn on the fifth rank had the power of play of a knight, on the sixth a bishop, seventh a rook, and on the eighth a queen.

When she declared checkmate, with her two queens, a bishop, and three knights, he clapped his hands and saluted her.

"And Drustan thinks you're a bampot," he murmured, smiling.

"He told you that?" she asked, feeling wounded. "Forget it," she added hastily. "It doesn't matter. Just tell me this: Do you know of anyone who might wish your clan harm, Silvan?"

"None. 'Tis a peaceful land, and the Keltar know no enemies."

"No clans who wish to conquer you?"

"Ha," Silvan scoffed. "None that would dare try."

"How about . . . um . . . the king?" she grasped at straws.

Silvan rolled his eyes. "Nay. James likes me. I performed magic tricks for the boy-king when last I was in Edinburgh. His council seeks no battle in our Highlands.

"Maybe Drustan angered someone's husband?" she pried none-too-subtly.

"Drustan doesn't tup married wenches, m'dear."

She smiled, pleased by that bit of knowledge.

"Or maidens," he said pointedly.

She scowled. "Can I tell *you* my whole story?"

"Nay." At her wounded expression he added, "Words cost nothing, they buy nothing. Actions speak truth. You neatly trounced me at progressive chess. Were I to suspect you of aught, it wouldn't be to think you mad but to believe you some sort of Druid yourself. Mayhap come to spy upon us—"

"First Drustan thinks I'm crazy," Gwen interrupted glumly, "now you think I'm a spy."

"—or, in the future, lasses are better educated. If you permit a man to finish, m'dear, you'll see that I was merely pointing out possibilities. They are endless. Time will have out. I am interested in your heart, not your words."

"You have no idea how nice it is to hear someone say that."

One silvery brow rose.

"Until I met your son, Silvan, I wasn't even certain I had a heart. Now I know I do, and that bonehead is going to marry someone he's never even met. She's never going to be as right for him as I am."

"Bonehead," he repeated, smiling faintly. His other brow rose. "You told me you didn't wish me to make him wed you," he said softly.

"I don't want you to make him. I want him to *want* to. I'm telling you, we're perfect for each other. He just doesn't remember that. If my story is true," she added archly, "I could be carrying your grandson. Have you thought of that, O wise one?"

Silvan burst out laughing. He laughed so long and loudly that Nell poked her head out, with a smile herself, to see what was going on.

When he finally stopped, he patted Gwen's hand. "None but Drustan has ever called me that in such a tone. Irreverent you are, clever and bold. Aye, Gwen Cassidy, I'll give him a nudge or two in your direction. I'd planned to anyway."

Gwen tucked her bangs behind her ears and smiled at him. "Again?" she asked.

As they began resetting the pieces, Nell came out on the terrace, depositing two mugs of warm ale.

"Join us, Nell," Silvan said. Nell glanced dubiously at Silvan, until Gwen patted the seat beside her.

For the next few hours, Gwen watched Silvan and Nell in what she was certain had become a longtime ritual: his head turned, hers wouldn't. Her head turned, his stayed down. They managed to look at each other only if the other wasn't looking. Not once did the older couple make direct eye contact. Somehow they were so attuned that Silvan could sense when Nell's gaze had wandered up to watch a golden eagle soar beyond the castle, and Nell could sense when Silvan was so intent upon the game that he'd not notice her watching him.

It was amazing, really, Gwen realized. They were so in love with each other, and neither of them knew it.

Maybe her own life was unraveling at the seams, but surely she could do something to bring those two together.

When the sun had nearly completed its lazy crawl across the sky, smearing streaks of rose and liquid gold across the horizon, Nell pushed herself up and went off to prepare the evening meal.

She cast a glance over her shoulder at Gwen and made a fluffing motion to her bodice. "Dinna be forgettin' to dress for dinner," she said with a wink. "He never misses a meal, and I made his favorite this eve—roast suckling pig, neeps, and tatties."

Oh, she'd dress, all right.

But Drustan didn't come to dinner that night.

As a matter of fact, the stubborn man managed to hide from her for nearly a week.

· 19 ·

Chaos had stormed his castle, dressed in lusciously low-cut gowns, silky slippers, and ribbons, Drustan brooded, raking his hair back and tying it with a leather thong.

None of his fortress's defenses were useful against her, unless he wished to declare open warfare, mount up the guards, and dust off the catapult.

At which point, of course, his da and Nell would laugh themselves silly.

He'd been avoiding her since the day he'd taken her to Balanoch.

The next time he touched her, he'd tup her. He knew that. He fisted his hands at his sides, inhaling sharply.

His only recourse was to avoid her completely until Dageus returned with Anya. When Dageus confirmed that no such battle had occurred, he would have her removed from his castle and sent far away.

How far will be far enough? a most unwelcome voice asked. He knew that voice well. It was the one that endeavored daily to convince him that he had every right to take her to his bed.

A most dangerous, frighteningly persuasive voice.

He groaned and closed his eyes. He enjoyed a blissful moment's respite, until her laughter, lifted by the buoyant summer breeze, soared through the open window of his chamber.

Eyes narrowed, he peered out, both dreading and anticipating what gown she might have donned today. Would it be purple, violet, indigo, lavender? It was almost as if she knew of his preference for the vibrant color. And with her golden hair, she looked splendid in it.

This morn she wore sheer mauve with a golden girdle. No surcoat, in deference to the sunny weather. Succulent, creamy breasts rose from the simple scooped neck. She'd piled her blond tresses atop her head and, threaded with violet ribbons, it tumbled in delightful disarray about her face. She sauntered across his lawn, as if all his estate belonged to her.

For the past week she'd been everywhere he'd wanted to be, driving him to seek seclusion wherever it could be found. He'd ducked into chambers in the castle he'd forgotten even existed.

She hadn't bothered to be subtle about it. The moment she saw him, she chased about after him wearing a ferocious scowl, jabbering away about "things" she had to tell him.

Daily her tactics grew more sly and underhanded. Last night the audacious wench had picked the lock to his chamber! Because he'd had the foresight to barricade the door with a heavy armoire, she'd then gone to his door in the corridor and picked that lock. He'd been forced to escape out the window. Halfway down he'd slipped, crashed the last fifteen feet to the ground, and landed in a prickly bush. Since he'd not had time to don his trews, his manly parts had taken the brunt of his abrupt entry into the bush, putting him in a foul mood indeed.

The wench sought to unman him before his long-anticipated wedding night.

His every movement, every thought, every decision was being directly affected by her presence, and he resented it.

Her finger was even in the food he ate in the garrison with the guards, safely away from her, as Nell had begun "experimenting" with new recipes, and he'd like to know what the blethering hell was wrong with the old ones.

And she'd begun learning to ride, had indeed coaxed the stable master to teach her (probably for the cost of a smile with a dimple on one side, for he certainly hadn't seen her shoveling out the stables). In midafternoon she could be found prancing about on a gentle mare across the front lawn of the estate, impairing his passage. He had to admit, she'd found her seat rather well. Any day now, when he vaulted astride his horse to escape her, she'd follow him.

His life had been so orderly before her arrival. Now his life was ordered about her schedule and how to avoid her. He'd been heading toward certain success, all the things he'd longed for. Just the day before she'd appeared on their doorstep, he'd been dreaming of holding his first son in his arms within the year, God willing that young Anya would catch a babe so quickly.

But now he dreamed of *her*. This morn, when he'd sneaked into his chamber for a change of clothing, he'd heard the splash of her bath. He'd paced from hearth to window and back again, convinced she was splashing far more than necessary just to force him to think of rosy breasts and thighs and silken gold hair, misted with glistening beads of water.

Drustan stared out the window, scowling. She was

driving him mad. How could so wee a wench create such havoc with his senses?

Last night, after he'd fallen out his own window, he'd tried to catch a short nap in the hall. A short time later, she'd wandered down. There he'd been sitting, feet propped up, staring with heavy-lidded eyes into the fire, seeing golden tresses in the flames, when he'd caught a whiff of her unique scent and turned to see her standing on the stairs.

Clad only in a diaphanous night rail.

Drustan, you can't keep avoiding me, she'd said.

Without a word, he'd leaped to his feet and fled the castle. He'd gone to sleep in the stables.

The laird of the castle, catching winks in the stables, by Amergin!

But had he stayed within the walls, he would have made short work of her sheer rail, kissed and suckled and devoured every inch of her body.

His traitorous father and Nell weren't making things any easier. They'd welcomed her into their lives with the enthusiasm of parents who'd finally gotten the daughter they'd longed for. Nell sewed for her, dressing her in luscious creations, Silvan played chess with her on the terrace, and Drustan had no doubt that once Dageus returned he'd like as not set to trying to seduce the lovely witch.

And Drustan would have no right to complain.

He was getting married. If Dageus wanted to seduce the lass, what right had he to argue?

He crashed his fist down on the stone window ledge. A sennight. He had only to avoid her until then. The moment Dageus returned, confirming there'd been no battle, he would pack the lass off to Edinburgh, aye— mayhap England. He'd send her with a flank of guards, finding some excuse to keep his flirtatious brother at home.

Thrumming with frustrated energy, he stomped from his chamber. He would go for another long ride and try to while away yet another eternal day, ticking them off on a calendar in his head: one day nearer salvation.

As he loped down the hall toward the servants' stairs, he stiffened and spun about. By God, he would *not* skulk out the back entrance again.

If she was fool enough to try something when he was in such a mood, she would suffer for it.

Drustan rounded the corner at a full charge and crashed abruptly into Nevin.

"Milord!" Nevin gasped, flying backward.

"Sorry." He grabbed the priest by the elbows and steadied him on his feet.

Nevin smoothed his robes, blinking. "Nay, 'twas my fault. I fear I was lost in thought and didn't hear your approach. But 'tis grateful I am for our encounter. I was coming to seek you out, if you have a moment. There's a wee matter I wished to discuss with you."

Drustan tamped down a flash of impatience, then got angry that he was feeling impatient to begin with. It was *her* fault. He'd whiled away many a fine hour talking with Nevin and not once suffered impatience; he liked the young priest. He took a deep, calming breath and forced a smile. "Is aught amiss with the chapel?" he asked, the cameo of patient interest.

"Nay. It goes well, milord. We have but to replace the altar stones and seal the new planking. It will be finished in ample time." Nevin paused. " 'Twas a different matter I wished to speak with you about."

"You needn't hesitate to speak your mind with me," Drustan assured him. Nevin seemed reluctant to broach whatever topic was worrying him. Had he seen the bampot chasing him about? Was the priest concerned about his upcoming betrothal? *God knows, I am,* he thought darkly.

" 'Tis my mother again. . . ." Nevin trailed off, sighing.

Drustan released a pent breath and relaxed. It was only Besseta.

"She's been agitated lately, muttering about some danger she thinks I'm in."

"More of her fortune-telling?" Drustan asked dryly. Was the estate to be overrun with addled women spouting dire predictions?

"Aye," Nevin said glumly.

"Well, at least now 'tis you she's worried about. A fortnight past, she was telling Silvan that my brother and I were 'cloaked in darkness,' or something of the like. What does she fear will happen to you?"

" 'Tis the oddest thing. She seems to think your betrothed will harm me in some fashion."

"Anya?" Drustan laughed. "She's but five and ten. And, I've heard, a most biddable lass."

Nevin shook his head with a rueful smile. "Milord, 'tis futile to seek sense in it. My mother is not well. If you should encounter her and she carries on like a madwoman, 'tis because she's worsening daily. I believe the walk to the castle is beyond her abilities, but should she somehow manage it, I beg you be gentle with her. She's ill, very ill."

"I'll warn Da and Dageus. Doona fash yourself, we'll simply guide her back home should she roam." He made a mental note to be kinder to the old woman. He hadn't realized she was so ill.

"Thank you, milord."

Drustan started down the corridor again, then stopped and glanced back. He enjoyed Nevin's philosophical mind and wondered how the priest reconciled a fortune-telling mother with his faith. It might also shed light on his tolerance for the MacKeltar. Drustan knew Nevin had been in residence long enough to have heard most of the rumors by now. Men of the Kirk generally held staunch views on pagan doings, but Nevin radiated some inner understanding that defied Drustan's comprehension. "Do any of her predictions ever come true?"

Nevin smiled serenely. "If there is aught of truth in her yew castings, 'tis because God chooses to speak in such manner."

"You doona think pagan and Christian are breached by an irreconcilable chasm?"

Nevin considered his answer a moment. "I know 'tis the common belief, but nay. It offends me not that she reads her sticks; it grieves me that she thinks to change what she sees therein. His Will will be."

"So has she been right or not?" Drustan pressed. Nevin was oft evasive, difficult to pin down. But Drustan sensed he didn't intend to be evasive, he was merely nonjudgmental to an extreme.

"If someone is to harm me, 'tis my Father's will. I shan't naysay Him."

"In other words, you won't tell me."

Nevin's eyes sparkled with amusement. "Milord, God doesn't bear any of His creations ill will. He give us opportunities. 'Tis all in the way you view it. My mother has a suspicious mind, so she sees suspicious things. Keep your eyes open, milord, for the chances He gives you. Keep your heart true, and I bid you, use what gifts He may have given you with love, and you will never wander from His grace."

"What do you mean, 'gifts'?"

Another calm smile, and some fascinating awareness in Nevin's clear blue gaze.

Drustan smiled uneasily and wound down the corridors to the Greathall.

Gwen had just walked into the hall and slumped into a chair when he came down.

She nearly fell off her chair, so startled was she to see him walking *toward* her and not skulking out the back entrance. Her first instinct was to leap up, fling her arms around his leg like a child, and cling so he couldn't get away from her. But she reconsidered, thinking he might just shake her off him and stomp her, if the expression on his face was a true indication of his feelings about her at the moment. He was awe-inspiringly large.

She decided to try the subtle approach. "Does this mean you've finally decided to listen to me, you pigheaded, stubborn Neanderthal?"

He walked past her as if he hadn't even heard her.

"*Drustan!*"

"What?" he snapped, spinning around to look at her. "Can't you leave me in peace? My life was fine, wonderful until you appeared. Flitting about"—his gaze raked over her bountiful curves, nicely fluffed in her gown—"trying to tempt me into making a fankle of my wedding—"

"Flitting? Tempting *you*? Could you show off your legs more? Walk around with no shirt on a bit more often? Oh, silly me, of course you couldn't, you're shirtless *all* the time."

Drustan blinked, and she saw the hint of her Drustan's grin tugging at his lips, but he fought it admirably.

Casually, he adjusted his sporran, hiking his plaid up a bit more. He tossed his silky black hair over his shoulder and arched a dark brow.

Her hormones broke out party streamers and kazoos.

She leaned forward, folding her arms beneath her

chest. She felt the edging on her bodice graze her nipple. *Two can play that game, Drustan.*

His silvery eyes changed instantly. Icy amusement was replaced by untamed lust. For a long, suspended moment, she thought he was going to duck his head, charge her, and carry her up the stairs to a bed.

She held her breath, hoping. If he did, at least then she might be able to soothe him enough to get him to listen—after, of course, they made love nine million times and her own hormones had been properly soothed.

She peeped at him from beneath her brows, her gaze a blatant challenge. A come-hither-if-you-dare look. She hadn't known she had it in her. But she was realizing there were a lot of things she hadn't known she had in her, until she'd met Drustan MacKeltar.

"You know naught what you provoke," he growled.

"Oh, yes, I do," she shot right back. "A coward. A man who's afraid to hear me out because I might prove inconvenient to his plans. I might dishevel his tidy world," she mocked.

The flicker in his eyes blazed into flame. His gaze raked over her exposed bosom. She nearly gasped at the savagery in his expression; he was shaking, vibrating with suppressed . . . desire?

"Is that what you want? You want me to tup you?" he demanded roughly.

"If that's the only way I can get you to hold still long enough to listen to me," she snapped.

"Were I to tup you, lass, you wouldna be speakin', for your mouth would be busy with other things, and I, of a certain, wouldna be listenin'. So give over, unless you're lookin' for a rough roll in the heather with a man who wishes he'd never laid eyes upon you."

He spun on his heel and stalked out the door.

When he was gone, Gwen sighed gustily. She knew

that for a moment she'd almost had him, had almost provoked him into another kiss, but the man's willpower was nothing short of amazing.

She knew he was attracted to her, it crackled in the air between them. She consoled herself with the thought that he must have some doubts or he wouldn't be so studiously avoiding her.

Whatever his reasons, too many days were slipping by with nothing to show for them, and the arrival of his betrothed drew nearer, as did his impending abduction.

Although she'd cornered him on two occasions, he'd jumped upon his horse and galloped away, and until her riding improved, it was an effective escape.

She felt like a fool, trying to be everywhere, watching for a glimpse of him. She'd picked the lock on his chamber door last night, only to find he'd slipped out the window and scaled the damn castle wall to get away from her.

When he'd crashed into the prickly bush, she'd stared with wide eyes, any thoughts of laughing firmly squelched by the sight of him nude. It had been all she could do not to fling herself out the window at him. He was magnificent. Watching him stroll around every day was killing her. Especially when he wore a kilt, because she knew from experience that he wore nothing beneath it. The thought of him hung heavy and naked beneath his plaid made her mouth go dry every time she looked at him. Probably because all the moisture in her body went somewhere else.

Her antics had not gone unnoticed, nor had she missed that several of the maids and guards had taken to loitering about the castle proper, watching with unconcealed amusement.

Love hath no pride . . .

Yeah, well, Gwen Cassidy did, and humbling herself wasn't a whole lot of fun.

She suspected that by the time she finally wore him down—as stubborn as he was—she was going to be downright pissed off.

Didn't he know how dangerous it was to piss off a woman?

· 20 ·

Gwen had a plan.

Foolproof so far as she could see.

She'd had ample time to reflect upon the errors of her ways. Although the list was long and inclusive of virtually everything she'd done since the moment she'd arrived in the sixteenth century, it was not beyond salvaging. She was still astonished by how thoroughly emotions could cloud one's actions. Never in her life had she done so many stupid things in such rapid succession.

But she was under control now, and soon to be in control of him.

She was going to tell him her story again, only this time he was going to listen to every single detail of it: From the moment he'd awakened in the cave to the moment she'd lost him, including what he'd eaten, said, worn, what she'd eaten, said, worn. And somewhere in it, she was convinced she'd find the catalyst that would make him remember. She'd pondered closed timeline curves for hours last night, along with the thermodynamic, psychological, and cosmological arrows of time. She was convinced the memory was imprinted in his DNA, and despite the arrows indicating one could only remember forward, not backward, she wasn't quite certain she believed that.

She was going to give it her best shot to prove the theory wrong. After all, the quantum was rarely predictable. Even Richard Feynman, winner of the Nobel prize in physics for his work in quantum electrodynamics, had maintained that nobody really understood quantum theory. Mathematical theory was vastly different than the world implied by such equations.

She'd concluded that there had never been two Drustans, merely two fourth-dimensional manifestations of a single set of cells. Rather like a solitary beam of light refracted by a prism, where the beam of light was Drustan, and the prism was the fourth dimension. Although the single light aimed into the prism would refract in multiple directions, it was still only one source of light. Were that light a person, why wouldn't his cells bear the imprint of his alternate journey? If the memory was there, perhaps remembering would be too confusing, so the mind would seek to resolve those "memories" by labeling them "dreams"; if recalled at all, discarded as nocturnal fancies.

Drustan was going to listen to every word, if she had to talk herself hoarse.

And she knew just how and where he was going to be doing it, she thought smugly, tucking the lance beneath her arm. She might be small, but she was *not* harmless. Enough shilly-shallying about, feeling wounded and ineffectual. It was time to do battle.

"Get in there and try it," Gwen told the guard.

He cast her a dubious glance.

"Go on, just try it," she said peevishly. "I'm not going to hurt you."

The guard glanced at Silvan, who was leaning against the wall, arms folded, smiling. At his nod, the guard sighed and did as he was told.

"Can you get out?" Gwen asked a few moments later.

There was the sound of muffled thuds, kicks, and punches, then, "Nay, milady, I canna."

"Try harder," Gwen encouraged.

More thuds. Soft cursing. *Good*, she mused. *Perfect*.

She and Silvan exchanged smug grins.

Drustan crept down the stairs, his bare feet silent on the stones. It was four in the morning, and although she was asleep, stealth was ever wise with *her* in residence. He'd heard her enter her chamber last eve, try the connecting door, then sigh and lean against it when she found it still barricaded. The bed ropes had squeaked for a time as she'd tossed, but finally all had grown quiet.

He'd stretched out on his back in his bed, hands folded behind his head, refusing to think about her sleeping nude on the other side of the wall. But the tricky part about refusing to think about something was that you had to think about it in order to remind yourself what not to think about.

And he knew she would. Sleep with nothing on, that is. She was a sensual wee lass who would enjoy the silky slide of velvet coverlets against her fine, smooth, creamy skin. Slipping with tender velvety abrasion over her puckered nipples, twining about her hips, probably twisting and turning to enjoy—

Exasperated, Drustan gave a vicious shake of his head. Christ, he was going mad, that was all there was to it.

Probably from being spied on all the time. She thought he didn't know she lurked about watching him all the time, but he knew. She was a living heat, strolling about his castle, all lush curves and temptation.

Thus such stealth to do a man's business. He could have gone outside, but it irritated him that he'd even briefly considered it. It was his castle, by Amergin! She was making him positively irrational.

As he rounded the corner, he stubbed his toe and cursed in five languages. Glancing down, he made a mental note to have the pile of lances moved out to the armory. He couldn't imagine why they were lying beside the staircase in the first place.

Shaking his head and muttering beneath his breath, he walked the few paces down the corridor and slipped into the garderobe.

⧽✿⧼

Aha! Gwen shouted silently. *Finally!* She dropped down from the stone arch in the corridor. People rarely looked up, and the darkness in the corridor had provided further camouflage. She landed lightly on the balls of her feet, hurried to the hall, and plucked up several steel lances that were piled flush to the wall of the stairs.

Creeping silently back to the door of the garderobe, she braced one end of the steel lance against the stone wall and then gently, oh-so-quietly, wedged it into place. She understood bracing and pressure points with the best of them.

Two, then three, then five—although only two had held the helpful brawny guard just fine. Drustan was a large man, and she wasn't taking any chances that he might crash the door down on her head.

A small giggle built inside her. Trapping the laird of the castle in his own garderobe appealed to her sense of humor. Then again, the fact that she'd been going without sleep for the past three nights, waiting for him to make a nocturnal journey, probably had a bit to do with it too.

She stepped away from the door and ducked into the Greathall, thinking to give him a few minutes of privacy and time to discover he was locked in and get the worst of it out of his system.

She soon found out she'd woefully underestimated how bad "the worst" would be.

~ ❦ ~

Drustan raked a hand through his hair and fumbled in the dark for the door. When it didn't budge, a part of him was unsurprised. Yet another part of him met the fact with a kind of glad resignation.

She wanted battle? Battle she would get. It would be a pleasure to have it out with her finally. Once he'd ripped the door from the framing, he would exact vengeance upon her wee body with gleeful abandon. No more honorable *I-won't-touch-you-because-I'm-betrothed.*

Nay—he'd touch her. Any damn place and any damn way he wanted to. As many times as he wanted to.

Until she begged and whimpered beneath him.

She'd been trying to drive him mad? Well, he was giving in to it. He would act like the animal she made him feel like being. The hell with Anya, the hell with duty and honor, the hell with discipline.

He needed to tup. Her. Now.

He slammed his body against the door.

It scarce shuddered.

Howling, he flung himself at it again. And again, and again.

It didn't give a hairbreadth. Furious, he slammed his fists on the door above his head. Another shudder, but nothing significant.

He stepped back, eyeing it warily, telling himself he did not feel a bud of respect blossoming. Might the canny wench have wedged braces between the wall and the door, *all* the way up? Christ, he'd never get out! He knew how sturdy the door was, it had been hewn extra thick for privacy.

"Open up!" he roared, pounding it with his fist.

Nothing.

"Lass, if you open up now, I'll leave you in one piece, but I swear to you, if you keep me in here *one more moment* I will tear you limb from wee limb," he threatened.

Silence.

"Lass! Wench! Gwen-do-*lynnnnnn!*"

※

Outside the door, Gwen eyed the five lances lodged at varying angles between the door and the stone wall. Nope. No way. He was never getting out of there. Not until she was good and ready.

But it was pretty darned impressive how much the door shuddered each time his body hit it.

"You might have to let him yell himself hoarse, m'dear," Silvan said, leaning over the balustrade.

Gwen tipped her head back. "I'm sorry, Silvan. I didn't mean to wake you."

He grinned, and Gwen realized where Drustan had

gotten his mischievous grin. "I wouldn't have missed seeing my son getting barricaded in the privy by a wee lass for anything. Bonny fortune with your plan, m'dear," he said with a smile, then ambled off.

Gwen eyed the shuddering door, then clamped her hands over her ears and sat down to wait him out.

※

"I brought ye coffee, lass," Nell shouted.

"Thanks, Nell," Gwen shouted back.

They both jumped at the next enraged roar from behind the garderobe door.

"Is that you, Nell?" Drustan thundered.

Nell shrugged. "Aye, 'tis me. Bringin' coffee to the lass."

"You're dismissed. Fired. The end. Hie you from my castle. Begone."

Nell rolled her eyes and smiled at Gwen. "Be ye wantin' breakfast, lass?" she said sweetly, loud enough that Drustan could hear it.

Another roar.

※

By ten o'clock she thought he might soon be ready to talk. He'd threatened, blustered, even tried to sweet-talk her. Then the bribery had begun. He'd let her live if she let him out immediately. He'd give her three horses, two sheep, and a cow. He'd give her a pouch of coin, three horses, two sheep, not just a cow but a milking cow, *and* set her up anywhere in England, if she would just leave his castle and not bother him again for the rest of his life. The only offer/threat that had perked her momentary interest was when he'd shouted that he was going to "toop her 'til her bonny legs fell off."

She should be so lucky.

But he'd been silent for fifteen minutes now.

Gwen eyed the door, knowing that she shouldn't instigate their little discussion. It would undermine her position as the one in control. No, *he* had to address her in a reasonable tone first.

And it wasn't long before he said, " 'Tisna verra pleasant in here, lass." He sounded pouty. She smothered a laugh.

" 'Tisna verra pleasant"—she imitated his accent—"out here either. Do you realize I've stayed up for the past three nights waiting for you to go to the bathroom? I was beginning to think you never did."

Growl.

She sighed and pressed her hand against the door, as if to soothe him. Or be closer to him. This was the closest they'd been in days, with only a door between them. "I know it's not very pleasant, but it was the only way I could think of to get you to listen. You escaped your chamber; where else could I trap you?"

"Let me out, and I'll listen to whatever you wish to say," he said quickly. Too quickly.

"I'm not falling for that, Drustan," she said, lowering herself to the stone floor. In a pair of someone's outgrown trews, she crossed her legs comfortably and leaned her back against the door. She'd been wearing them nightly, with a flowing linen shirt, as she'd clung to the stone arch above the garderobe.

"Plenty o' cream, as ye like it, Gwen," Nell said, placing a bowl of porridge, cream, and peaches beside her.

A roar from behind the door. "Are you serving her porridge?"

" 'Tis naught of yer concern," Nell replied calmly.

"I'm sorry, Drustan," Gwen said soothingly, "but this

is all your fault. If even once you had been willing to sit down and drink some coffee or have breakfast with me and talk, I wouldn't have to be doing this. But time is slipping by and we really need to get some things cleared up. Nell's leaving now, and it's going to be just you and me."

Silence. Stretching, taut.

"What do you want from me, lass?" he finally said wearily.

"What I want is for you to listen. I'm going to tell you everything I can remember about our time to-gether in the future. I've thought about it a lot, and there's got to be something that will make you re-member. It's possible that I'm simply missing whatever it is."

She heard a huge sigh from behind the door. "Fine, lass. Let's hear it all this time."

Drustan sat on the floor of the garderobe, his feet stretched out, arms folded over his chest, his back against the door. He closed his eyes and waited for her to begin. He'd worn himself down raging. Grudgingly, he admired her persistence and resolve. The fit he'd had would have terrified any lass he'd ever known. While he'd raged and flung himself at the door, he pictured her standing outside it, arms folded beneath her lovely breasts, tapping a foot, waiting patiently for him to quiet. Waiting hours—he felt half a day might have passed.

She was formidable.

And by Amergin, a bit too clever to be completely addled.

You know she's not addled, why doona you admit it?
Because if she's not addled, she's telling the truth.
And why does that fash you?

He had no answer for that. He had no idea why the lass turned him into a babbling idiot.

"I'm twenty-five years old," he heard her say through the door.

"That old?" he mocked. "My bride is but five and ten." He smiled when she growled.

"That's called statutory rape in my century," she said with an edge in her voice.

Statutory, he mused. Yet another unclear phrase.

"That means you can go to prison for it," she added.

He snorted. "Why would I care how old you are? Does that have aught to do with your tale?"

"You're getting the long version with a bit of background. Now, hush."

Drustan hushed, finding himself curious what she would tell him.

"I took a vacation to Scotland, without knowing it was a senior citizens' bus tour . . ."

In time, Drustan relaxed back against the door and listened in silence. He fancied from the sound of her voice that she was seated much the same, back to the door, talking over her shoulder to him.

Which meant, in a way, they were touching, spine to spine. The thought was intimate as he sat in the dark, listening to her voice.

He liked the sound of her voice, he decided. It was low, melodic, firm, and confident. Why hadn't he ever noticed that before? he wondered. That her voice contained a degree of self-assurance that had to have come from somewhere?

Mayhap because whenever she'd spoken to him, he'd been hopelessly distracted by his attraction to her, but now—since he couldn't see her, his other senses were heightened.

Aye, she had a fine voice, and he'd like to hear her sing an old ballad, he thought, or mayhap a lullaby to his children—

He shook his head and focused on her words, not his idiotic thoughts.

※

Nell silently handed Gwen yet another mug of coffee and slipped away.

"And we drove up the hill to the stones, but your castle was gone. All that was left was the foundation and a few crumbling walls."

"What date did I send you through the stones?"

"September twenty-first—you called it Mabon. The autumnal equinox."

Drustan sucked in a breath. *That* wasn't commonly related in the legends, that the stones could be used only on the solstices and equinoxes.

"And how did I use the stones?" he pressed.

"You're skipping ahead of me," she complained.

"Well, tell me, then go back. How did I use the stones?"

※

Above her, behind the balustrade, Silvan and Nell sat on the floor, listening. Nell was flushed from her many dashes from Gwen's side into the kitchen, up the servants' stairs, and around to join Silvan. All quiet as a mouse.

"I doona think you should hear—" Silvan whispered, but cut off abruptly when Nell pressed her mouth to his ear.

"If yer thinkin' I've lived here twelve years and dinna

know what ye are, old man, yer dafter than Drustan thinks Gwen is."

Silvan's eyes widened.

"I can read too, ye know," Nell whispered stiffly.

Silvan's eyes grew enormous. "You *can?*"

"Shh. We're missing it."

❦

"You'd collected paint rocks. You broke them open in the circle and etched formulas and symbols on the inside faces of the thirteen stones."

A chill brushed Drustan's spine.

"Then you drew three more on the slab. And we waited for midnight."

"Och, Christ," Drustan murmured. How could she have knowledge of such things? The legends hinted the stones were used for travel, but no one—save himself, Dageus, and Silvan—knew the how of it. Except now, Gwen Cassidy did.

"Do you recall the symbols?" he asked roughly.

She described several of them to him, and her descriptions, although incomplete, bore enough accuracy to unsettle him deeply.

His mind rejecting it, he floundered for something solid to think about. Something less disturbing. He grinned, striking upon a fine topic. He had no doubt she'd try to change it quickly. "You claimed I took your virginity. When did I make love to you, lass?" he said huskily, turning his mouth toward the door.

Gwen sat on the other side and turned her mouth toward the door. She kissed it, then felt utterly foolish, but from the sound of his voice, it seemed as if he, too, was sitting with his back to the door. And his voice had sounded closer that time, as if he'd turned his mouth toward hers.

"In the stones, right before we went through."

"Did I know you were a virgin?"

"No," she whispered.

"What?"

"No," she said more loudly.

"You deceived me?"

"No, I just didn't think it was important enough to mention," she said defensively.

"Bullshit. Sometimes not telling the whole truth is the same thing as lying."

Gwen winced, not liking having her own words tossed back in her face. "I was afraid you wouldn't make love to me if you knew," she admitted. *And you were afraid I'd leave you if I knew the truth about you. What a fine pair we were.*

"Why were you still a maiden at twenty and five?"

"I . . . I just never found the right man."

"And what would the right man be for you, Gwen Cassidy?"

"I hardly think that has anything to do—"

"Surely you can find it in your heart to grant me a few boons, seeing where you've kept me trapped for the day."

"Oh, all right," she said grudgingly. "The right man . . . let's see, he'd be smart yet playful. He'd have a good heart and be faithful—"

"Faithful is important to you?"

"Very. I don't share. If he's my man, he's mine only."

She could hear a smile in his voice when he said, "Go on."

"Well, he'd like simple things. Like good coffee and good food. A family—"

"You want children?"

"Dozens," she sighed.

"Would you teach them to read and such?"

Gwen drew a deep breath, her eyes misting. Life required a delicate balance. Her own had been painfully unbalanced. She knew exactly what she'd teach her children. "I'd teach them to read and to dream and to look at the stars and wonder. I'd teach them the value of imagination. I'd teach them to play every bit as hard as they worked." She sighed heavily before adding softly, "And I'd teach them that all the brains in the world can't compensate for love."

She heard him draw a harsh breath. He was silent a long time, as if her words had meant much to him. "You truly believe love is the most important thing?"

"I know it is." She'd learned all kinds of lessons in Scotland. A career, success, and critical acclaim—none of it amounted to much of anything without love. It was the necessary ingredient that had been missing all her life.

"How did I make love to you, Gwendolyn Cassidy?"

Gwen's lips parted on a soft moan. The simple words he'd just said had sent heat lancing through her body. He was beginning to sound like her Drustan. This intimate talk was melting her; perhaps it was melting his defenses as well.

"How, Gwen? Tell me how I made love to you. Tell me in much detail."

Wetting her lips, she began, her voice lowering intimately.

❧

Silvan grabbed Nell's hand and tugged.

Nay, she mouthed.

We can't eavesdrop on this, he mouthed back. *'Tis not proper.*

Proper be damned, old man. I'm not leavin'. Her lips were pursed, her gaze stubborn.

Silvan gaped but, after a few moments, sat back down.

And when Gwen spoke, he found himself ceding her a sort of privacy by imagining it was Nell telling him in such detail how he'd made love to her. At first he kept his chin firmly down, eyes averted, but after a time he stole a surreptitious peek at her.

Nell did not look away.

Brown eyes met blue and held.

His heart pounded.

"And then you said something to me, there at the end, that I'll never forget. You said the sweetest words, and they kind of shivered through me. You said it in that funny voice you have."

"What did I say?" Drustan moved his hand on his cock. His kilt was tossed to the side, his legs spread, palm around his shaft. He was so aroused that he thought he was going to explode. She'd told him in detail how he'd made love to her, and it had been the most erotic experience of his life. Sitting in the dark, watching the images in his mind's eye, he'd felt as if he'd been reliving it. His mind had filled in details she'd not mentioned, details that may have sprung solely from his imagination or from some deeply buried memory. He knew not.

He cared not.

It no longer signified if she was lying or telling the truth. He wanted Gwen Cassidy in a way that defied reason, in a way he refused to further question.

He admired her tenacity; he desired her with every fiber of his being; she made him laugh, she made him furious. She stood her ground; she believed him a Druid and desired him anyway.

By Amergin, he—thrice-jilted Drustan MacKeltar—

was being pursued by a woman who knew what he was.

He could no longer recall why he'd ever resisted her to begin with.

He struggled against an intense desire to bring himself to completion, to find release—a release he'd desperately needed since the moment she'd entered his home. But, nay, not in so empty a fashion. He wanted it with her. Inside her.

"What you said was *so* romantic," she said with a little sigh.

"Um-hmm," he managed. When she spoke again, it took him a few moments to realize what she was saying.

And when he did, he leaped to his feet, roaring, but she kept speaking: "If aught must be lost, 'twill be my honor for yours. If one must be forsaken, 'twill be my soul for yours. Should death come anon, 'twill be my life for yours. I am Given. That's what you said."

As she finished, Drustan doubled over. A spark of heat and light built inside him and spread, enveloping him. He couldn't talk, he could scarce breathe, as wave after wave of emotion crashed over him. . . .

ᙠᘯ

Gwen doubled over, as a wave of intense emotion crashed over her. She felt funny, really weird, like she'd just said something irrevocable. . . .

ᙠᘯ

"Och, Christ, Nellie," Silvan whispered, stunned both by Gwen's words and by the realization that he was holding Nell's hand, and she was *letting* him. "She just married him."

"Married?" Nell's fingers tightened on his.

"Aye, the Druid vows. I didn't work that spell, even when I wed my wife."

Nell's lips parted on a "why," but then they both peeked breathlessly over the balustrade, desperate to hear what would happen next.

· 21 ·

"Ahem," Drustan said after a long time. "Do you know you just married me, lass?"

"What?" Gwen shouted.

"Would you please let your *husband* out of the garderobe?"

Gwen was stunned. She'd married him with those words?

"Those were the Druid wedding vows you just said to me, a binding spell, and I doona understand how you knew it, but—"

God, he still didn't remember! she realized with a sinking sensation, even though she'd told him all of it, down to the minute details. "I knew it, you dolt, because you said it to me! And I didn't *know* I was marrying you—"

"Doona be thinkin' you'll be gettin' out of it," he said testily.

"I'm not trying to get out of it—"

"You're not?" he exclaimed.

"You *want* to be married to me? Without even remembering?"

" 'Tis too late. We are. Nothing can undo it. Best you grow accustomed to it." He punched the door for emphasis.

"What about your betrothed?"

He muttered something about his betrothed that warmed her heart. "But that's another thing I doona understand, lass. If what you claimed happened did indeed happen, I doona understand why I wouldn't have woven a spell for you to carry to me. I would have known the possibility existed that I might not make it back. I would surely have given you a memory spell."

"A m-m-memory sp-spell?" Gwen sputtered. Could it have been that simple all along? Did she have the key to make him remember, but he'd not told her how to use it? What hadn't she told him so far? She'd deliberately withheld a few details so she might have something to test him with should he suddenly claim to have regained total recall. Closing her eyes, she thought hard, sifting through details. Oh!

Have you a good memory, Gwen Cassidy? he'd asked her in the car as they'd approached *Ban Drochaid.* "Oh, God. Like something that rhymed?" she shrieked.

"It may have."

"If you'd given me such a spell, would you have told me how to use it?" she said accusingly.

There was a long silence, then he admitted, "Like as not, I wouldn't have told you until the last possible moment."

"And if at the last possible moment you melted?" she pressed.

There was a harsh intake of air, then an extended silence behind the door. Then, "Speak your rhyme if you have one!" he exclaimed.

She turned around and faced the door, then laid her palms and cheek against it.

Quietly but clearly, she spoke.

Drustan was facing the door, his palms spread against the cool wood, his cheek pressed to it. He'd whispered the Druid wedding vows back the moment she'd said them. There was no way she was getting away from him now. His former betrothal meant naught. He was well and truly wed. Druid binding vows could never be broken. There was no such thing as Druid divorce.

He braced himself, waiting for her words, hoping and fearing.

Her melodic voice carried clearly through the door. And as she spoke, the words shivered through him, mixing past and future with a cosmic mortar and pestle.

"Wither thou goest, there goest I, two flames sparked from but one ember; both forward and backward doth time fly, wither thou art, remember."

He hit the floor doubled over, clutching his head.

Och, Christ, he thought, *my head will surely split.* It felt as if he were being ripped in two, or *had* been ripped in two and some unseen force was trying to crush two parts back together again.

It was purest instinct to fight it.

Words from a dream place buffeted him: *You don't trust me.*

I do trust you, wee lass. I am trusting you far more than you know. But he wasn't. He was afraid he'd lose her.

Then images:

Another flash of those blue trews, a naked Gwen beneath him, above him. A crimson scrap of ribbon in his teeth. The white bridge.

You would fight me to the death. The counterfeit's lips moved soundlessly. *I see. I see now why only one lives. 'Tis not nature which is innately indifferent, but our own fear that causes us to destroy each other. I beg you, accept me. Let us both be.*

I will never accept you, Drustan roared.

He'd fought, viciously and victoriously.

Let us both be.

Drustan drew upon his Druid will, forcing himself to relax his defenses, forcing himself to submit.

Love her, the counterfeit whispered.

"Och, Gwen," Drustan breathed. "Love *Gwen.*"

Gwen eyed the door warily. There'd not been a sound from behind it since the moment she'd said the rhyme.

Worried, she scratched at the door. "Drustan?" she asked nervously.

There was a long silence.

"Drustan, are you okay?"

"Gwen, lass, open this door this very instant," he ordered. He sounded winded, out of breath.

"You have to answer some questions first," she hedged, wanting to know exactly who would be stepping out of the garderobe. "What was the name of the store—"

"Barrett's," he said impatiently.

"What did you want me to buy you in the store to wear?"

"I wanted purple trews and a purple shirt and you gave me a black T-shirt and black trews and hard white shoes. I didn't fit in your blue trews and you threatened to help me fit with my sword." His voice deepened smugly. "But I recall your threats ceased once I kissed you thoroughly. You became quite the amenable lass after that."

She blushed, remembering exactly how wantonly she'd responded to his kiss. A tremor of excitement raced through her. He was *her* Drustan again! "So what was the saleslady's name in Barrett's? The bitchy, unattractive one," she added, wrinkling her nose.

"Truth be told, I haven't the veriest, lass. I had eyes for only you."

Oh, *God*, what a great answer!

"Open the bletherin' door!"

Tears misted her eyes as she leaped up to hit the top lance and knock it loose. It clattered to the floor, followed by the second one.

"And what was I wearing when you made love to me?" she said, kicking the third and fourth out of the way, still unable to believe that she had him back.

"When I made love to you?" he purred through the door. "Nothing. But before that you wore tan trews cut off at the thigh, a chemise cut off at the waist, boots named Timberland, socks named Polo Sport, and a red ribbon I—"

She yanked the door open. "Removed with your teeth and tongue," she cried.

"Gwendolyn!" He crushed her in his arms and kissed her, a deep soul kiss that seared her all the way down to her toes.

When Gwen wrapped her arms around his neck, he cupped his hands beneath her bottom and lifted her, pulling her legs about his waist. She locked her ankles behind him. He was *never* getting away from her again.

"You want me, lass. Me. Knowing all that I am," he said incredulously.

"Always will," she mumbled against his mouth.

He laughed exultantly.

Their coming together was not a gentle thing. She tugged at his kilt, he tore at her trews, clothing flew this way and that, until, gasping for breath between kisses, they both stood naked near the staircase in the Greathall. Gwen glanced up at him, eyes widening, breath coming in short pants, as she belatedly realized where they were. Then her gaze drifted over his incredible body, and she forgot not only where she was but what century she was in. There was nothing but him.

Silvery eyes glittering, he grabbed her hand, tugged her down the corridor into the buttery, slammed the door shut with a kick, and flattened her up against the wall, leaving their clothing strewn about the hall.

Gwen pressed her palms against his muscular chest and sighed with pleasure. She couldn't get enough of touching him. During the time he'd not known her, it had been the worst sort of torture, looking at him every day, unable to caress and kiss him. She had a lot of lost time to make up for, and began by tracing her hands up over his shoulders, down his back, skimming to his muscular hips. His skin was velvet over steel, he smelled of man and spice and every woman's fantasy.

"Ah, God, I missed you, lass." He took her mouth roughly, hands bracketing her face, kissing her so deeply that she couldn't breathe, until he filled her lungs with his own breath.

"I missed you too," she whimpered.

"I'm so sorry, Gwen," he whispered, "for not believing you—"

"Apologize later. Kiss now!"

His laughter rolled erotic and rich in the dark buttery. He pushed her back atop sacks of grain and lowered himself over her, suspending his weight on his forearms. And he kissed her. Slow, intensely intimate kisses, and mad rushes of deep kisses. She drank him in as if he were the air she needed to survive.

Melting back against the sacks, she moaned when his muscular thigh slid between her legs. He traced hot, wet kisses down her neck, over her collarbones, across her shoulders. She wrapped her legs around his, rubbing against him wantonly, savoring the slick slide of him.

Drustan gazed down at her, marveling. She was so beautiful; her cheeks flushed, her eyes stormy with passion, her lips half parted on a soft gasp. She was his soul mate, smart, lovely, and tenacious. He would love her to his dying breath, and beyond if such was possible for a Druid and his mate. He would show her with his body all the things he felt for her, and mayhap she would murmur those tender words he'd so longed to hear back in the circle of stones when she'd given him her virginity.

She whimpered when he rasped his unshaven jaw against her nipples. She arched up, hungry for more. He shifted his body so the thick, hot length of him rested between her thighs, moving his hips in slow, even thrusts.

Then he pulled back, driving her mad, and proceeded to taste her from head to toe.

Starting at her toes.

Gwen tossed her head back in ecstasy. Long, velvety strokes of his tongue on her calves and ankles. Bending her legs, he traced silky kisses on the backs of her knees. Wet, hungry kisses on her thighs, teasing flickers against the sensitive skin where her hip met her leg.

Then deep, warm, wet kisses where she needed him the most. Lapping and nibbling, his hands glided up her body to tease her nipples as he kissed and tasted her until she shuddered against his mouth, arching her hips up for more.

Resonance built to an exquisite peak, and she shattered, crying his name.

While she was still resonating with tiny tremors, he rolled her over and ran his tongue down her spine to the hollow where her back met her hips. Then kissed and tasted and nipped every inch of her bottom. Kneading, plumping, caressing, dangerously near the hottest part of her. But not quite there. She was going to die if he didn't get inside her, she thought, gritting her teeth. She burned, she ached for want of him.

Slipping his hand between her and the sacks, he palmed her woman's mound and pulled her back against him, resting the heavy ridge of his cock in the cleft of her bottom. As he rubbed against her lush softness, he caught her tiny nub with his fingers, flicking lightly back and forth.

He savored the tiny cries she made, the soft pants and breathy moans, listened intently to discover just what touch elicited each sound, then played her again and again, bringing her dangerously near the peak—

—then denying for the pleasure of hearing her cries grow wilder, of feeling her hips buck back against him, of seeing such evidence of her desire. She knew what he was, and *still* wanted him with such hunger. It was more than he'd ever dreamed of having. If only she would say the words, those three simple words he longed to hear . . . Aye, he was a warrior, he was strong and manly, but, by Amergin, he *wanted* those words. He'd passed a lifetime believing a woman might never say them to him.

"Drustan!" she cried. "Please."

I love you, he thought, willing her to hear it. Willing her to say it. He traced a finger over her taut nub before slipping it inside her. He closed his eyes and groaned as she clenched around him. When she bucked back against him wildly, the last vestige of his control snapped. He became mindless with need. Wrapping his hands around her waist, he thrust into her in one sleek motion.

She sobbed with pleasure, begged him not to stop, then murmured something so raggedly that he nearly missed it.

But nay, he would not let such words slip by him!

Trembling, he stopped mid-stroke and whispered hoarsely, *"What* did you just say?"

"I said 'don't stop,' " Gwen whimpered, pressing back against him.

"Not that—the other thing you just said," he demanded.

Gwen went still. It had slipped out without conscious thought—an impassioned declaration of her feelings—God, how she loved him! She, Gwen Cassidy, was utterly and deliriously in love. She spoke quietly, savoring the warmth of her feelings, putting every ounce of her heart and soul into the words. "I love you, Drustan."

Braced on his elbows, Drustan swayed, the words hit him with such impact. "Say it again," he breathed.

"I love you," she repeated softly.

He sucked in a harsh breath and was silent a long while, relishing her words. "Ah, Gwen, my lovely wee Gwen, I thought I might ne'er hear such words." He lifted her hair away from her face and kissed her temple tenderly. "I love you. I adore you. I will cherish you all the days of my life," he vowed. "I knew even back in your century that you were the one for me, the one I'd longed for all my life."

Gwen closed her eyes, treasuring the moment, hugging his words to her.

When he moved again, thrusting into her yielding warmth, she arched back to meet him. Moving his hips, entering her slow and deep, he tipped her face to the side and kissed her with the same tempo. Increasing the pace, never breaking the kiss . . .

It was a mating of raw need and mindless melding. As if they could somehow crawl inside each other if they got close enough.

He thrust; she screamed. She clenched; he roared.

He slid his hands up her body and cupped her breasts, pulling her back against him as he drove inside her. The buttery was filled with sounds of passion, scented with the erotic musk of man and woman and sex.

When she peaked again, he exploded, crying her name.

He kept her in the buttery nigh as long as she'd kept him in the garderobe. Unable to stop touching her, loving her. Unable to believe that it had all worked out, that she'd indeed cared for him in her century, that she'd given him back the binding vows, that even though he'd failed to give her full instructions, she'd tenaciously persevered. Unable to comprehend that Gwen loved him for exactly what he was. Needing to roll it over and over in his mind as if savoring the finest brandy.

He made her tell him again and again as he reacquainted himself with every inch of her luscious body.

It was full night before he poked a cautious head out, retrieved their clothing, then swept her into his arms and carried her up to his bed.

Where she would sleep each night, he vowed, till the end of forever.

· 22 ·

Besseta Alexander sat motionless, one hand clutching her yew sticks, the other her Bible. She grimaced at her own foolishness. She knew which one was more useful, and it wasn't the fat tome.

She'd had her vision again. Nevin, blood dripping from his lips, the woman weeping, Drustan MacKeltar scowling, and that fourth nameless presence who seemed also to be troubled by her son's death.

What could one old woman do to defy fate? How could she, with too many years on her bones and too little vigor in her veins, avert the impending tragedy?

Nevin wouldn't heed her pleas. She'd begged him to give up his post and return to Edinburgh, but he'd refused. She'd pretended to be grievously ill, but he'd seen through her ploys. Sometimes she wondered that the lad had sprung from her loins, so implacable was his faith in God, so resistant was he to her "sight."

He'd forced a promise from her that she would not harm Drustan MacKeltar. In truth, she didn't wish to harm anyone. She only wanted her son alive. But she'd begun to realize that she was going to have to harm someone or lose Nevin.

She sat rocking for time uncounted as morning slipped away into afternoon and blended with gloaming, fighting the yawning darkness in her mind.

It was full twilight, the Highlands alive with the hum of frogs and soft hooting of owls, when she heard bells jingling, voices shouting, and the thunder of horses approaching the cottage.

Besseta pushed herself from her chair, scurried to the door, and opened it a crack.

When she saw the gypsy caravan, she closed it to a hairbreadth, for the wild gypsies frightened her. She counted ten and seven wagons in the caravan, gaily decorated and pulled by prancing horses draped in silks. They thundered past, toward Balanoch.

Nevin had told her some time ago that the gypsies camped each summer near the MacKeltar estate, where they hosted a trading fair in Balanoch, told fortunes, and mingled with the village folk. There would be wild dancing and bonfires and, next year, babes with dark eyes and skin.

Besseta shuddered, closed the door, and leaned against it.

But as a possibility slowly took shape in her mind, she struggled to rise above her fears. With the gypsies' dark arts, she could remove the threat without harming anyone. Well . . . not *really* harming anyone. The Rom sold powerful spells and enchantments cheek by jowl with their more ordinary wares. They cost dearly, but she knew where to find an illuminated gold-leafed tome that would more than cover the price for anything she sought. The longer she considered it, the more appealing the solution seemed. If she paid the gypsies to enchant the laird, she wouldn't really be harming him; she would just be . . . suspending him. Indefinitely. So that Nevin might live out his life in safety and peace.

It would mean she would have to seek those wild creatures out, brave their bawdy, sinful camp, but for her beloved Nevin, she would brave anything.

Silvan and Nell had fled their perch the moment Gwen released Drustan from the garderobe.

Nell hadn't needed to wait around to see what was going to happen next. During Drustan and Gwen's intimate talk, she'd been surprised the door itself hadn't gone up in flames.

She'd followed Silvan in a blind dash to his tower, where they'd collapsed on his bed, huffing and sorely out of breath from their mad race up the hundred stairs.

When her heart finally stopped pounding, she realized, with much consternation, where she perched. On the laird's bed! Next to him! She tensed to move away.

With strong hands on her waist, he caught her before she could flee and turned her face toward his with a firm hand beneath her chin. His eyes were brimming with emotion as he searched her gaze. Deep in their brown depths, tiny golden flecks glittered. She couldn't look away for anything. She gazed at him mutely.

Then slowly, so slowly that he gave her a thousand lifetimes to turn away, he lowered his lips toward hers.

Nell's breath hitched in her throat. It had been twelve years since she'd kissed a man. Did she even recall how?

"It has been long since I last kissed a lass, Nellie," he said huskily, as if sensing her fears. "I beg you be patient. You might need to remind me of the finer nuances."

Her breath came out in a sudden rush, ending in a

small moan. His admission dashed her fears. In all her years at Castle Keltar, she'd not once seen Silvan woo a woman. She'd thought he was simply discreet about his manly needs, mayhap went to the village to satisfy his urges, but was it possible he'd been as alone as she had? She wanted to ask how long but couldn't bring herself to voice the question. No matter, for he read it in her eyes.

"Since my wife died, Nellie."

She gasped.

"Would you kiss such an untried man?" he asked softly.

Not trusting herself to speak, she nodded.

His first brush was soft and tentative, much how she felt. And he didn't try to plunge right in, nay, Silvan kissed her as if she were made of fine china. Kissed her lips, brushing back and forth, kissed her nose, her chin, then her lips again. Kissed the corners of her mouth.

Then pulled away and regarded her soberly.

She tried a tentative smile.

His second kiss was warm and encouraging. By the third touch of his lips to hers, a part of her she'd thought dead was dancing a Scottish reel. And remembering how to kiss as if she'd never stopped. *He* certainly hadn't forgotten!

His fifth was deep and hungry with passion.

When he finally broke that kiss—she couldn't have for anything—he drew back and said softly, "Och, Nellie, there is a question I've been wishing to ask you. And if I am prying, well, then prying I'll be. 'Tis long past time we spoke freely with each other. Would you tell me, sweet lass, what on earth happened to you the night I found you?"

When tears misted her eyes, he wrapped his arms around her and held her tightly.

"There, lass," he whispered. "I've been a damn fool for far too long. So many things I should have said, but I was . . . afraid."

"Afraid?" Nell whispered incredulously. "What might Silvan MacKeltar fear?"

"Och, the possibilities were endless, the fears myriad. That I couldn't make all your hurt go away. That I might make a fankle of things with you, and you'd leave, and my lads loved you so. That you might think me strange—"

"Ye *are* strange, Silvan," Nell said seriously.

He sighed. "That you wouldn't love me, Nellie."

Words she couldn't bring herself to say trembled on her lips. Words that frightened her, words that would make her heart vulnerable again.

So she offered those words to him silently by pressing her lips to his, hoping they might roll off in the kiss and find their way into his heart.

⁂

Dozens of candles shimmered in the laird's bedchamber.

Drustan had made love to her yet another time, so many times, she'd lost count. Gwen's body felt deliciously swollen by kisses and thorough loving from head to toe. In the candlelight, his dark skin shimmered golden, his silky black hair gleamed. She gazed at him, marveling. She had *her* Drustan back. She still couldn't believe it.

"You really meant it when you said you were going to 'toop me until my legs fell off,' didn't you?" she teased, wondering if she would be able to walk by morning.

"By Amergin, Gwen, it was killing me watching you walk around the castle! I was obsessed with you. As much as you spied on me, I watched you. And had you stopped, I like as not would have begun stalking you instead."

"A shame I didn't stop, then. I was getting rather sick of humiliating myself."

He winced and stretched himself atop her, propping his weight on his elbows. Smoothing a wisp of hair behind her ear, he whispered, "Och, lass, forgive me."

"For what? Being a stubborn medieval man and refusing to believe me right away?" she teased.

"Aye, for that and many other things," he said sadly. "For not preparing you better. For being afraid to trust you fully—"

"I understand why you didn't," she cut him off gently. "Nell told me about your three betrotheds. She said they were frightened of you, and I realized the reason you didn't confide in me was that you thought I'd leave you."

"I should have believed better of you."

"For heaven's sake," she protested, "you'd just woken up to find yourself five centuries in the future. Besides," she admitted, "it wasn't as if I trusted you either. I tend to hide my intelligence. If I'd been more honest, you might have been too."

"Never hide it from me," he said softly. " 'Tis one of the many things I adore about you. But, Gwen, there is more for which I must seek your forgiveness."

"Marrying me without telling me?" she said lightly. "Have you any idea how flattered I am? We're *really* married?" she pressed. "Could we get married in a church too? Formally, with a long dress and everything?"

"Och, we're more married than the church could do, but aye, lass. I should like a church wedding," he agreed. "You'll wear a gown fit for a queen, and I'll wear the full Keltar regalia. We'll feast for days, invite the whole village. 'Twill be the celebration of the century." He paused, his silvery eyes flickering with shadows. "But there's still something more for which I must seek your forgiveness. There is the small matter of me abducting you and trapping you in my century."

She trailed her fingers lovingly down his chiseled jaw, then slipped her hands into his silky hair, grazing his scalp with her nails. They were nearly touching nose to nose, and his hair fell about her face, framing it. She tipped her head back for a quick kiss. Then two and three.

"Do you know," she murmured a few minutes later, "when you performed your ritual in the stones, at first I thought you had gone back to your century and left me behind in mine. I was furious. I was so hurt that you had left me. I thought you had begun to care for me—"

"I did!" he exclaimed. "I do!"

"My point is that if you'd told me everything that night in the stones, and had asked me to come back to the sixteenth century, I *would* have. I wanted to be with you wherever or even whenever that had to be."

"You doona hate me for not being able to return you?" He paused for emphasis. "Ever, Gwen. I can't return you ever."

"I don't want to go back. We belong together. I felt it the moment I met you, and it terrified me. I kept trying to find excuses to leave you but couldn't make myself go. I felt as if fate had brought us together because we were supposed to be together."

His smile flashed white in his dark face. "I felt the same way. I began falling in love with you the moment I saw you, and the more I learned about you, the more intense my feelings grew. That night in the stones when you gifted me with your maidenhead, when I gave you the Druid vows, I realized I would rather have a single night with you—even if it meant I was doomed to be bound to you, aching for you forever—than not know such love. I swore that if I were given the chance to have a life with you, I would treat you as befits a queen. That I would devote my life to making it up to you, what I'd taken from you. And I meant it, Gwen. Anything you want, anything at all . . . you have but to say."

"Love me, Drustan, just love me, and I'll not want for anything."

Later she said, "*Why* can't you go through the stones? You said they could never be used for personal reasons. What do you use them for?"

He told her, withholding nothing. The entire history, back to his ancestors, the Druids who'd served the *Tuatha de Danaan*, and about the war, and how the Keltar were chosen to atone and protect on behalf of all the Druids who'd scarred Gaea.

"The last time the stones were used, we sent two fleets of Temple Knights, carrying the Holy Grail, twenty years to the future so they might hide it away again."

"Did you say the *Holy Grail*?" Gwen squeaked.

"Aye. We protect. It would have been a war to end all wars had the king of France, Philip the Fair, gotten his hands on it."

"Oh, God," Gwen breathed.

"The stones may be used only for the greater good of the world. Never for one man's purpose."

"I understand." She paused a moment, then forced herself to go on. "I had to face a similar kind of situation once."

He kissed the tip of her nose. "Tell me. I want to know everything about you."

She rolled onto her side, and he stretched out on his, facing her. Their foreheads touched on the downy pillow, golden hair tangled with black silk. He laced their hands together, palm to palm. She told him all of it, which she'd never told another living soul. She confessed to her Great Fit of Rebellion.

There had been a time when, like her parents, she'd adored doing research. The pressure of their expectations had not seemed such a burden to her then. From the time she'd been able to talk, they'd made it clear that they expected her to be their greatest achievement, with a genius that would surpass theirs and enhance their reputation.

And until she was twenty-three, she'd toed the line they'd clearly defined. Her love of learning, of stretching her imagination to the furthest possible limit, had seemed adequate compensation for a strange childhood. She thrived on the rush of excitement whenever she discovered an alternative way of looking at things. And for a glorious time in her adolescence, she basked in her parents' approval and committed to joining them at Los Alamos and working by their side one day.

But as she'd grown older and learned more, she realized the danger of certain knowledge. And one night, as she'd worked in the lab, she had a terrifying realization. For years she'd been playing around with a set of theories, working toward a hypothesis that—if it held water—would change the way the world viewed everything.

Her parents had been delighted with her progress, demanding constant updates, pushing her harder and harder.

So engrossed had Gwen been in proving her hypothesis—for the sheer joy of proving it—that she hadn't given thought to all the possible ramifications until it had been nearly too late. In a moment of blinding clarity, she suddenly glimpsed all the potentials should she complete her work.

The fundamentals of it would make possible weapons to exceed all weapons. Infinite possibilities, not just to destroy the earth but to alter the very fabric of the universe. Too much power for man to own.

Late that very night, the lab at Triton Corp. caught fire.

Everything was destroyed.

The fire chief and arson investigator spent weeks picking through the rubble before writing it up as accidental, despite the unfathomable heat that had caused the foundation to explode.

There'd been too many chemicals stored on site to prove anything, and the burn patterns had been oddly random. A veritable *study* of randomness, her father had observed coldly when she'd informed him that all her research had gone up in flames and she'd failed to keep back-up Zip disks in the safety box at the bank as he'd taught her.

Five days later Gwen quit school and moved out into her own barren little apartment. Her father had refused to let her take so much as one piece of furniture.

She'd never looked back.

"I set fire to the lab I'd been working in and burned everything. I dropped out of my parents' world and took a job settling . . . er, disputes."

His eyes were glittering when she finished. He was stunned by what she'd just confided. Doubly stunned that fate had brought him such a woman who was his match in every way. Intelligence, passion, honor, courage to defy and do what she knew was right.

What children they would have, what a life they would have!

"I am proud of you, Gwen," he said quietly.

She smiled radiantly. "Thank you! I *knew* you'd understand. And that's why I understand about the stones."

They kissed slowly and passionately, as if they had all the time in the world. Then Drustan said softly, " 'Tis said that if a Keltar should use the stones for his own selfish reasons, the souls of the lost Druids—the evil ones who died in the battle—wait to take possession of such a fool. That they're trapped in a kind of in-between place, neither dead nor living. I know naught if it's true, nor dare I chance it. To reawaken such violence, such madness and rage—" He broke off. "There is much about Druidry even we doona understand. We doona tamper with the unknown. When Dageus died in the other reality, I could not break my oaths." He blinked and looked startled. "Dageus," he muttered, pushing himself up.

Gwen sat up with him. "He's alive, remember? You sent two hundred guards with him."

He rubbed his forehead. "Och, 'tis damn odd having two realities in here. I can see why the mind instinctively resists it. I hold all the grief of him dying yet the awareness that he hasn't." He blew out a breath, frowning. "Yet."

Gwen searched his eyes. "You're worried about him."

"Nay," he said swiftly, "I have my beloved wife—"

"You're worried about him," she said dryly.

He raked a hand through his hair.

"Has the battle happened yet? You never told me what date he died."

"Two days hence. The second day of August."

"Could you get there by then?" she pressed.

He nodded, clearly torn. "But only if I ride without pause."

"Then go. Bring him safely home, Drustan," she said softly. "I'll be fine here. I can't bear to think that he might die if you're not there. Go."

"You dismiss me from your bed so soon?" he growled

teasingly, but she glimpsed a brush of vulnerability in his eyes. She marveled that such an intelligent, attractive, passionate, sexy man could suffer insecurity.

"No. If it were up to me, I'd never let you go, but I know that if Dageus doesn't come home safely, I'll hate myself. We have time. We have the rest of our lives," she said, smiling.

"Aye, that we do." He stretched himself over her, suspending his weight on his palms, and kissed her with only their lips touching. Long and slow and delicious. The hot silk of his tongue swirled languidly against hers.

When he sat back, he was grinning.

"What?"

"Anya. I can both secure my brother's safety and tidy up that bit of business. No lass of five and ten will tolerate 'magic' well. I will induce her to break the betrothal, bring my brother home, and toop you till you can't move. For a sennight, nay, a fortnight—"

"You will come back, love me, then we'll get down to figuring out who plans to abduct you, because we still have a big problem, you know," Gwen corrected him as a chill of concern marred her dreamy contentment. She was so elated to have her Drustan back, had been so lost in their lovemaking that the danger he was in had completely slipped her mind. She pulled the coverlet about her waist and sat cross-legged, facing him. "Who abducted you, Drustan? Do you remember anything at all?"

His silvery eyes darkened. "I told you all I could recall about the abduction in your century. I never glimpsed my abductors. By the time I neared the clearing, whatever drug they'd given me had rendered me nearly unconscious. I couldn't even open my eyes. I heard voices but couldn't identify them."

"Then the first order on the agenda is that I will

personally prepare all your food and drink for the next month," Gwen announced.

He arched a brow. "I doona think I care to let you out of my bed that long."

"There's no way you're drinking or eating a thing that hasn't either been prepared by me or sampled by someone first."

"There's an idea," he mused. "After all, 'twas only a drug, not a poison. Our guards have been known to serve such a function in times of danger."

"I asked Silvan who might wish to harm you. He said you have no enemies. Can you think of anyone?"

Drustan pondered her question. "Nay. The only possibility I can think of is if someone thought to steal our lore, but that still doesn't explain why someone would enchant me. Why wouldn't they have killed me? Why make me slumber?" He shook his head. "I thought that once I got back here, I would see some hint of the threat. But still I can't imagine who it might be."

"Well, when the message comes, you won't go. We can send the guards to the clearing. What day were you abducted?"

"The seventeenth day of August. A fortnight after Dageus was . . ." He trailed off, his concern etched on his face.

"Go now," she urged. He looked so worried. "We can talk about it more when you return. Go bring your brother home. Silvan and I will put our heads together and list some possible suspects while you're gone, then when you and Dageus return, we'll figure it out."

"I doona wish to leave you."

Gwen sighed. She didn't want him leaving her either. She'd only just gotten him back again. But she knew that if she had a brother, and if her brother had died in some other reality, she'd need to be there to make certain he didn't die this time. She couldn't bear it if anything went wrong. Drustan needed to be there, and he needed her to encourage him to go.

"You must," she insisted. "I can't ride well enough yet, and I'd slow you down. You might not make it in time if you take me."

Raking a hand through his hair, he slipped from the bed, looking impossibly torn. His gaze swept over her; her skin flushed from lovemaking, lips swollen from kisses. She sat cross-legged amid the violet velvet coverlets, a creamy goddess rising from a purple sea. "A lovelier vision I've ne'er seen," he said huskily.

Gwen beamed at her magnificent Highlander.

"I'll be back, lass. I'd bid you doona move a muscle so I could find you looking just the same, but I fear it will be four or five days before I return."

"It might take me four or five days to start walking right again," she said, blushing.

He flashed her a grin of pure male satisfaction, dressed swiftly, kissed her a dozen times, then slipped from the chamber.

Then poked his head back in. "I love you, Gwen."

Gwen fell back on the bed, sighing dreamily. Love. Gwen Cassidy had a heart and was loved.

"Say it," he said anxiously.

She laughed delightedly. "I love you too, Drustan." His neediness about hearing the words was adorable. Her Highland hunk had such a charming vulnerability.

He smiled brilliantly and was gone.

In Drustan's absence, Gwen, Silvan, and Nell listed potential suspects: all the occupants of the castle, certain questionable personages from the village of Balanoch,

Drustan's ex-betrotheds, and several neighboring clans. After much discussion, each was ticked off for lack of a possible motive.

"Is it possible the Campbell had anything to do with it?" Gwen asked. "Because they killed Dageus in the other reality," she clarified.

Silvan shook his head. "I doona see those two events being related, m'dear. Colin Campbell has ne'er come against us, and his holdings are vast enough that even now he has difficulty protecting his territory. Besides, there's the issue of enchantment. 'Twould take another Druid or a witch to do such a thing. The Campbell have no such arts."

Gwen sighed. "So what are we going to do?"

"The only thing we can do—take all precautions. We'll triple the guard rotations. I'll send them out combing the countryside. And we'll wait. Now that we know there is a threat, it shouldn't be too difficult to avert. Drustan will go nowhere unaccompanied. Robert, our captain of the guard, will serve as his taster."

"And in the meantime," Nell said, taking Gwen's hand, "we women-folk will set our minds to happier things, mayhap select the room ye wish to use when ye have wee bairn."

Silvan turned a beatific gaze upon them. Gwen didn't miss the way his gaze lingered overlong on Nell. Nor did she miss the heated glance that passed between them.

Hmmm, she thought. *Seems they finally came to their senses, without my help.*

She might have been mortified had she known just *how* she'd helped them.

"Aye, now, there's a sound plan," Silvan said. "And rest easy, m'dear. We'll avert the threat."

For the next few days, Gwen immersed herself in

plans for the future. Drustan was a strong man, smart, and his castle well fortified. Now that they were aware of the impending threat, they would indeed unmask the enemy, and life would be all she'd ever dreamed it might be.

· 23 ·

Besseta's eyes were dark with terror as she watched the MacKeltar guard thunder past the cottage. The news she'd overheard in Balanoch earlier today was true! The guards were returning with Drustan's betrothed! She hadn't even known they'd ridden out to fetch her—thanks to Nevin's refusal to discuss the goings-on at the castle.

Now *she* had arrived—the woman who would kill her son!

Trembling, Besseta crept away from the window and nearer the fire. She rubbed her hands together, trying in vain to dismiss a chill that had nothing to do with the weather. The chill was in her heart, ne'er to be thawed lest she secure her son's future.

She'd bartered for the gypsies' services several days earlier, but, unaware that the laird's betrothed was arriving so soon—more of Nevin's fault for being so close-lipped—she'd not specified the date for Drustan's abduction. She'd planned to use herbs to drug the laird, then lure him to the loch where, helpless, he would be enchanted. Now she had a better idea. She would go to the gypsy camp this very night and instruct them to act immediately, take his betrothed, use her as lure, then enchant them both.

She snatched up her cloak in trembling fingers and hurried to the door. Nevin was still at the castle and would be for several hours if he stayed true to his schedule. Utterly oblivious to danger all around him.

She squeezed her eyes tightly shut, clutching the door and steeling her will. It was almost over. Just one more day, brave the gypsy camp one more time, and her son would be safe.

And mayhap, just mayhap, that horrible sucking darkness would finally leave her alone.

The evening Drustan returned, Gwen, Silvan, and Nell, alerted by the guard that rode ahead, waited on the front steps of the castle.

Gwen felt her heart might burst from happiness. Her gaze lingered long on the two magnificent men, talking, clapping each other on the shoulder, and jesting as they dismounted and the stable master led their horses away. *She'd* had a part in that, she thought, smiling. First goal accomplished. Drustan's brother was safe.

When Drustan reached the bottom step, she flung herself into his arms.

He swung her up into his embrace and kissed her hungrily. By the time he'd finished, she was gasping for air and laughing.

"My turn?" Dageus teased.

"I doona think so," Drustan growled. Then his scowl faded and he smiled at his brother. "By Amergin, 'tis like a dream. I still recall standing in her century, mourning you, brother. Have a care with yourself. I never want to suffer that again. I expect you to live a hundred years or more."

"I plan to," Dageus assured him. Then he smiled at Gwen, and she caught her breath. For a moment, she thought him nearly as gorgeous as Drustan. Those lion-like golden eyes of his . . .

She glanced up at Drustan, who had arched a brow, watching her.

"Oh, come on," Gwen said lightly. "I can't possibly not notice how attractive he is, as much as he looks like you."

Drustan rumbled deep in his throat.

"But I married *you*," she said pertly.

"Aye, that you did, lass. That she did, Dageus," Drustan said pointedly.

"Doona be getting yourself in a fankle," Dageus said lightly. " 'Tis plain her heart is only for you. If you'll recall, she didn't care for my kiss."

Drustan growled again.

Dageus laughed. " 'Tis thanking you I am, Gwen Cassidy. Drustan tells me he regained his memory when you said the spell. The battle occurred as you predicted. 'Twould seem I owe you my life."

"No," Gwen protested. "I'm happy I could help, and glad you're all right."

" 'Tis an old custom. I shall always protect you and yours," he said, his golden eyes glittering. "And there is the small fact that you have made my brother happier than I've ever seen him, so I'm thanking you doubly, lass. Welcome to our family."

Gwen's eyes misted. She was part of a family now. Drustan's arms tightened and he swung her legs up, cradling her. She tipped her head back for another leisurely kiss.

Dageus grinned and shook his head, turning to greet

his father. He paused, noticing Silvan's arm about Nell's waist.

Drustan noticed at the same time. His eyes widened and he glanced at Gwen.

She shrugged, smiling. "I don't know what happened, but ever since you left, they've been acting different. It seems they finally admitted their feelings to each other."

Dageus tossed his head back and gave a whoop of joy. He grabbed Nell and kissed her soundly on the mouth. Nell flushed, looking immensely relieved, and Gwen realized she must have been nervous about how Drustan and Dageus might feel about her relationship with their father.

"Stop that," Silvan growled. "Kiss her cheek if you wish, but doona be kissing those lips. They're mine."

Nell's laughter was joyous, and she and Gwen exchanged a purely feminine smile. Possessiveness in tiny doses could be delicious.

Dageus grinned. "So, our dolt of a da has finally opened his eyes."

Silvan looked sheepish.

Dageus plucked Nell up and twirled her around in dizzying circles. " 'Tis long past time you took your seat at our table, Nell."

"I take it this means you approve," Silvan said dryly.

"Oh, aye, we approve," Dageus and Drustan said simultaneously.

When Dageus deposited Nell near Silvan, only Gwen noticed the faint hint of sadness in Dageus's eyes, buried deep behind the golden glitter. She might not have noticed it at all had she not experienced it herself.

It was loneliness.

Where would Dageus MacKeltar, brother to a man who'd been jilted four times—

"You *did* break the betrothal, didn't you?" She tipped her head back at Drustan, narrowing her eyes.

"Aye, seems Anya didn't care for me calling down a storm during battle," he said, grinning.

—*Druid extraordinaire, gorgeous beyond words, find a woman to wed him in all of Alba?*

And Dageus knew it, although Drustan hadn't realized it yet.

"Did he make his eyes glow and everything?" she teased, eyeing Dageus thoughtfully.

"It was most impressive," Dageus informed her. "You should have seen him raise his arms to the sky and make quite a performance of it, when in truth it doesn't require much effort—an arrow with the right elements shot into a certain cloud formation."

"Oh, you must tell me," Gwen breathed.

They both laughed, tossing similar manes of silky dark hair.

"I didn't call down a storm. I told her that if she broke our betrothal, she could retain the bride-price to use as a future dowry." He grimaced. "It seems she didn't wish to wed me anyway, she'd been pining for another. She said her da gave her no choice, as they had need of coin."

Oh, Drustan, Gwen thought. Doomed never to be appreciated by the women in his century. And Dageus! There were going to be some serious matchmaking efforts in her future. Where on earth would she find him a wife? she wondered.

Then she wondered no more, for Drustan turned with her in his arms and loped up the stairs into the castle. To make immediate, passionate love to her, she was quite certain, and her entire body quickened with anticipation.

"Wait!" Silvan called after them. "I thought we could dine together as a family."

"Give over, Da. I doubt they'll be leaving the bedchamber till morn," Dageus said dryly.

Silvan sighed, then glanced at Nell. His gaze grew heated.

When Silvan took Nell's hand and hastened her toward the stairs, bidding a good night over his shoulder to his son, Dageus shook his head, smiling faintly, and withdrew a flask of whisky from his sporran.

Dageus sat on the steps for a long time, filled with a strange restlessness that even whisky couldn't mellow, watching the night sky twinkle with a smattering of brilliant stars.

If he felt lonely, in the vastness of things, 'twas a feeling to which he'd grown long accustomed.

Gwen welcomed her husband home in a time-honored fashion. They spent the evening in their chamber, where she lovingly bathed the dust of travel from him, then joined him in a fresh bath and showed him how very much she'd missed him.

They lit candles and drew the velvet bedcurtains, alternately making love and stopping to feed each other tidbits from a scrumptious dinner delivered personally by Dageus.

It was clear from the array of foods, Gwen decided, that Dageus had quite the erotic mind, just like his brother. For he'd brought them lovers' food: juicy slices of peaches and plums, baked meat tarts, cheese, and a crusty loaf of bread. He'd also brought honey, with nothing specific to put it on, a thing she'd not understood until Drustan laid her back upon the bed, drizzled a dab on that most feminine part of her, then proceeded to show her just how long it could take to lick it off. Thoroughly.

She'd peaked twice beneath his masterful, slightly sticky tongue.

Then there were cherries from the orchard, and she'd eaten a handful while trying her own hand at the honey.

Drustan had lain supine upon the bed for all of two and a half minutes before flipping her over on her back and taking charge of matters. She'd reveled in eroding his control. For such a disciplined man, he certainly came undone in bed. Uninhibited, passionate, his enthusiasm for sex was endless.

She'd fed him slices of roast pig, then given him small drinks of wine from her own lips. And when he'd whispered to her the same base, primitive words back that she'd said to him their first night together in the stones, untamed lust had consumed them both.

They'd rolled across the bed and tumbled to the floor, knocking over tables and candles and setting fire to the lambskin rug. They'd laughed and Drustan had doused it with the cooling bathwater.

And when she finally slept—spooned, her back to his front—with Drustan's arms around her, her last thought was *heaven*. She'd found heaven in the Highlands of Scotland.

· 24 ·

"*Mmm.*" **Gwen sighed contentedly. She'd been** having a marvelous dream in which Drustan was waking her by making love to her. Dimly, the realization penetrated—at the same moment he did—that it was no dream.

She gasped as, still spooned, he slipped into her from behind.

"Oh, God," she breathed as he increased the tempo. Deeper, harder, faster. He thrust into her, his arms wrapped tightly around her, and nipped the skin at the base of her neck. When he rolled her nipples between his fingers, she arched back against him, meeting his every thrust until they peaked in perfect harmony.

"Gwen, my love," he whispered.

When, later, he'd gone to fetch breakfast, intent on serving her in bed, she lay back, a silly smile plastered on her face.

Life was *so* good.

Whistling a cheery tune, Drustan balanced a tray laden with kippers and plump sausages, tatties and clootie dumplings, peaches and porridge, on his arm as he fumbled with the door. All had been prepared by Nell herself, all tasted by Robert.

Despite the fact that the threat loomed some distance yet in the future, he was taking no chances with his wife.

"Sustenance is here, and you're going to need it, love," he announced, pushing the door open.

The velvet bedcurtains were tied back, revealing a tangle of coverlets and linens, but the bed was empty. He glanced about the room, puzzled. He'd been gone a scant half hour, gathering food. Where had she gone? A quick visit to the garderobe? He had a delicious morning planned: a leisurely breakfast, a leisurely bath for his wife, who must be aching from so much bed play. More lovemaking only if she was able, if not, he would massage scented oils into her skin and gently minister to her tender limbs.

A chill of foreboding kissed his spine as he eyed the empty bed. Dropping the tray on a table near the door, he walked swiftly through the boudoir and into the Silver Chamber.

She wasn't there.

He pivoted and stalked back to his chamber.

Only then did he see the parchment propped on the table near the fire. His hands shook as he snatched it up and read it.

Come to the clearing by the wee loch if ye value her life. Alone, or the lass dies.

"Nay!" he roared, crushing the parchment in his fist. *'Tis too soon,* his mind protested. He wasn't supposed to be enchanted for nearly a fortnight! He hadn't even given the guards instructions to triple the watches and scour the countryside!

"By Amergin," he whispered hoarsely, "we've changed things somehow." By preventing Dageus's death, they must have altered the way subsequent events would unfold. His mind raced furiously. Who was behind it all? It made no sense to him. And what might the enemy want with Gwen?

"To get to *me*," he muttered grimly. They hadn't drugged him this time. Rather—because Gwen was there—she'd been used as bait.

Frantically, he crammed his feet into his boots and grabbed his leather bands, strapping them on. In the Greathall, he stuffed blade after blade into the slits as he raced to the garrison.

Alone, my arse, he thought.

I'll walk in alone, while my men sneak up behind them and destroy every last one of the bastards who took my woman.

ॐ

Besseta cowered behind the lofty oak, watching the gypsies prepare to work the spell she'd commissioned. They'd painted a large crimson circle upon the ground. Runes she did not recognize marked the perimeter—dark gypsy magic, she thought, shivering.

The moment Nevin had departed for his morning stroll to the castle, she'd hastened from the cottage and crept through the forest. She was determined to see the deed done with her own eyes. Only then would she believe her son safe.

She narrowed her eyes, peering at her enemy—Drustan's betrothed, who'd been plucked straight from his bed, she was fair certain, for the lass wore naught but a sheer nightrail. Soon the laird himself would arrive, the gypsies would enchant him and take him far away, to be interred underground, and her worries would be over. The gypsies had demanded extra coin to enchant the woman as well, forcing Besseta to pilfer from Nevin's charity box. But no transgression was too great to save her son.

A few yards away Nevin watched his mother with a heavy heart. For some time, she'd been worsening, her moods growing increasingly erratic, her eyes too bright. She watched him ceaselessly as if she feared a bolt of lightning might strike him at any moment. He'd done all he could to allay her fears that Drustan MacKeltar might harm him, but to no avail. She was lost in terrible imaginings.

He murmured a soft prayer of thanks to God for guiding him. He'd awakened with a niggling foreboding, and rather than immediately striking out for the castle, he'd lingered behind the cottage. Sure enough, moments later, his mother had slipped out, wild-eyed, her hair mussed, half-dressed, pulling her cloak tightly about her.

When she'd scurried off, he'd followed at a distance. She'd crept to the edge of the forest, where it opened into a circular clearing at the edge of the small loch. Now he watched, deeply uneasy. What was his mother doing? What involvement had she in gypsy affairs, and what strange designs were etched upon the sod?

He scanned the clearing, stiffening when a small group of gypsies moved apart and one broke away from the rest, carrying a bound woman toward the crimson circle. It was the wee blond lass Nevin had seen about the castle of late. When the gypsy briefly glanced in his direction, Nevin ducked deeper into the brush, deeper into the shadows of the forest.

What ominous events transpired? Why did his mother lurk here, and why was a woman from the castle bound? What terrible things had Besseta gotten herself ensnared in?

Smoothing his robes, he reminded himself that he was a man of God, and as such had a duty to work in His name despite his slight stature and mild nature. Whatever was about to happen, it was clear no good might come of it. It was his responsibility to put a stop to it before someone was harmed. He began to step forth from his hidden vantage, but no sooner did he stand than Drustan MacKeltar, mounted on a snorting black stallion, burst into the clearing. He vaulted from his horse and, unsheathing his sword, stalked toward the gypsy carrying the lass.

"Release her," Drustan roared savagely in a voice that sounded like a thousand voices. His silvery eyes blazed incandescently. 'Twas no normal voice, Nevin realized, but a voice of power.

Nevin ducked back again, blinking.

The gypsy carrying the blond lass dropped her as if burned and backed away toward the loch. The lass tumbled and rolled across the rocky sod, stopping a few yards from where Nevin stood.

And that was when all hell broke loose.

Besseta keened low and long as chaos erupted in the clearing. She wiped clammy palms on her skirt and watched in horror as mounted guards burst from the forest.

The gypsies, hemmed in by the loch at their back and guards on all sides, reached for their weapons.

Wrong, wrong, it was all going wrong!

She inched from the cover of the forest, creeping unnoticed in the tumult, toward the wagon that had been brought to cart off the laird's slumbering body.

The gypsies were aiming their crossbows.

The guards were raising shields and swinging swords.

Men were going to die and blood was going to flow,

Besseta thought, grateful that Nevin was safely in the castle working on his chapel. Mayhap rather than being enchanted, Drustan MacKeltar would be killed in battle. Not by her hand at all. Mayhap.

But mayhap was too weak a possibility to ensure her son's safety.

I will not harm the MacKeltar, she'd promised Nevin, and she was a woman of her word. If a son couldn't trust his mother's word, what could he rely upon?

She'd carefully planned the enchantment so that not one hair on the laird's head would be harmed. But now all her cautious plans were going awry. She had no choice but to try another option to save her son. If she could not remove Drustan MacKeltar before he wed his lady—well, she'd made no promises about that lady. And that lady was currently forgotten as the battle raged around her bound body.

Lying on the ground, she may or may not get trampled by the horses. May or may not get struck by a stray arrow.

Besseta was quite finished taking chances. *If* Drustan survived the battle, Besseta had to make certain there was no woman for him to wed.

She narrowed her eyes, watching the lass struggle with her bonds, and inched nearer the wagon.

With trembling hands, she plucked up a tightly strung crossbow and, summoning every ounce of her strength, leveled it at the lass.

❧

Nevin's eyes widened in horror. His mother, his own mother would do murder! She was truly lost in her madness! *Thou shalt not kill!*

"Nay!" he roared, plunging from the brush.

Besseta heard him and started. Her hand slipped on the cord.

"Nay! Mother!" Running, he catapulted himself through the air to shield the bound lass, and stumbled, landing sideways atop her. *"Naaaa—"*

His cry terminated abruptly as the arrow slammed into his chest.

❧

Besseta froze. Her world grew eerily still. The tumult in the clearing receded and grew hazy, as if she stood in a dreamy tunnel, she at one end, her dying son at the other. Choking on a horrified sob, her knees buckled and she collapsed.

Her vision swept over her again, this time in full, and she finally saw the fourth person's face. The person she'd thought had meant naught since she'd been unable to see it clearly.

She'd not been able to see the fourth person because it had been herself.

She was the woman who would kill her son. It had never been the lass. Och, indirectly, in a way, for had the lass not come, Besseta would not have planned to abduct the laird, and had she not set such plans into motion, she would never have shot her beloved son.

God's will will be, Nevin had said a thousand times if once.

But, trusting her visions more than God, she'd tried to change what she thought she'd seen and had brought about the very event she'd tried so desperately to avoid.

She fancied she could hear her son's ragged, dying breaths over the din of battle.

Oblivious to the warfare all around her, the arrows flying, the swords swinging, she crawled to her son's side and tugged him onto her lap. "Och, my wee laddie," she crooned, smoothing his hair, stroking his face. "Nevin, my baby, my boy."

Gwen struggled to sit up the moment she was no longer pinned by the man's body. A sob escaped her when she spied the arrow protruding from his bloody chest.

She'd never seen anyone shot before. It was horrible, worse than the movies made it seem. She tried to inch away, but her wrists were bound behind her, her ankles tightly tied. Scooting awkwardly on her behind was painstakingly slow going. When a horse screamed and reared behind her, when she heard the chilling *swish* of a blade slicing through the air, she went utterly still, and decided moving might not be the wisest course of action.

Drustan had been gone only a few minutes when the gypsies had slipped into the chamber and taken her captive. They'd subdued her with humiliating ease.

She hadn't seen it coming, but somehow, by preventing Dageus's death, they'd changed things. Plans had been accelerated, and rather than a message bidding Drustan to come if he wished to know the name of the man who'd killed his brother, *she'd* been used as the lure.

She stared at the weeping old woman, whose frantic, gnarled hands fluttered above the man's cheeks and brow. As Gwen watched, his chest rose and fell, then did not rise again.

" 'Twas me all along," Besseta wailed. " 'Twas my vision that did this. I should ne'er have bargained with the gypsies!"

"*You* arranged to enchant Drustan?" Gwen gasped. This gray-haired old woman with arthritic hands and rheumy eyes was their unknown enemy? "You're the one behind everything?" But the old woman didn't reply, merely stared at Gwen with loathing and madness in her gaze.

"Gwen!" Drustan roared. "Get away from Besseta!"

Gwen's head snapped back, and she saw him running toward her, a horrified expression on his face.

"Crawl, get away!" he roared again, dodging swords and ducking arrows.

"Stay back," Gwen screamed. "Protect yourself!" He would never make it through so many weapons.

But he didn't stay back, he kept running, heedless of the danger.

He was no more than a dozen yards from her when an arrow slammed into his chest, taking him off his feet. As he collapsed on his back, suddenly she was . . .

. . . on the flat rock, sunning herself, in the foothills above Loch Ness.

"Noooooo!" she screamed. "Drustan!"

"The release of atom power has changed
everything except our way of thinking . . .
the solution to this problem lies in the heart
of mankind. If only I had known, I should
have become a watchmaker."

—ALBERT EINSTEIN

*"The heart has its reasons—of which
reason knows nothing."*

—BLAISE PASCAL

· 25 ·

Gwen lay on the flat rock for time uncounted.

She was mindless, wracked with grief. When a sip of reality finally returned, it couched an impossible pill to swallow—reality without him. Forever.

How had she—the brilliant physicist—failed to see it coming?

How could she have been so stupid?

She'd been so thrilled to remain with Drustan in the sixteenth century, so lost in dreamy plans of their future, that her brain had gone on strike, and she'd failed to take one critically important factor into account: The moment she changed his future, she would change her own.

In the *new* future they'd created, Drustan MacKeltar was not enchanted. Was not buried in the cavern for her to find.

And so—in this new future they'd created—because

Drustan was not enchanted, she'd not found him, *and he'd never sent her back to him.*

At the precise moment the possibility of him being enchanted had reached absolute null, Gwen Cassidy had ceased to exist in his century. Reality had plunked her right back where she'd been before she'd fallen down the ravine. Right back *when* she'd been. No need for the white bridge. Sixteenth-century reality had spat her out, rejecting her very existence. An unacceptable anomaly. Drustan was never enchanted—hence she had no right to exist in his time. So much for the theories that claimed Stephen Hawking was wrong for advocating the existence of a cosmic censor that would prevent paradoxes from piling up. There was clearly some force keeping things aligned in the universe. *God abhors a naked singularity*, Gwen thought with a half-snort that quickly translated into a sob.

She clutched her head, suddenly fearing her memories might melt away.

But no, the scientist reminded her, the arrows of time remembered forward, and so her memory would remain intact. She *had* been in the past, and the memory of it was etched into the essence of her being.

How had she failed to realize that by saving him, she would lose him forever? Now, looking back, she couldn't believe she'd not once thought through to what the inevitable finale would have to be. Love had blinded her, and in retrospect she realized that she hadn't *wanted* to think about what might happen. She'd studiously blocked thinking about anything to do with physics, busy savoring the simple joy of being a woman in love.

"No," she cried. "How am I supposed to live without him?"

Tears slipped down her cheeks. She scanned the rocky terrain, seeking the ravine down which she'd tumbled, but even that was gone. There was no longer a crevice splitting the northeast face of the foothills. The gypsies must have had some part in creating it, she realized, perhaps lowered him though it, who knew?

What she did know was that even if she dug beneath the mountain of rubble upon which she perched, she would find no sleeping Highlander beneath it.

"No!" she cried again.

Yes, the scientist whispered. *He's five hundred years dead.*

"He'll come through the stones for me," she insisted.

But he wouldn't. And she didn't need the scientist to point that out. He *couldn't.* Even if he had survived the arrow wound, he would never use the stones. It would be like someone saying to her, "If you finish your research, create the ultimate weapon and unleash it upon an unsuspecting world, you can have Drustan back."

She could never release such capacity for evil, no matter the enduring grief.

Nor would he. His honor, one of the many things she loved about him, would keep them forever apart.

If he'd even survived.

Gwen dropped her head against the rock, scooped her pack into her arms, and clutched it tightly. She might never know if he died from the arrow wound, but if he hadn't died in battle, he'd still died nearly five hundred years ago. Grief smothered her, grief more intense than anything she'd ever imagined. She buried her face in the pack and wept.

≈

It was hours before she managed to force herself up from the rocks and hike down to the village. Hours in which she sobbed as if her heart would break.

Once in the village, she'd gone to her room and checked in but wasn't able to bear being alone, so she'd walked numbly down to the inn's cozy restaurant, hoping to find Beatrice and Bertie. Not to talk—she could hardly talk about it—but to be buffered by their warm presence.

Now, standing in the doorway of the dining room, she blinked as she glanced around the brightly lit interior. *I will not start crying again*, Gwen told herself fiercely. She would weep later, after she'd returned home to Sante Fe. She would fall apart there.

The restaurant felt strange and modern to her after having been in the sixteenth century. The small fireplace on the south wall of the dining room seemed miniature compared to medieval hearths, the neon bar decorations garish after weeks of soft candlelight and oil globes. The dozens of tables, topped with vases of fresh wildflowers, seemed too small to seat guests with any degree of comfort. The modern world felt impersonal to her now, with everything churned out in mass, uniform shapes and styles.

Her gaze drifted over a cigarette vending machine in the corner. Dimly, she realized she'd passed through the worst of withdrawal in the sixteenth century.

Still, she felt an utterly self-destructive urge wash over her.

Her gaze was drawn to a yellowed calendar that hung behind the cash register. *September 19.*

It was the same day she'd left. But of course, she thought. No time *would* have passed. Perhaps a mere few moments had slipped by in the twenty-first century while she'd lived the happiest days of her life in sixteenth-century Scotland.

She sniffed, perilously close to tears again. Glancing around, thinking Bert's rainbow ensemble should be easy to spot, she nearly missed the lone silver-haired woman huddled in one of the booths that lined a bank of windows, silhouetted against the gathering twilight. The gloaming cast Beatrice's complexion in bruised shadows, and Gwen was struck by how old she looked. Her shoulders were hunched, her eyes closed. Her wide-brimmed hat was crushed between her hands. As a car drove by outside the bank of windows, headlights illuminated the elderly woman's face, revealing the shiny trails of tears on her cheeks.

Oh, God—Beatrice weeping? Why?

Stricken, Gwen rushed to the booth. What could make cheerful Beatrice weep, and where was Bertie? From what Gwen knew of the love-struck couple, the only way Bert would leave Bea's side was if he was physically incapable of being there. A chill brushed her neck.

"Beatrice?" she said faintly.

Beatrice jerked, startled. The eyes she raised to Gwen's were red-rimmed from crying, deep with grief.

"No," Gwen breathed. "Tell me nothing has happened to Bert," she insisted. "Tell me!" Suddenly limp, she slumped into the booth across from Beatrice and took the older woman's hand in hers. "Please," she begged.

"Oh, Gwen. My Bertie's in the hospital." The admission brought on a fresh bout of tears. Plucking another napkin from the dispenser, Beatrice wiped her eyes, blew her nose, then deposited the wadded napkin atop a substantial pile.

"What happened? He was fine just . . . er, this morning," Gwen protested, having a difficult time keeping the date straight.

"He seemed fine to me too. We'd been shopping all morning after you left, laughing and having a fine time. He was even feeling . . . frisky," she said with a pained smile. "Then it happened. He went absolutely still and just stood there with the most startled and angry look on his face." Beatrice's eyes filled with more tears as she relived the moment. "When he clutched his chest, I knew." She wiped impatiently at her cheeks. "The damn

man never takes care of himself. Wouldn't get his cho-
lesterol checked, wouldn't get his blood pressure tested.
A few days ago, I'd finally managed to wring a promise
from him that once we got back home, he'd get a complete physical—" She broke off, wincing.

"But he's alive, right?" Gwen asked faintly. "Tell me
he's alive." She couldn't bear any more tragedy today.
Not one more ounce.

"He's alive, but he had a stroke," Beatrice whispered.
"Although they've stabilized him, they don't know how
much damage was done. He's still unconscious. I'm going back to the hospital in a few minutes. The nurses insisted I get a breath of fresh air." She flushed. "I couldn't
stop crying. I guess I was pretty loud and the doctor was
getting upset with me. I thought I'd get some soup and
tea before I went back for the night, so here I am." She
waved a hand at the plastic container of soup and sand-
wich-to-go.

"Oh, Beatrice, I'm so sorry," Gwen breathed. "I don't
know what to say." Tears she'd been holding back
slipped down her cheeks; tears for Drustan, and now
tears for Bea and Bertie.

"Dearie, are you crying for me? Oh, Gwen!" Slipping
over to Gwen's side of the booth, she hugged her, and
they clung to each other for a long time.

And something inside Gwen broke.

Wrapped in Beatrice's motherly arms, the pain of it
all crashed over her. How unfair to love so deeply and
lose. How unfair life was! Beatrice had only just found
her Bert, much as Gwen had only just found Drustan.
And now, were they both to suffer endlessly for losing
them?

"Better not to love," Gwen whispered bitterly.

"No," Beatrice chided gently. "Never think that. Better to love and lose. The old adage is true. If I never had

another moment with my Bertie, I would still feel blessed. These past months with him have given me more love and passion than some people ever know. Besides," she said, "he's going to be all right. If I have to sit by his bed and hold his hand and yell at him until he gets better, then tote his ornery butt to the doctor every week, and learn how to cook without fat or butter or a damn thing worth eating, I'll do it. I am *not* letting that man get away from me." She fisted her ring-bedecked hand and shook it at the ceiling. "You can't have him yet. He's mine still."

A bit of laughter escaped Gwen, mingled with fresh tears. If only it were so easy for her, if only she could fight for her man the way Beatrice could fight for hers. But hers was five centuries dead.

She became aware, after a moment, that Beatrice was regarding her intently. The older woman cupped Gwen's shoulders and searched her gaze.

"Oh, dearie, what is it? It looks to me as if you might be having a problem of your own," she fretted.

Gwen tucked her bangs behind her ear and averted her gaze. "It's nothing," she said hastily.

"Don't try to put me off," Beatrice chided. "Bertie would tell you there's no point once I set my mind on a thing. It's not only my problem with Bertie that's made you cry."

"Really," Gwen protested. "You have enough problems—"

"So take my mind off them for a moment, if you will," Beatrice pressed. "Grief shared is grief lessened. What happened to you today? Did you find your, er . . . cherry picker?" Beatrice's blue eyes twinkled just a bit, and Gwen marveled that the older woman could still sparkle at such a moment.

Had she found her cherry picker? She fought a bubble of

nearly hysterical laughter. How could she tell Beatrice that she'd lived almost a month in a single day? Or at least she thought she had. It was so strange coming down from the foothills to find that no time at all had passed, she was beginning to fear for her sanity.

Yet Beatrice was right: Grief shared was grief lessened. She *wanted* to talk about him. Needed to talk about him. How could she possibly confide her pain . . . unless . . .

"It's really nothing," she lied weakly. "How about if I tell you a story instead, to take your mind off things?"

"A story?" Bea's eyebrows disappeared beneath her silvery curls.

"Yes, I've been thinking about trying my hand at writing," Gwen said, "and I've been kicking around a story, but I'm stumped on the ending."

Beatrice's eyes narrowed thoughtfully. "A story, you say. Yes, I'd like to hear it, and maybe you and I will be able to figure out how the ending should go."

Gwen took a deep breath and began: "Okay, the heroine is a girl who was hiking in the foothills of Scotland, and she found an enchanted Highlander sleeping in a cave above Loch Ness . . . pretty far out there, huh?"

An hour later, Gwen watched Beatrice open her mouth several times, then close it again. She fussed with her curls, fiddled with her hat, then smoothed her pink sweater.

"At first I thought you were going to tell me something that happened to you today, that you didn't want to own up to." Beatrice shook her head. "But, Gwen, I had no idea you had such an imagination. You truly took my mind off my worries for a time. Goodness," she exclaimed, waving at the plastic containers, "long enough that I ate when I was certain I wouldn't be able to force a bite down. Dearie, you *must* finish this story. You can't just leave the hero and heroine hanging like that. I can't *stand* it. Tell me the end."

"What if there is no end, Bea? What if that's all of it? What if she got sent back to her time and he died and that's it?" Gwen said numbly.

"You can't write such a story. Find a way to bring him through the stones."

"He can't," Gwen said flatly. "Ever. Even if he lived—"

"Oaths are a lot of nonsense when love's at stake," Beatrice insisted. "Bend the rules. Just write that rule out."

"I can't. It's part of the story. He would become a dark Druid if he did." And Gwen understood how awful that would be better than most ever could. "Not one of his clan has ever broken the oath. They must not. And in truth, I'm afraid I would think less of him if he did."

Beatrice arched a brow. "You? *You* might think less of him?"

Gwen shook her head sheepishly, "I meant my heroine in the story. *She* might think less of him. He was perfect the way he was. He was a man of honor who knew his responsibilities, and that was one of the things she loved about him. If he broke his oath and used the stones for personal reasons, he would corrupt the power within him. There's no telling how evil he would become. No. If he lived—which I greatly doubt—he will never come through the stones for her."

"*You're* the storyteller. Don't let him die," Beatrice protested. "Fix this story, Gwen," she said sternly. "How dare you tell me such a sad story?"

Gwen met her gaze levelly. "What if it's not just a story?" she said softly.

Beatrice studied her a moment, then glanced out the window into the twilight. Her gaze shifted from left to right, over Loch Ness in the distance. Then she smiled faintly. "There's magic in these hills. I've felt it ever since we arrived. As if the natural laws of the universe don't quite apply to this country." She paused and glanced back at Gwen. "When my Bertie gets better, I might just take him up into the hills myself, under a good doctor's care of course, and rent a small cottage for the rest of the fall. Let some of that magic soak into his old bones."

Gwen smiled sadly. "Speaking of Bertie, I'll walk you back to the hospital. Let's go see what the doctors can tell us. And if you need to cry, I'll do the talking." Although Beatrice put up a token protest, Gwen didn't miss the relief and gratitude in her eyes.

Gwen was relieved too, because she suspected she might not be able to bear being alone for quite some time.

❦

Gwen spent the rest of her holiday in the village by the deep glassy loch with Beatrice, never looking up into the foothills, never venturing forth from the village, never allowing herself to even consider going to see if Castle Keltar still stood. She was too raw, the pain too fresh. While Beatrice visited Bertie at the hospital, Gwen huddled beneath the covers, feeling feverish with grief. The prospect of returning home to her empty little apartment in Santa Fe was more than she could bear to contemplate.

When Beatrice returned in the evenings, exhausted by her own worries, they comforted each other, forced each other to eat something healthy, and took slow walks beside the huge silvery mirror of Loch Ness and watched the setting sun paint the silvery surface crimson and lavender.

And beneath the wild Scottish sky, Gwen and Beatrice bonded like mother and daughter. They tossed around her "story" on more than one occasion. Beatrice urged her to write it down, to turn it into a historical romance and send it into a publisher.

Gwen demurred. *It would never get published. It's way too far out there.*

That's not true, Beatrice had argued. *I read a vampire romance this summer that I adored. A vampire, of all things! The world needs more love stories. What do you think I read when I'm sitting in the hospital, waiting to see if my Bertie will ever be able to speak again? Not some horror story . . .*

Maybe one day, Gwen had conceded, mostly to end the conversation.

But she was beginning to consider it. If she couldn't have the happily-ever-after in real life, at least she could write it. Someone else could live it for a few hours.

Despite her relentless grief, she refused to leave Beatrice's side until Bert was stable and Beatrice in better spirits. Day by day, Bert grew stronger. Gwen was convinced he was healing from the sheer magnitude and depth of Beatrice's love for him.

The day he was released, Gwen accompanied Beatrice to the hospital. His speech was impeded because the left side of his face was paralyzed, but the doctor said that in time and with therapy he might regain considerable ground. Beatrice had said with a wink that she didn't care if he could ever speak clearly again, as long as all the other parts were in good working order.

Bert had laughed and written on his erasable memo board that they certainly were, and he'd be happy to demonstrate if everyone would quit fussing over him and leave him alone with his sexy wife.

Gwen had smiled and watched with a mixture of joy and pain, as Beatrice and Bert rejoiced in each other.

Only after they'd wrung a promise from her that she

would visit them in Maine for Christmas—Beatrice had indeed rented a lovely cottage on the Loch for the fall—did Beatrice help Gwen pack up and tuck her into a cab for the ride to the airport.

As Gwen settled into the backseat, Beatrice shifted her ample bulk into the door and hugged her fiercely, kissing her forehead, nose, and cheeks. Both were misty-eyed.

"Don't you dare give up, Gwen Cassidy. Don't you dare stop loving. I may never know what happened to you that day up in the hills, but I know it was something that changed your life. There's magic in Scotland, but always remember: A heart that loves makes magic of its own."

Gwen shivered. "I love you, Beatrice. And you take good care of Bertie," she added fiercely.

"Oh, I plan to," Beatrice assured her. "And I love you too." Beatrice stepped back as the driver closed the door.

Once the cab pulled away from the curb, and she'd watched Beatrice until she was a small pink-clad speck in the distance, then gone, Gwen cried all the way to the airport.

· 26 ·

Although Gwen had known by the age of four
that objects derive color from their innate chemical
structure—which absorbs certain wavelengths of light
and reflects others—she now understood that the soul
had a light of its own that colored the world too.

It was an essential light, the light of joy, of wonder, of
hope.

Without it, the world was dark. Didn't matter how
many lights she turned on, everything was flat, gray,
empty. Sleeping, she dreamed of him, her Highland
lover. Waking, she lost him all over again.

Most days she hurt too much even to open her eyes.

So she stayed in bed in her tiny apartment, drapes
pulled, lights off, phone unplugged, reliving every moment they'd spent together, alternately laughing and
crying. On rare occasions, she tried to persuade herself
to get out of bed. Short of bathroom jaunts to attend a

queasy stomach, or stumbling to the door to pay the pizza guy, it wasn't working.

She was mortally wounded, but her stupid heart kept pumping.

How was she supposed to live without him?

She'd been deceived by platitudes and clichés. Time did *not* heal all wounds. Time didn't do a damn thing. Truth was, time had stolen her lover away, and if she lived to be a hundred—heaven forbid she suffer *that* long—she'd never forgive time.

That's silly, the scientist sniffed.

Gwen groaned, rolling over on her side and pulling a pillow over her head. *Leave me alone. You've never been any help to me. You didn't even warn me that saving him would make me lose him.*

I tried to. You didn't want to hear me. And I'm trying to help you now, the scientist said stiffly. *You need to get up.*

Go away.

You'd better get up, unless you want to sleep in that three-day-old slice of pizza you just ate.

Well, that was one way out of bed, a shaking Gwen decided a few moments later as she weakly brushed her teeth. Seemed to be the only way she got up lately. Squinting, she braced herself before turning on the light so she could see to wipe off the toilet. The light hurt her eyes and it took her several moments to adjust. When she caught a glimpse of herself in the mirror, she gasped.

She looked awful. Her hair was dull and tangled, her skin pale, her eyes red and swollen from crying. Her face looked gaunt, her eyes defeated.

She really needed to get herself together, she thought dimly.

If not for you, then for the child, the scientist agreed.

"Wh-what?" Her voice, so long unused, cracked, and the word escaped in a hoarse, disbelieving croak.

Child. The child, you idiot, the scientist snapped.

Gwen gaped, stunned, staring at her reflection. She peered at herself a long while, brows furrowed.

Shouldn't her skin look radiant or something if she was pregnant? Shouldn't she have gained a little weight? She glanced dubiously down at her flat stomach. Flatter than it had ever been in her life. She'd definitely *lost* weight, not gained.

Don't tell me you can't do the math. When's the last time we had our period?

Gwen felt a tiny bud of hope blossom in her heart.

She squelched it firmly. A dangerous feeling: hope. No way—she was not going that route. She'd hope she was pregnant, only to be doubly crushed when she found out it wasn't true. It would destroy her. She was in bad enough shape already.

She shook her head bitterly. The scientist was wrong this time. "I'm not pregnant," she told her reflection flatly. "I'm depressed. Big big difference." It was simply stress making her period late, nothing more. It had happened before. During her Great Fit of Rebellion, she'd skipped two periods.

Fine. So crawl back in bed, keep eating stale pizza, and refuse to wonder why you've been getting sick. Blame it all on stress. And when you lose our baby because you won't take care of yourself, don't blame me.

"*Lose* our baby!" she gasped. Fear knifed through her and her eyes flew wide. If there was even a remote possibility that she had a child of Drustan's inside her, there was no way she was losing it. And afraid though she was to hope—because of how awful the potential disappointment might be—she acknowledged that there was more than a possibility. There was a probability. They'd made love repeatedly, and she was not on birth control. If she hadn't been so lost in misery, she might have considered it sooner. If she was pregnant and did anything to jeopardize the baby, she would just die.

Stricken, she stumbled back into the bedroom, turned on the light, and took a good look around, thinking hard. Counting days, looking for clues.

Her bedroom was a pigsty. Pizza boxes, with half-eaten slices dotted the floor. Glasses with milk-encrusted bottoms were forgotten atop the bed table. Cracker wrappers were strewn across the bed: crackers she'd been nibbling in the morning to calm her queasy stomach.

"Oh, my God," she whispered. "Oh, please, oh, please let it be true."

The wait to discover if she was pregnant was interminable.

No at-home pregnancy test for Gwen Cassidy—she needed to hear whatever news it was directly from a doctor.

After giving both a urine and blood sample, Gwen tapped her foot and sat tensely in the crowded waiting room of her doctor's office. She felt wired from head to toe. She shifted position a dozen times, changed chairs, fanned through every magazine in the office. She paced. Periodically made sure the receptionist knew she was still alive.

The receptionist scowled each time she passed by, and Gwen suspected the woman thought she was mildly unbalanced. When Gwen had called earlier, nearly hysterical, insisting on seeing the doctor immediately, the receptionist had brusquely informed her that Dr. Carolyn Devore had no openings for several weeks.

Gwen had pleaded and sobbed until finally the frustrated receptionist had put Carolyn on the phone. Her dear, wonderful doctor since childhood, who'd become a friend over the years, had squeezed her in.

"Sit," the receptionist snapped, exasperated, as Gwen paced by again. "You're making the other patients nervous."

Mortified, Gwen glanced around at the roomful of people and slunk back to her chair.

"Ms. Cassidy?" A nurse poked her head around the corner.

"That's me!" She shot back up and trotted after the nurse. "That's me," she informed the receptionist brightly.

A few moments later, she took a seat on the examining table. Hugging herself in the chilly room, she sat, feet swinging, waiting.

When the door opened and Carolyn Devore stepped in, Gwen said breathlessly, "Well?"

Carolyn closed the door, smiling. "You were right. You're pregnant, Gwen."

"*I am?*" she breathed, scarcely daring to believe it.

"Yes."

"Truly?" she persisted.

Carolyn laughed. "Absolutely and unequivocally."

Gwen hopped off the table and hugged her. "I *love* you, Carolyn," she exclaimed. "Oh, thank you!"

Carolyn laughed again. "I can hardly take credit for it, but you're welcome."

For several minutes, all Gwen could do was repeat "I'm pregnant," a delighted smile on her face.

"You need to gain weight, Gwen," Carolyn chided. "I squeezed you in this afternoon because you sounded so awful on the phone. It worried me." She paused, as if searching for a delicate way to continue. "I know you lost both your parents this year." Her brown gaze was sympathetic.

Gwen nodded tightly, smile fading.

"Grieving takes its toll. You're ten pounds lighter than you were at your last checkup. I'm starting you on supplements today and putting you on a special diet. It's fairly self-explanatory, but if you have any questions, call me. Eat. Feel free to stuff yourself. Go overboard for a while." She gave Gwen a folder of menu suggestions and a bag of sample supplements to tide her over until she went to the drugstore.

"Yes, ma'am," Gwen promised. "Scout's honor. I'll gain, I promise."

"Will the father be helping you?" Carolyn asked carefully.

Gwen took a deep breath. *I am strong,* she told herself. *My baby is depending on me.* "He's . . . um . . . he, er . . . died." The word escaped in a soft rush of air; merely saying it hurt her to the marrow in her bones. *Five hundred years ago,* she didn't say. Carolyn would have packed her off to a cushy, padded hospital if she'd said that.

"Oh, Gwen," Carolyn exclaimed, squeezing her hand, "I'm so sorry."

Gwen glanced away, unable to meet Carolyn's sympathetic gaze. Simple kindness could undo her, make the tears come. Carolyn must have sensed it, because her voice changed, became briskly professional again.

"I can't stress enough that you must gain weight. Your body is going to need special care, and I'd like to schedule an ultrasound."

"An ultrasound? Why? Is something wrong?" Gwen was alarmed and her gaze flew back up to Carolyn's.

"No, nothing's wrong," Carolyn hastened to assure her. "In fact," she added, smiling, "depending on your

utlook, you might think it's something wonder-
ul. Your hCG levels lead me to believe you're
carrying twins. An ultrasound will give us a definite an-
wer."

"Oh, my God! Twins!" Gwen cried. "Twins," she repeated disbelievingly. Twins just like Drustan and
Dageus. A chill raced through her—not just one of his
babies, but two! *Oh, Drustan,* she thought, lanced by
piercing sorrow. *Twins, my love!* How he would have rejoiced in the news, how he would have celebrated the
birth of their children!

But he would never know, would never see his sons or
daughters. She would never get to share this with him.
She closed her eyes against a wave of pain.

Carolyn watched her closely. "Are you all right,
Gwen?"

Gwen nodded, her throat tight. After a long moment,
she opened her eyes again.

"If you need to talk, Gwen . . ." Carolyn trailed off,
waiting.

Gwen nodded stiffly. "Thank you, but I think it's just
going to take some time." She forced a weak smile. "I'll
be fine, Carolyn. I'll take care of myself, I promise."
Nothing would jeopardize her babies.

"I'll squeeze you in again on Friday," Carolyn said,
walking with her to the door. "I'll have my receptionist
call you this afternoon with a time."

Gwen thanked her profusely. "You have no idea how
much I needed to know this."

Carolyn gazed at the dark circles beneath her eyes. " I
think I do," she said softly. "Now go home, eat and take
care of yourself. There's more than just yourself to
think about now."

Gwen waved good-bye to the receptionist as she left.
She was pregnant. She had a part of Drustan inside

her. A child of his, possibly two, to raise, to love, to cherish.

Walking across the parking lot to her car, she was briefly stunned by how blue the sky seemed, how bright the sun, how green the grass.

Color. There was light in her soul again.

· 27 ·

A week later, Gwen was back in Scotland.

She sat at the base of the MacKeltar's mountain, perched on the hood of her rental car, gazing up, filled with trepidation.

When Carolyn had confirmed she was carrying twins, a surge of energy had flooded her. She'd cleaned her apartment, put the phone back on the hook, gotten her hair trimmed, treated herself to an eyebrow waxing, and gone grocery shopping. Then she'd called Allstate to tender her resignation, only to find they'd already fired her for not showing up for so many weeks. No loss there, she'd shrugged philosophically.

She'd called a Realtor and placed her parents' house on the market. The ostentatious showplace had been paid off years ago, and the sale of it would give her more than enough money to make a fresh start. She was done with Santa Fe. Done with insurance claims, done with it all. She was thinking of moving to the East Coast, maybe Maine, near Bert and Beatrice. She'd buy a lovely house with a darling nursery. Perhaps get a job at a local university teaching math and making it *fun*.

But before she could do any of that, before she could move forward, she had to somehow make peace with the past.

And the only way to do that was to lay to rest the questions that drove her mad at three o'clock in the morning when her heart felt heavy and her soul was inclined to brood.

Questions like: Had Drustan died from the arrow wound, or survived? And if he'd survived, had he ever married? She *hated* considering that one, because it left her feeling so torn. She would be crushed if he had remarried, yet at the same time, she would be crushed if he'd spent the rest of his life grieving. She loved him so much that if he'd lived, she wanted him to have been happy. It hurt her to think that he might have grieved for thirty or forty or fifty years. She realized that *she* was the lucky one: They'd both lost each other, but she alone had the precious gift of their babies.

More questions: Had Dageus had children? Had any MacKeltar descendants survived to the twenty-first century? The answer to that question could be a blessing, for if MacKeltars still lived above Alborath, she would feel as if they hadn't failed completely. One of the things Drustan had wanted was to ensure the future succession of his clan, and if by saving Dageus they had guaranteed survival of his clan, she could find some small measure of satisfaction in that.

Even more than finding answers, however, she needed to go sit by his grave, to lay sprigs of heather atop it, to tell him of their children, to laugh and reminisce and weep.

Then she would go home and be strong for their babies. It was what Drustan would want.

Steeling herself, she slipped back into the rental car.

She didn't delude herself, she knew that whatever she found atop the mountain was going to be excruciating. Because this was going to have to be the final goodbye . . .

As Gwen topped the crest of the mountain, her eyes misted.

The perimeter wall had been torn down, and the majestic stones of *Ban Drochaid* towered against the brilliant, cloudless blue sky.

There she had made love with her Highland mate. There she had traveled back into the past. There she had become pregnant, according to her due date.

She'd known that seeing the stones again would hurt, because a part of her was tempted to hole up in a laboratory and try to figure out the formulas that danced so far beyond her comprehension. The only thing that held her back was that Gwen knew—even as brilliant as she was—that she could devote the rest of her life to it, only to die a bitter old woman, never gaining the knowledge. She would *not* live her life like that, nor would she subject her children to it. The few times she'd pondered the symbols, she'd realized how far beyond her understanding they were. She might be a genius, but she just wasn't smart enough.

Nor would she plead—if modern MacKeltars still lived—with them to break their oaths and send her back, and unleash a dark Druid upon the world. No, she would be the woman Drustan had loved, honorable, ethical, loving.

Thus resolved, she accelerated past the stones and lifted her gaze to the castle. She sucked in a breath. Castle Keltar was even more beautiful than it had been in the sixteenth century. A sparkling, many-tiered fountain had been constructed on the front lawn. It was surrounded by a lush tumble of shrubbery and flowers and stone walkways. The facade had been renovated, probably many times over the centuries, and the front stairs were no longer stone but had been replaced with rosy marble. An elegant matching marble banister framed both sides. What had once been a huge wooden door was now double doors fashioned of burnished cherry trimmed with gold. Above the doors, a stained glass window detailing—her heart leaped—the MacKeltar plaid, shimmered brilliant purple in the sunlight.

She parked before the steps and sat gazing at the door, wondering if that small bit of MacKeltar heritage meant the castle was still inhabited by descendants. Suddenly the door opened and a young child, blond curls tumbling about a delicate face, stepped out, peering at her curiously. Inside the rented Volvo, Gwen squinted against the bright sunlight at the lovely little girl, who was followed closely by a boy of similar age, and an older pair of twins.

The eldest boy and girl took her breath away and eradicated any question in her mind about whether any descendants had survived.

They most certainly had.

Pure MacKeltar blood was apparent in both of the

older children—in the rich dark manes, the unusual eyes and golden skin. The boy could have been Dageus's own son, with similar golden eyes.

She closed her eyes briefly, fighting tears, feeling both joyous and sad. They hadn't failed completely, but the visit was going to be excruciating, she realized, massaging her temples.

"Hello," the little girl called, knocking on the car window. "Will you be getting out, or will you be sitting in there all day?"

Gwen snorted lightly, the pain easing a bit. She opened her eyes and smiled. The little girl was absolutely darling, peering in expectantly. *You're going to have two of those soon*, a comforting voice reminded her.

"Cara, get back from that car!" a blond woman who looked to be in her early thirties called, hurrying down the front steps.

She was heavily pregnant, and Gwen instinctively touched her own abdomen. Turning off the ignition, she tucked her bangs behind her ear and opened the car door. She realized, as she stepped out, that she'd not thought this far ahead: She had no idea what excuse she would offer for dropping in on perfect strangers. She would have to play it by ear, claim to be taken with the castle, then beg a tour. She was grateful that the woman was pregnant because she was willing to bet she would invite her in to visit without asking too many questions. Gwen had recently discovered that pregnant women were a breed unto their own, with a tendency to forge an instantaneous, deep bond. A few days ago, she'd chatted for over an hour with a pregnant stranger in the ice cream aisle of the grocery, discussing baby clothes and tests and methods of birth and all kinds of things that would bore a nonpregnant person silly.

"I take it these lovely ones are yours?" Gwen said, offering her friendliest smile.

"Aye, my youngest are Cory and Cara," she said, gesturing toward them. Cara said hello again, and Cory smiled shyly. "And these"—she waved a hand at the dark-haired teenage twins—"are Christian and Colleen." They chimed hello together.

"Plus I've two on the way in a few months," Maggie added. "As if it weren't obvious," she said dryly.

"I'm pregnant with twins myself," Gwen confided.

Maggie's eyes flickered strangely. " 'Tis easier that way," she said. "You get them over with two at a time, and I always wanted a dozen or so. I'm Maggie Mac-Keltar and my husband should be out in a moment." She turned to the steps and shouted, "Christopher, do hurry, she's here!"

"Coming, love," a deep baritone voice replied.

Gwen frowned, puzzled, wondering what Maggie had meant by "she's here." Had they mistaken her for someone else? Perhaps they were expecting someone, she decided, maybe they were hiring a nanny or a maid and thought Gwen was that person.

Cara tugged impatiently at Maggie's arm. "Mama, when are we going to show her—" Cara began.

"Hush," Maggie said swiftly. "Run along with you and Cory. We'll be in shortly. Christian, you and Colleen go help Mrs. Melbourne lay the tea in the solar."

"But, Mom—"

"Do I have to repeat myself?"

I'm going to have to clear up this case of mistaken identity, Gwen thought, watching the children go in. She didn't care for the thought of misleading Maggie MacKeltar. Then all thought fled her mind as Maggie's husband,

Christopher, stepped out of the castle. Gwen sucked in a breath, feeling suddenly faint.

"Aye, the resemblance is strong, isn't it now?" Maggie said softly, watching her.

A dark lock of hair fell over Christopher's forehead, and he had the same extraordinary height and muscled body. His eyes were not silver, but a deep, peaceful gray. He looked so much like Drustan that it hurt to look at him.

"Wh-what do you mean?" Gwen stammered, trying to compose herself.

"I mean he looks like Drustan," Maggie replied.

Gwen opened her mouth but nothing came out. *Like Drustan?* What did they know about her and Drustan?

"Och, Gwen Cassidy," Christopher said with a thick Scots burr, "we've been waiting for you for some time now." Smiling, he slid his arm around Maggie's waist. They both stood there, beaming at her.

Gwen blinked. "How do you know my name?" she asked weakly. "What do you know about Drustan? What's going on here?" she asked, her voice rising.

Maggie kissed her husband's cheek, slipped from his embrace, and tucked her arm through Gwen's. "Come in, Gwen. We have much to tell you, but I think you might be needing to sit while you're hearing it."

"Sit," Gwen repeated dumbly, her knees feeling weak.

"Good. Sitting would be good."

☙❧

But sitting didn't happen, because the moment Gwen entered the Greathall, she froze, gaping at the portrait that hung above the double staircase facing the entrance.

It was her.

Six feet of Gwen Cassidy, clad in a pale lavender gown, blond hair tumbling about her face, graced the wall at the landing between the two staircases. "Me," she managed to say, pointing. "That's me."

Maggie laughed. "Aye. It was painted in the sixteenth century—"

But Gwen didn't hear the rest. Her attention was caught and held by the family portraits covering nearly every inch of the walls in the Greathall. From ancient times to modern day, they stretched from chair rail to ceiling.

Eager to see who Dageus had married, and what kind of children he'd fathered, she hurried past the modern paintings. Dimly, her mind registered that Maggie and Christopher were trailing behind her, now watching in silence.

At the section displaying the sixteenth century, Gwen drew to a stunned halt. She stared for a moment, unable to believe what she saw, then smiled as tears misted her eyes. She fancied she could hear faint strains of Silvan's laughter in the air. And Nell, making some saucy response. The patter of children's feet on stone.

The painting that held her captivated was eight feet tall. A full-length portrait, Nell was seated on the terrace, Silvan was standing behind her, his hands on her shoulders. Nell held twins in her arms. "Nell?" she finally said, turning to look at Maggie.

"Aye. The lot of us descend directly from Silvan and Nell MacKeltar. He wed his housekeeper, so the records say. They had four children. We have twins an uncommon lot in this family."

"He looks pretty old to be having kids to me," Colleen said, wrinkling her nose as she bounded back into the Greathall, followed by her siblings. "The tea's ready," she announced.

Gwen's heart swelled. "He was sixty-two," she said softly. And Nell hadn't been a spring chicken either. Dear Nell had gotten her babies back after all, and it had been Silvan who'd given them to her.

She moved to the next portrait, but two empty spaces followed. The wall was darker where portraits had once hung. "What was here?" she asked curiously. Had they taken down portraits of Drustan to give her?

Christopher and Maggie exchanged an odd glance. "Just two portraits being touched up," Christopher said. "There's Nell and Silvan again," he said, pointing farther down the wall.

Gwen eyed them a moment. "And Dageus? Where is Dageus?" she asked.

Again, the couple exchanged glances. "He's a mystery," Maggie finally said. "He wandered off somewhere in 1521."

"Is there no record of his death?"

"No," Maggie replied tersely.

How very odd, Gwen mused. But she would come back to that later, for now thoughts of Drustan consumed her. "Do you have any portraits of Drustan?"

"Mom!" Colleen cried. "Come on, you're killing me! Let's get on with it!"

Christopher and Maggie grinned. "Come, we have something more for you."

"But I have so many questions," Gwen protested. "How do you—"

"Later," Maggie said gently. "I think we need to show you this first, then you can ask whatever questions remain."

Gwen opened her mouth, shut it again, and followed.

When Maggie stopped at the door to the tower, Gwen took a slow, deep breath to calm the racing of her heart. Had Drustan left something for her? Something she could give her children, from the father they would never know? When Maggie and Christopher exchanged a loving glance, she nearly wept with envy.

Maggie had her MacKeltar; Gwen longed for some small token to remember hers by. A plaid with his scent, a portrait to show her babies, anything. She shivered, waiting.

Maggie withdrew a key from her pocket, dangling on a frayed and threadbare ribbon.

"There is a . . . legacy handed down over the centuries at Castle Keltar. It has been the source of many young lasses' romantic dreams"—she arched a brow at her eldest daughter— "and Colleen here has been the worst—"

"Not true. I've heard you and Dad mooning over it tons of times, and then you both get that disgusting look in your eyes—"

"Might I remind you, that disgusting look heralded the advent of your wee life," Christopher said dryly.

"*Eww.*" Colleen wrinkled her nose again.

Maggie laughed and continued. "Sometimes I think the sheer love of it has blessed all who've ever lived within these walls. The tale was carefully told from generation to generation as they waited for the day to come. Well, the day has arrived, and now the rest is up to you." Smiling, she handed Gwen the key. "It's said you'll know what to do."

"It's said you've done it *before*," Colleen added breathlessly.

Perplexed, Gwen inserted the key with trembling hands. The lock was old and gritty with time, and it took her a few minutes to work the lock.

As she opened the door, Christopher handed her a candle. "There's no electricity in there. The tower hasn't been opened in five centuries."

Suspense growing, Gwen accepted the candle and gingerly stepped into the room, dimly aware that the entire MacKeltar clan was hot on her heels.

It was too dark to see much, but the glow of the candle fell upon a pile of old fabric and the silvery flash of weapons.

Drustan's daggers!

Her heart lurched painfully.

She bent over and fingered the fabric upon which they lay. Tears stung her eyes when she realized it was his plaid, and atop it lay a small pair of black leather trews that would probably be a perfect fit.

He'd never forgotten that she'd wanted a pair.

"That's not all," Colleen said impatiently. "That's the least of it. Look up!"

"Colleen," Christopher said sternly. "In her own time, lass."

Blinking back tears, Gwen glanced up, and as her eyes adjusted completely, she noticed a slab in the center of the circular room. Her heart slammed against her ribs, and she surged to her feet.

"Oh, my God," she choked, stumbling toward the slab. It couldn't be. How could it be? She glanced frantically at Maggie, who smiled and nodded encouragingly.

"He waits for you. He's waited five hundred years. It is said you know how to wake him."

Gwen began to hyperventilate. Spots swarmed

before her eyes and she nearly collapsed where she stood. For several moments she could do nothing more than stand there and stare in shock. Then she thrust the black trews she hadn't realized she was clutching at Maggie and scrambled up onto the slab.

"Drustan," she cried, raining kisses on his slumbering face. "Oh, Drustan! My love . . ." Tears slipped down her cheeks.

How had she awakened him? she wondered frantically, unable to believe that he was really there. She touched him with shaking hands, afraid he might just melt away, afraid she was dreaming.

"I'm not dreaming, am I?" she whispered weakly.

"No, lass, you're not dreaming," Christopher said, smiling.

Gwen stared at Drustan, trying to recall exactly what had happened in the cave. She'd fallen down the ravine and landed squarely on top of him. She'd been fascinated, had touched him, shamelessly running her hands over his chest. Then she'd leaned back so the sun could fall on him, so she might get a better look at the devastating man.

"The sun! You must help me get him outside," she said urgently. "I think sunlight has something to do with it!"

It took their combined strength to carry the enchanted Highlander down the winding stairs, through the library, and out onto the cobbled terrace. They were huffing by the time they deposited her mighty warrior on the stones.

Gwen stood for a moment, just gaping down at him. Drustan was *here*! All she had to do was figure out how to wake him! Dazed, she slipped astride him and placed her palms flush to his chest, exactly as she'd done in the cave. The sunshine was falling directly on his face and chest.

But nothing happened.

The symbols remained, etched clearly upon his chest. Back in the cave, they'd begun disappearing. Why?

She narrowed her eyes and peered up at the sun. It was brilliant and clear, a cloudless day. She glanced at Maggie. "He didn't leave any instructions?" She needed him awake *now*.

The MacKeltars shook their heads.

"It was thought he feared someone might wake him before it was time," Maggie said. She cast Colleen a wry look. "Like my daughter who's been infatuated with him since she first peeked through the slit in the tower and saw him slumbering."

Closing her eyes, Gwen thought hard. What was different? She opened them again slowly and gazed down at his chest. Everything was the same: the sun, the symbols, her hands. . . .

Blood. There had been blood smeared on the symbols from her cutting her hands up when she'd fallen through the rocks. Could it be that elemental? Human blood and sunshine? She knew nothing about spells, but blood figured prominently in myths and legends.

"I need a knife," she cried.

Colleen dashed into the castle and returned swiftly, clutching a small steak knife.

Mumbling a prayer beneath her breath, Gwen lightly ran the edge over her palm so drops of blood welled up. With trembling hands, she smeared it across the symbols on his chest, then sat back anxiously, waiting.

For a moment, nothing happened.

Then one by one, the symbols began to fade. . . .

She sucked in her breath and glanced up at his face.

"Good morrow, English," Drustan said lazily, opening his eyes, his silvery gaze tender. "I knew you could do it, love."

Gwen's eyelids fluttered and she fainted.

· 28 ·

When Gwen regained consciousness, she was lying on the bed in the Silver Chamber. Drustan was bending over her, gazing down with so much love in his eyes that she gasped and began crying.

"Drustan," she whispered, clutching at him.

"She's awakened, Maggie," Drustan said over his shoulder. "She's all right." Gwen heard the door shut as Maggie left, giving them privacy.

She stared up into his silvery eyes wonderingly. He was looking at her as if she were the most precious thing in the world.

"How?" she managed to ask, cupping his face in her hands. She traced her fingers over every plane and angle, and he kissed them repeatedly as they passed his lips. "How?"

"I love you, Gwen MacKeltar," he whispered, catching her hand and planting a kiss in the palm.

Gwen laughed through her tears. "I love you too," she whispered back, flinging her arms around him and holding him tightly. "But I don't understand."

In between dozens of kisses, quick sips, long leisurely ones, he told her.

Told her how he'd watched her disappear as he'd lain on the ground, the battle raging all around. Told her how the arrow had been deflected by the metal disc on his leather bands and had been but a flesh wound. Told her how they'd discovered who the "enemy" was.

"That old woman," Gwen murmured. "She said she'd hired the gypsies."

"Aye, Besseta. She made a full confession." He kissed her again before continuing, sucking gently on her lower lip. "Besseta claimed she scryed in her yew sticks that a woman would bring about the death of her son. Since I was soon to wed, Besseta decided my betrothed must be the woman in her vision. She warned Nevin, but he laughed it off and made her promise not to harm me. To her ailing mind, bespelling me wasn't harming me, so she purchased the gypsy's services to enchant me so she might prevent the wedding. In the first reality, when Anya was killed by the Campbell, Besseta must have thought the threat had passed. I suspect, however, that sometime shortly after Anya's death, Besseta must have had her vision again, and realized that as long as I was alive and might yet wed, the danger would never pass. So she proceeded with her original plan to have me enchanted."

"So she drugged you and sent the message bidding you come to discover the name of the man who'd killed Dageus."

"Aye. I was enchanted, you found me, and I sent you back."

"But in the second reality," Gwen exclaimed, "since

Dageus and Anya weren't killed, she must have heard you were coming home with your betrothed—"

"—and stepped up plans to have me abducted. Unwilling to take any chances; she wanted my "betrothed" gone too. As you were in my bedchamber, they assumed you were Anya."

Gwen shook her head, amazed. "It was her belief in her vision that made everything happen, Drustan! If she hadn't believed in it, she would never have enchanted you, I would never have been sent back, and Nevin would never have given his life to save me."

"Aye. 'Tis why the gypsy are o'ercautious of fortune telling. They make it clear that any future they scry is but one possible future: the most likely one, yet not writ in stone. For Besseta, driven by lifelong fear, it was indeed her most probable future. Fear drove her to have me enchanted. Having me enchanted resulted in me sending you back. Once you were there, Nevin gave his life to protect you. Her fear drove her to fulfill the possibility."

Gwen rubbed her forehead. "This hurts my head."

Drustan laughed. "It hurts mine too. I'll be most happy to ne'er muck with time again."

Gwen was silent a moment, thinking. "What happened to Besseta?"

Drustan's eyes darkened. "After you disappeared, she plunged into the battle, and though the men strove not to harm her, she was determined to die. She impaled herself on Robert's claymore." He frowned. "She confessed before she died, and we were able to piece the story together."

Fresh tears gathered in Gwen's eyes.

"You would weep for her?" Drustan exclaimed.

"If not for her, I should never have found you," Gwen said softly. "It's sad. It's sad that she was so afraid. But at the same time, I'm so glad I found you."

He kissed her again, then told her the rest of it. How he'd grieved, how he raged. How he'd stormed to the stones and stood arguing with himself for hours.

Then his mind had struck upon an idea—so temptingly possible that it had taken his breath away.

The gypsies. They'd made him sleep once for five centuries. Why not again? And so he'd tracked down the wandering tribe and commissioned their services. The gypsy queen herself had performed the spell for a pouch of coin.

"For a pouch of coin!" Gwen exclaimed. "How dare they charge you? They were the ones who—"

"Who sold a service, nothing more. The Rom hold themselves to a strange code. They maintain that blaming them for Besseta commissioning them to enchant me would be akin to blaming the blade for drawing blood. 'Tis the hand that wields the dagger, not the dagger itself."

"Fine way to evade personal responsibility," Gwen grumbled. Then she sucked in a shallow breath. "Your family! Silvan and Nell and—"

He cut her off by kissing her. "My choice was painful to them, but they understood."

He'd not once wavered. He'd spent several months saying his good-byes before being enchanted. And implementing plans that would bear fruit five centuries later, plans to ensure a fine life for him and his wife. But there would be time to tell her of that tomorrow, or the next day or the next. "They bid me give you their love when we were reunited."

Gwen got misty-eyed again, then thumped his chest with her fist. "Why didn't you leave instructions for Maggie to find me weeks ago?" she cried. "My heart broke. I've been back for over a month—"

"I wasn't certain when you would return to your

time. I couldn't decide if the month would pass for you in both centuries."

"Oh," she said in a small voice.

"And I wasn't willing to take any chances of summoning you before you'd met me. Och, but what a fankle that would have been. You wouldn't have known how to wake me. You wouldn't have even *known* me if we'd sent for you too early. Seemed safer to let you come."

"But what if I hadn't come? What if I'd never come back to Scotland?"

"I left instructions that if you hadn't arrived by Samhain, my descendants should find you and bid you come. They were to look for you in America and bring you here."

"But—"

"Are you going to talk me to death or kiss me, wife?" he asked huskily.

She opted for the kiss.

When his lips claimed hers, her body quickened with desire. He paused only to strip off his linen shirt, while Gwen made short work of his plaid.

"Lay back," she commanded when she had him completely naked. "I think I should like to be on top." He complied, flashing her a sexy grin that dripped promises of fantasies about to be fulfilled. She sat back on her heels, gazing at him, sprawled across the bed. His bronze skin and silky dark hair gleamed against the white linens. Six and a half feet of Highland warrior lay before her, awaiting her pleasure.

Yum.

Years of not understanding the equation of life culminated in one perfect moment of clarity—life equaled love plus passion squared. Loving and being passionate about what one did was what made life so precious. She would be perfectly content to devote the rest of her life to the proof of that equation.

"Touch me," he purred.

She touched. Lightly, gliding her hands up his muscular thighs. Tracing each muscle, each ridge, then lowering her head to taste in her hand's wake. She cupped him and swept her tongue up the underside of his hard shaft, delighted when he bucked beneath her.

"Gwendolyn!" he thundered, cradling her head with his hands. "I willna last a minute if you do that!"

"Och, nay, my braw laird," she said in a lilting Scots accent. "Be still. 'Tis my pleasure you serve—ack!" She burst into laughter when in one swift motion he rolled her onto her back.

"I bid you recall I've been needing you for five hundred years, whereas you've been waiting only a month."

"Yes, but you didn't know time was pass—" she began, but he kissed her words away. He covered her body with his own, sliding her shirt up, kissing each breast as he bared them. Alternately returning for a searing kiss to her lips, then moving lower.

When at last he buried himself inside her, he groaned with ecstasy. He'd have waited a thousand years, nay, eternity, to have this woman as his own.

Much later, Drustan held her in his arms, marveling at how she completed him. She'd had her way, and had the top—the third time—informing him he was her "own private playground," then explaining what a playground was. He had much to learn to fully integrate himself into her century. He suffered no fear on that score; rather, was exhilarated by the challenge.

Emotion flooded him, a sense of rightness and completion, and he kissed her, putting all his joy into the kiss. He was surprised when she pulled away, but then she took his hand and gently placed his palm over her belly.

He shot straight up in bed, searching her eyes. "Are you telling me something?" he exclaimed hoarsely.

"Twins. We're having twins," she said, bubbling over with joy.

"And you waited till *now* to tell me?" he roared, then threw his head back and whooped. He swept her into his arms and danced her about the room. He twirled her, kissed her, danced her more, then stopped and gently placed her back on the bed. "I shouldna be tossin' you about like that," he exclaimed.

Gwen laughed. "Oh, please, if our loving didn't jostle them, a little dance certainly won't hurt. I'm a little over two months along."

"Two months!" he shouted, leaping to his feet again.

Gwen beamed; he was so elated. It was what every woman should get to experience when she told her man she was pregnant—a man utterly ecstatic to be a father.

He stood grinning like a fool for a moment, then sobered and dropped to his knees before her. "Will you be weddin' me in a church, Gwendolyn?"

"Aye, oh, aye," Gwen sighed dreamily.

And this time when they made love it was tender and slow and sweeter than e'er before.

❧

"Where will we live?" she asked finally, combing her fingers through his silky hair. She simply couldn't stop touching him. Couldn't believe he was here. Couldn't believe the sacrifice he'd made to be with her.

He grinned. "I took care of that. The estate was divided into thirds in 1518. My third is to the south. Dageus oversaw the construction of our home. It awaits us even now. Maggie and Christopher assured me they opened it and all is in readiness."

Dageus, Gwen thought. She needed to tell him about Dageus vanishing, but there would time for that later. She didn't want anything to spoil the moment.

"You doona mind living in Scotland, do you, lass?" he teased lightly, but she sensed a hint of vulnerability in his question. It would be hard for him to adjust to a new century. It would be even more difficult if she dragged him off to America. In time, she suspected he would like to travel, for he was a curious man, but Scotland would always be his home. Which was fine, she had no desire to go back to the States.

The enormity of what he'd done, how much he'd given up for her, overwhelmed her.

"Drustan," she breathed, "you gave it all up—"

He pulled her onto his chest and brushed his lips against hers. "And I would do it all over again, sweet Gwen."

"But your family, your century, your home—"

"Och, lass, doona you know? Your heart *is* my home."

Dear reader:

I'd like to share with you a letter that neither Gwen nor Drustan have yet seen. I'm sure you noticed the connection between the two portraits missing in the Mac-Keltar hall, and Dageus "vanishing" in 1521.

There are actually *two* legacies handed down over the centuries, but rather than spoil Gwen and Drustan's reunion, Maggie and Christopher agreed to hold off on revealing the second one.

You see, they have a letter addressed to Drustan and Gwen, from Silvan, as well as two shocking portraits of Dageus to show them. Yet they wished for Gwen and Drustan to have a few more stolen moments for loving before their new journey begins.

Turn the page for a peek at Silvan's letter, from *Dark Highlander,* coming in the fall of 2002. . . .

Drustan, my son:

I have missed you. I wish you could have met your brothers and sisters, but your heart was with Gwen, and 'twas where it wisely belonged. I wish the two of you every happiness, but rue to tell you your trials are not yet o'er.

First, the gentler news. Beloved Nell consented to be my wife. She has made every moment a joy. We left a few things for the two of you in the tower. Count over three stones on the base of the slab, second stone from the bottom. Life has been rich and full, more than I e'er dreamed. I have no regrets but one.

I should have watched Dageus more closely after you went into the tower. I should have seen what was happening. There you slumbered, enchanted, waiting for your mate, here I sat, with mine.

Yet Dageus grew e'er more solitary. Blinded by my own happiness, I didn't see what was happening until it was too late. I shall be scant with the details, but suffice it to say as time passed, he became . . . obsessed with you. He worried that something would happen to prevent you from surviving until you found Gwen again.

And it did. I have no memory of it, mayhap an odd wrinkle in my mind, but he confessed to me that three years after we placed your enchanted body in the northeast tower, that wing of the castle caught fire and you were burned and died.

Dageus broke his oath, went back in time through the stones to the day of the fire, and prevented the fire from occurring. He saved you, but in so doing, turned Dark. The old legends were true.

If you are reading this, he succeeded in his course, for he appointed himself your dark guardian, his sole purpose to see you safely to Gwen. He vowed to watch over you, then disappeared. Dageus is a strong man, and I believe such a vow has kept him sane.

I hope it has, for I tasted the evil within him.

I believe, however, the moment you awaken and are reunited, there will be nothing to hold his darkness at bay. His purpose accomplished, the thin thread that binds him to the light will snap.

Och, my son, 'tis sorry I am to be sayin' this, but you must find him.

You must save him.

And if you cannot save him, you must kill him.

SOURCES

Flatland: A Romance of Many Dimensions, Edwin A. Abbott, Dover Publications

A Brief History of Time, Stephen Hawking, Bantam Books

Infinity and the Mind, The Science and Philosophy of the Infinite, Rudy Rucker, Princeton University Press

The Fourth Dimension: A Guided Tour of the Higher Universes, Rudy Rucker, Houghton Mifflin Company

Stephen Hawking's Universe: The Cosmos Explained, Stephen Hawking, Basic Books

The Handy Physics Answer Book, P. Erik Gundersen, Visible Ink Press

The Celtic Reader: Selections from Celtic Legend, Scholarship and Story, John Matthews, ed., Thorsons

A Celtic Miscellany: Translations from the Celtic Literature, Kenneth Hurlstone Jackson, ed., Penguin Classics

The Story of the Irish Race, Seumas MacManus, The Devin-Adair Company

ABOUT THE AUTHOR

Bestselling author KAREN MARIE MONING graduated from Purdue University with a bachelor's degree in Society & Law. Her novels have been nominated for 3 prestigious RITA awards. Her debut novel, *Beyond the Highland Mist* won the Romantic Times Best Historical Time-Travel award, and the Waldenbooks Bestselling Debut Romance Author Award. Her third novel, *The Highlander's Touch*, debuted on the USA Today National Bestsellers Expanded List.

Karen lives in Cincinnati, Ohio with the cat who rules the earth, Moonshadow, and is currently completing her fifth novel.

Visit Karen online at:
www.kmoning.bizland.com/tartan.